D

BO

BY W. & W. GREGORY

***

***

ORIGINALLY PUBLISHED IN POLISH AS DWUSWIAT BOOK I - PRE-WAR
TRANSLATED AND PUBLISHED IN ENGLISH WITH PERMISSION.

***

PAPERBACK ISBN: 979-8-9869299-2-7
EPUB ISBN: 979-8-2018445-2-3

***

WRITTEN BY W. & W. GREGORY
PUBLISHED BY ROYAL HAWAIIAN PRESS
COVER ART BY TYRONE ROSHANTHA
TRANSLATED BY RAFAL STACHOWSKY
PUBLISHING ASSISTANCE BY DOROTA RESZKE

***

FOR MORE WORKS BY THIS AUTHOR, PLEASE VISIT:
WWW.ROYALHAWAIIANPRESS.COM

***

Table of Contents

Chapter 1 Inco

“I don't have good news for you," Dr. Steavans said, tossing his used disposable gloves into the trash.

Anxiety appeared on Jasmin's face. She was lying in just her underwear on an acrylic glass couch covered with a linen bedspread. *What went wrong?* - she mused. She felt like asking a question, but only pressed her lips together and turned her gaze toward the window. She always did that when she was choosing her words. This time, however, it was completely dark outside, and it didn't help. The light, shimmering in the distance, made a rather depressing impression and made it impossible to focus. She glanced tentatively back at the doctor. The news, still unspoken but already sounding like a verdict, would surely change her life.

“It's a multiple pregnancy," the black-haired doctor continued. “It's rare and I can't remember the last time I dealt with three babies of the same sex.”

Steavans fled with his eyes toward the prenatal testing apparatus. He focused on the clear, spiral hose. He took a cloth soaked in blue gel from its metal packaging and began to use it to wipe the sensor protruding from the hose, gleaming with lifelong sterility. The polishing looked like a mere distraction. The doctor acted as if he didn't want to look into those big amber eyes at that moment, which were filling up with tears more and more with each passing second, until they were dropping streams of sadness down his cheeks. This sight was not unfamiliar to him. Most of the previous cases he had witnessed had been single pregnancies. If twins did occur, they tended to involve siblings of both sexes. Jasmin's precedent clearly took him by incredible surprise.

"I need to enter the data into the computer module. Okay?" He asked with palpable concern.

She nodded her head. He took that as acceptance. The device he turned on had a body with several buttons, a mini-projector, and a keyboard. Immediately, a small light came on. It cast a narrow beam of white light towards the wall, creating a screen. On it, after a moment, appeared a brown background and the white heading of the Gender Control Office, followed by the code for authorization.

"Jasmin Kozllov, daughter of Irmina and Omar, wife of Addam. Age: three and a half. You look good," Steavans said with a sincere smile on his face.

"Thank you."

The sentence she heard awoke the patient as if she had been somewhere else a moment ago. She quickly rubbed her eyes.

"You are very nice," she added.

"Let me get your report card. I have to collect twenty *entitys* for the visit. In that case, there can be no postponement. You understand. And get dressed."

Jasmin knew it was no use pretending she had forgotten her card. Some time ago the Government had introduced a quick solution to several plagues plaguing society. All it took was one very serious problem. Such trifles as theft, rape or causing harm to someone ending in permanent disability had to be efficiently and definitively eliminated. Therefore, for all these offenses the following punishments were set, chosen at random by the judge presiding over the trial: life in a maximum security prison, the same in a labor camp, or possibly the gallows. It worked. Since then there have been practically no petty thefts, if only on a large scale. A sign of the times was the fashion for transparent bags. Jasmin also wore one. Dr. Steavans, like everyone else, could easily tell that inside the pouch lying in his office next to the couch was a pink communicator, branded air fresheners, one for the mouth and one for the hand, two red regeneration bars and the report card in question. The multifunctional document looked like a metal plate with a glass chip located at one of its edges. It was used to open the house, to contact the bank, the insurance company, and - which until recently was not so obvious - as a symbol of identity. With a full health history. And most importantly, it was easy to identify in the pannier.

Jasmin struggled to rise from her semi-reclining position and sat down on the couch. After a moment, she sighed, took out her card, and handed it to the doctor. Dr. Steavans inserted it into the reader located on the front of the computer module and pressed the black button. All of the patient's information appeared on the screen, including her account balance, where she had accumulated twenty-six thousand entitys. The doctor made a slight grimace, as if surprised to see that amount. However, he quickly realized that his reaction might have looked inappropriate, and smiled rather clumsily in return.

"Done. Expected delivery date..." Steavans just double-clicked the keys, took the card out of the reader and handed it to the patient.

At this time, the computer module announced with a short beep that it had begun printing a serious-looking report.

"Are you going to tell me?" She asked, zipping up her dress.

"What does it matter? You have to be brave.

The doctor turned off the screen and pressed the big red button located in the middle of the desk. At that moment, a shrill sound rang out, which apparently boded more bad news. When it stopped, the door opened and a veined female GCO officer rushed into the office, without any questions, waiting in the hall like a runner in the starting blocks. Her brown, perfectly tailored and pressed uniform and her implacable expression heralded trouble.

"Ms. Gibbondy, take a look at this report," Dr. Steavans announced dryly and pointed to the printout lying on the desk in front of him.

"Three? Well, well."

The officer looking over the doctor's shoulder smiled broadly, as if she were excited. She turned to Jasmin.

"In the waiting room is a rack of bait from the doctors who work with us. Not like Dr. Steavans..."

"Which you would most like to take away your license, but you know as well as I do that you can't do that," the doctor interrupted her. "Too bad, right?"

"I do not understand this sarcasm. You are indeed a respected gynecologist, but glorifying doctors who are not part of a national program, in my opinion, is just plain wrong. You are indifferent to what happens to the human race. Yes. To me, you are just a hypocritical turd and I am waiting for you to be caught breaking the law!" she shouted with a grimace on her face, then smiled artfully at Jasmin.

"Pretty, you have twelve days to get things done. There are such modern methods now. Nothing will hurt."

At that moment Jasmin realized that in the emblem of the Gender Control Office the letters g, c and o were placed in a border in the shape of a human heart. She perceived this as a gaffe or at least a gaffe of the author's intentions. Meanwhile, Mrs. Gibbondy took out a communicator from the side pocket of her uniform and proudly reported a woman named J. Kozllov, age three and a half, to headquarters. Jasmin didn't want to hear it anymore. She put on her rag sandals, took one last glance at the doctor and left the office with her head lowered. In the waiting room, she noticed that it had become crowded in the meantime, despite the evening hour.

The women - in fact, most of them - waiting for their turn looked worried. She did not know whether it was because of the sympathy they felt for the patient who was leaving the doctor's office or because they feared a similar fate awaited them.

***

On her way out of the building, Jasmin didn't even notice that there was a light fog outside and not much to see. When she left the apartment where she and her husband lived an hour earlier, the temperature and humidity did not bode well for a change in the weather. Although in general the fog didn't annoy much and usually lasted a short time, the women of this part of town got angry when it shattered the effect of a laborious hairstyle. Jasmin was a white-haired woman. Her one-fifth elbow-long strands - most of them carelessly flopping in different directions (only some of them were tousled in a controlled manner) - were never bothered by unannounced changes in weather conditions. Even more so now, when she had a far more important affliction than any hairstyle. In the milk of the fog she was walking as if she was walking on a string. It was as if her body was moving along a path known by heart, while her thoughts were going somewhere else. Addam did not suspect that she was planning to visit Dr. Steavans. It was supposed to be a surprise. Should she tell him? How would he react? She knew she had a week and a half to think about it. That was the amount Officer Gibbons had given her. *Mean* that's what she thought of her. If Jasmin didn't comply with the order by the deadline, there would be a financial hold on her report card, a hold against future draconian taxes. The same will happen to Addam's card. Until the matter came to light, Jasmin had a chance to think about what she should do. It's just that they say it's not hard to terminate a pregnancy. But she had known several friends who had been crippled forever by such a procedure, even when it was done early in their pregnancies. They would never be able to bear children. The gynecologists working with GCO are torturers, not doctors. Dr. Steavans was supposedly different. She went to him on the recommendation of a close friend.

When she reached the suite, she decided not to show from where she was returning. She threw herself around Addam's neck and kissed him hard. He didn't ask for anything. The man she thought was an intelligent beast always made as good an impression on her as he did today. She loved him wisely. The feeling was a combination of desire and the promise of providing dignity, respect and the satisfaction of feeling safe. It was for Addam that she had decided to marry, and later considered offspring, though previously alien children had caused her mild disgust. They were excessively expensive, too rambunctious, and usually mean. She knew this because she had repeatedly noticed these traits in her friends' offspring. Each of the planned grandmotherly get-togethers always ended the same way - with the company of a promiscuous shithead, a self-centered egotist. *This was probably a sign of a reprieve from the cold-bloodedness that was fashionable in those days, and also from the discipline that had been instilled since kindergarten,* she thought. The nasty brats eventually caused her to stop keeping in touch with their mothers, without harm to either side. She has since stopped using the word friend.

It took her a long time to decide to have a child of her own. All in all, she wanted her and Addam to become a real family, not just a couple. There were whispers that there was something wrong with her. She was a little concerned, though she pretended not to care about the rumors. However, she was not sure if this was the time. Especially since Addam had behaved for a long time like a spoiled youngster, the youngest child of his overprotective parents. Eventually she realized that age three and a half was time for a change, so she discontinued the contraceptives. In her mind, she told herself that she did it for Addam because he wanted a son. When the first signs of pregnancy appeared, she was happy not only because it would please her husband and his family. She also thought of fulfilling the dream of her mother, who repeatedly insinuated that she would not live to see her grandchildren. Jasmin imagined a whole, happy family celebrating life under new circumstances. Before her upcoming appointment with Dr. Steavans, she even started addressing the baby, though she wasn't sure about him yet. She called him guest, in a whisper. Before, such behavior would have seemed absurd to her, an idiotic invention of immature women. She explained it to herself by the emerging bond. The thought puzzled her. *Apparently it's hormones or some kind of embodiment of the affection she had for Addam*, she thought.

Her husband was a yellow-haired man, not very handsome, but well-built and healthy, like the rest of his family. He had a modern, medium-length haircut and a thick beard. She first fell in love with his analytical mind, only then did she like his other qualities. But she was reluctant to accept the flaws that, one by one, began to surface and nestle into their relationship. The malicious rumor had it that the middle-class girl had married Addam because the Kozllov family was well-off and respected in the community. The Kozllov family also got along well with the authorities. Addam received a spacious apartment from his parents as a reward for completing his studies, and he moved in with his wife after their marriage. His two much older brothers held senior corporate positions and had sons, which only added to the family's glamour.

"Such a gene," he joked repeatedly, "no daughters are born in our family.

Jasmin dismissed all bad thoughts and focused only on her husband that evening. They made passionate love that night. For the first time since time immemorial she agreed to all his desires.

***

In this world, many areas of life were arranged in even numbers. Two communities lived in two lands, of which Inco made up nearly a quarter of the small planet's surface. This is why it was colloquially referred to as the quarter, sometimes the southern quarter. The second land, Floris, which made up the other three quarters, was called the countryside or even the hollow in Inco. The people living there were called the Boonies, sometimes fools, and most rarely Florians by the inhabitants of the neighboring country. Inco was divided centrally into four zones called districts.

In the middle of the country-first district, stood a huge metropolis full of luxurious skyscrapers. Their lower parts were office areas, while on the upper floors there were multi-level apartments of the richest part of society. In this part of Inco, public transportation was completely unnecessary. Young people usually walked, usually on wide pedestrian streets, arranged in a regular grid of squares with collision-free, multi-level intersections. The elderly, who were not healthy enough to walk on their own, were hidden in houses so as not to pose a threat and not to make the society obsessed with physical activity worse. Occasionally one could see vehicles hovering a little above the ground, but this was rare and concerned rather people connected with the Government or state services.

Further from the center, the so-called second district, was a slum, rightly called the filter. Multi-storey buildings, one next to the other, housing workers' families and a whole bunch of social outcasts, filtered the sand and dust coming from the distant outskirts, that is the third and fourth districts, not allowing them to get to the clean district one. Only in the slums was there public transportation based on endless multi-level conveyor belts. If they worked, they were mostly used by the elderly. Government vehicles did not appear here, but the sight of various means of transport of the garda, the local police, was rather not alien to anyone. This is where the fire and rescue services had the most work.

The third district consisted of clusters of factories producing food and technological goods, generating and accumulating energy from *Hello* rays for use in factories, and for extracting and distilling water from nearby dead lakes. An army and border guard base in one was also located in this district. It was a modern unit, fully automated and dominated by robots. They were managed by a small group of professional officers, mostly male. They had a variety of weapons made with available technology at their disposal. The government never spared on border protection.

The final fourth district, the one furthest from the center of Inco, consisted of implacable rocky steppes with access to essential minerals and a small desert. Inco was almost completely devoid of any vegetation or animals. The border between this land and Floris ran through a difficult mountain range and only in one section along the wide, life-giving Ethne river along with the high Pinati waterfall. Due to poor ventilation, the whole of Inco was covered in a grey smog, regularly blown away by autonomous, flying bird-shaped machines with large, moving wings. They worked around the clock.

Inco was self-sufficient. Poor quality fresh water was always in abundance, although it was relatively not cheap. In the western part of the third district, food production took place in several state-owned plants. It consisted of regeneration bars - red, high-protein ones, fondly called slush, and green, based on carbohydrates, which were simply called fodder. Standing near the dead lake, a huge factory complex produced about a hundred million of each type every day. The pleasure of eating was exchanged for a rush toward health. The bars provided the optimal, calculated amount of ingredients necessary for life. It was enough to eat one a day. The rest of the diet consisted of supplements. After all, for many generations, in fact since the beginning of the twenty-fourth era, which is when the Chemist Party funded by the drug cartels came to power, the plethora of drugs and supplements for all ailments was virtually incalculable. After the twenty-second era, when it was realized that society was dying too quickly from obesity, slimness became a national obsession. It worked. Mortality rates declined rapidly, and the average age lived by Inco citizens doubled.

The language of the community has always evolved to some degree, although at different rates in different areas. There were local dialects, different meanings of the same words and different grammatical forms. It is difficult to speak of unity in a nation that used different words to describe the same phenomena or values. Three eras before the beginning of the world, i.e. the division into two lands, a council composed of the sages of that time decided that not only should the language be unified, but also the features of particular life laws should be given identical names. First, an order was established regarding the units of time. Up to that time, some measured it in days, others in weeks, still others in months. Although the units could be arranged in a logical whole, there was always a problem with them.

After much discussion, the Council agreed that the *Omniearth* travels in its orbit around a star called *Hello* in a repeating cycle. During this wandering, the planet had two distinct seasons. One of them, lasting exactly one hundred and twelve months, was called almost everywhere the same: the bloom. The other, a complement to their year, lasting only two months, was spoken of differently in practically every quarter: cleansing, renewal, restoration, purification. To make matters worse, in the western quarters and almost all of the northern quarters, this time of year was treated as more important and short-lived, so it was in this quarter that time was measured. It was said there that something took one purification, which meant that approximately one lap around *Hello* had passed. Not everyone understood how it was possible that a purification was a year, but also a shorter season. In order to avoid confusion, and to prevent people from mixing up the two meanings of one word, it was established that purification from now on would be called a full year, and the seasons that comprise it would be renewal and bloom.

Each day was divided into five seasons: morning, noon, afternoon, evening, and night. During a single purification, the duration of each time of day varied according to the position of the *Omniearth* relative to *Hello*.

The time between each co-moon - that is, the days when during the night three of the four visible moons formed a single line in the sky - was called a month and lasted four weeks, eight days each. There were one hundred and fourteen such months during the entire purification, one hundred and twelve of them during the flowering, and two of them during the renewal. One era lasted exactly one hundred purifications. After these arrangements, order finally came. When this burning issue was dealt with, in a flash the entire language was unified and in this form it has functioned ever since.

The bloom was the dominant season of the local year, during which it was usually warm and sunny. Rain, if it fell, was brief and infrequent, basically only at night. Sometimes there was fog in the evenings. During the renewal, first the temperature rose rapidly, even setting in severe heat. Immediately thunderstorms came, strong winds blew, and it rained heavily. Then it got colder and colder, almost icy. Everything would freeze and after a few days, some said, "after a few *Hello's*," or "few *hellorises*" it would suddenly come back to life. Again the bloom would begin. And so on and so forth. During the renewal, this short season, all plants would die, while creatures would fall asleep in their burrows. This ritual also applied to the human species.

Florians lived in harmony with nature, meaning that they regenerated in burrows during the recovery period. In Inco, this customary life function for the species was passé. Back in the eighteenth era, it was considered a waste of time. A way to wait it out was invented. But everyone knew that during this time of year, the bodies and minds of living creatures needed to be refreshed, to eliminate accumulated bad emotions and toxins. Nevertheless, a change was decided upon and no one ever dared to propose a return to the roots.

Since people in Inco replaced natural processes with new rituals, they began to live shorter and in poorer health. No connection was made between these two facts. It was supposed to be more modern, so it was. Action chased reaction. As people began to get fatter and their health declined, the way to longevity was invented - medicines. Genetically modified hormone-controlling supplements became a staple of the Inco man's diet. Pills appeared for everything. For all kinds of pain, obesity, for bad moods. Even drugs related to sexual desire had many different versions. A twenty-point scale was created to take into account all possible states, ranging from a complete lack of desire through low and medium desire to constant hyperactivity. The entire body could be controlled. Every hormone, every organ and its action, at every time of day. Medicines had their own brands. The better ones for the richer, and the mass ones for the poor from the slums, who over time began to lose their teeth. This condition was explained by a change in their lifestyle. After all, they had been chewing rather than biting for at least two cleanses.

Ostensibly to reduce the amount of vital energy consumed. It was supposed to be the answer to longevity and prevent possible obesity. They believed.

Over time, they began to need something more. How long can one live in drug-controlled apathy? Twelve purifications earlier, Metachemie, a conglomerate run by one of the drug cartels, had launched a modified hybrid drug called *Ray*. It was supposed to be a remedy for all ailments. It made you not want to eat, but it gave you a lot of energy. People taking it were easily successful and happy. It was accepted quickly.

***

The next morning, while Jasmin was still asleep, Addam smeared his body with a cream containing a good dose of nutritional value, vitamins and minerals, thickly in some places, creating a slippery coating that he did not immediately want to absorb. He patted the excess, not without pleasure, especially on his thighs and around his buttocks. Once he was sure his body was no longer sticky, he put on an outer garment that looked like a latex suit with short pants. Biting through the slush, he peeked through the glass wall at the Inco skyline. The view was stunning. The glass buildings reached for the clouds. Colorful boardwalks winded between them, protected from above by an energy glow. On this kind of obscurity, zany displays of all kinds of services and products were occasionally projected from large projectors. They were clearly visible both from the luxury apartments located at the very top of the skyscrapers and from the bottom for people strolling along the promenade. These baubles almost screamed that in this city the ideal of beauty is not a woman, but a man, preferably young and well-built. Whether it was a middle-aged boy or a swarthy, muscular bearded man with a mature, penetrating gaze, each proudly displayed his masculinity, making the recommended product or service more attractive. The biggest part of this 24-hour spectacle was the bait-and-switch associated with the supposedly accessible cyber technology available to everyone. It seemed that people didn't have to work at all, because all activities could be performed by robots - whether they were based on artificial intelligence with a high empathy index or soulless *humaans* used in border guards, emergency services and *garda*, or simple machines for cleaning or ionizing air. On the other hand, prostitution was by far the most recommended service. Since the beginning of the tenth era, when the government realized that there was no need to make a fuss about it and it was enough to impose appropriate taxes, this service became completely legal. For a good five purifications, due to the declining interest in the female sex, the profession had been practiced almost entirely by men or humanoid robots with male facial features and a transparent shell imitating skin. This was just another stupid fashion, promoted on the example of transparent panniers - after all, if everything is visible, there is no concern about impure intentions of the manufacturer. In fact, it was a decree related to the superiority of the human race over cybernetics. So that no one would mistake a human for a machine and eliminate it by mistake, robots were given transparent mouths. Many women who could afford to buy a robot taught to love flamboyantly did not like this solution. To cover up the insensitive looking mechanisms and to feel a substitute for a real male face, they painted over the carelessly transparent shell with flesh-colored paint. Occasionally, one could see used robots or parts of robots with peeling or scratched paint on the garbage dumps.

Before Addam left for work, he stood for a moment beside the low, flat bed occupying most of the ascetic bedroom sectioned off in the living room. Sleeping in it was Jasmin, on her stomach. She was naked. Her delicate body, partially covered by a tulle bedspread, looked innocent yet phenomenal. Her only mole on her whole body, located perfectly in the middle between her shoulder blades, on her spine, tempted to check if it was real. It gave the impression of being unique. Addam stopped his gaze on it, almost as if it were every day. He smiled tenderly and kissed Jasmin gently on the shoulder. She did not feel his lips on hers. She was still in a deep sleep at this hour, though this was not an ordinary sight in her case. She had planned to take this day off from work. She was convinced that the news she would give to her husband the day before would make them celebrate until the morning. That did not happen. When Addam had fallen asleep the night before, exhausted by the intoxicating caresses, Jasmin had been restlessly moving from side to side for a long time.

***

Suddenly there was the loud sound of a metal gong made of several centrally mounted copper rings. When Jasmin had chosen it, the sound had seemed more subtle to her than it did today. This time it was triggered by brown-haired Luicey Biedermann, who was anxious to hear the news of a potential pregnancy. It was she who had recommended Dr. Steavans to a colleague. Before Jasmin opened the door to the suite, she covered her naked body with a tulle quilt. The friend ran inside and flew like lightning straight to the cooler. That was the name of the room used to hold the supply of recovery bars and hectoliters of drinking water. Luicey took one of the small bottles with a label that read encouragingly, "Pearl. From the purest springs of Floris." She unscrewed the cork and gulped down the contents, astonishing her hostess.

“Well, speak at last, or I can't stand it,” fired Luicey in one breath, after which she took several deep breaths.

“Why haven't you been in touch?” Jasmin asked coldly.

“Check the communicator,” Luicey said indignantly.

Jasmin walked over to the bed. From under the bedspread she pulled out a small pink device that looked like a flashlight with several buttons, she pressed one of them. A streak of blue light came out of the communicator, which Jasmin projected onto the wall. It acted like a micro-router. You could see a list of recent calls. Most were from Luicey.

"Indeed. How did you know I was home?" She asked and turned off her communicator.

"I was at your office."

Suddenly she saw a soft smile appear on Jasmin's face.

"What do you wonder? I couldn't sleep a wink. I ate three feeds out of nervousness and now I have to catch up on water levels." Luicey seemed unhappy that her friend didn't appreciate her commitment. "Are you going to say something, or do I have to beg you?"

"All right. What do you want to know?" Jasmin asked.

" Everything. How was it? How's Dr. Steavans? And you know..."

"It was even tolerable. It's not my favorite examination," she murmured shyly.

"But specifics, specifics..." In Luicey's voice one could clearly sense a hint of malicious irritation. "It's a boy?"

"No," Jasmin answered shortly and hid her face in her hands.

This was not the answer Luicey expected. However, she decided to lift her friend's spirits.

"A girl is not a problem. It could always be worse. If it was the second or twins... The first child is not a total tragedy yet. You're rich, you can handle it. What does Addam say?"

"He doesn't know."

"Oh, shit. But will you tell him?"

"Yeah, just..." Jasmin didn't feel like continuing the conversation anymore, she purposely made a bored face.

"At the most, we will find you some proven doctor who will relieve you of the problem."

Luicey was unable to elicit any positive emotions from her best friend, so she quickly decided to relent.

"I'm coming. Remember, you're still young. Bye, sweetie," she said and made a secret bow, remembered from her childhood days, hoping it would make her laugh. It didn't help.

Jasmin closed the door of the suite in complete silence. She glanced at the unmade bed and headed for the cooler. She pulled one of the green candy bars from the shelf, unwrapped it, and took a gentle bite. It didn't taste good today. She put it back on the shelf involuntarily and went to refresh herself.

In the wealthier part of the metropolitan area, the recovery rooms looked more like a gymnasium. Exercise equipment stood in it, used without clothing. It was more hygienic that way. After the workout, it was enough to activate the flushing module, which in the form of rain falling from the perforated ceiling washed away not only the sweat from the body, but also from the machines. After the entire process, a blower was activated to dry the entire room along with the exercisers. Such a fashion. It was completely different in the poorer part of Inco, the slums. There were no rooms, and the regenerative devices themselves were rather small in caliber. A portable, multi-functional head, looking more like a curling iron than a shower handset, was used to wash, possibly fumigation or deworm, and later to dry human bodies. All one had to do was change the given program and use within the allotted water and energy level. Refreshing with this method had two disadvantages: it simply took longer and the head often clogged. Besides, district two often ran out of water, and what's more, it was expensive.

That day Jasmin, for the first time in a long time, was not going to exercise. She got out of the pancake made tulle quilt and immediately turned on the body rinse module. The stream of falling drops, however, was a little too strong. Apparently Addam had set that particular program. The woman did not change it, but quickly interrupted the refreshment. When she turned on the drying program, the module demanded to complete the previous process and crashed. Jasmin wrestled with the device, cursing at Addam that it was his fault. She pressed more buttons, but the screen kept displaying the unfinished program. With each attempt, Jasmin grew more and more furious, until she finally gave up out of helplessness. She left the room naked and wet.

Just by touching the wall, which looked like a piece of concrete overgrown with artificial vegetation, the wall retracted into the ceiling, revealing access to the dressing room. When Jasmin stepped inside, she was still a little annoyed at the refreshment system. The bad mood didn't pass quickly, even when she saw hundreds of variations of outerwear in various shades of grey and a shelf of shoes. As a rule, that sight made her feel better. Not today. She slipped the first better dress over her wet, firm body and began to think about her choice of sandals. Suddenly she heard a familiar sound. It was the communicator informing her of an upcoming call. Its signal was synchronized with the small light blinking on the mirror located in the dressing room. Without leaving the dressing room, Jasmin paired the devices together by touching the small sensor in the lower right corner of the mirror.

“Are you finally up, sleepyhead?” asked a male voice.

It was a familiar timbre that could sometimes soothe her nerves. She smiled at her thoughts.

“Is that you? Hang up, because my husband will be here in a moment," she joked, although her tone of voice did not sound very cheerful.

“Very funny," Addam said with a laugh.

“I haven't slept like this in a long time, honey. How was the office? Is everything okay?” She asked.

“We need to talk.”

Jasmin was deeply disturbed by his businesslike tone. She didn't like him. He usually didn't bode well. Since Addam started the conversation that way, it means that either something terrible happened, like he lost his job, or he found out he was pregnant. Just from whom? Did Luicey talk herself out? Or did the GCO bitch make a fuss that a high-ranking employee of the Public Opinion and Public Attitudes Research Bureau was going to have female triplets? - she mused.

“Okay," she whispered briefly, though her voice sounded like it was stuck in her throat.

“What are your plans for today?” Addam artificially kept up the conversation, which always irritated Jasmin.

“Can you say that again?” she answered with a question he hated because she didn't want to continue the masquerade.

“I have to go. See you tonight," he muttered and hung up.

“Well, bye," Jasmin said to herself. “See you tonight.”

She was sure this was going to be one of the longest days of her short life. She had no desire to go outside. The weather forecast at Inco was extremely precise and accurate. The temperature for today was forecast to be about six hundred Meyer degrees and a light breeze. That is, the same as yesterday, the day before yesterday, and for the last sixteen days. Tomorrow, on the other hand, the day off, is supposed to be six hundred and thirty degrees and a brief evening rain. There will be some variety. She and Addam had planned a visit to an art gallery. She was looking forward to it.

As an industrial city, Inco offered little in the way of activities for the experience-hungry, bored residents. There were no restaurants. Because what for? Who would want to eat recovery bars at a beautifully decorated table and candles? There was one inn, decorated in an old-fashioned style, and damned expensive. It sold meals made with imported ingredients from Floris, but basically only Government representatives ate there when they hosted a delegation from a neighboring country. Consumption of real food for the people of Inco usually ended in severe pains. No wonder. The digestive systems of the officials, as well as of every resident of this land, were limited to digesting candy bars.

Since there were no places to eat, where did the elite of this city meet? Only in art galleries offering the only kind of art allowed, that is, a hybrid of painting and sculpture. Thanks to the graciousness of the Government, few artists were given a license to create their works. They tended to focus on the technique of four-dimensional painting, or spatial painting, which was able to mutate over time. These were truly labor-intensive cakes. It took a quarter of a purification or more to create a single work, the size of, say, a person, depicting a time-shifting story several minutes in length. Nevertheless, when this masterpiece was completed, there was no shortage of those willing to interact with it, even repeatedly. Other artistic disciplines were in short supply. In fact, the Inco government did not recognize the artistic arts; indeed, it forbade the study of any kind, especially those favored in Floris, such as sculpture, pottery, and song. Something like music, that is, undulating sounds forming harmonic vibratory sequences, was available to the general public, but only during important state ceremonies. These sounds replaced the country's anthem. It was always presented in conjunction with another symbol of national identity, the white flag. Of the other attractions to choose from, there was still *theatremania*, with four channels controlled by the ruling camp. The first channel broadcast over and over again the accomplishments of the Government or the Chemist Party, linked to the drug cartels. The second on the list was a sports channel. It reported on interesting events or games of various disciplines. These did not only involve human competition, but also various types of robots. They took place in the company of journalists, whose opinions were interrupted by baits. The third channel featured staged, moralistic stories. The fourth channel contained programs about health, advice on raising sons, and weather forecasts.

With a voice command, Jasmin activated the first channel of *theatremania.* Immediately there was a big screen displayed on one of the white walls. A news program was in progress and the commentator was, as every day, praising the merits of the Government. Suddenly the picture disappeared. After a while a picture of several officials appeared and a commentary on the lower bar: "Concealment of the truth. Government to resign!" Jasmin couldn't believe her eyes. Was this intentional? After all, the ruling party had stood its ground for many purifications, with the officials always looking the same, only their heads had changed. No one had ever fired anyone, no one had ever resigned. Boredom. The propaganda of the party's success was done exemplarily, based on the best standards of marketing. Jasmin could appreciate their craftsmanship. She herself worked in one of the corporations responsible, among other things, for the promotion of a series of supplements helping to reduce dental plaque.

She turned up her voice. Nothing could be heard. After a moment, another picture appeared on the screen. This time it was the then Prime Minister, Barney Clifford, with a not very friendly face. The still image was quickly deleted and after a brief pause, accompanied by irritating noises, a barrage of varicose vein massaging devices appeared. Jasmin only thought that someone's head would fly for such an unfortunate picture of the most important person in the state. She turned off the *theatremania* and began to wonder what it was all about. Later that evening there was a clarifying announcement that channel one had mistakenly broadcast unready material, planned as a moralizing story for channel three. At the time, none of the Inco residents attached any significance to the incident.

When Addam came back from work, it turned out to be about this hacking attack on theatricality and the mention of the government resignation that he wanted to talk to his wife about. He didn't dare to do so via instant messenger. Jasmin breathed a sigh of relief.

“These juvenile antics are just the tip of a thicker scandal," he said. - A journalist, incidentally, who has just lost his job, has come across some material that links the Government's activities to the problem of the reduced number of births of boys. There is talk of a Y chromosome.

“Y?” she wondered.

“This much I know. The GCO has disassociated itself from these revelations.”

Jasmin felt that Addam was not telling her the whole truth. He looked involved and full of doubt. This was suspicious. But if he knew anything, he could not share that knowledge even with his own wife. Jasmin this time attached more importance to the fact that she had a secret too. Although she was aware that her husband was also hiding something, she did not feel justified.

“When do you think things will clear up?” She asked, watching Addam closely.

“I suspect we'll see another episode within the next week or so. Well, let's say two.”

Jasmin was already sure that since there was a declaration of dates, it meant that her husband's entire office really knew a lot.

***

Just before the visit to the art gallery, Addam had been very anxious. Jasmin thought it was again about topics related to the government scandal. But he had been keeping a close eye on his wife. A few times he glanced casually at her stomach. Although he mirrored her gently, she did not like it. As she fastened the impressive ruby necklace, she felt his critical gaze on her. She decided not to wait any longer in uncertainty.

“Addam, is something bothering you?” she asked.

“I don't know if I'd call it anxiety. It's more like I'm totally fucked up," he mumbled, not hiding his ominous tone.

“Something about the affair?”

“It's about trusting those closest to you.”

"And what, are you going to punish me now? When will I get the honor and you will kindly tell me what you mean?"

"When were you going to tell me you visited Dr. Steavans?"

"In due course."

"Why do I need to hear about it from others?"

"From whom?"

"Never mind!" shouted Addam and started nervously walking around the living room.

He was dressed in a festive uniform that he wore only on occasions like today. And it was this pressed and stiff outfit that made him doubly anxious. He quickly undid all four buttons at the collar and breathed a sigh of relief. Jasmin knew there were only two possibilities. Either Addam had found out from the doctor or that Gibbondy bitch, or her friend said. In the first case, he probably learned the whole truth, while in the second case, only part of it. Only one question could quickly dispel the doubt.

"What if we had a daughter?" She asked and swallowed her saliva.

"That's impossible! It would have to mean that something was broken between us. No one in our family has ever had a girl. Boys have always been born. Even more so now that there are such restrictions, it would be irresponsible."

"You don't pay tax for one girl," Jasmin said nonchalantly, recognizing that Luicey was not to be trusted.

"Yes. But for a boy we could get a high social security benefit. Besides, another child would be a risk. Let me remind you that you can only have one girl. You can have boys all you want, but no girls! Have you forgotten?!"

"We can afford it! We earn a lot!" she shouted, but after a while she calmed her tone. "You wanted to have several children."

"Yes, but boys." Addam saw the sadness in Jasmin's eyes. He walked over to her and embraced her tenderly.

"That's the only thing there is no cure for. You can't choose your gender. What is this whole pharmaceutical industry for?" she asked in a whisper.

"Come on, now. I love you. Have you thought about having an abortion?

And all the charm associated with his tenderness hit.

"Fuck you!" She shouted and turned her head away.

This time it was Addam who grimaced. Her determination reassured him that there would apparently be a first girl in the family. Ever since he met Jasmin, and that was back in school, he knew that he would always have to practice argumentation. Otherwise his will would lose to the stubbornness of the ambitious girl. Then all his classmates looked up to her. He thought they matched, although she came from a poorer family. Sometimes he would tell her that she wanted to rise too quickly, but he was actually impressed. In front of his own family he always defended her, explaining that she had class and was more concrete than the others, although his father told him not to marry if he was not sure of his feelings. Even when they quarreled or insulted each other, he never even for a moment considered that they could separate. They had grown close in their own way. He knew that if she insisted on something, there was no force that could dissuade her from it. On the other hand, the birth of a daughter was a harbinger of serious problems, not only financial.

For some time in this country, only girls and very occasionally boys were born. Children were also born who had organs of both sexes but were incapable of reproduction. They were called "*hermas.*" The government, which had definitive solutions for all ills, decided to deal with the problem quickly. It introduced a decree prohibiting the registration of children without a clear sex. Consequently, to the despair of parents, intersex infants were disposed of. Their bodies were cremated while still on the hospital grounds, a few rooms away from where the birth was received. This was supposed to help. Rumor had it that the male proportion was less than twenty percent of the population and steadily declining. The exact figures were not known to the public because the Government was hiding them. It was said that far fewer boys than girls were being born, far fewer than seniors were leaving this world. In order to prevent society from turning into a country of amazons, the Government introduced the Gender Control Decree. According to its rules, one family could have a maximum of one daughter. Sons could be had at will, but that hardly ever happened. If a family had more than one girl, they had to pay a high tax for each additional girl. On the other hand, each son was entitled to social benefits so high that they could support a large family, including grandparents. In the case of families with two daughters and more, the parents had to work hard and still lived in poverty. Everything was supervised by the Gender Control Office. Representatives of this institution supervised the work of every gynecological office in the state, because in the past there had been cases of fraud. The system of abortion of unwanted "taxes", as girls were called, flourished. It was more humane that way. To protect the species.

“Everything will be fine," Addam said tenderly and hugged Jasmin.

Chapter 2 Floris

The family of Fahid, a poor dirham farmer in the western quadrant of Floris, was expecting a long-awaited visitor. A few days ago Mahmud, the host's father of seven purifications, died. Unfortunately, according to the Patri rite, the body of the deceased could not be mummified without the participation of the priest. To prevent his father's body from beginning to rot in this warm climate, Fahid carried it to a burrow hollowed out in a small hill, where it was customary to keep food during the bloom. *Let father eat before his last journey, he looks so miserable,* thought the God-fearing, white-haired son.

"He's coming! He's coming!" shouted Sumi joyfully.

Fahid ran outside the hut where his large family lived. In the distance, across a field that stretched all the way to the horizon and looked like a purple sea with ribbons of uneven stony paths, he saw the silhouette of Kadu, priest of the goddess Patri. He rode on a three-wheeled cart pulled by a pair of animals. Fahid could not immediately recognize them, even though he had been farming since childhood and used them in his daily work. They were simply too far away.

In this colorful land, three species that looked quite similar were domesticated. They had the same pale white coat color and almost identical bodies. As a result of evolution, their backs developed a seat that made it easy for the rider to make even the most arduous journey without hurting the animal he was riding. The comfortable edge of each of the three types of back was covered with a protective mane that looked like intertwined, narrow strips of dark algae. It fitted the rider like a saddle. Beneath the creatures' torso was a belly with sagging skin and four pairs of small breasts. Each had three tubular nipples capable of feeding a large litter. Two pairs of asymmetrically placed, muscular legs ended in three-toed feet. Each of the exceptionally flat toes concealed a sharp claw to help navigate slippery surfaces and even climb steep slopes. Two fingers on the front, one on the back of the paw, and a membrane between them, provided a sense of stability in any terrain. All three species were unisexual. They reproduced by nucleation. When an animal reached reproductive maturity, it gave birth to numerous offspring. Up to fifteen individuals. Only once during its lifetime.

These species differed in agility, pulling power, and head shape. The fastest ones were not suitable for farm work, but for fast travel. They were most often used in the military or used as a means of transport for couriers of the local post office. Their head was slender, disproportionate to their muscular body. They had long, pointed, sinew-filled ears that served as reins when ridden on horseback. They were called *okurai*. The slowest but strongest were the *tine*, with a round head and ears covered by a membrane. They tended to be used as pulling power for primitive tillage equipment, and younger individuals were used to play with children. The more adorable pets were even given names. An intermediate species was the *hydapi*. They had an elongated head and spindly auricles shaped like punched bladders. They were used to work underwater and also in the mountains because of their resistance to harsh weather and low pressure. All three species were bred to have an interchangeable means of transportation, as livestock, or as a food source. Their milk mixed with blood made an excellent energy drink called *keeffi*, while meat and offal proved to be an indispensable part of a high-protein diet. The names of these animals were not conjugated. Whether it was one individual or a whole herd, they were always called *okurai*, *hydapi* or *tine*.

As Fahid watched Kadu approach, he wondered when he had last seen a stranger on the farm. From what he could remember, he had appeared when he and his father had built a large windmill to produce the energy needed to control the irrigation system for the fields. Today, their joint creation was a little haunted by its clumsiness and archaic workmanship. *It could use some new fillings*, Fahid thought, and remembered that Sumi, his beloved daughter, was also born then. The priest of Kadu, who had come to perform her nuptials to the goddess Patri, was the very stranger last seen in his household. Apart from him, no one had passed this way for many purifications. Similarly, none of Fahid's family members had ever ventured far. About once every half cleansing they traveled, usually himself or with his father, to the nearest Litrijis settlement to exchange crops for needed items or gray stones, the local currency. From time to time they would see their neighbors. They lived a few days away and belonged to a family.

"Go to your mother, have her prepare food. And help her," Fahid said to Sumi.

The visit of the priest was an interesting event for the curious girl, so she did not feel like going home at all. She hesitated for a long time what to do. She wanted to personally greet Kadu, who had once performed the ritual of her birth. Besides, she had never seen anyone but family members in her life. On the other hand, her father's words were equally sacred. To reconcile the two, she decided to help a little and return quickly. Before she was given the task of fetching some treats from her mother, she peeked through the window opening to see if, by chance, a visitor had already arrived. This was not the window familiar from Inco, as glass was not used in Floris. The openings were used to ventilate the houses. They were covered with a mesh that defended the entry of insects that made life difficult.

Sumi ran toward a small hillock thickly covered with yellow moss. On its almost vertical slope hung *shuri* shoots. She swung them open like a small curtain. Hidden behind them was an oval wooden door, leading to a deep cave hollowed in the brown rock. It was in such places, during the short season called renewal, when the land was haunted by hail storms, heavy rains and frost, that the Florians would fall asleep. They were then subject to the regeneration of their bodies, minds and souls. Without water or food. During the heyday, or dominant season, the burrow served as a handy larder.

White-haired like all her siblings, Sumi couldn't make up her mind. The cave hid so many fragrant foods. On the wooden shelves there were baskets full of various edibles, woven from shuriken stems. She didn't know what their guest liked, so just in case, she took her favorite treats, a little bit of everything. She took one last look at her grandfather's corpse lying in the burrow and left. When Kadu got close enough for Fahid to recognize that the harness was drawn by *hydapi* animals, she was already standing back next to her father.

“Good morning, Kadu," Fahid greeted his guest.

“Good morning. Isn't that the little girl we married to Patri once, probably one purification ago?” asked the tired priest dressed in a penitential robe.

“It's me," Sumi reported, but her face was not happy at the sight of such a disgusting person.

“We're glad you were able to come so quickly," said the host, distracting the guest from his frightened daughter.

***

Rita, not a very pretty but warm-looking woman, Fahid's yellow-haired wife had, as usual, made a great effort. The big feasting platform placed on the stone terrace on the side where *Hello* was shining the strongest was overflowing with food and drink. On its wooden top one could see cakes made of *mao* flour, platters of juicy gray *sandi* fruit, and tuberous purple puke vegetables, the foraged variety of which served to supplement the diet of pregnant livestock. In the middle of the platform stood a ceramic flask of fat that looked like black lard. It was a delicacy of the local community, made by evaporating charcoal-colored *okurai* milk. It was because of the speed of the animals of this breed, and thus their excellent metabolism, that it was the most essential and tastiest. Over the entire terrace hung a small canopy of vines. Their long, edible, sweet-smelling thorns served as holders for hanging pieces of roasted *tine* meat and braided cheese rolls. There was also a smear of purple *dirshna* flowers. After all, Fahid's family specialized in growing this life-giving rush. A full bowl tempted with its smell not only the hosts, but also the surrounding *moree* birds. It was rich.

Kadu refreshed himself after the tiring journey. He took off his penitential robe, which looked like a dirty beige bag made of stem fiber, and put on a festive version, special for such occasions, of similar cut but embroidered with gilded thread. Despite these treatments, he still looked disgusting, at least seven cleans, though he had only six. His skin in many places resembled scaly, inflamed wounds from the burn, and his brownish-gray eyes and sparse teeth seemed to scream that the priest had just returned from some abyss. When he saw the feast so lavishly prepared and the corpse covered with cloth next to it, he smiled warmly at the host, compensating for the uninteresting face. He knew that the poor family attached great importance to rituals and did not skimp on their goods if they were to be used as an offering made for the dead. He did not count on them drinking for Mahmud's soul. He saw that Fahid, like his father before him, shunned all stimulants and alcohol. When he gave the sign that the ceremony could begin, the large family consisting of parents and ten children stood around the platform and began to sway, mumbling seemingly meaningless syllables. The priest at this time discovered Mahmud's body. On one of his stringy legs, near the ankle, he noticed a funky leather bracelet decorated with unusual ornaments. He glanced in the direction of his host, who only shrugged his shoulders.

"The last will of the deceased. He wanted to take a family heirloom with him," he said.

Kadu was not happy with this turn of events. After all, religion forbade taking any worldly goods with him. Eventually he agreed to such a deviation from the rules. He began to sprinkle his body with a powdered mixture of *radda* herb and dried *dirshna* flowers. The powder, which looked like magic dust, was removed with his fingers from a small tin box with a decorated lid. Fahid's children glanced jealously in the direction of the ritual. They would also like to play at mummifying the dead. Besides, there was nothing unnatural about it. In Floris, death was treated as something pleasant, the beginning of a new, better life, a person's journey to Patri.

“Mahmud, my friend, are you ready for your final journey?” Kadu asked, turning his head towards Mount Saandreal, visible in the distance.

“I am," replied the son of the deceased according to the ritual.

“Do you feel rested and full?” continued the priest.

“I feel.”

“Has your body rid itself of all evil and do you have a clear mind?”

“Twice that.”

“So, before I cover you with the balm of light and you go to Patri, worship *Hello* and this rich land.”

Fahid's family in complete silence and reverie began to bow to the invisible spirits in all directions of the world. At this time Kadu was wrapping Mahmud's naked body with pieces of bark from a *mohair tree* soaked in green sticky oleum. It was elastic like a cloth and stuck easily to the skin. When Kadu finished poulticing the front of his torso, he turned his body over and continued on his back. At this time the family members did not stop bowing.

“Goodbye!” shouted Kadu.

“Goodbye!” Fahid and his wife answered him with a chorus.

Rita looked at her husband and gave him a tender smile. The priest sprinkled another small pinch of magic dust in the direction of the food platform and then finished the ritual. With Fahid's help, he packed Mahmoud's body onto the cart and covered it with a cloth. The family could finally begin the celebration. The priest did not intend to fast that day, on the contrary. He stuffed himself as if he had not eaten for days. When he reached for the keeffi, he made a face of disappointment each time, as if he were hoping for another drink to sip.

Suddenly, there was the sound of flapping wings and a few grunts, as if an aerial brawl was taking place several cubits above the revelers. A strangled *raidi* creature fell near the food platform. It was a quarter of an elbow long and had green and white plumage. Sumi glanced up at the sky and noticed four *moree* birds flying in circles at a low altitude just above the house.

"Oh, it's a furry one. This one's a glutton," she said.

"Give him a pie, or he won't detach himself," her father said.

Kadu glanced toward the birds, but had to squint because *Hello* was glaring at him. Meanwhile, Sumi tore off a piece of *mao* cake and threw it up in the air. A burly *moree* bird swooped down toward the treat and caught it in flight.

"They would cut themselves for such a treat," said Rita proudly, but Kadu was not impressed.

It is noteworthy that the people of Floris learned to use - not domesticate, but harness - predatory, four-eyed, scale-covered *moree* birds. They helped hunt the many species of flying, colorful creatures useful on the farm, which were inedible because of the hairy texture of their flesh. They were all called the same thing: *raidi* creatures. They were used to make cloth for clothing, but also rope. *Moree* birds had no beaks, but razor-sharp talons, one on each of their four wings, and dwarf horns on their heads, usually two. Although there were also those that grew a third, spiral, curved horn, as if under the chin, and only when the bird lived to a ripe old age. For this species it meant more than one cleansing. Their hunts looked quite unusual. When they caught up with their prey, they would embrace it with all four wings and strangle it. Since they couldn't fly in such a situation, before they strangled their prey they would fall several elbows with it, sometimes all the way to the ground, shattering its body and breaking its wings. Rarely did any bird survive such a fall. *Moree* had no legs, so you could say they were always in flight. They even slept, swaying slightly in the wind or hanging head down, hooked by one of their claws on a tree branch. It was easy for humans to learn how to lure and exploit them; they were greedy for food. All they had to do was make cakes of *mao* flour with *dirshna* smear and toss them into the sky. Out of gratitude, they would bring their prey and throw it under people's feet. Although they were not enslaved, they cleverly kept close to human settlements. In fact, few individuals of this species lived quite wild. They have been seen near the Asaran Gorge, among other places. They fed on pink-blue *turlin* fruit, which grew in bunches only in that region.

Kadu did not stay long after finishing his meal, even though his hosts urged him to listen to Sumi's vocal talent.

He explained that he had to reach the Litrijis settlement before evening. As he watered and fed the *hydapi*, Fahid's children excitedly threw more pieces of *dirshna* cake into the air, and the *moree* birds showed off their agility by catching them in flight. Kadu measured the sight, collected the funeral fee, and departed.

***

The world began when, after a conflict over access to science, the surface of the *Omniearth* was divided into two countries: Inco and Floris. Since then, the two communities have grown apart. Although they all spoke the same language, they wrote it differently. Inco was founded by people looking for answers to their questions about existence. There, they began to abandon faith in favor of dizzying progress explained by the wisdom of men, not the laws of God. In Floris, life continued at its old pace. There was no interest in technology. Agriculture, local culture based on religion, and the artistic arts were strongly developed. Schools, teaching only useful professions, were not compulsory. No attention to fitness in the form of sports was known here. Nobody worried about bad weather or worse crops. After all, the inhabitants were protected by the goddess Patri, and on earth her counterpart: Ae - the High Priestess of the *Omniearth*. She lived with the Church Council in Patrix, the capital of the country, which looked like a network of hollowed out caves connected by corridors. Patrix was located inside a sacred mountain called Saandreal, just below the Golden Temple in the shape of an inverted pyramid with stone steps located on the inside. They served as a resting place for the priests during their daily prayers. Above the golden, inverted temple was the Diamond Shrine, arranged symmetrically with respect to it. It was the top of the hill. None of the inhabitants of Floris could cross its threshold, only the High Priests. This is where Patri herself was believed to reside. She surrounded herself with all the souls of the dead. Although no one but the High Priests had ever seen this place, all the people of Floris believed it existed. News of it was passed down orally from generation to generation. It was only known that the Diamond Shrine was the most magnificent and sacred place in the world.

Not only the highest hierarchs of the Church lived in Patrix. There was also a school, in which future priests were prepared for their ministry. The recruitment was always done by letter, in the form of an invitation. No one ever refused. A family that received a letter with the vocation of one of their children, gave their child away forever. Despite the painful loss, this gesture was associated with pride. After all, a priest in this country was the epitome of holiness. After training, which lasted one cleansing, the newly minted representative of the Church first did military service which lasted another cleansing, then he was sent to the assigned district. Always in the opposite direction from his hometown. The focus was to be on ministry, not on feelings or family relationships. This applied to both male and female priests. To ensure that their mission did not end in a loss of faith due to feelings for another man, after graduation the priests were injected in the neck with a poison called holy venom. It was designed to eliminate sexual desire, and over time it also destroyed the cells that regenerate the outer shell of the body, making it age faster and become unattractive.

The religion associated with the Patri cult was combined in its own way with the symbol of statehood. The High Priestess of the *Omniearth* - like her predecessors before her, mostly men - apart from her authority over the Church, was treated as an unquestionable leader, and the priests responsible for the subordinate regions as loyal representatives of her power. Everyone in the land not only respected the decisions of the Church, but believed in them and trusted that they were the right ones. Modern forms of communication were not recognized in Floris. All correspondence, including the decisions of the Ae, reached the various lands only by letter. It was always handwritten, in the old language. The priestess paid great attention to detail and always used a style adapted to the addressee. Letters of a decisive nature were written in the form of a poem, riddle or poem, whose moral or point was the correct message to be read. To the mid-level local priests, which is what Kadu was, she wrote in a flowery and mysterious manner, with a hidden message. To the low-ranking priests, who constituted the core of Floris' army, she sent short, specific letters with sentences that mimicked commands. To members of the public, on the other hand, she wrote in language simple enough for any child to understand, though not everyone in Floris could read.

Ae didn't look spiffy like the other priests. She was a handsome brown-haired woman with a shapely figure. When a venom-poisoned pin was driven into her neck after she finished her training, fate spared her body and mind. This was the first such case in history. It was considered at the time to be providential or simply a Patri decision. I guess that's why Ae rose quickly in the structures until she finally became the most important person in the state at a rather young age. The members of the Church Council preferred to be ruled by an ugly person with luck rather than a nasty unlucky person. The Florians treated this fact similarly. They fell in love with it. The ceremony of the beginning of each bloom became an ideal opportunity to meet with the faithful. The priestess was treated almost like a Patri.

***

As Kadu drove away with Mahmud's body towards Litrijis, Fahid was bursting with pride that his father had embarked on his most exciting journey at the right time. He rejoiced in his good fortune. He did not yet feel any longing. He also knew that his father would be there for him when the need arose. It had always been this way. According to Patri's belief, when the mummified bodies traveled to the Asaran Gorge for their final resting place, the souls of the deceased had the opportunity to experience every pleasant adventure they wished. After arriving at the place where the mummies were stacked, the fulfilled souls of the dead would travel to the Diamond Shrine on top of Mount Saandreal, home of the goddess Patri. Then they became ambassadors for their families and could beg from her prosperity, happiness and health. However, if the relatives did not bid farewell to the body of the deceased with the proper ritual, they had no chance for protection, and the soul of the deceased was sent to the abyss, the opposite world. A few families created memorials for people who had passed away. They looked like stone graves, each piece of which symbolized a different dead person. One could easily read that the bigger the pyre was, the luckier the family was, as it meant more souls in the goddess' house. Fahid's family also owned one. On the north side of the broad courtyard, under a ten cubit tall, spreading dew tree many purifications earlier, a common grave had begun to be piled. It looked like a pile of stones. Each was a memento of a particular dead person. Fahid knew he had to find a stone that matched his father's character, who was hardworking, strong and had principles. All his life he had said that family was the most important thing. He was very close to it. He could not imagine ever giving up any of his children to study to be priests. Fahid did not always agree with his father, but on this issue they were of a similar mind. He promised him that he would not give any child to the goddess Patri. Before he began his search for a suitable stone, he wanted to enjoy for a moment more the sight of his family, who were just finishing a feast in honor of the deceased. He smiled at Rita, and she stroked his shoulder affectionately. He glanced toward the hearth some more. He noticed that some dried *dirshna* stalks needed to be donated. *Today's fire will be of a very different nature from the previous ones*, he thought.

***

The daily ritual of burning bonfires took place just after dark. It was supposed to provide solace after a busy day and an opportunity to pray together to the goddess Patri. That evening there were two more rituals in Fahid's family. One uncommon, the other unusual. First, a few words had to be said about his deceased father. Secondly, there was a supermoon that night, and this phenomenon was connected to a particular family custom - telling favorite stories. Until recently Mahmud had been doing this, but now it was time for his son to do it.

The family prayed briefly to Patri. Then Fahid spoke a few sentences about his father, but he wasn't going to get all chatty. He noticed that the children were already bored. They were waiting for the promise to be fulfilled, that is, an interesting story for a good night's sleep. Fahid had learned them all by heart. He had listened to them from the time he was little until now. When he became a father himself, he continued to give way to Mahmud. This was the family custom, always told by the eldest male of the family. All the stories were interesting and always had a moral. Fahid's children liked the one about the banner the most, they always asked for it. When he saw that everyone was seated comfortably and began to look at each other in agreement, he began his story.

"In the beginning, the banner of the *Omniearth* was a gray-bearded *moree* bird on a purple background. The bird had four wings and each wing symbolized one of the quadrants: south, west, north and east. Exactly in the middle, between the quadrants, stood the sacred mountain Saandreal, where Patri lived. It was like the head of a bird. The goddess had her observatory from which she could look into people's homes, in all four lands. These were the eyes of the bird. About two hundred cubits below the very top were the four trumpets of order, or claws. If any of the quarters fell under Patri, the goddess played the trumpet corresponding to that quarter to call the people living there to orderly and moral behavior. These were called the trumpets of Waesstoria. Patri had another instrument for disciplining the people - the Gondoluu bell. One day some of the people wanted to separate themselves from the *Omniearth*. Patri was furious and rang the bell all day, but they would not listen. They occupied the southern quarter, established a settlement there, then a country they called Inco. The people in Floris worried that Patri would be angry not only at those who left, but at all the people of the *Omniearth*. They began to give her a tenth of the honor of their harvest, and with that they somehow cowed her. As a sign of the new order, they decided to change the banner.

They decided that it should symbolize the newly created land lacking one quarter. But no one knew what it should be. Then it was remembered that a crescent moon would be best. On the new banner three moons were painted in one line and one next to it, that is three quarters of Floris and separately of Inco, which left the *Omniearth*. Such a banner has been preserved until today."

"Now tell us about the savages," asked Sumi.

"And won't you be afraid?" joked Fahid.

"No," the kids replied in chorus, giggling with excitement.

"Right. The savages are kind of farmers too, but they don't have fields like we do. They live somewhere in the northern quadrant, in a forest that looks like a big orchard. It grows different varieties of nut trees, but *shaedor* nut trees are the most common. It has branches growing in pairs and hard leaves in the shape of big lobes - he showed two joined hands - from which the savages make their shoes. The nut-trees have delicious fruit, that is to say, seeds, but it is difficult to get at them, for they are protected by shells so hard that they could be used for strewing paths instead of stones. But nobody uses them for that purpose. Can you imagine what would happen if someone started a fire? It would quickly spread and burn not only the orchards but also the roads. The savages have to be careful not to start a fire. They would have no place to live, after all, they have houses among the trees."

"And how do they split these nuts?" asked Sumi, causing consternation in her father, who opened his eyes wide with surprise, as if he was hoping to see the answer.

"To tell you the truth, I don't know," he finally breathed out, scratching his head.

"Now tell us about the *pokuns*," suggested Tamadur, Sumi's younger sister.

"No, because you will dream," Rita forbade.

Fahid just shrugged his shoulders and smiled sassily, as if to say it wasn't his fault.

"But please!" said white-haired Abdul, Fahid's eldest son, almost one and a half purifications old.

"Well, but only a little," agreed the father. "In the eastern quadrant you can find the Toothless," he began in an ominous tone. "They have no teeth, because they painted them black and they fell out. They don't live in permanent houses like we do, nor do they live like savages in trees. They live in tents among the lakes, which are innumerable in this quarter. And they breed temptations. The end. Ha, ha."

"What's not enough," fretted Ragir, a boy of just over one cleansing age.

Rita winked at Fahid, signaling for him to tell something else.

"All right. But not about the *pokuns* anymore," he said, glancing at his wife in agreement. "The *pokuns* collect and dry *harann* algae growing near the shores only in shallow water, where the healthiest rays of *Hello* reach. When they manage to harvest all of them by a given shore, they move elsewhere. And so on and so forth. In this way, they constantly wander from place to place around the great lakes in search of food. They sell some of what they manage to collect to the northern and western quadrants. I ate once. Unpalatable. And how bad are the larvae that the savages take out from under the bark of the nut trees. Shocker..."

The children laughed to their hearts' content when Fahid made an exaggerated grimace of disgust. Rita glanced at him affectionately and smiled at her thoughts.

"That's it, time for bed," she said. "In two hours east *Hello*. Father needs to sleep before work."

Fahid added a thick piece of wood and two bundles of dry *dirshna* stems to the fire. It was to last until morning. As they headed for home, Sumi hummed the beloved refrain of one of the Sundrian songs, the same as every day last.

Chapter 3 Dilemma

The only person Jasmin could truly confide in and count on her understanding was her mother Irmina. When her father Omar was still alive, her parents repeatedly criticized the Government's actions. They were both supporters of the natural order of the world. Hardly anyone knew about it, because they carefully hid their views, but they allowed themselves to be honest with their daughter. Their worldview was to be the foundation of her humanity, the basis of her existence.

Jasmin's parents had no more children. They spent their entire adult lives absorbed in work, and they spent each free day learning another, more or less useful skill. This was what Jasmin had learned, and that was probably why Addam drew his attention to her. "Beautiful and wise, my white-haired girl" - that's what he often said about her. Omar Manduarra, Irmina's husband, completed his engineering studies fairly late in life and got a job in the R&D department of Sky Robotics Co. There, due to his academic performance, knowledge and, above all, practical experience, he was quickly promoted and became the head of one of the most important departments dealing with smooth movements. Whatever that meant, it sounded serious. Omar was respected by his colleagues and neighbors. After two purifications, he was allocated an apartment in the Inco center, which was paid for by the corporation. They celebrated the move from the second district for a very long time. Such social promotions did not take place very often in their environment. Jasmin had half a purification then. Since then, she has never ventured into a slum again.

"I'm pregnant," she said.

Her mother hugged her as tightly as she could. This is good news for a woman who has been professionally active for many purifications and has been bored alone in her apartment since she switched to the so-called senior allowance. She even made purchases remotely. She repeatedly returned to the slum, where she would have a chance to meet her peers, friends from the old days, but her daughter discouraged her effectively, explaining the danger that had been growing since two purifications. Irmina liked neither the Inco center nor her apartment, which is still paid for by Sky Robotics Co. It was too modern for her. The only things she accepted about all this technology were artificial animals and insects. Every now and then she would buy one toy for herself. She collected animarobots that mirrored the real animals, reptiles, insects, and birds that once lived in Inco and now only in Floris. She already had a small okurai, a sahadi, a hydapi, a moree bird, as well as a perfect imitation of a chckenei, a *dirshna* flower pollinator, an insect that looks like a little bird. She kept them all together in a large glass aquarium. She dreamed of a pokuna, but these toys cost three times more than others. Only chckenei were on a one-to-one scale, the rest were miniatures. They had limited functions compared to the larger ones, but could not afford a large okurai or a medium-sized moree bird, although they were available on offer. She didn't even have a place where they could move freely. She started collecting animarobots after her husband's death, out of boredom. Earlier, he had disapproved of the artificial creatures, his concern was working on, running around their apartment.

"I hope you will bring my granddaughter to me from time to time?" She asked timidly, counting on confirmation of gender.

"Mom, it will be triplets. All the girls," Jasmin said, and she felt herself hugging the Ice Queen. Her mother, upon hearing the news, began to tremble and instinctively move away from her daughter.

"You cannot give birth to them, little girl," said her mother dryly.

"Life matters. Do you remember? These are your words. Who raised me like this?"

"For the sake of your father's memory, please don't do this." The mother was desperate and, in a way, implacable.

"But what memory?" Jasmin got angry. "The more dad would never allow himself such advice. Who are you?"

Jasmin was disappointed with her mother's attitude. This was not the reaction she had expected. "Do people get dumber in old age?" - she wondered. "Is she sick? Probably not". Irmina looked good for eight purifications survivors. She had natural copper-blue hair unlike most older ladies her age who wore clever plain colored wigs. She walked slightly stooped, but not with a cane, gracefully. She always adorned her face and wore age-masking gloves made of thin latex-like material for two purifications. In them the hand looked younger, with no discoloration and always perfectly painted nails. The gloves were expensive but indestructible. Nobody would believe that Irmina is that age.

The mother looked at her daughter critically, gasped as if to say something, but hesitated. It was evident that he wished her well, and despite the fact that Jasmin had been an adult for a long time, she still felt responsible for her.

"If you give birth, the whole family will suffer. Not only you and your husband. Everyone will bear the consequences of such a choice. Addam's parents, his brothers, their wives and children. You know it will be like that. You can't just think about yourself."

Jasmin stood up abruptly. She glanced at her mother, lowered her head, and slowly started walking towards the door.

"Wait. You must know something," said her mother calmly.

The daughter stopped and looked up. There was an unease mixed with unfathomable anger on her face. She waited motionless, sending her mother a critical look.

"Your father wasn't born in Inco," Irmina began, driving Jasmin out of anger into disbelief combined with embarrassment. "Only at Floris. He grew up there. He escaped from there because he didn't feel well. He has always been interested in science, and as you know, in this rural country hardly anyone has ambition. Fishermen smuggled him. He was always so practical. I miss him so much."

"It's not true! Why are you telling me this now?" Jasmin asked.

"Because when I fell in love with this young, passionate engineer, my family made a condition. If I marry him, they will disinherit me and I can forget about them."

"You said that you grew up in an orphanage, that you did not have relatives. Why were you lying? I have always envied my friends who had grandmothers and grandparents. I only had you." Jasmin's head was buzzing with all the vague thoughts that had been remembered from all her short life.

"For neighbors or colleagues, Omar was simply a good man, a great specialist. Why? Because no one knew about his origins. You are aware of the opinion of the Florianians. Only my parents and I knew. To them, he was always nothing. No matter how much he achieved, what he did not receive honors, they contemptuously called him a "fool", sometimes "a lying immigrant from the village" who took jobs from honest Inco residents.

"What? Why did you never tell me about this?" Jasmin was furious.

"For your protection. If you had known, you would never have been so successful. The stigma of an outcast severely cuts the wings. Father and I did not want this to affect you. You have achieved so much. You have a wonderful, loving husband, you live in a beautiful apartment, you have a bright future ahead of you that many people do not even dare to dream of. Do not waste it."

Jasmin became sad. The world she had known had just collapsed. Everything it based its existence on turned out to be worthless. Throughout her life, her parents instilled in her that truth and life are the most important values of this corrupt world. How disappointed she was. And what was she to do with this pregnancy now, even if the mother was against it? Before leaving, Irmina showed her one of her father's notebooks as proof that she was telling the truth. It was written in the old language, that is, with characters used so far only in Floris. Omar had beautiful handwriting, but neither his wife nor daughter had any idea what he wrote.

***

The blue, cloudless sky and the bright rays of Hello filled her with optimism, but the communication promenade along which Jasmin was heading towards her apartment deprived her of hope. It was full of attractive, slender women of all ages, dressed in white, black, or one shade of gray, usually monochrome. There was sometimes a man between them. Rarely. He didn't usually walk alone, but no matter how many women he surrounded himself, others followed him with a sigh. It was evident that society was consumed by harmful hyperactivity and lust. There was a mixture of women's perfumes in the air, masking the effects of angry hormones. The women looked at the men like a hunter for game. Neither knew what discreet flirting was. The intensity of jealousy for male representatives has reached a dangerous level. Jasmin believed that under normal circumstances no woman would look back for Addam. However, under these circumstances, he became an object of sighs. She felt a desire to fight for belonging, as if defending her own toothbrush. Personal. She would kill if someone took advantage of it, but then she would have to throw it out of disgust. She thought so. Over time, ordinary human care for belongings - this is how she associated everything related to a sense of security - turned into jealousy. Jasmin knew that in Addam's office most were fair sex. Anyway, wherever they went together, the longing eyes of mischievous schoolgirls or mature women, even at the age of five purifications, looking at her husband, were the order of the day. She was never used to the fact that he always reciprocated with a gentle gesture, a smile or a wink. When he left for work, she looked for a job not to think about it. He said the flirtation offers merely amused him. He often compared such incidents to seeing desperate women walking by the hand with a male-faced robot. Jasmin didn't quite trust him.

When she reached a multi-level intersection, she felt a slight tremor under her feet. It moved through the protruding pillars from the underground to the metal platform along which it was heading. She knew that it was the effect of the passing queue, which transported various goods on a network of perfectly connected underground connections. She remembered seeing them from childhood and that it was her father who had taken her underground to show this logistic, elaborate solution. Omar was very curious and it was probably this attitude that developed the same trait in his daughter. None of colleagues had ever seen the underground railway or other devices hidden from the public necessary for the functioning of the first Inco district. Only Jasmin. And only thanks to the father. Too bad he was dead, he would surely know what to do, she thought. At this point, her communicator, hidden in a transparent pouch, began to blink a blue light and make the familiar sound of an impending conversation. Jasmin took it out, pressed one of the buttons, and heard a familiar voice.

"Hey, love, I have a doctor for you. Basically a woman doctor. She's not like those butchers. Her name is Meilly. I don't know how to read it," Luicey said.

"But I..."

At that moment Jasmin saw a woman with two girls. They looked homeless and lost. A humanoid robot in a navy blue guard uniform stood in front of them straight as a string. He emanated superiority. It had no eyes or an imitation of a nose or mouth like models intended for domestic use. His head, if you could call it that, resembled a sphere stuffed with all sorts of sensors. The woman, with a trembling hand, handed him the registration card and waited with downcast eyes to see what would happen. The robot has read the card.

"According to the Government decree," a squeaking voice came out, "you have no right to be in this place. Please don't resist."

"I just wanted to show my daughters," said the woman.

Suddenly, humaan grabbed the older girl by the rags and began to drag her towards the cage marked "Garda" made of glass bars reinforced with a circonium. The woman put out her hand to grab registration card from him, but she didn't make it. Humaan pushed her so violently that she fell to the ground, severely injuring herself. The second daughter furiously kicked the robot in the lower limb, which did not make any impression on him. Jasmin was stunned at the sight, she didn't hang up the conversation, just dropped her hand with the communicator in her hand. "Unheard of," she said to herself.

"Jasmin, what's going on there? You there?" Luicey recalled herself.

"Wait," she whispered into the communicator, and only heard mumbling in response.

"Everything is forbidden. The fine for staying in a forbidden place is two hundred and sixty entitys for one female." The squeaking voice from the humaan faded every syllable.

The girl suddenly released her grip and quickly ran in the opposite direction, then disappeared around the corner of one of the skyscrapers. At that time, humaan was standing by her mother and was holding her by the throat.

"You are responsible for the offspring. Your registration card has been blocked," a squeaking voice came out. "Please don't make it difficult. For this, there is a fine of one hundred entitys per person. Please get in."

Jasmin glanced at the woman and her daughter for a moment more. The glass cage they entered closed and lifted slightly above the ground. Humaan marched towards the skyscraper behind which the older girl was hiding. The cage with the woman and her younger daughter followed him at a short, equal distance.

"What's the name of the doctor?" Jasmin asked on her comm, although it was obvious she still couldn't believe what she saw.

"Meilly, but I told you I'm not sure you read it like that," Luicey replied.

***

Inco's treatment system was private, though completely subordinate to the Government. Each visit paid in accordance with the centrally approved tariff had to be recorded in the database. If, by chance, one of the doctors forgot to draw up a study report, he would immediately join the ranks of those convicted for acting to the detriment of society and would work physically for Inco at one of the state-owned establishments until the end of his miserable life. The government controlled not only the health service, but also many other areas of life, including education. Jasmin and Luicey graduated from high school in one cleanup. They taught a simplified history, rules of spelling, counting and one, non-engineering profession. Jasmin learned the principles of marketing, Luicey learned the social sciences. There were also the rules of teaching, treating, decorating and, of course, knowledge of chemistry useful in the pharmaceutical and food industries. In the remaining schools, usually technical, the chosen profession concerned engineering. After all, Inco was a technological mecca and robotics, automation and telecommunications were the most important areas of life. Addam was the chosen one. Like his slightly older cousin, Haenry, with whom he had a better relationship than with his more than one purification brothers, he graduated from the same elite school of state administration reserved only for children from wealthy families. After graduating from such a university, each graduate always received a lucrative position with a high salary in one of the state offices controlling particular areas of life or branches of the economy. Working for the Government was responsible and stressful. It could be lost in the event of acting "to the detriment of the state". Unfortunately, it was only up to the representatives of the Government and heads of individual departments to interpret what this term meant.

"Hello, we have an appointment with Dr. Meilly," Luicey said as she followed Jasmin into a dingy doctor's office on the outskirts of the First District.

"The visit has been canceled," said the assistant, without looking up from the newspaper she was reading.

"Ma'am, this is a very important procedure." Jasmin was trying to be nice.

"Yeah, I get it, but the system isn't working." This time the assistant looked up graciously and looked Jasmin straight in the eye.

"What system? We came here for the procedure. Where's Dr. M-e-j-l-i?" Luicey spelled.

"GCO system has a breakdown or something. Anyway, nothing works. All state systems are blocked from remote access. Please come tomorrow."

"Tomorrow, this girl will have a card lock. Let the lady be humaan." Luicey did not give up, but changed her tone.

"Come on," Jasmin said, then grabbed her friend's hand and started pulling her towards the door.

"Come on?" The companion was surprised, airing out ordinary cowardice.

All the way back, Luicey was chattering grinning that you can't believe anyone and that life always brings bad solutions. Jasmin wasn't listening to her. She wondered what had caused the system to crash. Did what Addam knew but refused to talk about affected the nationwide paralysis? Why was there no GCO officer in this office?

When Jasmin returned to the apartment, she turned on the theatremania. All four channels displayed the message "Continuation of program in a moment". It was signed by the Inco Ministry of Indoctrination of the Society.

Chapter 4 Guest

"You summoned me, my lady?" Asked Kifor, the tallest of the high priests of almost six purifications.

As he closed the door to the chamber that was the office of the High Priestess of the Omniearth from the inside, he noticed that Ae was sitting at the stone table, writing a letter. As usual, she was exquisitely calligraphed.

"New invitations to the priesthood," Ae replied, noticing his surprise. "Hard times are coming. We need more support for our community."

"What are you talking about? What hard times? Has Patri passed something on to you?" Kifor asked, stepped closer, blocking out the light coming from the little torch.

However, he noticed his mistake. He stepped aside, letting the rays reach the table top and the papyrus on it.

"Don't be silly, Kifor. You and I know perfectly well that Patri does not convey anything directly during a vision." Ae looked extremely mysterious.

Kifor thought for a moment. He knew the priestess very well and knew that this person's election as a saint was not the result of strong faith or paranormal abilities. Ae came from a poor family that dealt with doorstep juggling. She was ashamed of her roots, but surely a part of the artistic gene had seeped into her mind. When she said what seemed obvious but impossible, it was to be assumed that it was due to her inherited talent for acting. Kifor, like most high priests, knew that the visions of Saint Ae that Patri reportedly conveyed to her were just the magic of her sublime politics.

"How many new priests do we need?" Kifor asked.

"It seems to me that about two thousand conscripts would be good."

"I don't understand. After all, this is more or less the number of children we invite for each recruitment. It is just a natural replenishment of the ranks of the priests who left for Patri."

"This time I am thinking of another additional list. Can you bring me records of girls born one purification ago in the western quarter?"

"This is the fifth recruitment with only girls."

"Do you doubt Patri's wisdom?"

"No, my lady."

Kifor looked down and went to the archives. Ae made sure he was not eavesdropping and summoned Jusif, hidden in an adjoining room. The slender man in the clothes of a merchant gave the impression of a trusted person. Ae took a small purse from her dress pocket. She handed it to Jusif, signaling him to go away. He bowed and disappeared imperceptibly behind the curtain.

After a while, Kifor returned to the chamber. He was carrying a few scrolls, he didn't look happy. Ae guessed what was bothering him. The high priest was from the part of Floris she had asked for. He probably saw in one of the engravings the name of one of the members of the former family. The former, because every priest from the moment of poisoning became a member of the new. Patri family.

"Is something bothering you?" She asked courteously.

He answered nothing. He was just waiting for the sentence. It should seemingly indifferent to him, because these are not his roots anymore. If he had, or should, anything, it is rather joy. After all, the service of Patri is an honor for the family. As Ae looked through the engravings, he held his breath. She deliberately stopped exactly on the most important card for him. There was the name of his younger brother's daughter. He knew them well because he had full access to the archives. He repeatedly checked who was born or died in his family or neighborhood that he remembered from his childhood. Ae narrowed her eyes as if to show that she hesitated. She felt Kifor was waiting to be executed. It was up to her to decide. This time, she was not going to hurt this important priest. She knew she would need it, that he had no doubts and must be loyal. She looked him straight in the eye and turned the card over. When Kifor saw another engraving with the Manduarra family tree drawn out, he breathed a sigh of relief and nodded his appreciation for the gesture.

"Let it be Sumi, Fahid's daughter. And that's interesting..." Ae was surprised. "Fahid is the son of Mahmud, whose brother Omar has no further connection. How it's possible?"

"Perhaps he died?"

"There is no mention of it. And that's just..." the priestess was surprised again. “In this era, none of the Mahmoud family members served Patri. Isn't that villainy?" She sneered.

"Whose area is this?" Asked Kifor, who had already calmed his breathing.

"Kadu. Hmm, good Kadu added this little girl to her family tree. He will surely be pleased with this news. I'll write him a letter too."

"What if her family doesn't agree? It's just an invitation. Nobody is required to accept it."

"You're mocking, aren't you?"

Kifor nodded and smiled fake. Ae was pleased with this turn of events.

"Okay, who's gonna be next?" She asked, and began leafing through the scrolls of engravings again.

***

Hello was already on the way to the west when Kadu finally reached Litrijis. This was the name of the only settlement in the district for which this priest was responsible. It was located close to a large dam built together with an artificial, though life-giving water reservoir in the Ethne River bed. Several dozen families lived and lived in the settlement, mainly fishing and herding nimo. The shells of this freshwater shellfish were used to make building materials for houses. Before the nimos reached their proper size, however, humaans grazed them on underwater algae pastures. Their foraging lasted almost continuously for many long weeks - for this reason, the precious herd was watched over by groups of underwater shepherds riding hydapi. They were equipped with primitive weapons and apparatus designed to breathe underwater, sold cheaply by a crafty corporation in a neighboring country. Since bathing in dead Inco lakes was banned, cameras became unnecessary there, and here they found a second life. Anyway, it was no exception. Many more or less useless inventions or machines that had become obsolete in Inco were forced into the gullible inhabitants of Floris. It was similar with the drives for fishing boats. They broke frequently and spare parts were missing. They were thrown into the river, where they lay at the bottom. Only the nimo shepherds were aware of the scale of the phenomenon. Nevertheless, no one believed them. Their minds became confused from being under water for too long, and they were treated as madmen with unpredictable behavior.

Kadu was glad to be commuting to Litrijis. He stayed in this settlement most of the time and had his home there. Before going to bed, however, he decided to water the animals. They had been dragging the wagon with Mahmud's body for a long time and were exhausted. He reached the river bank in a rather secluded place surrounded by trees. As he descended from the wagon to undo the hydapi, a boat appeared around a bend in the river. It was starting to turn grayish, but you could clearly tell that a terribly thin, black-haired man rowed it. He did not look like a fisherman, although he was dressed in their outfit, consisting of a single, cleverly wrapped piece of cloth designed to mask many folds of fat. The mischievous called them the "belly carrier". On Haris, for that was the name of the five-cleansing man, the characteristic fisherman's outfit hung like a rag.

"Hello, priest. Where are you going to?" Haris asked.

"To Asaran. I am carrying the body of this lucky one so that his spirit will meet the goddess Patri. Did you have a good catch today?" Kadu asked searchingly.

He knew all the fishermen, but this one seemed strange to him. He also did not have such a compliant mouth as other representatives of this profession.

"I caught a few macaboules and one rhisma," Haris said, then grasped the fish in his hands and lifted it up so that the Kadu standing on the shore could judge it. It was pink and an elbow long.

"Nice. I haven't eaten the rhisma for a long time." Kadu was still distrustful.

"I can sell it to you, cheap," Haris said, but he quickly averted his gaze, which did not bode sincere intentions.

"I wouldn't have anything to pay with," Kadu said, then unhooked the Hydapi from the wagon and led it to the water.

He knew he had to hold them well, because hydapi loved bathing. As one of the few species of animals that can breathe underwater, they were looking for opportunities to dive. In addition to washing and cooling the body, they treated immersion in a freshwater river as cleaning their respiratory system of residual dust. The filter organ was located in the alveolar ears. When it was not clear, it did not function properly and the hydapi grew tired quickly.

"Anyway... I'll give it to you," Haris said. "It's not worth one macaboul. Just come closer. It's too shallow for my boat here."

Kadu was surprised. He tied a hydapi harness to a nearby tree and took a few steps towards the boat, careful where he was walking. The water in this place only covered his ankles, but the stones at the bottom were very treacherous. Some are slippery, others with razor-sharp edges. Suddenly the priest felt a pain in his head, he staggered and fell into the water with all his force. Haris, who had hit him with an oar a moment ago, jumped out of the boat. He grabbed Kadu's robe and dragged him ashore, cutting his body against angular stones. He walked over to the wagon and with one jerk took off the cloth covering Mahmud's body. The sight of the mummy terrified him, but after a while he began to tear off pieces of bark that had been stuck to it. He was in a hurry as if he didn't have much time. He glanced every now and then at Kadu to see if the other had woken up. The last piece wouldn't peel off, so Haris tore it off, tugging it very hard. When he finished, he struggled to lift Mahmud's body and began to carry it towards the boat. At one point, he apparently stepped on something sharp. Pain spread across his face. He hissed shortly and moved on. Mahmud's body was thrown into the bow of the boat and he sat on the side of the boat himself. He glanced at the bloody foot. It didn't look bad. He grabbed the oar, rested it on the bottom, and began to push the boat away from the shore. She quickly picked up the pace and came out to the depth where he could begin rowing. When he reached the middle of the river, he stripped naked. He tied the garments to Mahmud's leg on one side and to a heavy anchor on the other. He threw it all into the water with effort. There was no audible splash, but he looked prophylactically towards the shore. The priest was still unconscious. Haris waited for the body to sink into the water. When he was sure it did not come up, he began swinging the oars in the opposite direction. He swam back to shore, climbed onto the wagon, and began to cover his body with the uncooked pieces of bark. They didn't want to stick too much, so he quickly gave up and wrapped himself in the cloth that had previously covered the mummy.

When Kadu opened his eyes, he was surprised that the night had passed and dawn greeted him with dew. He didn't remember how he got to this place or what happened last night. He was lying on the bank of the river, and his hydapi grazed a few cubits away. One had already eaten everything around the tree to which he was attached. The priest had scratch marks on his body and had a headache. At the bottom of the boat was a coiled net and a basket of fish. He was glad to see them. Apart from the pink one, the rest of the fish were blue in color, with bulging eyes and a zigzag dorsal fin. "It's an expensive species, hard to catch," he thought then, and felt his head ache again.

***

The young courier, tasked with delivering the letter from the priestess of Ae, was wondering how to find the addressee. He first went to Litrijis. Every child there knew Kadu and you could count on them to help him in his search. Especially that for help in finding the fastest okurai in the whole land could be a reward. And that's what the postal couriers had at their disposal. When he got to the settlement, it turned out that Kadu had left this unusual place some time earlier. Before he did so, he washed the wounds and applied a rope leaf wrap to his head, which was effective in treating the excruciating pain. The children knew everything. The courier also heard that Kadu had eaten one fish and had sold a few at the market, because they would have spoiled on the way to Asaran Gorge. For the four gray stones he obtained, he bought a bag of puke tuber seeds and dried sandi fruit. He also provided himself with two skins of fresh water, two barrels of a liquor called tinghao, and a bowl of black lard.

The courier was worried at first that he had to go back, as Asaran was very close to where he had just arrived. He was surprised when he realized that they might have missed each other. He decided not to waste time unnecessarily arguing with his own fears and moved on. Urging okurai as hard as he could, he smiled at his thoughts.

***

"Should be all the way back and forth. At most I will eat turlin fruit," thought the priest, and put the rest of the provisions in his bag. He took a deep sip of the drink he had bought at the inn, lay down on the edge of the wagon, and narrowed his eyes. His hydapi knew the way very well. He could take a nap without fear. They knew the purpose of their journey anyway. The next day he was awakened by the flutter of a moree bird flying quite low. Kadu noticed that a good amount of puke and some sandi fruit were missing from the opened bag. This fact, however, did not disturb him. The old priest just smiled. He decided that the alcoholic drink made him clumsy, that he forgot to close the bag and lost some of the food he had taken on the road. And then he saw Asaran, wide across the horizon, in the distance. "Half a day and I'll be there," he thought, and chased the hydapi away. He was always happy to see it. He associated it with a good deed. This majestic gorge at the foot of Mount Saandreal was one of the most beautiful places he had ever seen. Its uniqueness was only the Golden Temple in Patrix and the great Pinati waterfall on the Ethne River near the border with Inco. When he was nearly there, he stopped the car at the edge to peek down. The ravine two hundred cubits deep was filled in half with the tens of thousands of mummified bodies lingering from many cleansing mummified bodies, arranged casually as if someone had thrown them off. There is a reason why this famous place was situated in the foothills of Saandreal. According to Patri's beliefs, the spirits of the dead had the shortest possible path to the goddess's home from there. Ae's predecessor, the priest Vishare, when he proclaimed himself a saint, declared that Asaran is a tremendous source of energy from the dead and that only he can benefit from it. However, he never proved the truth of these words. He died of a heart condition just a few months after his appointment as High Priest of the Omniearth.

There was a peculiar smell in the air - a mixture of incense, bark and dried herbs. He was off-putting, but not to Kadu. While he was savoring the scent, on the other side of the gorge he noticed a wagon drawn by six tine animals. They moved slowly and heavily. They gasped as if carrying an inhumanly tiring load. That coachman, a woman, in fact, as ugly as Kadu, was also a priestess of Patri. She had a district somewhere in the northern quarter. You could tell by the color of the garment, navy blue. They greeted each other from a distance with a short gesture. Her wagon reached a narrow wooden structure over the ravine. It looked like a bridge, light, easy to take apart and move to another place.

Probably the point was that the spilled corpse should evenly fill that great hole in the ground. Kadu thought he would wait for the priestess to complete the sacred rituals. He wasn't sure the bridge was stable enough to hold as many as two body deliveries.

The northern quarter priestess stopped her cart. She put on a formal robe, raised her hands, and began to bow. It took quite a while. Too long for a simple ceremony, thought Kadu. However, when the priestess threw off the linen cover, it was found to cover not one but several mummified bodies, including two young children. The priestess made some eloquent gestures and released the little lever. The horizontal landing on which the body lay leaned slightly back. The mummies were glued and did not want to slip off. The woman glanced at Kadu as if she were afraid of criticizing what she was about to do. But she pushed the body closest to the edge with her hand. Did not help. She climbed onto one of the tall wheels, gripped the sides tightly, and kicked it mercilessly. The body immediately peeled off, releasing more. After a while, the carcasses began to slide off the platform and fall, making an echoing clap sound. The priestess looked at Kadu once more, bowed gently, and drove away.

"Now you, Mahmud," said Kadu, and yanked the reins.

The Hydapi pulling the wagon started along the road that led close to the rocky edge of the ravine towards the bridge. Suddenly a head popped out from under the cloth covering the mummy of Mahmud. The bark, which was poorly taped, basically fell off in one go. Kadu turned pale. He was convinced that Mahmud had come to life. He knew it was impossible, but nothing else came to mind. After a while he realized it was Haris, who at that very moment decided to take a breath. He had been suffering from pain in his gut for some time, but the stench from the ravine did not help at all, it even made him vomit. The priest was surprised. He still didn't know what was going on. Haris vomited long and painfully.

"What's that stinky in here?" He asked, wiping his hand over his mouth.

"Where is Mahmud?!" Kadu answered question with a question. "What did you do with his body, you bastard?"

"I threw it in the trash. I had no other idea," Haris said nonchalantly.

Blood was clearly boiling in Kadu. Suddenly he rushed to the neck of the man lying on the cart. A scuffle ensued, as Haris's body immediately fell off the carelessly stuck bits of bark. A completely naked man appeared to the eyes of the Kadu. The sight knocked him off the beat only for a moment. Hydapi began to snore anxiously. Haris tried to release his grip, but Kadu gripped the reins with one hand and tied them around his neck. He learned this trick while serving in the army as a young priest. Haris, however, began to tear himself away. He jerked the reins left and right. The frightened hydapi kicked, stamping nervously on the rough, though rocky ground. After a while, a piece of the escarpment with one of the animals broke from the edge and fell down, dragging the cart behind it, as well as Kadu and Haris hugging each other. The second hydapi saved himself for a moment longer by digging in its claws. The weight he was trying to support was too heavy, and he was quickly tugging on the rest. The animals, despite the fact that they were digging their claws deep into the rock, could not stop. They slid down, making a piercing scratching sound coupled with a panicked squeal. They were balancing their bodies awkwardly, but that didn't help much. Haris broke free from the priest's grasp and grabbed the manes of one of them. He quickly realized that the problem was the heavy cart that Kadu was holding onto all the time. He decided to get rid of the ballast. As he began to undo the individual straps holding the structure, the priest climbed onto the second hydapi. He started hitting the intruder with his fists, screaming as if they were skinning him. Several wild birds of the Moree became interested in this quarrel and flew closer.

"It's a holy place! There can only be embalmed bodies in it, you unfaithful bandit!" Kadu shouted furiously.

"Shit on it!" Haris answered him and unhooked the last handle.

The wagon crashed to the very bottom and, despite the amortization of the soft ground, which was a pile of corpses, broke in several places. The two hydapies Haris had stripped of their shackles, with the riders on their backs, began to brake sharply until the deeply driven claws stopped for good. Kadu tugged at the reins, signaling the climb. Haris did the same. His hydapi climbed faster. It was slim and therefore lighter. It only took a moment to get to the top. After climbing onto the shore, the animals began to snore violently. It was a sign of dissatisfaction and excruciating exhaustion. Haris looked Kadu straight in the eye.

"How can you eat it?" He asked, pointing to the spilled grains with his hand.

He waited a brief moment, yanked the hydapi's mane, and slowly began walking towards the bridge. As he drove across, he didn't even look back. He was consistently walking towards Mount Saandreal. The priest only glowered after him. He stood dumbfounded and broken. He lost everything in an instant: the wagon, the bag with provisions, the body, which the deceased's family had given him with gratitude and trust. And worst of all - an untainted, long-standing reputation. In addition, some thug, apparently an Inco fugitive whose purpose was unknown, stole his animal and drove away completely naked. Kadu stood at the edge of the Asaran Gorge, looking down. On top of the swarm of bodies lay the desecrated sacred place the remains of his three-wheeled car and a torn off piece of rocky cliff. "How do I get it now?" - he wondered. If anyone finds out that this is the priest's work, he will have no use returning to his district. He will be banished from the community and never end up in Patri.

Then he heard a familiar voice. It was a courier headed his way. He was playing an annoying thumping instrument that announced the delivery of the mail. Kadu froze. Had the priestess of Ae foresaw what would happen and called him to

Patrix? It looks like the courier did not see what happened before. Perhaps it would be better, thought the priest. He quickly picked up the parcel and with one move he untied the bow from the roll in which the letter was rolled. Kadu did not notice that the courier had time to say goodbye and go away. The priest took out a folded papyrus and read the coded riddle cursily.

He learned from the letter that he was to come to Patrix, but for a completely different reason. He should have breathed a sigh of relief, but penitent thoughts swirled in his mind. He was given the task of fetching another candidate for a priestess. Apparently he did it many times, but this time the choice fell on Sumi, Fahid's daughter. Whether her father agreed or not, it was his duty to bring her back alive and whole. But how do you pick up a family member who has just believed him and he has just let her down? They handed over Mahmud's body to take it back to Asaran, and he just lost it. The soul of the girl's deceased grandfather was to go to Patri, and it probably wanders somewhere near Litrijis, guarding its body. The priest could not refuse Ae's command, but there were no sensible solutions to his martyred mind. After all, he will turn out to be the worst liar. When he gets to Fahid's farm, the family will surely ask how the burial was done. Kadu glanced once more at the remains of the wagon lying on the pile of mummified corpses. "It will be a memorable purification," he thought.

Chapter 5 Revolution

"I have some good news for you." Dr. Steavans smiled in his unique style.

Jasmin was lying on the couch. She was waiting for such a message. This was how she imagined the moment when she planned an appointment with a famous gynecologist, about which neither her mother nor her husband had a clue. Only Luicey.

"It'll be a son. Have you ever wondered what his name will be?"

"I don't know." Jasmin exuded happiness. "And yours?"

"My? Hmm... It's too common, and your son will surely achieve a lot. He can't be called Jon."

"Yeah. It is actually a terribly boring name." Jasmin was still stunned and didn't even realize she was being tactless.

Dr. Steavans responded with an understanding smile. This guy was just classy. At this point, an uninvited Gibbondy entered the office.

"And what?" She asked inquisitively. "I was looking forward to it."

"A boy. In a moment I will enter his data into the computer module."

Mrs. Gibbondy looked inconsolable. She was probably counting on a little scandal, but nothing here. She left, glaring furiously at the patient. Jasmin was smiling radiantly at her thoughts like a child. Suddenly her eyes began to water heavily, and a grimace of sadness appeared on her face. It is not how it suppose to be. She wanted to enjoy the happy news, but her body refused to obey. It wanted her to cry. She fought him for quite a long time. It was a tiring moment that would last for all eternity. Finally Jasmin succumbed to emotions that burst from the inside out like an exploding volcano. She began to sob. Meanwhile, Dr. Jon Steavans was entering data into the module, completely ignoring her crying. He was still glad that another boy would be born. Jasmin narrowed her eyes to stop them from producing more tears. She heard, as if from another world, a rather softly sounding voice coming from theatremania. She opened her eyes and looked around. She wasn't in the gynecologist's office at all. She was lying in her bed while Addam watched the morning news projected on the wall.

"Oh, you're awake," he observed. "You screamed a lot."

For a long time Jasmin could not come to terms with the fact that it was only a dream. She closed her eyes one more time to go back to that moment, but Prime Minister

Clifford's voice coming from the theatremania speaker was effectively bringing her down to earth.

"Dear compatriots, I must deny all rumors about the alleged crisis. The state is functioning perfectly. It is not true that hooligans broke into our information system."

"Only theatremania works," said Addam. "The rest of the systems are still infected with viruses."

Jasmin did not realize for a moment what her husband had just communicated. When Addam turned off the projector, she felt his words hung in the air all the time waiting for her reaction.

"What happens now?" Jasmin asked.

"If the Prime Minister of the Government claims that there is no crisis, it means that it has been there for some time. Different scenarios are to be expected."

"Is it about the Y chromosome?"

"You're not getting up?" He asked, running away from the answer.

"I still feel bad. I'll stay another day at home."

"It's been going on for quite a long time. Your boss, the ice queen, will start to suspect something."

"I'll go to work tomorrow."

"What do we call her?" Addam decided to change the subject to an equally touchy, but at least with a more distant ending.

"Her?" She repeated, as if she did not understand the question.

"Well, the baby you are carrying."

"I haven't thought yet. Maybe after your mom?"

Jasmin realized that she hadn't even mentioned to her husband about visiting her own mother, Irmina. The remorse of the piling secrets prompted her to make amends, which were merely a compromise.

"So there is never enough good news," he ironized.

His relationship with his mother had deteriorated a bit, but he continued to confess everything to her. Jasmin didn't understand that. He knew that since his wife had proposed that the baby be named after his mother-in-law, it meant Jasmin was not taking the matter too seriously. Because they didn't like each other.

"And you? What do you think?" She asked with concern.

"I can't accept it yet. I didn't expect to have to come up with a name for the girl. I'll ask my mother."

***

There were two political groups in Inco: the Chemist Party and the Labor Party. In the elections, which took place every half of the purification, eighty percent of the population voted for the first, i.e. the entire first district, and only the inhabitants of the second district voted for the second. Barney Clifford was elected Prime Minister of the Government three and a half purifications ago. Nobody was surprised then, and neither did the next re-election. He came from a wealthy family related to pharmacy. He was also one of the most effective leaders in Inco, chairman of the Chemist Party. There were rumors that he had sold himself and that he would have to repay the pharmaceutical cartels. The people who preached them quickly joined the ranks of the mining brotherhood. They were condemned for treason and sent to labor camps, where, in the sweat of their brow, they died of circonium, a precious metal used in the production of precision machining and cutting tools, as well as light weapons. Clifford ran the Government fairly efficiently. He was well educated, had charisma and a sense of a predatory politician. Everyone was afraid of him. When the first hacker attacks appeared in the theater, he lost his heart. His hypocritical surroundings wished him imminent demise. More candidates have already been seen to replace him. One of them was Petar Rubby, the Minister of Home Affairs. They met frequently in private meetings in the prime minister's apartment. Clifford trusted him immensely, though he never allowed them to be called by their first names.

"Prime Minister," Rubby began. "In the northern part of the second district, we quelled the riots. People took to the streets. They are demanding the truth."

"What kind of people? They're trash," said Barney Clifford outraged. "I understand you know who's behind this."

"Of course. I just can't connect it with a journalistic investigation."

"Can you finally enlighten me? I have no time for unnecessary introductions." The prime minister was clearly impatient.

"Behind these brawls are Black Hand's military group."

"I don't understand. After all, it is a secret group that we created ourselves. It was your idea. Pretty successful. Have we made a mistake?"

"In a way, yes. Black Hand Agents are still operational. Someone is controlling them all the time."

"Don't tell me that one of my ministers is overseeing a secret organization that neither you nor I know about. In addition, the case comes to light when there is a serious problem with the leakage of data on the Y chromosome."

"I don't think it's a coincidence. Who has supervision over the Public Opinion and Mood Research Bureau, which controls theatremania addiction?" Rubby said casually, pretending he wasn't interested in Clifford's reaction.

The prime minister's face turned red immediately. He took a few nervous steps, pulled out his communicator, and pressed one of the buttons.

"I am calling a brief meeting in the morning with the Ministry of Home Affairs, Health and Indoctrination of Society," he said into a microphone inside a small device.

"Yes, sir!" There was a short answer.

"Tell me everything you know about these military groups," he said to Rubby.

The Minister of Home Affairs reminded the prime minister of the entire story. Well, when the Inco people reacted badly to the creation of the Gender Control Office, a secret organization called the Black Hands was created. They were the most saucy and cunning women. Their task was to penetrate the structures of opposition groups and cause their slow destruction. The infiltration was successful. Three more so-called Mother Riots, triggered in the slums by opponents of the ban on the birth of girls, were nipped in the bud with the help of the Black Hands. The UTCOMP project and subsequent directives depriving residents of their privileges spread exponentially. A gentle modification to a drug called Ray also helped. The improved version had a calming effect on possible outbreaks of maternal hormones. Over time, people have forgotten what hurts them. They have adapted. The Black Hands project was closed, but apparently its members never stopped working. They still actively participated in controlling the social mood among the poorer part of the inhabitants of the second district. Rubby argued that this time they were the source of the conflict that was just developing, but they acted against the authority that created them.

"The most interesting thing is that the first march to expose the alleged truth passed the day before the hackers attacked theatremania." Rubby finished his story with those words.

"You are the Minister of Home Affairs, tell me the hell who is financing all this?! After all, these women did not organize themselves!" Clifford was furious.

"I have fewer and fewer people. Most of the tasks are carried out by humaans. They are not ready for spying. It's not the garda it used to be," explained Rubby. "This responsibility lies with the Minister of Indoctrination of Society."

"I see. Is there any news from Haris?" Asked the Prime Minister, trying to change the subject.

"Unfortunately not." Rubby looked sad.

"You still believe in him?"

"And what's left for me, Prime Minister?"

***

When Addam left for work, Jasmin tried to remember some interesting names for the girl. She could think of only the kind had those around her, and they all seemed too common. All in all, she was pleased with the name that her parents had given her. She didn't know anyone named Jasmin. It finally became clear why she had it and why she had a hair color so rare in this country. After all, her father came from Floris - apparently that name was popular there, and the white-haired people were no exception, as in Inco. Perhaps the name reminded him well, with some aunt, grandmother or sister. Jasmin was surprised by the information she heard from her mother. This was not what she had expected when she went to her for pregnancy counseling. In passing, she began to wonder about her father's origins, and even for a moment the idea of a trip there crossed her mind. It would be nice to meet the family. All her life she envied her friends who told about aunts, uncles, cousins and even aunts. After a while, however, she chased away the thought of visiting. She remembered how different the two communities were. She immediately went down to the ground. After all, the people of Floris were rightly treated like freaks. They did not want to learn. They preferred to farm. They took no drugs, only herbs. They ate the flesh of smelly animals or on dried, pickled, or coal-roasted plants. These old-fashioned foods lingered and rotted in their digestive systems. She imagined the stench in her gut. She also remembered that the Florians didn't care about the Inco people. They treated them as wise men who for a moment separated themselves from the motherland and acted like a modern state. Idiots, she thought. "Just for a moment? This was already in the twenty-fourth era, and it was not going to change. Inco will absorb Floris sooner than the other way around. Why do you believe in these fairy tales about deities?" she thought. "We are so different." She sighed deeply. She also decided not to tell Addam about her origins. She was fed up with being mocked about the slums she grew up in anyway.

Only three people knew that Jasmin was carrying female triplets in her stomach. That ghastly GCO officer, Dr. Steavans, and the mother. "What an irony of fate," she thought. Neither her husband nor her closest friend, whom she shared many times, but not always, knew about it. Luicey was a good man, but she was not to be trusted. "She's the greatest gossip girl ever. If she had known the truth, the entire first quarter would have been raving about it immediately," she thought bitterly.

When Jasmin visited Dr. Meilly, she was determined to terminate the pregnancy. Now she wasn't sure she was ready for such a step. How will Addam react? Will he condemn her?" She wondered. She was sure of his loyalty, but no feeling could compare to the threat that would hang over them if she chose to give birth to triplets. She preferred to convey this message to him at the right moment. She hoped they would make a decision together, although deep down she hoped that some solution would be found to save all three innocent babies.

There were many differences in the outcomes of having a male and a female child. It was enough to remember the most important ones. Depending on the age, the Inco Government allocated five or eight hundred entitys a month to support the boy. In addition, the child was provided with medical care and access to the best vaccines, vitamins and drugs. The situation of the birth of a female child was completely different. The girl's parents could not count on free treatment, and the monthly tax for each subsequent daughter, except for the first one, was one thousand entitys. With good earnings, in the order of two to three thousand entitys a month, this amount was quite a challenge. This difference was most noticeable in the kindergarten, where the children spent practically the whole day. The boys and girls played in separate rooms. Each boy wore a mask. It was intended to protect against potential dangers of childhood. Built-in special carbon filter protects against viruses and bacteria. In addition, the mask was equipped with a system of sensors detecting an increase in temperature or potential diseases. If the child was losing normal immunity, he was immediately automatically given an appropriate dose of minerals or vitamins necessary for the proper functioning of the body. These masks were paid for by the government. The girls' parents could not afford them, especially the current replenishment of applicators. In a kindergarten that lasted half a purification, one caretaker was tasked with looking after just two boys or twenty girls. It was just that nobody cared for the girls except their parents. If one were mutilated or died, no one would care. Jasmin despaired of what would happen to her daughters if their mother was not there. She was struggling again with her thoughts as to what she should do. She was sobbing in her mind as if she was mourning the end of her happy life. She remembered all the most wonderful moments. She was particularly fond of Addam's proposal - the most enjoyable moment so far.

Such a ritual took place only in one unique place. On the outskirts of the first district, in the historic part of Inco, there was a Glass Dome so large that it could accommodate a small town. A large part of the surface hidden under the glass was a lake with deep, crystal clear water, full of colorful, freshwater fish. In the land part, you could experience contact with live fauna and flora, which, apart from the dome in the entire Inco, was impossible to see. Many cleanings ago, for fear of plague, diseases and impurities, the government issued a decree on the elimination of many species of animals, mainly rodents and birds. Therefore, all the water, land and flying creatures living inside this dome were basically the only ones in the whole land.

It was a magical place. This relic was built at the time when Inco was connected with Floris. Back then, there was a common religion, the cult of Patri. After all, after ages of oppression, who doubted that Patri did exist, she was definitely banned from Inco in the eighth era. At that time, the dome was a kind of chapel, where colorful, paper boats were launched on the surface of the water. They were innocent, symbolic sacrifices made to smaller local deities responsible for health, love and wealth. After all ancient beliefs were made illegal, the dome remained unused for many cleanings. Still, somehow the water never got dirty, and neither did the creatures die out. With time, the youth began to return there and again, this time secretly, pray for love. The then government took advantage of this pseudo-religious act and turned it into an element of its policy. The custom of making offerings or praying for love has turned into a secular tradition of negotiating a marriage. It quickly became iconic.

That day, Addam and Jasmin were still engaged. When he announced that he was inviting her on a boat trip on the glass-domed lake, she couldn't help but tear happy. It was the most expensive version available on the market. Only the most eminent families could afford it. A cruise on the lake in this boat, made of light but strong and the finest materials, was quite an expense. Despite the cost and long waiting times for their turn, many men chose this option. He was synonymous with luxury. Poorer fiancées borrowed small rafts for a few moments, which they could move only a few elses from the shore, and after repeating a short oath, they returned. Addam did the best he could, in one day. When they got on board with Jasmin and a group of a dozen or so young people, many of the girls cried with emotion. After reaching the middle of the lake, the official announced that the ritual could be started. It was kind of simple. Potential bride and groom lay on the deck close to each other and waited as if for deliverance. Their bride and groom, so far hidden under the deck, were supposed to find their fiancé with closed eyes and kiss him on the mouth. Men were not allowed to give any hints. Many brides were wrong to give the others an excuse to cheer. The mistake meant that the couple would be betrayed, which is why rarely any girl decided to continue the relationship. In turn, the longer she looked for her chosen one, the worse it was supposedly. This meant that their marriage would face many obstacles in life, and the husband would have to work hard for the family. There were couples who never found each other. In such a situation, when the impatient young lady finally uncovered her eyes, it meant that she gave up the proposal, though not necessarily out of love. Jasmin found Addam in record time, which bode idyll. Other couples that day looked for much longer. The entire atheist Inco society knew that the proposal procedure was superstition. However, no one dared to give it up. It was too rooted in tradition.

***

Before Gibbondy joined the Office for Gender Control, she was an activist at the Ministry of Health, then Sports and Interests. Everywhere she made sure that the nation developed properly, that it eliminated unhealthy tissues itself. "Mollies", she thought of them many times, as she put on pounds while exercising on a multi-functional muscle training machine. "Life does not pamper you," she would say to herself, which is why she always did all the exercises very thickly dressed.

That afternoon, the wet inside outfit was sticking to her body, and the growing choking sweat was a sign that the exhausting training session should be over. After that, it was enough to undress and turn on the flushing module. She loved the moment when drops of icy water thrown from the ceiling with high pressure bombarded her skin. Then she really felt alive. She did not like the drying function, so she rarely used it. She associated it with a warm, tender touch that she disliked. After taking a bath, she went straight to the living room. Naked and wet. Her wardrobe was filled with brown uniforms of the UTCOMP, pressed into a crease. They hung freely, not too tightly filling the entire room. At the bottom of the wardrobe stood a row of shiny composite boots laced up to the knees. On the other hand, there were caps for all occasions on the top shelf. The field version was practical, it was used for day-to-day activities, including tracking and prosecuting combiners. The birthing machine, more resembling a scarf, was used during routine checks in hospital rooms, as well as in gynecological offices. Gibbondy was a high-ranking officer, she did not have to control the work of doctors, but she did it selflessly after hours. Out of pure passion for the cultivation of meanness. She used the gala cap only for all parades, which, thanks to the involvement of the Ministry of the Indoctrination of Society, took place a lot.

She dressed quickly. She still had some time to stare out the window. The view from one of the last floors of a tall skyscraper pleased her cold heart. She looked at the swarming crowd below with open contempt and disgust. She knew a lot would change soon. With this positive thought, she ran out of the apartment. Along the long, narrow corridor, she marched inspired. She wanted to fly, not take the elevator. It was mercilessly going down the hundred floors. As she stepped outside, she quickened her pace. The people she passed, mostly from good families, and such lived in her neighborhood, were practically transparent to her. The meeting was to take place at the Gender Control Office. As usual, after working hours. But for Gibbondy, service was the number one job she did.

When she entered Noovack's office, she was first as usual. Its boss, the Director of the GCO, and also the Deputy Minister of Health, looked pleased. Gibbondy nodded slightly in greeting and took her seat at the great council table.

"Are you aware of this moment, Claire?" Eva Noovack asked.

"I've never been more sure what we are doing is of the utmost importance," she replied.

"We will have a lot of work now."

"I'm prepared for anything."

After a while, four women, aged between three and a half and five purifications, entered the office. One of them was dressed in a border guard uniform with an officer rank, the other in a guard uniform, and the others appeared to be civilians. Gibbondy was extremely excited. If she hadn't killed herself with hard training earlier, she probably would have gone mad with excitement now. The women took their seats. Eva Noovack walked around before she sat down with them.

"Can we talk freely?" She asked.

"Yes. I blocked the eavesdropping," replied Natalia Tatarczyna, guard officer.

"Excellent," said Noovack, and finally sat down on the last of the empty seats at the table. "My dear," she continued. "A bomb will go off tomorrow morning that will sweep away the remnants of the old system. In a few days, I will propose to the Council of Advisers the formation of a new Government. The pharmaceutical cartels will defend themselves, but the Black Hands have already made sure that in the near future pharmacy ceases to play such a key role as it did during the recent purges. We have the support of several important tech corporations, but I can't reveal any names right now. We can also count on the Minister of Sport and Interests, as well as the one from the economy. The files will have to be left with them. The rest will, as is known, be shared. The dust after the bomb will settle quickly. Are there any questions?"

"When should I turn off the theatremania?" Asked Kimberly Davis, the current head of the Public Opinion and Sentiment Research Bureau. "The Ministry of Society Indoctrination will push for an exclusion right away. I think it would be good for the nation to know the truth."

"Good point." Eva Noovack thought for a moment.

"What if they try to force it off?" Davis continued considering the possibility.

"The humaan garrison will be ready. I've already reprogrammed them," Tatarczyna flaunted.

"Way to go. This is what the country needs," said Noovack proudly. "And what is the situation with a virus in computer modules?"

"They won't be able to dig out of the blockade by tomorrow. They are still convinced that they control theatremania, losers. Upgrades of all systems for IT, radio and telecommunications support only wait for a signal. Once we play, no one will break in. Only me and the future prime minister have access codes." Nadine Bleur, a dry, brown-haired, Oriental beauty, took out a small envelope and handed it to Noovack.

"Thank you and congratulations, the future Minister of Digitization and Telecommunications," said the boss and smiled significantly.

"Will we be able to incorporate the superior state system, i.e. the UTCOMP?" Gibbondy absolutely wanted to remind of her existence.

"Of course, but that's not your concern anymore, friend."

The officer only smirked. Her thin lips and bony cheeks, combined with this grimace, were supposed to communicate that this ferocious predator was just waiting to hunt down the enemies.

Chapter 6 The crack

Hello hasn't come out well yet the horizon, and Fahid has been bustling around the farm a long time ago. He had time to pray to Patri and see if the night fire had burned down completely. Then he visited the stable where he kept the animals. This time six hydapis, two tine and four okurai stayed there. Only one representative of the latter species stayed outside the stable, in a small pen. It was pregnant and could give birth to children at any moment. It wouldn't be very safe for toddlers if adult animals, especially other species, were interested in them. Therefore, when his abdomen was severely swollen, the okurai was separated. Cannibalism has not been reported among animals, but adult animals have been trampled underfoot because of their too noisy behavior. In this family, the responsibility of caring for the pregnant creature always fell on Sumi or one of her sisters. Even so, their father always liked to check that nothing was wrong. He did this while the children were still asleep. After making sure all was well, Fahid returned to the hut to eat a nutritious meal and take care of daily hygiene.

The people of Floris are only wrong in the morning, before work. This was the custom not to contaminate the dirty, sweaty body of Mother Earth, who fed them. The place for daily ablution was next to the windmill. It was a huge barrel filled with water. *Dirshna* flowers were floating on its surface just to give a feeling of freshness. Every farmer in the area had access to virtually unlimited amounts of water, thanks to the canal system excavated many generations before. There was also one flowing through Fahid's farm, twelve cubits wide, four deep, and also a small stream.

Fahid took off his clothes. It looked like a suede made of the toughest material imaginable. The fabric made of raidi was virtually unbreakable. These flying creatures, hunted by moree birds, had a hair-like structure of muscles. Their fibers were split, dried and twisted in the spinning process and then wound on a skein. Later it was similar to materials of plant origin: they were colored with the use of natural dyes, they were woven and the resulting material was used by men to tie a rope or sew clothes. No woman was strong enough to control such a hard and difficult to process material. When Fahid emerged from the bath, he smeared his whole body with sirra oleum. This treatment was designed to create a protective layer for the skin, as well as to preserve the inside of the garment. All that was left was to trim the hair on the head and beard, a tedious habit of wanting to please my wife. For generations, all the men in Floris wore skimpy hairstyles and perfectly trimmed beards. If any of them ventured out in this regard, they were either a bachelor or a widower. There was no other option, the tradition was so deeply entrenched in society. A bald man was always associated with a priest. Poison sooner or later stripped the hair and stubble of each of Patri's servants.

The morning passed for Fahid until his meal, following the same daily rite. Then it was different. Either he dealt with animals or *dirshna*, that is, he planted it, chaffed it, collected flowers, cut down or reclaimed the soil. This type of rush, grown on fields that were flooded two cubits high, was associated with his family for generations. They specialized in it and put all their affection into it, and the plant reciprocated them with good crops. During one purification, their life-giving soil usually produced its crops thirty times. The cultivation cycle, from the planting of small plants to the post-harvest rehabilitation, was basically a timekeeper for these simple folks. On that particular day, the harvest of flowers from which food was made was planned. None of the petals could go to waste, which is why, two eras earlier, the people of Floris ordered a simple technology to facilitate harvesting from Inco. Fahid's family also finally collected the necessary amount of gray stones to buy a machine for collecting and processing fleshy flowers, and a few cleanings later for cutting the stems, reclaiming the substrate and planting new plants. The machines were quite primitive, they were drawn by animals. Only the one, intended for the collection of purple flowers - as the only one that works with energy obtained from Hello rays - hovered right above the plants. The chckenei, the pollinators that played from dawn to dusk among the flowers, feared her only. Their hum was heard a good fifty cubits from the field. The machine looked like a platform. Arches of grippers protruded from underneath. On its upper part there was a stand for the operator and a small silo for storing the collected flakes in the form of ground pulp.

Fahid waited until Hello was high enough to give enough power from its rays to activate the machine. He had only tried it once before, but the too weak source of morning light only choked the mechanism. The repair cost a few handfuls of gray stones, the amount he got from selling one crop. It was a lot. He decided never to make that mistake again. When Hello reached the center of the sky, he activated the machine. Her sound was soft but unpleasant to perceive. Even the best-oiled parts rattled and rattled unbearably. It was because of their age. Renewed and glued many times, they gave the impression that they would soon fall apart.

The farmer climbed onto the platform and sat down in the operator's station. You could see everything from here. Both the individual gripper zones and the inlet of the output into the silo. He drove to the edge of the field and began harvesting. The grippers stripped the flowers from individual petals very agile and quickly. The pulp processed by the sequentially operating screw kneaders was transported with precision to the silo, which filled up quite quickly. Even so, Fahid was aware that he could not afford a break. He should complete this phase of the cycle within the next three days. Another two will take him cutting the stalks to be used after drying for smoking. Then the local Patri feast, one of many when it was forbidden to work in the field.

Fahid managed to reach the opposite end in the machine and began the uneasy turning process. At that time, a courier with mail arrived at his hut. Rita took the letter from the high priestess. She wasn't going to open it until her husband arrived, though the letter bothered her greatly. Besides, she couldn't read. It seemed unnecessary to learn this skill. She knew that she would work in the field all her life anyway. Why study? It was enough that her husband could do it. "Let everyone do what they are made to do," she quoted her father. She knew Fahid was angry when he was disturbed at work, but she decided to send the eldest of her sons, Abdul, for the husband. The boy mounted an okurai and ran along the stone path towards the large flower-harvesting platform, seen from a distance. He persuaded his father for a long time to stop working. By the time they got back to the hut, Rita had prepared a short meal and a pot of Keeffi for her husband. The whole family gathered on the terrace. Fahid took a few sips of the energy drink and unwrapped the bow. Rulon was sealed with a matte black wax that only the priestess of Ae used. The papyrus looked grand as usual. The host sat down comfortably and began reading aloud.

"Dearly beloved friend of mine and my friend Fahid, and you, beautiful and wise Rita, wife and mother of ten lovely children." At this point the farmer paused to unfold another part of the papyrus. "Thank you for punctually and scrupulously paying our temple a tax of a tenth of your harvest. I am also proud that in the Patri community that I have led, there are people as religious and righteous as you. I know you love your goddess and you trust me, so I let you bow down to myself and..." He paused again and took a deep breath.

"Skip those titles, Father, and get to the point!" Abdul said impatiently, but his ears dropped quickly when he saw his short, disciplining gaze. Fahid resumed reading.

"I invite your large family to sacrifice one of daughters, Sumi."

Everyone froze in no time. Fahid looked at Rita and at beloved daughter.

"I believe," he continued his reading in a shaky voice, "that she will be the perfect candidate for a priestess. Before my faithful servant Kadu, whom you surely know, comes for her, enjoy her presence, for she will never come back. Fahid, greetings to your father Mahmud. Thank you for your generosity. May Patri be with you."

***

As it did every morning, the Golden Temple was filled with high-level priests dressed in festive robes. They entered according to rank. First, those with the shortest seniority and estimate, then more importantly. Kifor came at the end, and Ae last. It stood exactly at the bottom of the chapel, resembling an inverted pyramid. After reaching the appropriate level, each priest took his place. When Ae gave the signal to begin the daily prayers, each of them folded their hands in front of their chests and closed their eyes.

"Patri, bless our land," she began.

"Bless you," replied the other priests in chorus.

"Patri, bless our water," she continued.

"Bless you."

"Patri, bless our people, the most beautiful women and the most industrious men, as well as their offspring."

"Bless you."

And so on. Ae listed all the important parts of the land, sides of the world, animal species, even the biggest pests, and the names of the plants grown. This time she added one more request at the end.

"Patri, bless our Inco neighbors to find the way to faith and true happiness, which is reconciliation with you."

"What are you saying, lady?" Outraged Rados, a not very important but talkative priest standing on one of the middle steps. "They are eternal enemies. They don't care about our religion. They don't care about the dead, they don't care about Mother Nature."

"Shut him up, Kifor," she replied shortly, bowed and left.

Joy was ashamed. He was sure the rest of the priests would join his protest. But no one dared to oppose the High Priestess of the Omniearth. Apparently, if she prayed for these heretics, it meant she had a purpose in it. Walking down the Golden Temple after praying, at the sight of Kifor, Rados looked away. He refused to meet his eyes when this important priest gave him information about some severe punishment, such as the removal of several important quarters from management. Each of the high-ranking priests, and there were exactly forty of them in the entire council, managed a few or even a dozen territories. The loss of some of them was associated with a decrease in the hierarchy, as well as a decrease in the proceeds from tithing, a percentage of which always went to the pocket of the chief administrator. None of the lower and middle priests knew about this. Kifor had the largest and best organized network of middle-level priests under his management. Of its districts located in the eastern quarter, the most taxes were received. That is why he held the honorable position of Ae's deputy. She invented this position in the structure so as not to contact everyone. She treated him as her intermediary. Kifor only clapped Rados on the shoulder.

"Keep your head down, brother, or you will end up in the far frontiers as a mid-level priest."

The threat sounded convincing. Rados swallowed panically, bowed and retired to his chambers. Meanwhile, Ae had reached the bedroom. Her maidservants had already made the large bed and prepared a morning bath of tine milk, this time in a shade of pale purple tinged with pink. It was immediately apparent that the animals were fed only with the stalks of the *dirshna*, the favorite plant of the High Priestess of the Omniearth. Ae fell in love with her because of her amazing color. When the maidservants had the choice of making a bath with the milk of animals fed with *dirshna* or fodder puke vegetables, they chose a milk color that was closer to light purple than purple. In honor of her beloved bulrushes, Ae had the same-colored guards' robes, which henceforth referred to as "purple" or "purplats". Its core consisted of the strongest low-level priests who decided to abandon their clergy career in favor of the service and protection of the most important person in the state. When Ae entered the bath and one of the maidservants named Pirna poured her warm milk, the chief of the guard knocked on the door.

"Who's there?" Asked the priestess.

"It's me, lady," he replied.

"Come in, Zenit."

She was not ashamed of him. Every priest lost his sex drive right after taking the poison, so she knew that when this strong man looked at her with adoration, it wasn't because she was a beautiful, sexy woman. He just loved her like a monarch whom he faithfully served.

"We captured a naked man from Inco," said a big strong man at the age of five. "He was hanging around the neighborhood. Moments later, we found his pet."

"How do you know it was his?" She was surprised.

"One of the mail couriers says he passed a naked man traveling on a heavily handled hydapi."

"Interesting. How did he get here?"

"I think someone helped him."

"Get that courier. And I would like to see this man too."

"Of course, lady. We locked him in a dungeon, in a checkered room. He was given some water and a modest meal, but ate nothing. He's raving about a mission all the time."

Ae got impatient. She sent Zenit an urgent look. He understood immediately that instead of speaking, he should act. He left quickly and came back even faster. She did not manage to get dressed, so she kept her guard behind the door for a moment. She wore a long gown sewn with silver thread and light shoes adorned with bird feathers. She wanted to see how this outfit and a string of precious stones around her neck would make a stunning impression on the guests. She was not wrong. The young courier who entered with Zenit forgot his tongue. He didn't even say hello.

"Did you see anything disturbing?" Asked the priestess.

"I don't understand, my lady," the courier muttered.

"Before you saw the naked Inco man, did you pass something, or maybe someone you thought suspicious?"

He just twisted his face. Ae realized that she had just lost her alertness in choosing her words. A trait that set her apart from that whole bunch of idiots with which she surrounded herself.

"What did you do before you saw the Inco man?"

"I was going okurai to Patrix."

She breathed a sigh of relief.

"Okay. And before?"

"I was going too... I was delivering a letter from you, lady."

"To who?" There was a furiously growing impatience on the priestess's face.

"To the priest."

"What was his name?! Where was it?" Even Zenit, the most punitive and patient guard in the world, has lost his temper.

"Kadu. I was delivering the letter to a priest in the west quarter. When I was looking for him in Litrijis, I found out that he had gone with the body to Asaran. In fact, he was there, but he had no car. He was sitting on a hydapi that gurgled as if he had just been trying to catch up with the okurai. It is known that this is impossible."

"What did he do?"

"Nothing."

"He just stood there? And you, what did you do next?" Ae had had enough of those tales of Moss and Fern."

"I drove. A short while later I stopped by the stream. I drank some water. I was breathing. I drank okurai and moved on. I drove left, then straight, then..."

"Enough." The priestess motioned to Zenit for someone to lead this idle talker away.

Zenit called one of the door guards who, as he led the courier out, could hardly refrain from laughing for a moment. It turned out that you could hear everything outside.

"What do you think, my friend?" She asked.

"I suggest sending a small squad to scour the area. Maybe they will find something," Zenit replied.

"Right. In the meantime, let's go talk to that rider from Inco."

***

The news of Sumi's invitation to the priesthood shattered all the layers of her father's faith. In an instant, he hated the High Priestess of the Omniearth and the organization she managed. He decided not to give his child to waste. He tilted the pot of Keeffi all the way down so as not to look into his wife's teary eyes. Rita suffered no less than he did. The daughter whom the Church claimed was not the eldest or the youngest child in this family. Unfortunately, she was just the perfect age to begin her priesthood studies. Abdul and Ragir were too old. If that can be said of children less than one and a half years of purification. Younger children should always feel threatened by potential recruitment. If the parents did not accept the invitation on behalf of the child, which was unlikely to be done, the priestess could punish the entire family. She would have blamed her decision on Patri's anger as usual. Sometimes she ironically called such an act her kindness. It meant an increase in the tax or an order to return all children who did not pass the magical age of one purification. This was reportedly done with wayward families who, for example, shirked tithing or challenged God's laws.

"We will not agree." Fahid finally decided to break the awkward silence. "My father also lost a member of his family once and suffered all his life."

"He became a priest?" Ragir was surprised.

"No. His name was Omar, also Manduarra. He was my father's brother and it was this uncle who taught him to read and than me, and also build a windmill or repair a farm machine. Even flying. He was a very wise man. He knew not only about mechanisms. With time, our family home stopped talking about him, but I know that my father never forgot about him."

"What happened to this Uncle Omar?" Sumi asked.

"He left and didn't come back. Nobody knows where."

"You never told me about him." Rita felt betrayed.

Fahid just looked at her with buttery eyes as if to beg her forgiveness.

"We'll tell Kadu we'd like to accept the invitation, but Sumi will learn to be a singer. We'll send her to school in Hambarra."

"You really want to send her there? It's days away from here." Rita looked concerned.

"At least she'll come back from there," he replied.

Sumi was pleased with the idea on the one hand, but worried on the other. She always dreamed of singing. She had never dreamed that her parents would ever think seriously about her passion. She never considered separation.

***

A grotto with many checkered chambers was located in one of the lowest caves. It couldn't be lower. It was cold and damp. Illuminated by torches, which gave a substitute for warmth. Ae didn't like being around bad guys, but it was safe to lock every potential rogue in isolation. No one ever escaped from there. The bars were unbeatable because of the bars made of the stretched backbones of the sahadi lizards. These long, subterranean, predatory creatures were famous for not being cut in half with even the sharpest tool available in Floris. Hunting these reptiles was not easy either. Anyway, what for? They weren't tasty at all. Nevertheless, when the properties of their core were discovered, many daredevils were involved in this practice. The backbone of one lizard cost twenty gray stones in the open market. So it was worth fighting for such a trophy.

The sahadi backbone grating that Haris was held in was not made perfectly. She looked lopsided. It was difficult to process this hard, though organic material without the use of tools, which only belong to Inco. The prisoner was lying in his own faeces. His hands were tied to his legs. There were many flogging marks and many bruises on his back. He was naked. The sight moved Ae.

"What's your name, good man?" She asked to gain an ally.

"Call me "animal." That's how you treat me."

The priestess felt as if someone had shot her in the face. And this is in the presence of witnesses. She couldn't remember the feeling. It immediately triggered bad memories.

"I came voluntarily to talk to you, and your people have captured me, imprisoned me, and tortured me."

"Voluntarily?" She was surprised, but when she cast a meaningful look in the direction of Zenit, she understood that the man was telling the truth. Despite the lack of sufficient light, it was possible to see that the chief of the guard's face was the same color as his robe resembling the uniform of a security guard.

"So you say you came to talk to me. About what?" She asked.

Haris didn't answer for a long time. One of the guards hit him with a thick wooden stick, but the prisoner was clearly unimpressed. He just spat contemptuously. After a moment his eyelids closed and his head fell to the stone floor.

"He must have eaten nothing in days," Ae thought aloud.

At this point, she remembered the pain she felt after tasting one of the Inco food bars. She began to understand Haris's dilemmas. She even felt sorry for him. It was the first time she had seen someone act this way. She had seen madmen wanting to get to the goddess Patri faster, but none of them showed such desperation. "Probably because he is an unbeliever," she mused.

"Please bathe him, clothe him and feed him. After all, we have these longitudinal culinary delights in the event of guests visiting."

"Yes, lady," confirmed Zenit.

"And please lock him in one of the chambers. Have ten men watch over him. It is not known who he is. And with you," she whispered to the chief of the guard, "I'm disappointed. You know I do not accept fact coloring."

The purple boss just sighed deeply. He was always faithful and loyal to his mistress like no one else. He did not intend to colorize any information he gave her. It came out by itself. Without the control of his cold mind. Only when he felt a strong need for her to pay attention to him. When he felt invisible.

***

The rocky hills of the western quarter of Floris were lush. Rather, it grew on the slopes. If there was even a small flat piece of field in this varied terrain, the farmers immediately developed it. The hydapi carrying the priest Kadu walked along the stone-reinforced road. It was evident that the animal enjoyed it. The route meandering at times across the slope, and at times crossing a rather steep hill, was the best way to diversify the tedious hike. Unlike the animal, Kadu was not in a good mood. He decided to obey the priestess Ae and bring Sumi, daughter of Fahid, whom he had said goodbye a few days ago, to Patrix. His farm was extensive. This time it took ages to get to the host's house. The flooded fields looked like a flowery meadow stretching to the horizon, bland with blood purple. When he got close enough to count all eight wings of the huge windmill near the yard, he paused for a moment. He sighed deeply. He closed his eyes and began to pray fervently for the success of the mission. When finished, he summoned the spirit of Mahmud. It was his body that should have rested in the Asaran Gorge, not a three-wheeled corpse truck. He hoped Patri would understand it wasn't his fault. If the mission that Kadu was now to perform had failed, it would have meant that the priest had fallen out of favor with his goddess, which would have been a great waste. Patri surely would not want to lose her most staunch believer and preacher.

Rita greeted the priest as he entered the yard. She was standing in the doorway of the cabin with three curious toddlers.

"Hello, what brings you to us?" She asked.

"You probably know. I have come to fulfill the will of the High Priestess. Have you received a letter?" He asked timidly, glad in spirit that no one was asking him about Mahmud from the very beginning.

"Yes. It was brought by a courier, but I can't read. I'm waiting for my husband."

"And where is Fahid? Doesn't pick flowers? I thought I saw a *dirshna* harvesting machine a few hills from here. It's not yours?"

"Our. Abdul and Ragir help their father with the harvest. My husband and his daughter went to Hambarra. She is a smart girl. She will study to be a singer, and the most famous school is there."

Kadu thought about it. At first he thought Patri was mocking him. Was the goddess really angry for losing

Mahmud's body? Not. This, however, could not be true. Fahid has never traveled that far. In fact, Sumi was said to have a talent for singing, but to leave the farm in the care of an illiterate wife and burden the boys with the harvest? It wasn't that farmer style.

But Kadu wasn't about to embarrass Rita.

"When are you expecting your husband back?" He asked.

"He said he'd be back in about twenty Hello sunrises. So come over then."

"Okay, then there's nothing here for me."

This time the lack of hospitality of the woman was clearly visible. "Was she hiding something? She can't lie either," Kadu thought, bowed low and turned the hydapi.

As his pet took a dozen steps, he heard the question he was afraid of.

"Is my father-in-law Mahmoud doing well with Patri?" Rita asked.

He didn't even turn around. He only grunted briefly and rudely, as if to avoid an unequivocal answer. He was furious that the woman must have remembered this right now, before he left her yard. He jerked the reins, and the animal quickened its pace.

Rita waited a moment for the priest to go to a safe distance. After a long moment, he was too far to see what was happening in the yard.

"He drove!" She called out loudly.

At this point, Sumi emerged from the burrow, followed by Fahid.

"You did well," said her husband, hugging the still slightly shaky Rita. "Let's trust he believed. We've got twenty Hello rises to figure out what to do next."

"Maybe we shouldn't have a campfire tonight? It will be visible from afar. Kadu himself will think that it is impossible for boys to be able to do it."

"Don't be silly. How can you not light the night campfire?" The host said indignantly.

And the ritual was not so much rooted in social consciousness as sacred. The Florinians gathered every day at dusk to light a fire in honor of the goddess who arose from the rays of Hello. The whole families, warming up after the end of the day, prayed. Then the host added so many shrub stalks or logs that the fire would not be extinguished during the short night in this phase of its flowering. This has always been the case and every day. It is believed that each of the fires emitted rays similar to those from Hello. While burning, it gave the stars the rays borrowed during the day, while illuminating and heating the yard.

***

Haris was unlucky with the costumes he used on missions in a neighboring land. This time he was given a woman's outfit. Seemingly smaller than male, but also too big for a man so sick in the eyes of the Florians. He, as befits an Inco inhabitant, was simply fit and ate as much as his body needed. Exactly two food bars a day. Nothing more. Unlike men from a neighboring country who liked to eat a lot and eat well, and also used their muscles only for physical work, not for sports.

When Ae entered the room that served as the makeshift prison, she immediately wondered if she knew this man. Washed and dressed, he looked completely different. He was reminiscent of someone she knew; someone she has already met. She just couldn't remember under what circumstances. As High Priestess of the Omniearth, she had attended numerous meetings with representatives of the Inco Government, but Haris certainly never sat at the table with her.

"Thank you," he said, and bowed slightly.

It was evident that he had come back to life, although the bruise on his cheek made him not forget what he had experienced in the dungeons.

"How did you get here?" She asked, but he just sighed. "How many of ours did you kill before reaching the holy mountain?"

"I didn't kill anyone. I know your habits a bit, so it was easier for me."

"Yes? Where from?" She was surprised.

"My father was a border guard officer. When I was a boy, we lived on the other side of Ethne, at Pinati Falls. Have you seen this place?"

"Once. Also in childhood. I don't remember much."

"That's where our worlds intertwine. People know each other, they are even friends. I had a friend on your side. We were fishing together. Then our family moved to the city of skyscrapers. It wasn't so much fun anymore."

"Don't we know each other from somewhere?" The uncertainty haunted her.

"Of course. My name is Haris Sagavara. I had the pleasure of communing with you twice during the summit meetings. I have been a member of the Diplomatic Corps as Personal Assistant to the Minister of Home Affairs and adviser to Prime Minister Barney Clifford."

"As I understand it, just because you know our habits?" Ae felt satisfied. "Then why did you struggle like a fugitive?"

"I'd like to tell you, but only in private."

Haris nodded at the purpletes guarding them.

"I don't understand," said the priestess. "I trust these people. They pledged allegiance to me."

"For sure?" He asked sarcastically, as if to say that she shouldn't believe anyone. "Dismiss those eavesdroppers outside the door as well."

Ae just snorted. She was not going to agree to his terms. Even if he wanted to tell her something important, she couldn't be alone with him. Haris, however, looked adamant. She was impressed that he was ready for anything after the torture. She even thought that for the mission he would be killed. He, however, decided to make the worst possible impression to provoke Ae into submission.

"How good the poison has spared you, my lady." He felt he could allow himself to digress about the aftertaste of irony.

Ae's face appeared a little tense. "How could this man from a foreign country know such things? Besides, how dare she challenge the authority of the High Priestess of the Omniearth, even with the guards?" She thought.

"Hang him up," she said shortly and left the room.

Chapter 7 The coup

From this morning Addam acted as if he knew what was going to happen. He woke up early and couldn't go back to sleep. As if he was awake. His heart was beating faster than usual, though it never gave him any trouble. He was very anxious.

"Why do not you sleep?" Jasmin asked.

"I can't."

"Why don't you take some sleep medication?"

"It's useless."

Jasmin felt that the situation was starting to get unbearable and that there would be a great climax soon. And it wasn't a problem with her pregnancy. Something equally important, rather related to Addam's work, was around the corner. "We are both having a rough time," she thought, and resolved not to share the bad news. "Poor. He is still convinced that he will have one daughter. If he knew the whole truth, he would surely withdraw into himself, as he sometimes did," she thought. Meanwhile, she could not bear the emotional separation. In this difficult period, she needed close-ups. They supported each other, although they were both unaware of what the other side was struggling with. For them, the most important were the will and the bond that united them. I'm sure everything will be clear in the end.

When Addam left for work, she couldn't find a place for a long time. She was a little bored alone at home, but she didn't want to go back to the treadmill at the marketing corporation. If it turned out that she would get a project to create a campaign for another drug for something that does not solve the problem of humanity, she would have to spit her boss in the face. Jasmin had had enough the empty slogans she produced by the thousands. Always in the same style. Brazenly deceitful and primitive in its own way. Their task was to reach everyone and encourage them to buy. Only business mattered. "Where the fuck is mankind?!" She cursed herself for the first time since time immemorial. In order to distract herself from her thoughts, she turned on theatremania passion. This time she immediately lowered her voice. She did not want to listen to propaganda crap. It was another boring drug show. All she could see was the picture. Some reporter was showing a vial of Ray. Groundbait again? "You have no shame, sellers," she thought of all the journalists and pressed the button to turn off the projector. She has never defiled herself by taking this remedy. Father believed that it was doing nothing good. She obeyed him then.

***

It was a morning that all Inco would not forget for the following eras. A report by Luigi Pierone, a journalist and discoverer of the greatest scandal in history, was broadcast over and over again on all four channels. Nothing worked except for the theatremania. All IT systems were shut down. Even state-owned, operating on completely different principles than generally available. All services were completely paralyzed.

Barney Clifford was packing trunks of clothing. He wasn't even mad at the whole situation anymore. Concerned about the life of his wife, son and himself, he intended to implement the evacuation plan that had been prepared for some time. At this point, he was focusing more on getting to the hideout than on what was happening in the country under his management. If he could pray, he would certainly do so.

The first reactions to the report were rather indifferent. Everyone in Inco who was interested in politics at first did not believe what they saw on theatrical screens. It was believed that a well-known journalist had been dismissed and was only paying off. He invented another insignificant scandal and that's it. He always had a push to the front pages. The Prime Minister of the Government, however, had more complete knowledge on this subject. Pierone wasn't kicked out at all. He hid at the moment when he learned the truth and realized that this knowledge could be dangerous for him. The Ministry of the Indoctrination of Society had to somehow cover up the absence of his columns in a popular journal, so there was a post about the dismissal. They also wanted to exaggerate him a bit. Luigi Pierone was always looking for scandals. He was labeled the master of cheap sensation, so hardly anyone paid attention to his texts. He was rebellious to the authorities, but needed. Thanks to him, the image of the state was not so flawless. Due to these insignificant scandals, it seemed more real than the one shown by intrusive propaganda. Clifford accepted the antics of this magazine. However, as it turned out later, pseudo scandals led him to a real bomb. They were nothing compared to the one that would change the image of an ideal state forever.

"The investigation is one thing, but who made it easier for Pierone to record the reportage and broadcast it in the theatremania?" Rubby said basically to himself, because the operator of the machine they came for Clifford and his family didn't even understand the message.

They stopped almost in front of the building where the prime minister lived in the state-paid apartment. They were greeted by the crowds of journalists standing in front of the apartment building from the early morning.

"Ladies and gentlemen," Rubby said to the audience. "Please fan out. There is nothing interesting to watch here."

He was wrong. The sight of the vehicle in which they arrived was surprising to onlookers. Most of them had never seen such a machine. It was equipped with eight gravity-operated magnetic motors to keep the metal and glass platform low to the ground. Through the glass it was clear that there were fifteen rows in the middle, each with two comfortable seats. The platform was covered with a roof made of series-connected cells used to collect Hello energy. There were only three of these in Inco. Usually hidden from the world. They all belonged to the Chemist Party.

"Will the prime minister resign?" One of the hacks asked Rubby.

"For what reason? Are you crazy?" The Minister of Home Affairs absolutely did not take such a scenario into account. After a while, however, he realized that he must not show his nervousness. "Everything is under control. The report is a fiction created to fight a potential threat. Such a test of strength. You really have nothing to do?" he tried to downplay.

The matter was serious. Pierone somehow found out that the direct reason for the emergence of demographic problems was the introduction to the market of a modified hybrid drug produced by Metachemie. Ray, because that was the name of the drug, caused a drastic reduction in the birth of boys, as well as the emergence of a third sex, crippled children looking like girls-faced boys with developed organs of both sexes, unable to reproduce. For several generations, each of the adult Inco residents has been taking the product regularly, a real substitute for happiness and good luck. Unfortunately, it contained a chemical mutagen that somehow collided with the Y chromosome. It destroyed one of its chromatids, as a result of which the human genetic code began to mutate. And it just emerged that the Government had known about everything for a long time. In fact, the last four cabinets related to pharmaceutical cartels controlling the market have not tried to stop this pathology. Business mattered. When it was realized that the situation was getting serious, a recovery program was set up. So far, however, it has not brought the expected results. Rather than nip the problem in the bud, new ideas were created just to mitigate the effects. No attempt was made to eliminate the cause. For example, when it was analyzed that fewer and fewer boys were born and that men became rare, robots with exclusively male features were produced and called "humaans". So that they associate better. It was just one of the temporary solutions. Each subsequent one was even dumber. The consequence of demographic changes turned out to be an involuntary mutation of the entire state system and its main assumptions. It was then that the system of benefits for the birth of a boy and taxes for the birth of a girl, as well as the GCO, were created. Because more and more intersex people, known as "herms", roamed the slums, they were ordered to be eliminated. There were also attempts to change sex, but the experiments turned out to be too expensive and did not give the most important result - the ability to reproduce. The only idea with any chance of success was carried out by a research team led by Professor Romm Nakamuru. This eminent geneticist worked near the Floris border in a secret laboratory experimenting with the connection of a human gene to an animal reproducing by virgin birth. Nobody was aware that in the pen next to his clinic there was a large herd of species living in the neighboring land: tine, hydapi and okurai. Even when Nakamuru was buying animals from the Floris farmers, no one suspected exactly what he was doing.

***

Luigi Pieron's report caused an avalanche. The vast majority of the Government, including the prime minister and more important ministers, melted like camphor in the blink of an eye. Even the heads of Economy and Transport and Sports and Interests ministries, when caught destroying documents, had no idea where the rest of the cabinet was hiding. All the more important buildings, where individual ministries, offices or departments had their seats, were surrounded by a guard. Hundreds of humanoid robots armed to the teeth were guarding the most important places in the nation, including factories of strategic importance. Interestingly, the head of the Inco army, or more precisely, the border guard, also disappeared. The staff of officers ordered double vigilance. They didn't know if they should turn on and on which side to stand. Ultimately, they decided to wait for a decision on what to do next. As predicted by the Director of the Public Opinion and Mood Research Bureau, there were several attempts to exclude theatrical addiction, but they were unsuccessful. When the chaos was in full swing, a legacy of lawyers stepped in to defend the pharmaceutical cartels. Their pitiful thrills only lasted two days. Black Hands provoked a controlled public attack on Ray's network of outlets in both inhabited neighborhoods. Windows were destroyed, supplies were set on fire, and a few innocent sellers were hanged. This has silenced the industry for a while.

***

Addam returned quite late that day. Jasmin was concerned if something had happened to him. She had no contact with him because of the network failure. Despite his exhaustion, he went to exercise. All Jasmin heard him yell at the trail simulator. He called out to them vehemently. It's not his style. She hadn't seen him like this for a long time.

He was dry and fragrant when he left the recovery room.

"Do we still have upper?"

It did not surprise her to ask about a forbidden drug with a narcotic effect, definitely stronger than Ray's soothing and positive attitude. Addam looked like he was plowing the concrete floor with his own hands.

"I don't know, I'll check," she replied and walked towards the coolant.

"I need to restart."

"Can you tell me what's going on?"

"You know I can't," he replied, though he was eager to share his fears with his wife.

When she brought a small glass box through the sides of which the contents could be seen, his eyes glazed with joy. The box contained narrow strips of colored papers. Addam sat comfortably on the floor, resting his back against the wall. He took out a blue strap and held it to his forehead. His eyelids slowly drooped and his body became flaccid. The hand that was pressing the paper trembled slightly. The strip quickly began to fade, as if it was giving up its color as the drug was released. After a while, he turned completely white. Jasmin knew the sight. She was even a little jealous. They used upper with Addam many times, even though it was forbidden. Just in the case of this drug, she did not refuse. Her parents never knew she had a soft spot for it. It was a short but tumultuous romance.

Upper was made a long time ago. First, it was produced by pharmaceutical cartels. It had various effects, for example the red stripe was very stimulating, the green one relaxed, and the yellow one caused unimaginable hallucinations. The version Addam used produced the slightest symptoms. It was undetectable by the sensors built into every guardian. It acted on the subconscious. It stimulated the brain to turn the negative nature of challenges into an opportunity for development. It was enough to take it, and from then on, even the most difficult problem, which you wanted to forget, became a goal that you are willing to pursue and want to achieve. Regardless of the consequences, even after a disgraceful failure, you felt a spectacular success. The blue upper changed the perception of the current problem the user was struggling with forever. Due to concerns about the decline in revenues from the sale of Ray and similar inventions, the pharmaceutical cartels have abandoned the sale of the drug. Its production went underground. As you might have guessed, taking has become illegal and punishable by high fines. It was relatively cheap, but not easily available. In order not to lose its power, it had to be kept in a low temperature.

"I can't tell you, darling, what's going to happen, but it's going to be awsome," said Addam at last, drooling like a preschooler. "I have a wonderful prospect. I'm glad we're having a baby."

Jasmin didn't believe a word, though the last sentence sounded nice enough. She would like her husband to pronounce them sober. It would be even more nice if he praised his wife for triplets. But he still didn't know anything. He just started to say something about overcoming fear. She decided it was time to go to sleep. During this time, the upper will stop working on her husband. In the morning, she will finally be able to get rid of the tiring secret. With a hangover after an upper, Addam would make it easier to assimilate, she thought.

When she opened her eyes the next day, he was gone. She turned on this boring theatremania again. She breathed a sigh of relief. Finally, there was nothing about the Pierone affair. This time, the baits of new machines for exercising shoulder muscles were presented. They looked like a pair of wings and needed to be attached to the hands. When turned on, they simulated natural conditions for birds that have not been seen in this area for many eras. The work on the muscles was to consist of persistent twisting of the hands in order to obtain the most optimal flight trajectory. If it was not possible to set the right angle, which resulted in a virtual fall, you had to wave your arms very intensely like wings. A bit of exercise for feel, a bit of logic, and a bit for the muscles in question. To make it more interesting, you could buy a chip with a moving image displayed on the wall. The eye of the camera placed on the bird's head made the feeling of flight more real. Jasmin just thought it was stupid, unwrapped the red bar and took a bite. When she sipped it with water, all channels were turned off in the theater and a board with the words "The continuation of the program in a moment" appeared. At this point, she heard the familiar sound of her chime. It was Luicey that Jasmin didn't want to see today.

"My Haenry says there will be a new Government. Does Addam know anything?" Luicey asked, astonishing the hostess at getting straight to the point.

"Probably. But he doesn't want to tell me anything. He had known about this action with Ray for months."

"If it were my husband, I would not forgive him for hiding something from me."

"Yes, my dear. If..."

At that moment, an image appeared in theatremania, without sound for a moment.

"Oh, something's going on," Luicey said.

The screen showed a festively decorated room where the Council of Advisors used to convene. This small Inco parliament, whose task was to support the executive power with its experience, was basically a dead entity that hardly anyone took into account. It existed because tradition demanded it. It consisted of the oldest representatives of various environments. With the disappearance of Prime Minister Barney Clifford, the Board of Advisors temporarily assumed a management role. Exceptionally. She replaced the Government until a new one was appointed. Several notables in clerical uniforms could be seen on the screen. One of the older women spoke, but her voice was not heard. Jasmin grew impatient. Finally, something crackled, and after a while you could recognize a woman's voice.

"...That is why we are glad that the new cabinet was built so quickly," said Ms Duddlemayer, Deputy Chairman of the Council. "I am proud to present the new prime minister of the Inco Government. This is Eva Noovack."

Luicey and Jasmin exchanged glances.

"No elections?" The hostess was surprised.

At that moment, a strong woman standing proudly appeared on the screen. The other members of the Council, as well as journalists, turned their heads towards her. Close up, she looked like a charismatic, real leader. Everyone held their breath. It was an unprecedented event. For the first time in many generations, a woman was proclaimed Prime Minister. Plus, it was not promoted by any pharmaceutical cartel.

"Hello Inco citizens," Noovack began. "Not all of you know me, so let me tell you a few words about myself. Since last purification, I was the Director of the Office of Gender Control, as well as the Deputy Minister of Health. The Board of Advisors recognized that my specialization, experience and determination to save the human species could prove beneficial to our community. I come from a slum, but I do not intend to single out any of the districts as my predecessor did. I am also not connected with business or any party. I am not caught up in any shameful obligations. My goal is to save the human species. We'll clean up this mess and save the world."

At this point, there was a thunderous applause. Eva Noovack stroked as if she had already achieved tremendous success. Everyone knew that for her it was just the beginning of an arduous journey. She didn't care about their opinions. She has achieved something that no one before her has ever achieved. From an ambitious official coming from the commune, she was promoted to the position of the most important person in the country. And at such a young age. It was only five purifications, though she looked like four and a half.

"I would like to introduce you to the remaining members of the Government. We all know which area should be a priority. So let me start with a person who will have as much responsibility for the success of our mission as mine. I am thinking of the health department, of course. Here are the Deputy Prime Minister and Minister of Health, Mrs. Claire Gibbondy. Nobody is as dedicated to the cause as my longtime colleague. Hardly anyone knows that he has a lot of successes in the fight against pathology."

Jasmin felt a little faint. She slumped slightly to the floor. Luicey's faint scared her, but when she was sure the hostess preferred to be alone, she decided to watch the rest of the broadcast in her apartment. During this time, Eva Noovack presented the next members of the cabinet. Jasmin wasn't listening. It was focused only on the previous information. She could not believe that the persona presented in such a crystalline way was the same GCO officer who joyfully encouraged her to terminate her pregnancy and threatened her. It was only now realizing to Jasmin that Gibbondy had gained enormous power. "If this nasty old bag, who talks about murdering children with such ease, is to be responsible for health, who will be the minister responsible for the law? Bandit?" she wondered. She didn't like this Government anymore.

New people introduced by Prime Minister Noovack appeared on the theatrical screen. Natalia Tatarczyna, experienced in the ranks of the guard, became the Minister of the Home Affairs and State Organization. Her ministry was to deal not only with the exercise of power over the guardians of peace, as was said about the humanities of guard, or prison, but also over the department of labor and social policy. Nadine Bleur, once the number one public enemy - a recognized hacker, is appointed Minister of Digitization and Telecommunications. After her alleged conversion, the Clifford Government decided to take advantage of these unprecedented opportunities. Once her loyalty was assured, she was given access to control of all systems. It was even said that Bleur had seduced the Prime Minister, but it was probably just rumors. The Ministry of Indoctrination of the Society has been entrusted to Kimberly Davis, former Director of Public Opinion and Sentiment Research, head of Addam and Haenry. This news was a long-awaited catch for Jasmin. She felt something was up. Her husband had been acting strange for a long time. What will his future fate be? He respected his supervisor a lot and it was obvious that she also appreciated him. Was there a chance to be promoted to the Ministry? Jasmin wanted to call her husband on the communicator, but when she started searching, she remembered that the network was down.

Apart from Georg Donville and Kurt Schlagen, the only men who retained their former portfolios of the Ministries of Sport and Interests and the Economy and Transport, the rest of the Government consisted only of women. The Minister of Defense was the officer of the Border Guard Julia Fagot, the Minister of Law and Justice, the Head of the Gender Policy Committee, a certain Maria Monssantoo, and the Minister of Treasury and Finance, Harpia Duecklenbourg, a long-term Finance Director of one of Sky Robotics Co.

Meanwhile, Noovack briefly discussed the individual Committees and Departments and what they are responsible for. She hasn't introduced new bosses yet. She had left this information for her next speech scheduled soon. She wanted the society with which she intended to be in regular contact had a complete picture of the situation. Jasmin didn't want to see anything else. Even if there was information about who would be her husband's new boss, she preferred to rest for a while. She turned off the theatremania and decided to take a short walk. She needed some fresh air and exercise. It would be good for the children, she thought.

As she left the apartment and finally descended the elevator, she saw an unprecedented sight. The city was deserted. It mean, there wasn't a single man in sight. Only humaans. They went about their duties, mostly cleaning up after the last brawl. As Jasmin passed the drug stores, she realized that Inco would look completely different from now on. How will people behave, who so far have derived all their appetite for life from pills? She felt sorry for them. She - basically thanks to her father, because he has always been an opponent - did not take this substitute for happiness. Different Luicey. A friend with whom they never agreed on this matter was convinced that thanks to the drug she felt calmer, she always saw everything in positive colors and was successful. Addam felt the same way. He never admitted he saw the advantages of not taking it. After all, Jasmin, like her father Omar, also managed in life, although they did not need pharmacological support. "Were other drugs, besides Ray, also modified, and did they have any effect on genetic changes? What will the change in the position of the Minister of Health bring? Where are Prime Minister Clifford and his associates hiding?" These and many other questions were born in Jasmin's exhausted mind.

***

Immediately after the presentation, Eva Noovack went to the Meeting Room, where, together with the rest of the cabinet, she intended to begin the first official deliberations of the new Government. Journalists did not leave her step. She wasn't going to be rude. She very delicately told them to give her a week to present the program. How flirtatious she talked to them. It was evident that she was a great strategist. She has mastered the art of gently washing out. Neither felt offended.

"As you know," she began when the last uninvited guest left the room. "The program of our government has been ready for a long time, but maybe in the meantime some new ideas have emerged. I'm all ears."

"Yes," replied Natalia Tatarczyna. "I already know that we need to expand the prison system."

"Why?" The Prime Minister was surprised.

"I think the lack of access to Ray will increase crime. We have too much of Humaans. Just reprogram them, but there is not enough space in prisons. The cells are overcrowded. It is similar in labor camps. And we have to turn off the monitoring, the sensor system will not be able to grasp it," said Tatarczyna.

"Can you clearly, friend?" Duecklenbourg asked.

"Hardly anyone knows about it, but there is hormomonitoring in the first and second district. It detects hormonal changes so the garda can react faster and before anyone thinks they might do anything wrong, a little humaan patrol hangs around him. When people stop taking Ray, the amount of hormones we read will crash our system."

"We are introducing a new law. The list of crimes for which we will punish death can be expanded," suggested Kimberly Davis.

"You see. Great idea. And hormomonitoring needs to be turned off for a while."

Noovack's disarming joy with which she approved of the most inhuman solutions encouraged Gibbondy to take the floor.

"I do not dare to go ahead, but do all my friends know that we have a marriage decree prepared?"

"Of course. This is one of the main points of our new policy," recalled the Prime Minister.

"Exactly," Gibbondy continued. "We are introducing consent to polygyny. This will give us new perspectives. The genetic material of men cannot be wasted. They should be able to impregnate many women, not just one wife."

"Get to the point, ma'am," Georg Donvill said impatiently.

"I would consider one more idea. What do you think, colleagues and gentlemen, about the total prohibition of procreation in the comfort of your home?"

"What a nonsense? Is it forbidden to have sex?" Kurt Schlagen was surprised. "I think it's a joke."

A scowl of indignation appeared on Gibbondy's face, but after a while it turned into full happiness. She dreamed up.

"Imagine," she continued, "that each fertilization will be controlled by us. It will be a huge time and energy saving. Contrary to appearances, we will be burdened with much less work. Unnecessary pregnancies will become a thing of the past and will not need to be terminated. We will just act one step earlier. If a couple wants a child, they will have to give us genetic material. Only the GCO will be able to fertilize. Ectopic. If the embryo passes the appropriate tests, it will be applied to the mother. We have been able to recognize the sex of a child for a long time, when it is still a small, barely fertilized cell."

"Brilliant," replied Duecklenbourg.

This spontaneous reaction by the Minister of Treasury and Finance pleased Gibbondy, but the Prime Minister's cold face cooled her enthusiasm.

"Yes, brilliant," Noovack said. "But we have to be vigilant. Social trust must be gained first. Let's not start with the bans. Let's give people new rules that they will love. Only when they believe us will we begin to implement difficult reforms."

Gibbondy was inconsolable, but she trusted the political sense of her longtime boss. They've been through a lot together. It was Noovack who introduced significant changes to the Gender Control Office, and a faithful collaborator implemented them. Always first and one hundred percent. Every modification, even the most difficult one. They also shared some secrets in common.

"Dear Claire, we'll still triumph. Now focus on another brilliant idea. We must gain full control of Dr. Nakamuru's work. Summon him to the ministry and inform him that he has been promoted. Make him someone like the Director of Medical Experiments. The program must start immediately. I will ask you to keep me informed about its effects. I also hope that you will tell me how the professor reacted to your innovative ideas and what came out of them."

The Prime Minister winked at Gibbondy. The new Minister of Health smiled gently and briefly hid her pride in her pocket. She had just realized that managing such an important ministry had its advantages. On a small scale, proprietary programs can be implemented without consequences. She had already imagined which idea she would start with.

"So what, I guess we can turn on all the systems, right?" Noovack felt like a mistress of the world.

***

When Addam returned home after a difficult afternoon, Jasmin was waiting for him at the door of the apartment. She had been mad at the lack of communication all day. Addam's face made up for everything. He greeted her with a happy smile. After all, what he was going to tell her was one of the best news since they had been together.

"Good morning, wife of the Director of the Public Opinion and Sentiment Research Bureau," he said in one breath.

"Oh, Director, that's wonderful," she replied with a slightly lascivious smile and kissed him passionately on the lips.

They greeted each other for quite a long time.

"My promotion isn't signed yet, but it's a matter of formalities. Tomorrow, the last time Kimberly visits our office, I'm due to be nominated. Everyone knows already."

"I guess Luicey already knows too. And your wife is the last to know. Scandal."

Jasmin made a mock gloomy face, but it was only for a moment. She couldn't hold back another burst of joy.

"I like your boss. She would be fit to be a minister of indoctrination. She's not bad," she judged professionally. "Since when did you know about these changes?"

"I only found out about the fact that I would be the director of the office at the time of the coup. Before, I could only imagine something there. It was not certain how the fate would turn out. The action, which had been prepared for a long time, was completely secret. It was enough for someone to speak out and everything would backfire. I suppose rightly Kimberly gave me no illusions."

"Where did this journalist... What's his name?"

"Luigi Pierone."

"Yeah, Pierone. How did such a dupe discover the revelations of such a great rank? Could it be...?"

Addam just smiled and made a small gesture as if to say it was another mystery. Jasmin nodded. She couldn't hide her joy. The message she had just heard fell on her like a bolt from the blue. Everything was starting to fall into place. Her husband's promotion was associated with an increase in his earnings. And Jasmin did not intend to return to work at all, because the pregnancy, in addition multiple, was associated with the risk of termination in full health. Money will always be useful, but the position offered new perspectives. Due to the fact that Addam was attached to such an important person in the state, his family could be exempted from inconvenient taxes. It's always been the case at Inco. The penalties never applied to prominent persons. It looked really good.

Just as she thought this was the time for a sincere conversation, both her and Addam's communicators made a short sound at the same time, symbolizing the arrival of the message.

"Oh, the system works. Finally," Jasmin was pleased, but at this important moment she was not going to check the content of the message.

Addam, by virtue of his profession, has always been doubly alert. He took out his communicator and flashed a message on the wall. It sounded like the worst dream.

"Information from the Treasury and Finance Ministry..." he began to read, focusing on each letter. "Your account has been blocked. In order to restore its functioning, please contact the Gender Control Office". What?! It is impossible. I think something has gone wrong."

Jasmin remembered the date Gibbondy had set. She checked her communicator quickly. She received exactly the same message as her husband. Apparently, when the GCO system resumed operation, the soulless program noted that the designated cut-off date, the time for termination, had passed. "How do I tell him now?" - she wondered. Until now, she had repeatedly wanted to shed the yoke of secrecy, but had found no opportunity.

At this point, Addam's communicator started signaling an incoming call. The man clicked the button and heard a familiar voice.

"This is Kimberly, what did you guys use up there?" The voice sounded from a small speaker.

"I don't understand. What is it about?" Addam was still treating the block as a mistake.

"Did you forget that GCO blocks the account in case of the planned birth of another daughter? I just received a report that my candidate for director was placed on the list of social outcasts."

"Don't believe them. This is only the first pregnancy," he replied with a disarmingly sincere smile on his face.

He glanced knowingly at Jasmin. First she looked away, then lowered her head meekly. This gesture did not bode well.

"Very funny," Kimberly said. "Clear this topic quickly. At this point, we don't need any complications. I will not be able to sign the promotion if your name appears on the file as a debtor to the state."

Kimberly hung up. Addam did not take his eyes off his wife all the time. His irreconcilable gaze pierced her right through. She looked scared but also terrified. This was not how she had imagined this moment.

Chapter 8 The awakening

Ae couldn't sleep that night. And not only because she was irritated by a fugitive from a neighboring country. She just had a bad feeling. She had known for a long time that something was wrong at Inco, the spies regularly reported it to her. Still, that was clearly not what made her sleepless. As the High Priestess of the Omniearth, she was an unquestionable authority among a godly society. Even if anyone thought of her not very flattering, never showed it for fear of her mighty face. Haris Sagavara was the exception. The outsider mocked her divinity in the presence of cardinals. How will this affect the perception of her position? Will the news of this pride's nonchalance spread to Patrix? Shouldn't she just in case get rid of a dozen witnesses to this unusual event, the most loyal and best trained defenders? Not. Since they were dedicated, they must have kept the incident to themselves. Rather, in their eyes, which saw what they were meant to see, this man was just an impudent individual. It was a pity to waste so much energy for such a dodger. It was enough to punish him for inappropriate behavior and everything would be back to normal. She invented a number of punishments that were tempting to implement them quickly. However, on the other hand, curiosity as to why this man was visiting, haunted her. The thought won easily. Ae clearly understood the message that he would only be able to talk to her when no one would hear them. She was impressed by his steadfastness. She appreciated it.

There were few places in Patrix that would meet this requirement, and at the same time did not raise any suspicions. It was then that she remembered the old tower, which had been terrifying with its neglect for many long eras. It once served as a belfry, but has not been used for a long time. There was too much risk that when someone set in motion the ancient bell of the Gondoluu hanging there, the structure of the tower would swing to the rhythm of the rocking iron and fall with it. It was an ancient bell, hung even before the beginning of the world. He announced the start of all holidays in the country. Once. Nobody was going in now, because the belfry was in danger of collapsing. Ae believed that Patri would protect her if she did so. She also knew that none of the eavesdroppers would follow her upstairs, fearing not so much for her life as for possible disability. Only there she could talk freely with this insolent scoundrel. "But what if he seizes the opportunity and hurts her or runs away," she mused. “He came voluntarily. Why would he run away?" And in such a restless spirit, her thoughts circled all night. In the morning, right after morning prayers, she decided to deal with this challenge immediately. She wasn't going to waste another night thinking.

"Zenit, please bring the prisoner to the old belfry. All the way to the top. I'll talk to him there."

"But lady..."

"Enough. He is to be chained to the right-hand bell of the Gondoluu and wait for me. Do not be afraid. He won't steal it. It's too heavy," she joked.

She signaled him to go away. Zenit was not pleased, but he trusted his priestess. This impudent man from Inco must have had some important information for her to pass on if she wanted to meet him in isolation. It must be for our own good, he thought, and gave orders to his men. Moments later, he was able to report that the task had been completed. Haris was already waiting in the place designated by Ae.

"You didn't have to chain me," he said as he saw the priestess ascending the last steps.

She just sighed briefly, as if to remind her that she decides what's best for him.

"I wonder if I'll find out anything new," she sneered. "Please don't waste my precious time."

"As you wish. Since many purifications in Inco, practically no boys are born, but only girls."

"There was going to be something I don't know."

"People in this country blame politicians that no one can solve the problem. There may be times when members of the Council of Ministers have to hide from enemies who are just waiting for them to stumble."

"Can you cut to the chase?"

Ae seemed to know a lot, but that didn't surprise Haris.

"Prime Minister Barney Clifford is asking for your help, lady. Of course not for free. He is a very wealthy man. He would like to buy himself some time. The problem will be serious soon. It would be very good if he could wait it out in isolation, for example, in a household in Floris. With my family and some important officials. During this time, we will clean up the whole mess and he will be able to come back."

"What does he offer in return?"

"It's no big secret that the people of Floris use our machines from time to time. We could help you on a much larger scale. I am thinking of the automation of agriculture, the production of tools, building materials. Of course, no one can know about it. So are your people. Our compensation should be taken as your merit alone. The Floris community will appreciate it."

"Are you implying that my people do not trust me now and do not appreciate what I do for them?" Ae was clearly agitated.

"I know your habits. I know how important you are in the country. Rather, I meant to provide your divinity for further purifications." He looked up at the sky as if looking for inspiration. "I can imagine it already. Ae, the priestess who revolutionized Floris. They will teach about you in schools."

"You have disappointed me. I believed that you really respect our habits, which made you seem like an interesting person to me. If you knew our habits, you would know that our school does not teach about former priests or their merits. We don't teach history to children at all. There is no need. It is enough for them to learn religion."

"You didn't understand me, lady."

"I understood well. Besides, I know, and you probably too, that your government will never come back to power. This is the end. There is no chance. Why should I help them? For the few wretched machines they'll steal from your country?"

"But..."

"You have a family?"

"Two sisters. No, I don't have a wife or kids, if that's what you mean."

"So there's nothing keeping you there. Come to us and you won't regret it."

"How do you imagine it? It is impossible to live with you."

"Offer your government to join Floris as before. The Omniearth will be one nation again. I will be her High Priestess and Inco will become the fourth quadrant to return to the motherland. Clifford would be able to manage one of the more important areas, you could get another one, but under my authority. We will introduce our customs, religion and value system. Only then will you survive."

Haris held back from laughing for a long time. In the end, he couldn't stand it.

"What are you laughing at?" Ae inwardly tugged his hair.

"You don't understand anything, lady."

"How are you going to survive? One more, two generations and it will be after you." Ae was convinced of her point, she spoke with commitment.

"If I do not make my appointment at Pinati Falls within the next five days, our agents will provide your priests with answers to some of their questions. For example, who helped you become a High Priestess? How did Vishare, your predecessor, die? Why didn't the venom really poison your body after you completed your priesthood training?"

***

The settlement of Litrijis looked just like any other settlement on the shores of a large body of water, only it was larger. The walls of the fishermen's houses were made of braided shuri shoots, and the roofs of dried, spreading algae leaves. Carelessly hung nets dried on rows of stakes stuck in the ground. The fishermen's boats in the form of hollow canoes were anchored perpendicularly to the route running along the port, all the way to the wide pier where the inn was located. They only served tinghao, an alcoholic drink with the taste of fermented milk combined with fish oil. He was terrible, but quickly felt relaxed after the hardships of backbreaking work. It caused weight gain, but no one attached importance to it. This typically masculine world of a fishing village was softened by the sight of curtains made of colorful seashells hanging in the window openings, as well as children's toys hanging around the houses. Made of anything you could pick out. And there were many possibilities. From many species of freshwater fish to crustaceans, to slimy looking but tasty stout grubs. All species of creatures caught in this area were sold to traders who came to pick up the goods every morning. It was possible to live honestly and with dignity from fishing. The fishermen were rather compliant and good-natured. You might think that it was for the company of these very people that Kadu decided to live in Litrijis permanently. Nothing could be more wrong. His little beach house, nearly a thousand yards from the secluded place where he had once met Haris, was only a hundred yards from the inn of his favorite drink. He didn't have to walk far.

Kadu decided to wait a few days in Litrijis before returning to Fahid's house after Sumi. He dropped by the inn for a few small pots of tinghao. He felt good in this place. Before he could enter, he smelled the smell of the mixed sweat of amateurs of the drink with the customarily brought snacks in the form of smoked pieces of rhyme in the doorway. Fishing trophies hung on the walls of this unusual place, and the ceiling was adorned with old torn nets with bits of nimo shells. Kadu sat down as usual in his favorite spot at the makeshift bar and ordered a drink. He drank it down. Then another. At that moment he heard someone telling a kind of familiar story deeper in the room. He decided to listen.

"I was swimming in the middle of the river bed, not very successful," said the old, slimy fat fisherman. "At one point I noticed a body on the shore. I thought that the man lying face down in the sand was dead. He was skinny and naked. I swam closer to see who Patri had taken with her at such a young age. Then he pounced on me."

"So he came to life," another fisherman joked.

"He was faking it. He tore the rags off me and threw me into the water. Then he quickly swam away with my catch. By my boat."

"But you said the boat was found," another fisherman chuckled.

"Yes, but there were no anchors or fish in it. Then I caught eight macabules and one rhisma. It was a stranger," said the old fisherman. "He must have crossed the line at Pinati Falls, and then swam all the way here."

Kadu remembered Haris immediately. The very thought of this man made his blood boil. "When I finish my mission, I will find him and bring him to Ae," - he thought. "Not because this criminal threw the harness into the Asaran Gorge. First of all, because he stole Mahmud's body and you don't know what he did with it." - Kadu gulped down another pot of his favorite drink. Then another two.

***

The High Priestess of the Omniearth was mad, but only in her mind. Outwardly, she was not going to show either anger, or fear, or a desire for revenge. This brazen villain, Haris, first humiliated her in front of the guards, setting the terms of the conversation. Then, when she even intended to forgive him and made a proposal for a peaceful settlement of the conflict, which meant for him a promise to take over an important district, he boldly began to blackmail her. Fearing his long tongue, Ae ordered him to be left in the bell tower. She forbade him to be fed and watered. The message she heard from him awakened the vigilance that accompanied her throughout the first purification since her promotion to the High Priestess of the Omniearth. For a long time she had not felt even the slightest anxiety. Haris's suggestion sounded like a worst nightmare. She had thought that the problem had long ago been solved, but he had revived at the most unexpected moment. It turned out that a few of its deeply hidden secrets were known to any strayer. She was curious what else he knew and how many people were initiated. From the moment she talked with Haris, she began to look at each passing priest. Whenever anyone looked away from her or stared in her direction for too long, she saw him through the eyes of her mind as a potential spy from a neighboring country or someone who knew too much. She became obsessively suspicious. It made her unable to concentrate on solving the problem. "Should she succumb to Haris' blackmail and help members of the Inco government escape? Or maybe shorten it by the head and in this way send information to other potential blackmailers that you must not mess with the High Priestess of the Omniearth?" - she fought with her thoughts. Nervously, she couldn't concentrate, she couldn't make any decisions. Kifor was the best for her moods. This pretty smart, high priest in her opinion often had good ideas. He seemed impartial, devoid of emotional intentions.

"What would you do if someone you trusted found out to be plotting against you?" She asked as soon as he came to her chamber.

Kifor paled immediately. The question struck him as if he had something on his conscience. She didn't notice it. She sent him a urgent look.

"I think that such a person should be monitored to make sure if it is true."

"Okay, but let's just say you made sure?"

"I would punish," he said shortly and swallowed.

"Right. What if someone blackmailed you into spreading some non-true, harmful information about you, if you didn't give them a reward?"

"I'd also like to be sure." Kifor was tempted to ask who it was, but he didn't dare. He was afraid that if he showed intrusiveness, he would attract attention. He preferred to play uninterested.

"What if you didn't know if it was true or not, because you don't remember? For example, something did actually happen, but it was apparently not your fault."

"It does not matter. I would have no mercy."

Ae considered his answer. Kifor was sure he could feel safe. The priestess would not speak to him like that if she suspected his disloyalty. At that moment, she began to soften in his eyes. He felt her weakness. She was clearly afraid of something. Her hitherto tough, charismatic way of being turned into a plastic, friendly mass that began to spill and cling to every obstacle she encountered. It was evident that the priestess was fighting internally. The priest watched as she hid deeper and deeper behind the barrier of uncertainty with each passing moment. He clearly towered above her, but not for long.

"We're facing a very difficult time, Kifor," she broke the awkward silence. "It's not good with our neighbors. Their country is plunging into chaos. We will also feel the effects."

"After all, we live in one world."

"That's true. We are connected to each other. We have to help them. If we do not do this, the Universe will be destroyed."

"What do you mean, my lady?"

At that moment Zenit knocked on the door and, not hearing the consent, entered inside. Kifor took it as an affront. He glanced at the priestess, but she ignored that fact.

"What's wrong, my friend?" She asked, tearing her thoughts away from the vision of the collapse of the entire planet.

"The squad that was tasked with scouring the Asaran Gorge has returned."

"Yeah. I forgot about it. And what did they find?"

"The holy ravine has been desecrated. Someone threw a wooden cart to transport the corpse inside."

Ae and Kifor froze as if the news had something to do with the absolute worst possible.

"The traces of the daredevils who have done this heinous act separate," continued Zenit. "Some lead to Patrix and I think they belong to our prisoner; and the other to the priest who went to the west quarter."

"It's Kadu." The priestess remembered her conversation with the postal representative.

"We must notify the Council immediately," said Kifor.

"I know. Zenit, please send couriers. Let them find Kadu. He is to be here immediately. You, Kifor, summon all high priests. We will meet in the Golden Temple and deliberate what to do."

Before Ae reached the appointed place, she ran into the bell tower for a moment. Haris was clearly waiting for her. His smile only lit up her.

"The guards say you threw the harness into the Asaran Gorge."

"It fell alone. It was not my fault, nor the fault of this priest."

"How dare you!" Ae showed her emotions.

"It can be pulled out. They're just dead bodies."

"You don't understand anything! I won't be able to let you go to Pinati Falls in time! The Council is sure to put you to death. Goodbye."

Ae nodded slightly and started down the stairs, calming her breath.

"But I didn't throw that fucking car in! There must be a way out! After all, I saved this bald man! Don't tell me that for you some skeletons are more important than human life!" He shouted for her in helplessness, but she didn't hear it anymore.

***

Sumi walked nervously from corner to corner. It was obvious that she couldn't find a place for herself.

"When can I start packing?" She asked.

"Patience, little daughter," Fahid replied.

Her father, who had been thoughtful for a long time, didn't even look in her direction. He stood like a stone in the center of the sleeping room. He clearly looked embarrassed, though he tried not to show it. He was better at hiding his fear. He was really scared very much. After all, something terrible has happened. It was basically a series of uninteresting events. It started when the High Priestess of the Omniearth asked for his daughter. Then he and his wife lied to someone for the first time in their lives. In addition, an innocent priest who merely obeyed. Finally - to reassure the family - Fahid promised to take his daughter to Hambarra. And that was not what he was going to do. She was still too young. Who would take care of her in a strange city? Several days had passed since he and his daughter hid in the burrow to wait out Kadu's visit, and he still didn't know the solution. For the first time since he was collecting *dirshna* flowers, the harvest was practically self-limiting, without his help. That is, he was performing certain actions, but unknowingly. Being thoughts elsewhere entirely. This has never happened before. In the past, he put his heart into every activity. When he remembered again that he was working without any involvement because he was too preoccupied with problems, he felt for the first time how much he missed his father. If he were still alive, he would have known what to do. Fahid was an experienced farmer, a good husband and father, but he did not have the flair for solving problems like Mahmud. Anyway, what problems has he had so far? Sometimes with animals or when the children quarreled and he had to drill them. Suddenly, the machine broke down once and one tine died for an unknown reason. That's all. Life was slow. Subsequent cleanses passed peacefully. They did not go down in history, because the past was not mentioned in Floris. At most what someone remembers. Only divine laws, earthly customs and parables were passed down from generation to generation. But for someone to be interested in who, for example, was the previous High Priest of the Omniearth, it was rather unheard of. Each farmer working his field focused on what was around him. On the simplest of things. To survive each day well, to avoid conflict situations and, as often as possible, to bestow your loved ones with tenderness. And, of course, to live in harmony with the goddess Patri and her priests. If any of the hosts lost a child, or even a few, to the Church, he would accept the fact, because the majority really perceived the loss as a social advance.

When Fahid thought about this soulless tradition, he realized that something unexpected had happened to him and that he must be special. Earlier he had had this obnoxious thought on his mind, but the problem had never come this close. He really decided that he was not going to give any of his children to perdition. He was probably the only one among the people he knew who did not accept the sentence. Well, of course, except for Father Mahmoud and Uncle Omar, but they were dead. The thought made slightly unsure whether he knew himself well. He felt alienated. As if he had stepped out of his former self and saw that former Fahid looking rather pitiful. He didn't want to be. He wanted to become the new, strong father of the family, knowing what he wanted. He realized that now he would have to face something unimaginable for him. He has to clash two extreme attitudes - roles that did not know about each other. Faith and obedience to the religious organization had to compete with his fatherhood. He decided which of the two attitudes would prevail, but he was too simple a man to figure it out properly.

"But are we going or not?" Sumi did not give up and knocked him off the beat.

"I don't know," he grunted.

She took offense at her father and ran to her mother to complain. Rita was busy preparing the food, but she accepted the criticism of her husband with understanding and quickly found words of encouragement. At this point, several siblings entered the hut and were playing in the yard. Khalid appeared first. It was just a rascal, well over half a cleansing age. Not like his twin sister Adila. The boy approached Sumi and pulled her hair. She chased him away. In the blink of an eye, she forgot about her dilemmas. After him, the couple of the youngest toddlers, Hassan and Malik, entered the hut. They were both barely able to walk, stumbling awkwardly. In keeping with the custom in Floris, the children learned the various necessary skills by themselves. Among other things, walking. Therefore, Rita, like other busy parents, did not react. As the boys entered, Malik, who could not yet speak, signaled that he was thirsty.

"Give him some water," said mother, still holding her hands on the table where she was making mao-flour pancakes.

Tamadur, the fourth-oldest daughter of Fahid and Rita, who had just returned from the farm, took care of it. She fed a pregnant animal in solitary confinement.

"I think it will be soon. Okurai is barely panting," she said.

"It needs to be seen more often," replied his mother. "Call the rest and your father. Time for a meal."

Tamadur ran out of the room. After a while Sumi returned, followed by other family members. Fahid was the last to enter. The kids looked happy. The sight cheered him up. He sat down between Fatima and Nadir. He lowered his head and began to pray as usual. After a while, he realized that this time he was doing something against himself. The thought surprised him again. He paused in prayer and opened his eyes, arousing the curiosity of the children. He looked around and motioned for them to eat. Rita cast a short, uneasy look at him. She smiled artificially at Malik and handed him a bowl of *dirshna* liniment. It was just an unusual sight. A boy at such a young age managed to spread the cake on his own.

***

The Golden Temple was not only for prayers. High priests also gathered there to give advice. After all, it was a place just outside the Diamond Sanctuary, home of Patri. Its closeness could not be underestimated when making the most important decisions in the state. This time the problem was serious. Asaran has been desecrated, a ravine that has been filled since the beginning of the world with the bodies of the dead. Two eras ago, when one of the wild moree birds burst in, it was accepted that animal carcasses could eventually end up there too, but that was the only exception. According to the prophecy, when the ravine is filled with embalmed corpses, the world will end. So what to do with the three-wheeled wagon that fell there? Because of him, the prophecy might not be fulfilled. By the way, no one could come down to get him out of there. It would also be sacrilege.

"Brother priests," Ae began. "There are two topics. One simple. The Inco man who is imprisoned in the bell tower is suspected of throwing a wagon. He needs a hearing on this matter."

"Waste of time. He should be punished immediately. What he has done is unforgivable." Ali Ude, one of the oldest priests in the Council, was ruthless in his judgment.

"True, but he says it was an accident," Ae said.

"Why did he come here at all?" Kifor asked, looking sharply at the priestess.

Ae hesitated for a moment as to what to say. She did not want to explain herself to these old men, although, unfortunately, this was the tradition. It was weary of her. She preferred to make some independent, quick decisions and give Haris a chance to go to the appointed place. She was no longer afraid of this blackmailer. Like his supervisor, Clifford, she also wanted to gain time and figure out the network of agents. At that moment, she was puzzled by the fact that she had not yet realized that the net existed at all. I think I'm getting old, I've become too trusting, she thought, and thought back to her deputy's question.

"At Inco, things get more confusing than you might have expected. Their government is asking us for help," she said.

"They only have themselves to blame. They are heretics," said Namali, one of the elders.

"True, but let us, venerable priests, invite their prime minister here. Perhaps we will need such a gesture of little significance to us. Then we'll decide what to do next."

"A wise thought," Ali Ude replied. "And let us condemn this rogue to death."

"To death," replied the priests in chorus.

"Okay, then to death," Ae replied, but she was not at all pleased with the way things had turned out. "There is a second point," she continued. "What are we going to do with this harness that fell into the ravine?"

"That's true. What are we going to do?" Kifor asked with concern. "We cannot fly, and fruit and flower harvesting machines are not suitable for that."

"We are simple priests. We know a little about military, but not engineering." Ali Ude no longer sounded like a calculated master.

"Maybe the Inco guy knows some way?" Rados asked.

Ae had expected just such a reaction. She smiled inwardly.

"What do we do if he finds a solution? Shall we let him go?" She asked timidly.

"It is his fault. To death," several priests reacted.

"Do you think that knowing what fate awaits him, he will agree to help us?"

Many priests nodded with understanding, as if to say that the thief had to be summoned and then he would see him. He was quickly brought to the Golden Temple.

"We really shouldn't be talking to you," Ae began. "Do you realize that you have desecrated our holy place?"

"I did it to save your priest. Otherwise he would have fallen with the cart," Haris replied.

These words caused a stir among the audience and uncertainty as to the proper assessment of his deed. Ae sensed the clever swindler had time to find the hook. No matter if it was a lie. It worked. "He's smart," she thought.

"Could you build a machine that could pull the wagon pieces ashore without contaminating the bodies of the dead?"

"I don't know if I have that much time. I must be back at the border in a few days. You know that, lady, don't you?"

Ae felt his pin pierce her through, but decided not to owe him.

"If you get away quickly, you can make it. If not, you will be executed," she said with an expression that said she was not afraid of his blackmail.

***

Ae decided to personally supervise the unusual operation. Besides, she was curious what Haris would do. She was impressed and at the same time very pissed off by this clever blackmailer. When they arrived, she found a secluded spot to watch him do. In order to ensure success, she told Haris that if anything else fell into the ravine, he would immediately be the next one to land on the pile of corpses. Haris was getting bored with the constant death threats. He did not have an engineering degree. However, he knew the basics of mathematics and physics very well. The knowledge he possessed was sufficient to judge that the easiest way would be to move the demountable bridge intended for throwing in the bodies. Putting it right above where the cart lay and letting someone strong on the rope tie the pieces to the rope would do the job in his opinion. Unfortunately, the priests who were involved in the demolition of the bridge and assembly elsewhere thought it would take too long. After all, the ravine was two hundred cubits wide. It is estimated that such an operation will take approximately thirty Hello sunrise. Haris could not wait that long, so he proposed to build a simple crane with a reel. Ae watched curiously as he drew out all the necessary elements of the structure. She was very impressed with his craftsmanship. She was no longer surprised why such a raider had become a secret envoy of the Prime Minister of the Government. Haris first ordered a wooden structure to be assembled on the shore, which was later transported to the edge. At the end of the rope slung over the reel, one of the strongest low-level priests was lowered. When he went all the way down, he picked up the pieces of the wagon one by one and tied them to a lowered extra cord that pulled all the pieces up. At the end, there was the problem of a piece of rocky cliff that was too heavy to be lifted with even the thickest rope, and too good to attach. Breaking it to pieces was out of the question. Haris suggested tying several loops of a previously calculated diameter, capable of hugging the boulder. It succeded. After pulling up a piece of the cliff, the priests thanked Patri for a long time for help. Nobody to Haris. Ae was surprised by their reaction. She felt sorry for her brethren that they had underestimated the professionalism of the foreigner. Not so long ago, she was going to scold him for disgracing. Then for blackmail and insolence. And at the end, for the stupidity, which was close and he would have to give up his head. At that moment, she was proud of him and happy that she didn't have to kill him.

"We're waiting for your Prime Minister," she said, hoping Haris would return.

The released prisoner rushed the okurai towards Pinati Falls. He had limited time to make it to the agreed place. They both knew it.

***

Kadu reached the Patrix and appeared before Ae. It had only been a few days since he was summoned, but for her it took forever. She was impatient and irritable. Jusif, her trusted man who had always known everything faster than the others, has disappeared. It was certain that it was no coincidence. It could only mean one thing. From then on, she couldn't count on him. In addition, she began to feel unsure whether Haris had arrived on time. Kadu's questioning about the car didn't really matter. After all, everything was explained and ended well, the pretext for a disciplinary conversation and for making an impression on an insignificant priest appeared on his own. It turned out to be the subject of Sumi that had not been brought on time.

"I got your orders, lady," he said as soon as he entered Ae's chamber.

"Then why didn't you make them?!" In the tone of her utterance, the High Priestess of the Omniearth announced that her irritation had reached its apogee.

"When I received your letter, I hurried to the Manduarra family. Unfortunately, neither Sumi nor her father was at home. The girl's mother claimed that they went to school together, where she was to learn to be a singer," he recited.

"Do you understand the priesthood well? What is the eighth paragraph of the canon?"

"A good priest knows everything that happens in his quarter. He listens to people who listen to him."

"He listens to people!" She screamed. "Have you not been taught to question until it is complete? People are to tell us everything: what they do, what they think, who they share the bed with and what they dream about. If they don't want to talk, you have to remind them that Patri wants it that way and end of discussion."

"I'm sorry to offend you, lady," he stammered out in an uncertain voice.

"You insulted our goddess, you idiot. Suddenly twenty fellow moons

of bloom have passed, and you act as if your head hasn't been blown out by the previous purification."

"I don't drink as much as I used to, my lady. I swore to Patri."

"Of course," she sneered. "You followed them?"

"No. I am convinced that they have not gone anywhere. Or at least not too far. I decided to wait and visit them unexpectedly. It was at this time that you called me, lady," he stammered, less and less confident.

"Do you realize that even one family that opposes us can plant a seed from which something bigger will be born?"

"Yes, lady."

"What am I going to do with you, Kadu? You help the villains to desecrate our holy place, you do not follow my orders, you excuse yourself like a lying schoolboy, that you waited for the right moment, although everyone knows that you have not left the inn for several Hello rises. What would you do, if you were me?"

"It's not what you think, lady."

"Do you know better what I think?"

Kadu was devastated. He actually did take a few shots, but he didn't feel he was doing anything wrong. It was supposed to be just an innocent form of relieving stress, although in fact it was a bit longer.

"I promise, lady, that I will bring this little girl, even if I have to do something really unworthy."

"I have one more question: what happened to a man named Omar Manduarra? This is the grandfather's brother of that girl. We lost him in the papers."

***

As it is commonly known, after completing the training, each future priest had to undergo venom poisoning. After a short recovery, he learned the soldier's trade and for one cleansing he became a soldier of the Floris army, a low-ranking priest. The soldiers were stationed on the other side of Saandreal in the underground barracks. There they perfected their craft during many hours of training. Less often they participated in religious parades or as a logistic aid. If one of the priests liked the service, he could apply to remain in it forever. Not everyone was allowed to do so - only the most eminent and talented soldiers. All the rest of the priests, after their termination of service, received one of the territories to administer. They became Patrix's representatives on the ground, both spiritually as well as in exercising control and authority as mid-level priests.

The practice of soldiers was the last, indispensable stage of priesthood training, although it began right after poisoning. In the eastern wing of the Patrix cave network there was a military craft school. It was managed by Ling Gui, Kadu's cousin, the most hideous-looking priest in all of Floris. Apart from the remains of venom poisoning, characteristic of the clergy, he had many memorabilia after more than one duel. His entire body was scarred innumerable. Many of them never healed. Besides, he didn't really care about it. They made him feel more terrifying, and the constant, unbearable pain kept him feeling constantly participating in the fight. In the last three purifications, since he had the honor of fulfilling his function, he has raised many warriors of both sexes. However, he referred politically to the differences in body builds between men and women. The fair sex, although the young priestesses could hardly be called attractive, was, according to Ling Gui's decision, kitchen or hospital facilities. In his opinion, female cadets had a certain drawback: a squeaky voice they produced to cheer themselves up during their superhuman exertion. He couldn't take that groan off. However, if any of the women wanted to become, for example, a member of an elite reconnaissance group, and this one was specially trained, she had to pay the highest price by deciding to cut her vocal cords. Thanks to this procedure, her voice became acceptable to the head of the school. Shorter, slightly hoarse and quiet, similar to the male. In some cases it was gone forever. For people who dreamed of a career in the secret services, it was an indispensable element of war equipment like a uniform or a weapon.

During the training with Ling Gui, the adepts learned mainly hand-to-hand combat and the use of available, slightly archaic weapons. Most have been used since the dawn of time. Besides, there was no need to improve it. The potential enemy was well known. This is the neighboring land of Inco, which did not invest in soldiers, but in machines. The modern form of combat was downplayed in Floris. "No technology can replace human muscles and cleverness," Ling Gui used to say. However, his knowledge of the potential enemy army was nil. He was sure they were fighting in a fairly similar way to Floris. He did not try to find out if, by chance, a neighboring country had refined technology or war tactics. Like most of the people, Floris couldn't see anything but the tip of his nose. And since since the beginning of the world, when the border was established between the lands, their authorities had successfully discouraged the people of one side from the other, and vice versa, neither of the peoples was eager to conquer the other. Armies were basically an unnecessary toy in the hands of power. They were trained in the event of war only to make the population feel that the rulers care about security. In this respect, Inco was almost identical. The very modern border services of this land gave the public confidence that no enemy would ever dare attack their country. Both armies were not numerous. At least that's what the spies reported.

The school's armory was in a darkened cave. Seemingly next door, in fact, in one complex with the headmaster's private room. Ling Gui loved being there. He imagined himself in the middle of a great battle, heard the clash of the weapon alive. When Kadu visited him and asked for help, the teacher felt appreciated and excited about the challenge. He broke away from monotony and routine. Finally, some action. He would have liked to take part in it himself, but he knew that he was not allowed to leave the school.

Kadu needed an assistant, preferably two. They were to facilitate the task he had received from the High Priestess of the Omniearth. It was banal. It was necessary to bring a little girl. Preferably voluntarily and necessarily alive. It would seem easy, but Kadu foresaw complications. Despite the fact that Fahid, Sumi's father, came from a godly family, he had already shown his waywardness and his insubordination was to be reckoned with. The priest wanted to take advantage of the acquaintance with his cousin and be sure that the task would be done perfectly. Anyway, his further career, and maybe even a decent life, depended on it.

"I will give you two of my best students to help you, who should be perfect for such a task. If you're planning a surprise attack, no one will do better than Hara and Nate, the two biggest france to ever hit our school."

"Women?" Kadu was surprised.

At this point, the priests heard a knocking at the door, and after a while two people entered the dark chamber. Kadu stared hard for a moment, but when he realized that his behavior might seem intrusive, he looked away. He quickly realized that the two warriors in no way resembled women, but rather wiry, muscular men, whose mere gaze could do a lot of harm. Hara, the taller one, had gray eyes, dark skin full of scars, and a few gray wisps on her head. Nate was slanted. The color of her eyes was impossible to discern by the narrow gaps between her swollen eyebrows and swollen cheeks. Her skin looked as if it had been smeared with livestock manure. Basically because of the one-color tattoo that covers practically her entire body.

Both of them were dressed scantily, practically, as if in constant readiness for a mission. Hara bowed low. At that moment, Kadu noticed the poorly fused scars from the amputation of the breast. He shuddered slightly, though he had seen similar ones many times. The fair sex, who became priestesses, often cut out the remnants of their femininity for themselves, because after the sacred venom passed through the glands, their pain became unbearable. They did it themselves or asked another priestess. It was a simple procedure. Like having your ears pierced. Without any hygiene requirements. Later, it was enough to burn the wound with a red-hot sword, and soothe the pain with Radd's herb.

"These two women will be happy to help you. They get bored and need a little adventure. Then they will start their service," said Ling Gui.

Nate sent the teacher a contemptuous glance to remind him that the word "woman" had long ago been considered offensive.

"When do we go?" Hara asked, though her voice sounded like the gurgling of a drunken toper.

"As soon as possible," replied Kadu.

Ling Gui was delighted to open the gates of the armory, a forbidden place for adepts. On large piles sorted by subject matter, one could see, among others: four-sided axes, various types of swords, two-handed hammers, spiked ball slingshots, poison darts crossbows, spears, halberds, hoofstars, nets, harpoons, as well as shields of various sizes. Each of the warriors had their favorite weapon. Hara first reached for a short sword, usually hung on the back on a leather belt. His name was sirius. It was easy to operate. It was light, as comfortable as a dagger, and sharp as a scalpel. Then she walked over to the booth where strange irons lay. She chose the swordfish, a tool to split bones mercilessly. The tip of his long, narrow blade branched into small axes. Despite its monstrous size, it did not seem heavy. She took it easily in her hand.

Nate decided to take a favorite on such short expeditions, the grubber. This specific machete with a series of hooks secured by a blade caused a slight smile on her cool face. The favorite set still lacked only a double whip, made of the scales of an armored creature, pokuna, connected with a thick rope raidi. During the fight, this whip split into two parts, each lashing the enemy in a way never predictable to him. Hara and Nate felt distinguished and happy. Kadu glanced at his armed guard and thought that he had never felt as safe as he has today with just two women.

Chapter 9 Blockade

Jasmin's morning ritual that day was the same as before the pregnancy. She woke up quite early and decided to exercise before going to work. Addam was gone. And that's good. She didn't want to talk to him. Anyway, they had been passing for a good ten days. From the moment he found out the truth about the triplets and shouted out all the regrets in his gut. He had stayed at his parents' house twice since that day, and when he returned, he looked like an eternally angry predator looking for an opportunity to take revenge. Probably not only because both with Jasmin had their accounts blocked. Also, not because his promotion was canceled, probably forever. As he screamed the worst epithets she had heard in her life, she learned that her nonchalance had put their long, happy relationship at stake. Jasmin wasn't quite sure if she herself wanted these children or not. One day she loved them, the next she hated them. However, he did not know about it. She instinctively teased him. And also, with herself, with her ego. Why should she not decide about her own offspring? Her boisterous nature told her to do exactly despite others. Mother, husband, his friends from work, even his closest friend, not to say a friend, all expected her to decide on an abortion as soon as possible.

Before training, Jasmin sipped a little Pearl water. It amazed her that she drinks a lot. The glass bottles were gone so quickly. In the past, she wouldn't have bothered about it, but since the account was blocked, the inventory was gone faster than usual. At least she thought so. To chase away the piling up of bad thoughts, Jasmin undressed in the living room and after a while entered the regeneration room. She started with gentle exercises. She didn't want to push herself too much. Stretching and a short run, then the same spine kit as usual, but in double the dose. In case you have to carry heavier loads, she thought. She checked if the tummy was visible. She smiled at her thoughts. She was fooled again. Like everyday. She knew rounding off at the end of the first trimester, much faster for triplets, but it was only the seventh week. There was nothing to show from her slim figure. Not a single fold. However, she was not disappointed. She turned on the flushing mechanism.

The road to work was exceptionally long. It is unbelievable how quickly the changes in the city have progressed. Just ten days ago, a new Government had arrived, and the Inco center looked completely different. And it started with seemingly insignificant but annoying details. At every corner there was a humaan guard patrol, whose task was to randomly control passers-by. Jasmin didn't like robots.

"Please stop." She heard an artificial sounding voice. "I would like to see your registration card."

She complied with disgust and reluctance. The robot has read the card.

"You've got a lock. Please go to the Gender Control Office."

"Yes. I know," she replied, hiding her eyes from the prying eyes of other passersby.

"What are you doing here?"

"I live."

"On the boardwalk?"

"I'm going to work."

"Have a nice day then."

"Fuck you," she said in a whisper.

She was sure the robot understood her words and only thought that she had lowered her voice unnecessarily. She didn't want to give him any satisfaction. He wouldn't be offended anyway. Guard robots had no built-in empathy module. She would not have received any fines for insulting an artificial creation. She should have known that. She regretted a little. Before reaching the building where her marketing corporation was based, she had to show her registration card three more times. It spoiled her mood completely. Plus, she wanted to pee halfway down the road, and those metal can checks delayed everything.

"You're late. Did something happen? Are you feeling bad?" Agness Vinnetre, head of department, asked with mock concern.

"If not for these constant checks, I would be on time."

"I'm taking your half a day's wages."

"Yes? So, I'm going out. I'll be back at noon."

"Why?"

"If I'm supposed to be unpaid for a half a day, why should I sit here?"

"You do as you think. I had an interesting assignment for you. Katterina will get it."

Jasmin just huffed in disgust and left the office. However, she sat down in the corridor in front of the entrance. She already wished she hadn't acted so stupidly. Something made her be rude. Against her will. She blamed her garda for everything. It was because of them that this day started not very well. She wondered what else bad would happen and what should she do now? Come back? How about getting in touch with her husband? No. It would be embarrassing. Come to her mother? What for? To tell her she still can't make up her mind? Or maybe visit Luicey at her work? No idea made sense to her. "Are these the first symptoms of pregnancy?" - she wondered in her thoughts. She wondered if the fact that she had become so cranky was a normal reaction to hormonal changes, and if the children were sucking her brain out of her to build their coils, and therefore she couldn't think of anything that sounded logical. She assessed herself reproachfully. According to her subjective, but reasonably honest judgment, she considered that she had become a hesitant, critical, hormone-raging idiot. A boring woman with an embarrassing lack of control over her own being. For a while, she didn't even like herself. Those were depressing thoughts. In order not to tempt fate, let alone come across another control, she decided to go back to work with her tail tucked up. At the sight of her, Agness only smiled slightly. Rather not too lenient. It looked like a manifestation of pride.

The day at work passed much faster. Jasmin, however, received a new project and was happy to do it. "Finally, a challenge worthy of a champion," she thought. It got her in so much that she did not think about pregnancy, offended husband, malaise and uncontrollable moods. She was tasked with preparing for the new government a preliminary concept of a social campaign on popularizing the approved family model. The project, of course, was classified at this stage and Jasmin had to sign a confidentiality clause. If it leaked in an unfinished form and at the wrong time, it could have colossal consequences for the entire country.

"I miss the data," Jasmin said.

"Which ones exactly?" Agness was surprised.

"Since we are to tell a sad story about the fall of mankind, I need information about the true participation of men. How many boys are born, and how many girls? What is the average age of mothers? I mean simply demographic and sociological data."

"Dear Jasmin, the concept is to be presented in three days and the material is ready in a week. What do you have a husband for? Contact him. After all, he works at the Public

Opinion and Mood Research Office. They definitely have all the numbers you need."

"Addam also signs the confidentiality clause."

"But you can go to him officially. The fact that he is your husband will surely help."

"Is that why I got this project?"

Agness didn't answer. Jasmin didn't like the idea of the formal inquiry, but she knew her husband would definitely not answer her. Even if they weren't in an argument. On the other hand, she was very curious about the data and was happy with the great campaign idea that came to her mind. She was tormented only by the question of who to address the letter to. Kimberly Davis was no longer the director of the Office, but a minister. The director should be Addam, but due to the blockade, his promotion was postponed. Jasmin hadn't spoken to him in days, so she had no idea what had happened there and whether or not someone had been promoted in his place. There was also no information in the official ministry announcements.

***

"Am I so strange to you that instead of asking me outright, you resort to embarrassing solutions?" Addam asked when he returned to the suite that evening.

"Because you're not talking to me," Jasmin replied.

"You ruined our future. What do you expect? That I'll be nice to you?"

"I haven't ruined anything yet. I haven't made my decision yet."

"Without informing me about pregnancy, in addition to triple pregnancy, you acted like a thief who has something on his conscience. What are you looking at? I judge you like a thief. You robbed me of my dreams!"

"If you don't like it, get divorced!" She screamed.

"Tempting but..."

"Tempting?! You bastard. I hate you!"

"Slum upbringing is coming out."

"Fuck off my family, good house swell."

"My family took you in. They accepted you for who you are. Why? Because they knew I wanted to be with you. And that was the most important thing for them. Your mother never respected me."

"She just likes you very much and is on your side when it comes to pregnancy."

"This is interesting. And you didn't listen to mommy?"

Jasmin sighed heavily. She sat down on the floor and closed her eyes. She began to calm her breathing.

"What happened? Something hurts you?" He asked with concern.

"Give me a break. It's not your life. If you want, get divorced. Leave me."

"What are you saying? I love you. It was a joke with that divorce."

"I cried with laughter. Next time, let me know so I can prepare some handkerchiefs."

"Jasmin, you hysterical. I love you and I don't want us to hurt each other." Addam embraced his wife. They hugged each other.

"And what about your promotion?" She asked after a moment.

"They promoted Haenry. At least the position will stay in the family."

"What? Luicey wasn't telling me anything," Jasmin was surprised.

"Because I asked her to."

Instead of expressing regret and in any way showing that she was sorry for the loss of her promotion, Jasmin pulled away from Addam. It did not surprise him. He knew her fits of jealousy. He ignored them as usual. He never understood what the fuss was about. However, she thought it was perfidy. As every time he acted like this, this time she too felt an unimaginable dislike of him. The man of her life has just confessed that he had once again conspired with her only friend. Luicey had been hit too, mentally. Only she knew the marriage had quiet days. "She probably took his side yet. What a comforter," Jasmin grew angry in her soul. "And Haenry? Completely unfit for director. Not only is he ugly as a guy, he is also so sloppy. How good that Luicey has no children with him." Jasmin realized again that she was whining. She was smashed, her head hurt. She went to bed.

Addam escaped in watching theatremania. He didn't notice when she fell asleep.

***

Another nightmare made Jasmin wake up tired. She dreamed of Addam murdering three girls. He used a previously detached upper garda's humaan limb. She realized that until she decided about pregnancy, her life would be a bundle of nerves. All her friends, husband and mother advised against giving birth to triplets. In her mind, she fought a whole group of her abortion enthusiasts. She felt lonely in this fight. If just one person wanted to be her ally, perhaps a balance could be found. Only such a state of affairs would allow her to reliably assess the situation and think over this extremely important matter. She remembered the gynecologist examining her. Dr. Jon Steavans seemed to be the perfect candidate as a counterweight. She decided to visit him after work, under the guise of examining whether everything was okay with the pregnancy. She knew his office should have all the test results, but she took the printout from the computer module with her just in case. If the GCO system somehow broke down, she wouldn't have anything to talk to her doctor about and perhaps would have to re-examine her, and she didn't have a single unblocked entity. "A simple conversation will cost you nothing," she thought.

After a difficult day at work, full of difficult discussions with her boss about discipline, she went to Steavans' office. When she reached her destination, she took her place in the line. The waiting room was full of women of all ages and stages of pregnancy. Most of them were smiling, but not every face showed that it was going to be a boy. Jasmin sat down next to the brown-haired girl, aged slightly more than two cleansing, who looked distressed.

"Daughter?" She asked.

"Does all Inco know? I will kill him," the brown-haired girl replied.

"Who?"

"My husband. He is telling all his friends that I am crazy. He even won over my family. They urge me to remove it because we already have one daughter. But Ursula wants a little sister."

Jasmin was surprised by the honesty.

"And what do you want?" Jasmin asked with clearly palpable empathy.

"I know we can't afford it. I guess I should abort."

The brown-haired girl smiled fake, then closed her eyes and shed a tear, drawing the eyes of the others waiting for their turn.

"The belly is big now. What week is this?" Asked the GCO officer sitting in the corner.

"Nineteen," she replied, wiping a tear brown-haired.

"It's irresponsible. This is the last bell."

"I know! I have an appointment in three days," she said and made a non-obvious grimace that was a mixture of contempt, sadness and madness. Then she shed another tear, then another.

"Then why did you come here?" Asked the redheaded old lady who looked like a happy future grandmother.

"I wanted Dr. Steavans to show me how our Olivia is developing."

"Why do you need to know?" The GCO officer asked.

"I do not know. I had to come here." The brown-haired girl wiped one of the tears that managed to reach her chin.

Suddenly the door to the office opened. Dr. Steavans appeared smiling. He beckoned the brown-haired girl with a gesture. She returned a smile that was not too intrusive and followed him inside. The women in the waiting room exchanged glances. Some whispered among themselves. Jasmin realized that she felt alienated in this company. Like an outcast. She glanced contemptuously at the woman in the brown GCO uniform. She didn't look like Gibbondy. She was definitely prettier and younger. She had a sympathetic expression on her face suggesting a friendly disposition. She was not like that soulless creature. "It's easier to trust to her," Jasmin thought. "They resort to charm through nice appearance. Pure marketing. Bastards."

At this point, the garda's humaan entered the waiting room.

"I would like to see registration cards."

The women obediently showed the documents. Jasmin did it last.

"Did something happen?" The GCO officer asked.

"Please leave this place. Directive seven-GUHJY-eighty-two."

"But I waited two weeks for my visit!" One of the future mothers was outraged.

"The visit has been canceled."

The nice-looking GCO officer checked something in her communicator.

"Ladies, you will receive a message to when the visit was postponed. Please don't make it difficult," she said.

At this point, three more humaans entered the waiting room, their automatic weapons loaded in their upper limbs. Upon seeing them, the room was immediately abandoned in a panic. Jasmin also ran outside, mentally insulting the soulless system. She decided to wait. She was curious about the further course of events. After a few minutes, Dr. Steavans was led outside. He wore energetic shackles on his wrists and around his ankles. As he passed Jasmin, taking small steps, he smiled as if to say that everything was fine. Nothing was right. Jasmin thought so. She felt that something unfairly unfair awaited him. Humaans pushed the prisoner into a glass cage filled with other detainees.

"Please separate. Assemblies are forbidden."

Jasmin looked around. She quickly noticed that she was alone. "What kind of gatherings was this stupid robot fucking about?" She wondered. She looked down, pretending to be looking for something. Humaan moved away. After a while, brown-haired came out, she looked scared.

"What happened in there?" Jasmin asked.

"Gardobot entered the office and said that the doctor was under arrest for treason. What will happen to him now?"

"I'm sure everything will be clarified."

Jasmin smiled inwardly as she repeated the word gardobot in her mind. She had never heard anyone call that an electronic law enforcement officer before. She liked the nickname. She decided to use it. She was even going to come up with her own version, but after a while she became sad. She realized that Dr. Steavans' days were numbered. He messed up with the wrong person, Gibbondy. And she didn't seem to be willing to let anyone go. In addition, she became the second most important person in the country. Jasmin felt sorry for the esteemed gynecologist.

"Have you seen the baby?" She asked.

"Yes." For the first time the brown-haired girl exuded unimaginable happiness. "Olivia is so awesome. I will not give her back to anyone. What's your name?"

"Jasmin."

"Nice. My name is Tarya. You can see immediately that you will have boy."

***

The first days in Claire Gibbondy's new job did not go as she had imagined. Instead of immediately starting to act, at the urging of Noovack, she underwent a boring, unnecessary, thorough public relations training. Earlier, she had learned that her appearance and lifestyle did not go hand in hand with well-understood care for health. And such features should be a credible-looking health minister. At least she had to learn to fake empathic reactions, since such feelings were alien to her. She did not expect to have to use this new skill too often, but she obediently obeyed, or if you prefer, her boss's request. When she saw the pathetic poor thing as she glanced in the mirror with disgust, she decided it was time to end the secret experiment. Eva Noovack also recommended a change of appearance. To her own despair, Gibbondy had to give up the brown uniform in favor of a costume exposing the female body and replace the lace-up boots with comfortable women's shoes. However, the most difficult changes to introduce were not related to the wardrobe, but to the attributes of femininity. Gibbondy should start decorating the nails, preferably in accordance with the current fashion, i.e. covering them with a metallic coating, and also necessarily changing the hairstyle. The previous gray, sometimes black, usually loose, and sometimes tied in a careless braid, long hair was to be tied into a bun, preferably of a uniform color. She chose black hair because it seemed more distinguished to her. There were no more guidelines at this stage, though Noovack considered a few more ideas. However, she did not intend to kill her loyal friend.

She went to the first meeting with the new band Gibbondy with the intention of a quick rattling through. Without unnecessary tenderness and creating new bonds. Cool, quick and ready to go. The seat of the Ministry of Health was shaped like a cross. It consisted of a grand edifice and three smaller buildings joined by horns. Between them was a concrete atrium with several permanently attached benches and a small monument. The entire complex was spacious. Wide corridors and high ceilings made the interior monstrous. When Gibbondy appeared in the hall, she caused quite a stir. Not because it was noon already. Those who knew her well were amazed at the effect of her transformation. Many did not even recognize her. Moreover, they ignored the appearance of a differently dressed woman. People who did not know what she looked like but had only heard about the raw appearance of the new Minister of Health, agreed that she did not look very young, but she did not scare, as the legends about her said. Gibbons with a surprisingly pleased expression noted some flattery about herself. That day, it didn't matter to her whether they were sincere.

"Good morning, friends," she began with a fake smile on her face. "I am happy that we will work together. I would like to tell you about my plans, but I have a lot of arrears and would like to catch up quickly. An organizational meeting will take place in a few days. Let everyone do what they have done so far."

After these words, Gibbondy walked away towards her new office. She knew where she was because she had passed him many times on her way to her boss's previous office, after all, Noovack had been on duty there once a week. Small smirks, expressions of doubt, even dissatisfaction appeared on the faces of the welcoming committee set for a longer speech.

"Nicola McKinley!" You could hear Gibbondy's scream. "To me."

An unattractive, but competent-looking secretary, aged two and a half purification, raced, notebook in hand, toward the new boss's office.

"Close the door," Gibbondy said, effortlessly moving her desk closer to the window.

Nicola stopped short for a moment. However, she quickly reflected.

"What did they say?" Gibbondy asked.

"Who?"

"People. Who am I asking about? What a mess," Gibbondy said to herself, but aloud.

"I understand now. Everyone is waiting for some decisions. Who will be the new director of GCO and what is the plan to crack down on pharmaceutical cartels."

"And good. Let them wait. From today on, I want to have a complete picture of what is happening throughout the office. Is it clear?"

Nicola looked embarrassed and a little disgusted.

"I don't know if I understood correctly," she stammered timidly. "I have six faculties, including medical science."

"Yes. I know that this is a very responsible and complex function. Not everyone is suitable. If you fail, you will surely find a job that is much more appropriate to your competences."

The razor-sharp words cut Nicola into thin slices. She was recovering for a while. Meanwhile, Gibbondy was checking the contents of the drawers. Only once did she glance at the girl with narrowed eyes like a detective. It looked like a sign of impatience.

"Please forgive me. I had no bad intentions. When I started working in the ministry, nobody offered to report on my colleagues."

"At least you'll learn something. Your faculties will be of no use to you. Do we understand each other now?"

Nicola nodded.

"Did this Nakamuru get here?"

"Yes. He's been waiting in the auditorium since morning."

"Excellent. Where it is?"

"You have to go to the atrium, walk around the monument, and then the second door on the left."

"Monument? It is here, indeed. Filthy. I don't want to see it until tomorrow."

Nicola froze. A stone statue of a nursing mother and baby has been standing in the center of the atrium for nearly eighty purifications. It was a respected symbol of the ministry. Ex libris with its image has long been treated as a logotype. It was on all official documents, both paper and electronic.

"Will we have a new symbol?" Nicola asked.

"I can see that you are learning fast," the Minister of Health replied dryly.

***

Romm Nakamuru was lightly falling asleep. He was sitting at a high desk with his elbow resting on a thick wooden table. His head rested on the palm of his outward curved hand. It was evident that he had spent many hours in this position. His medium-length, stiff yellow hair twisted into a funny tangle. As Gibbondy entered the auditorium, her rhythmic footsteps woke him immediately. He stood at attention, his head bowed as if to bow. After a while he picked it up and looked sleepily. He was short for a man. He had bulging eyes that squinted as he made them accustomed to the light. He took out a monocle with a thick glass and placed it between the cheek and the eyebrow of his right eye. Gibbondy looked at him with a slight mockery, as if she was taller not by a head but by two. If someone had looked at this couple, he would have no doubts as to who is truly charismatic.

"Professor Nakamuru, I'm glad we will work together."

"I don't know on what yet," he answered quickly.

"I appreciate your achievements in the field of genetics. I've read all your works. The ones I had access to. The rest, as I understand it, you will also pass on to me. I want to create a new vision of a ministry able to heal this sick country. Not with drugs for everything, but with genetics."

"This is an important area. I am glad that you share my opinion in this regard."

"You will hold a new function. Chief geneticist, boss of bosses, alpha and omega."

"You flatter me. Unnecessarily. But thank you. What exactly are we supposed to do? Will we continue my virgin reproduction project?"

"Also. But it won't be yours, but someone else under your supervision. Your knowledge is too valuable to be squandered on one topic. I have a lot of experience and have seen a lot. I think my ideas may surprise you."

"You are the boss of all bosses."

"Come on. Enough of these flatteries. I only have one small request. I'm sure you will understand me."

"How can I help you?"

"Help?" She was surprised. "No. You worked for the previous authority. From today you are working for me and I am asking you to..."

At this point, her communicator made a sound to symbolize an incoming call. Gibbondy checked it was Eva Noovack.

"Get out, sir. Oh. Please do not, under any circumstances, tell that it was better in those days. We understand each other?"

Nakamuru nodded and headed for the door. Gibbondy activated her communicator.

"What's with this monument?" The Prime Minister's voice was recognizable from the communicator mini-speaker.

"I'm cleaning up. You said yourself that this mummy with the baby annoys you."

"That's true. Okay, take it out. But slow down a bit. Please give us time to seal the system."

"Yes, boss." Gibbondy smiled, glanced at the fingernails adorned with metallic notes, and shook her head. "I'm sick of getting up the ass of all those sugar-coated morons."

"Ha ha ha. Patience, friend. Patience. I would forget, the operator of the rig Clifford and his minions escaped had finally confessed that he had left them in the third district. I think they hid there."

"We'll find the bird," Gibbondy replied, frowning at the disdain she had for the former prime minister.

***

Two days' walk from the border with Floris there was an abandoned mine of bidrite, a mineral from which technical glass was melted. It was used to build Hello energy-absorbing cells, as well as structural elements of modern coolants. This type of glass, thanks to its unique properties, achieved better insulating parameters with relatively economical thickness. The color and structure of bidrite resembled old, rotten wood, but contrary to appearances, it was very hard. It was smelted in a steel mill at a temperature of nearly eight thousand Meyer degrees. It was processed by robots, and the smelting site was far away from people, in the total wilderness of the fourth district. Despite the complicated and expensive treatment process, bidrite was one of the most important minerals used in this land. Thanks to it, Inco went so far in technological development. Glass panes, consisting of two thin panes connected by a transparent foil, covered each facade and the roof of all high-rise buildings in the first district. They took Hello rays directly, and the inverters connected to them converted them into energy in an amount greater than required. The surplus was sent to the second district with minimal losses along the way.

One of the three depleted mines have become an ideal hiding place for government officials. Two hundred cubits deep. The only structure sticking out of the ground - the drill shaft - was situated on the edge of a rocky steppe covered with occasional clumps of dry, thorny grasses. Rarely has anyone looked there. Contrary to popular belief about the harshness of this place, Clifford and several of his most trusted associates and their families chose to hide from the first wrath of society. The place was not accidental. Haris had planned them - long ago, when the first nervous signals of potential leaks had surfaced. After several long days of hiking through the rocky steppe, the team arrived at their destination. It was considered a perfect idea.

"It seems to be safer here than in the mountains, but I suggest that we set up guards. We'll all be on duty," Clifford said.

"Of course, Prime Minister. Children too?" Rubby asked.

"Yes. Every person matters. Until Haris returns, we're at the mercy of this terrifying place. I would not like it to become our mass grave."

"One of us should stay afloat. We must listen to news about the situation in the country. Communicators don't work here underground, we won't find out anything."

"Right. No wonder you were in charge of internal affairs," Clifford said, and smiled genuinely.

The guards have been posted. The escapees, divided into groups, hid in small hiding places, substitutes for intimacy. A strange place, economical light, cool climate, light humidity, fear for the future. Such feelings were experienced by several families hidden underground. Clifford proposed that their isolated community meet for a common evening consumption. There was no such custom in Inco, but in exile it could have come in handy. Who would like to sit at a symbolic table to eat a bar and wash it down with water? No one. But in this extraordinary place, where none of the refugees felt comfortable, a forgotten ritual could lull the vigilance for a moment and give the impression of security and a kind of unity. He chose one of the walking opencast chambers as the site. Dinner lasted for a while. No celebration, just chewing. Without a word.

"It must have been interesting times once," Clifford said. "People were integrating at a table full of food. Perhaps they talked to each other, tasted life. However, many generations ago, real food and the rituals associated with it were forgotten. Maybe it's worth coming back to them?" He dreamed.

His companions only made puzzled expressions. As if no one understood what he meant.

"Everything passes," he continued. "Time is running wild and can not be tied down. Decisions made once have their consequences in the future. Our life will never be the same again. Even if we manage to restore order in Inco, we will be forced to change."

"Haris, Haris is here!" You could hear Rubby's son's voice in the distance. He was acting as a guard now.

All eyes were turned towards one of the entrances to the chamber. At first, you couldn't see anything for a long time, then there was the sound of not very measured footsteps. After a moment, Haris's head peeked out from behind the rocky passage. He looked exhausted. He moved closer, only shuffling his feet.

"Give him something to eat," Clifford said.

Haris nodded as if to thank for understanding. He couldn't say anything. He took a quick bite of feed and washed it down with a few sips of water. He chewed and repeated the action. As he swallowed, he felt the eyes of the impatient onlookers hungry for sensation.

"Good to see you," said Clifford.

"It worked," Haris began. "Ae will take us in and give us shelter."

"Whew, the blackmail worked. She believed?" Rubby responded.

"How much will it cost us?" Clifford asked, as if wishing the uninitiated would not learn the truth about Ae.

Haris understood his intention.

"I used final arguments, but only to convince the priestess. Their Council needs to get something to believe. They don't need anything but technology."

"How will we get there?"

"I have a plan. What about Mr. Goeffrey?"

"He's tearing through the mountains," Clifford replied. "We start at dawn. Now rest, my friend."

Haris nodded, finished a bar, then ate another. He sniffed his hands. They smelled bad, fodder. An imitation that did not resemble food, although it gave a feeling of fullness. It solved one of the existential needs. Stripped of colors. In the eyes of a man who has seen, smelled, and even tasted real food more than once, the regeneration bar was like an ascetically made painting, seen in the poorer houses of Floris, in fact a stretcher painted with only one color. Haris could not devote too long to reflecting on culinary tastes, as four girls and two boys caught up with him. Children between the ages of half and a half of purification had a lot of questions for the only man who returned from abroad and was considered a walking encyclopedia of knowledge about the unknown world.

Ultimately, he did not have time to rest. All night long he talked about colorful landscapes, vegetation, animals, and the habits of the people of Floris. Of course, he paid the most attention to the kitchen. Contrary to appearances, he did not condemn the peasants for the lack of interest in science and sports, as well as their faith. He based his story about the habits of the neighboring society on cultural differences and tolerance. The children were surprised. For the first time in their company, no one insulted or criticized the inhabitants of neighboring Floris. They listened to Haris's story with bated breath. Whenever he signaled that he was finishing because he had exhausted the topic, another question would immediately appear. At dawn, when the march was scheduled, he suggested - citing his experience - that all evidence of their presence in this place be removed, just in case. But no one listened to him.

***

Haenry was an underrated member of the Addam family. He was treated similarly at work. Kimberly Davis did not have to wonder for a long time which of the two oldest employees, and at the same time cousins, should succeed her as the Director of the Public Opinion and Mood Research

Bureau. She chose Addam because he was smarter, but less experienced. However, the scandal with pregnancy cut off his promotion. The new Minister for the Indoctrination of Society eventually had to do something against herself and choose another member of the same family clan. Jasmin had no difficulty explaining her decision. Apparently, Haenry was promoted to keep a disappointed Addam from inciting workers against the new boss. He wouldn't do that to his cousin. "It was a smart move", Jasmin thought. But this idea did not suit her for another reason, based on a private basis. Haenry was Luicey's fiancé. This insult was hard to bear. Jasmin treated it as a failure. Lost in internal rivalry between girls. It was known that Luicey, eternally jealous of Jasmin's successes, would be swaggering. She will trumpet the victory so loudly that the whole district will roar. They knew each other inside out, from the beginning of school. At first it was wonderful. They did everything together. After some time, a boy from a wealthy family, Addam, appeared on the horizon. They were both crazy about him, but he chose the one with the white hair. Dating the three of them was not conducive to a relationship or friendly relationships, so the idea came up to bring Haenry, an elderly, copper-haired cousin on his mother's side by a different name Freejay. It worked. Jasmin could get a break. Firstly, she got rid of the chaperone, and secondly, to some extent, an unwanted rival. She would never have gotten to that specific family member herself, but Luicey Biedermann acted as if she had moved into another world. She felt that her life changed. It was not a love relationship, but a sense unspoiled so far. A well-planned family creation project. Over time, Luicey liked Haenry, although Jasmin still had the impression that her friend was looking for a resemblance to Addam in her man.

"We're getting married," Luicey announced as she burst into Jasmin's suite unannounced that evening, and their men were still at work.

"Fantastic," Jasmin said with mock delight.

She was sure that her friend, who was on the wave of success, felt a strong need to dominate a depressed, pregnant woman with her joyful news. She obviously had no mercy. "Jealous witch. What does she think?" Jasmin was furious. "That I will enjoy her happiness? My world is collapsing and she...?"

"If Haenry hadn't been promoted, you wouldn't have been getting married?" She asked with a hint of irony.

"He has invited me to the Glass Dome many times, but since he is going to be the director, I finally agreed."

"I'm so lucky for you. And when the children?"

"Certainly not now. Haenry has new responsibilities. There is so much going on in the country. Becoming pregnant at such a time would be an act of irresponsibility."

Luicey bit off extremely well. Not as usual. It was evident that her confidence had opened dusty nooks and crannies in the network of long-lost neurons in her brain.

"Thank you, love." Jasmin wanted to throw Luicey out the window.

"You're welcome. Will you be my bridesmaid at the wedding? Addam agreed. I can already imagine it. We are in front, you are behind us. Together. We will be a family."

Jasmin couldn't listen to this nonsense anymore.

"You know, I'll go to bed. Addam is back in a moment. A difficult conversation awaits us. I need to regenerate."

"Of course. These quarrels of yours. I know everything. Give up this pregnancy and everything will work out."

"We'll see," Jasmin replied and closed the door behind Luicey, lightly pushing her out into the hallway.

She lay down, though she wasn't feeling sleepy at all. She quickly got up and took a few nervous steps. She was furious with herself. Thanks to her decision, it is a longtime friend who will become the director, not her. The tiring woman will now choke her with her happiness. "Why can't I make up my mind?" She wondered. You also had to find a guilty one. It was father. It was Omar who developed the humanitarian foundations in her. At that moment, she felt angry with her entire family, wherever they were. For some unknown reason, she rejected the human foundations in which she was brought up. She preferred to be born in a slum, in some pathological family, or even as a mixed breed, a social outcast who did not care about human life, principles or a good heart. Why did fate endow her with a moral backbone and a character-tolerant attitude that could not bear pressure? She kicked the wall out of helplessness.

"What's happening here?" Addam asked from crossing the threshold of the suite.

Why did you agree to be Luicey's best man?!" She screamed.

Addam said nothing, as if he did not want to take part in the shouting match. He changed into informal clothing and, watching his wife writhe in the torment of her internal war, ate one bar. He only lit her up with a dismissive attitude.

"Are you my husband or not?"

"What is that question?"

"Couples agree such things."

"What are you talking about? This is my cousin. Should I be asking you?"

"I would have asked."

"Write a formal application to see if you can be best woman of Luicey. I'll think about it," he joked.

"Speaking of the official letter, when will I get a reply on the data?"

"I have to ask the new boss, and he will probably ask his fiancée."

The malicious tone of Addam's tone only confirmed Jasmin that she did not want to have children with him. "Thank you, insensitive wise man. You helped me decide. I'll terminate the pregnancy, and then I'll divorce you," she said in her mind, turned on her heel and went to sleep.

The next morning, when Jasmin woke up, a blue briefcase lay beside her bed. It interested her. "Was Addam left something by accident, or did he do it on purpose? Oh, it doesn't matter," she thought. She decided to look inside. It was the report she had been waiting for. The first page read:

"Secret. Copying and distribution prohibited under penalty of imprisonment". She wasn't going to waste a single second in bed. She dressed quickly and went to her work like on wings. She couldn't wait for Agness to appreciate her efforts. She really needed kind words. She passed four garda's humaans blockades on the way. This time, nothing upset her. She even smiled at one of the robots. It's good that his software did not anticipate such cases and did not perceive it as the suspicious behavior of an enthusiastic madwoman who probably has something on her conscience. Agness greeted her at the door. Chilly. She looked surprised, as if Jasmin had taken an ace from her sleeve.

"Today you are ahead of time," she noted.

"I couldn't sit still at home. I have to deal with the concept," Jasmin said and pointed to the report in her hands.

"Do you have the data?"

"I have them."

"Excellent. Show me."

"I thought that I would prepare a presentation and then we will follow it together." Jasmin vented the trick.

"You know, because there is such a case." Agness squirmed like an eel. "This topic, however, will be continued by Katterina. Give her your notes."

"It's my project. I need it. Only I have the necessary data. What's wrong with all of you?" She was indignant.

"You understand."

"Pregnancy is not a disease!" I can work.

"Not any more. New directives came yesterday. You are on the wrong list."

"Are you firing me?"

"I regret it very much, but..."

Agness bit her lips and entered her office without a word. Jasmin froze, the report in her hand. She didn't know whether she should follow the boss right away or find peace in some isolation and come back stronger. She didn't hesitate for long.

"How can you do this to me after what we've been through together?!" She yelled as if she wanted to be heard within three hundred cubits. "My successes mean nothing to you? Who will plan your campaign now?"

"Calm down or..."

"Or what? You will call the garda? On me?"

"Jasmin, can I have you come to my office?"

When she entered, the documents for her signature were on the desk: termination with immediate effect and transfer order. This second document made her wonder. She began to read briefly. Agness saw it.

"You will get severance pay, but so that it does not soak in the depths of the blockade, we will transfer it to your mother's bank account. This is the only way I can help you."

The boss smiled briefly but sincerely and pushed both documents closer to the edge of the desk.

Chapter 10 Kidnapping

Pirna, the most devoted servant of the High Priestess of the Omniearth, acted suspiciously from the very morning. As she poured her mistress's milk for her daily bath, she spilled a good portion of it on the floor. Though she scrubbed it exceptionally long and laboriously afterwards, the greasy stain was reluctant to remove. Ae noted the unusual sight of a girl bustling in hot water. It puzzled her. She had been alerted and suspicious from the moment of the difficult conversation with Haris. She pronounced the sentence immediately. The maid was up to something, she decided. Just what? It was then that she remembered that Jusif had spoken well of her when he recommended her. That she is so hardworking and devoted. She, in turn, often smiled at him. The priestess quickly connected the facts.

"Do you know where Jusif is?" She asked.

Pirna twitched slightly, as if the question had caught the middle of her uneasiness.

"I don't know, lady. I was wondering what happened to him."

"Remind me where did you meet?"

Pirna realized that if she lied and the priestess found out about it, her moments would be numbered. In turn, if she tells the truth, she will bring her mistress's anger not only on herself but also on her entire family. Either from Ae or Jusif - one of them will feel cheated. Both variants were associated with a gloomy end to her stay in this world. She chose the version that apparently gave more time.

"I told you, lady, that I grew up in a poor family."

"I know. Often you had nothing to eat because your father died when you were little and your mother did not accept any of the suitors."

"Yes. There were eight of us. One morning, Jusif was passing through the village where I lived. Together with my sisters, I was washing the robes of wealthier families on the banks of the river. I had one and a half purification then. I was well developed for this age. I think I caught his eye. He offered my mother to buy me for a hundred gray stones. She agreed without hesitation."

"Has Jusif ever hurt you?" Ae asked, though she wasn't sure she wanted an answer.

"He said it was for my own good, so I don't think so. I was his property. He could do what he wanted with me. When he got bored he brought me here, lady."

The priestess was not entirely convinced that this quite good-looking girl was telling the truth. She knew Jusif and knew that if he got bored with anyone, he would rather not give it to anyone as a gift. He would have gotten rid of it sooner. When Ae met him two purifications before, he was just a bastard. He received orders from her that took him to the top of finance, but he never gave up his nasty thug character. They've been through a lot together.

Jusif was an extremely useful bastard. He could arrange everything, find out about the most hidden secrets, kill the most inconvenient witness or force unworthy behavior on righteous people. He was a master in his rogue trade. He impressed Ae. She even thought she liked him. Now she was disappointed in him. When she needed him to help her unravel the network of Inco agents, he suddenly disappeared. As if he knew what she could expect of him. He clearly did not want to perform such a task. As if he were involved in it or he was part of a great swindle that in the eyes of the power-hungry priestess was becoming ever wider.

When they met, she didn't trust him at first. He came out of nowhere. He himself offered to work for her. She was still a student then. An inexperienced, unfledged future priestess who was fond of praise and a career vision. She didn't sense any bad intentions. Nor did she expect to achieve so much with his help. She was convinced that this was the strength of their tandem. Her cunning and shrewdness and his ruthless and effective nature. She always rewarded him generously, though she didn't have to. The tasks he received from her were carried out with passion. As if they were food for his soul. He loved spying, reporting, bribing, theft, and especially eliminating her enemies. He did it differently each time. Let there be no boredom. "How did he survive? Nobody knows about his true identity," she wondered many times. The environment of the High Priestess of the Omniearth considered him a merchant who would bring her favorite fragrances, liniments and treats from time to time. In fact, he was coming to report the execution of the order and receive a new one. By the way, he reported what was happening in the far corners of Floris, as well as in the neighboring Inco. He had his informants, he paid them a lot, but he sold the revelations they gave his priestess for a much higher price. It was a mutual addiction.

At this point, Ae realized that only Pirna knew the truth about Jusif and knew a lot about her private life. It was quite inconvenient knowledge for such a shy girl. "If she really came from a poor family, how would she know what to say and what shouldn't even be thought?" Ae considered. The priestess did not believe in the talent of a minister of diplomacy, or in her inherent modesty, qualities that could possibly support this girl in loyal service. Only now has everything started to fall into place. The priestess was furious with herself mentally. How could she be so naive? Why had she not yet noticed the potential danger posed by this reckless mutual familiarity? She trusted Pirna because Jusif trusted her. But was it worth believing him? It was already known that not entirely. Ae realized another inconvenient point. Pirna witnessed several times Jusif bringing men to the priestess' chamber at night. Secretly. It was she who helped him arrange it so that no one would be aware of the true intentions of these visits. Even that nosy Kifor, who was hanging around all the time, as if out of concern.

"When was the last time you shared the bed with Jusif?" The priestess asked suddenly.

Pirna looked down. Ae no longer had any doubts. This accurate question confirmed that the girl did not work for her from the very beginning. She was apparently Jusif's concubine, and also a spy who followed her every move while he was away. Ae mechanically thought it was time to call on Jusif to get the job done right as usual. However, she quickly remembered that her court cleaner of problems had been absent and turned out to be a traitor. The thought even made her laugh.

The servant girl began to cry. Though it looked like a distraction, Ae turned her gaze back to the greasy milk stain. She did not want to take part in this performance, but to wait until the girl calmed down. Mentally she was tearing her apart. When Pirna was sure that the priestess could not see her, she wiped one of her tears with a trembling hand. She reached into a small pocket and took an ampoule out of it. She glanced at Ae one last time, hurriedly pulled out the plug and tipped out the contents. When the priestess realized the crying was no longer heard, she turned away. She saw Pirna lying on the stone floor. A mixture of frothy saliva and blood was coming out of her mouth. The girl seemed to have relieved her of her trouble. Or was it the beginning of another one? In any case, she left for Patri pretty quickly.

***

The animals that had stayed in Fahid's stable since dawn were restless. Their snoring increased, becoming more and more unbearable with each passing moment. The first one woke up Sumi, even before his father. She did not want to leave the bed in which she slept with a little younger Tamadur. She prodded her sister, signaling that it was her turn today. It didn't help, so she jabbed her thumb in the ribs.

"Ai!" Tamadur responded.

"Check," she said shortly and signaled her sister to listen to the sounds coming from the stables.

"I feel bad, wake Adila."

Sumi knew that this was not a task for the host's only third daughter. She struggled with her thoughts for a moment, but the snoring became extremely bothersome.

"I would go for you, but you will owe me another debt. And I would have to tell the father you're going out."

"I'm coming, you witch."

Sumi smiled at her thoughts and covered the bedspread to reduce the noise. Tamadur put on sandals and squinted outside. Meanwhile, louder and louder babbling sounds began to come from the room for the youngest children. It's Malik with Hassan. Even if any of the family members did not wake up to the sounds of the animals, surely the chirping of these two children could wake anyone up. After a while, the whole house came to life. Nobody was aware anymore that only animals could be heard. The family effectively drowned out the sounds coming from the stables.

Fahid was gifted with a keen hearing, but it was of no use to him in the general tumult. He decided to leave the sleeping room and come closer to the front door. As he entered the walk-through kitchen, he saw an unusual sight. There was an uninvited guest at the table. It's Kadu. He waited for everyone to wake up. "When did he enter?" The host thought. The priest was acting strange, not as usual. He never entered the house uninvited, he never showed up at dawn, much less feasted infrequently. Fahid's face said it all. Even though he was expecting this visit, he felt surprised.

"Good morning, my friend," said Kadu.

"What brings you so early?" Fahid asked as loud as he could.

Rita, still lying in bed, understood the signal from her husband. She wanted the moment when she hid from the priest in the bedroom to last as long as possible. She walked into the toddlers' room almost silently and motioned for them to be silent. There was total silence in the house in no time.

"I came for your daughter. Did you get the invitation?"

"Yes. Forgive me, but we won't take advantage of this boon. Sumi will study to be a singer."

"The priestess will be disappointed. We don't want to hurt her, do we? She asked me to do it personally. You don't know Ae's anger."

"We only have ten children, and my wife's sister no one. You understand. Someone has to stay with us and with my parents-in-law."

"Since your eldest daughter is important to you, give up the other children and I'll explain it somehow."

At that moment, Sumi remembered that she had sent her sister to the stables. "Has she arrived at the place? What will happen when she comes back?" She wondered. The little girl's head was full of bad thoughts.

"I will not give up a single child, priest," Fahid said.

"Tamadur, is that the name of one of your daughters?" Kadu asked, squinting.

Fahid nodded. In his mind, anxiety and disbelief and a desire to annihilate the impudent visitor fought each other.

"It could be Tamadur. It's two more and it'll be okay."

"Tamadur!" Fahid called his daughter.

Terror appeared on the face of Rita, listening from the neighboring children's room.

"Tamadur! Where she is?" Asked the host.

In response, he only heard the snores of animals. Fahid threw his hands on Kadu. He squeezed his neck and began to choke him.

"Hara!" Kadu only managed to scream once, then his voice withered in his throat.

Suddenly the door opened and a female warrior appeared in the kitchen.

"Let him go," her almost male voice came.

Fahid saw a nightmarish figure, armed to the teeth and looking like a ghastly murderer, that he would not want to see even in his dreams. He quickly released the priest. He just shrugged nonchalantly, as if to say that this is life. "This is supposed to be a priest?" The host thought.

"If you do not give of your's own volition, we will take by force. Two more. And don't argue." Kadu was implacable.

Suddenly Sumi entered the kitchen.

"I agree. I will go with you but give back Tamadur."

"Beautiful, my lady," rejoiced the priest.

"How's it beautiful?" Hara was clearly disappointed.

She was counting on a little brawl, and here is such a happy ending. Suddenly, Rita's cry came from the next room. Fahid held back his emotions for a moment but gave up. He also shed a tear. His soul howled in pain. He looked at his daughter and could not accept the thought that he would lose her.

"Bring that girl over there!" Kadu shouted at the top of his voice.

After a moment, Nate appeared in the doorway. Fahid paled. Looking like a predatory creature, neither woman nor man, she held the terrified Tamadur by the hair with one hand and gagged her mouth with the other. Fahid, in a pleading gesture, threw himself at the feet of his daughter's torturer. It only amused her. She looked happy with the power she held in her hands - an innocent child. Unlike Hara. This one did not like anything. Nor that partner flaunted as if she were the mistress of life and death. Or that it all ended in such a boring way and took no one's life. And yet she really wanted to do so.

While Hara chained Sumi, Nate released Tamadur. The girl immediately threw herself into her father's arms. Fahid pressed her as hard as he could, as if he wanted to stick with his daughter so that they would never part. After a while, Rita entered the kitchen, followed by the other children. Everyone started cuddling. Fahid went out to the yard to say goodbye to Sumi. The girl was just getting into a small two-wheeled car. She turned for a moment and shed a tear. She already knew that she was going to meet an unknown, evil world. Fahid felt he was losing a part of himself.

Suddenly there were screaming noises from the farmstead.

"Okurai is giving birth!" Tamadur shouted.

Fahid didn't react for a long time. His thoughts were with his beloved daughter who was going to eternal damnation. Plus, with bad people. There was nothing he could do. He felt weak.

Rita suddenly snapped him out of his trance. She tugged at his arm as if she wanted him to focus on what was most important now and throw away any bad thoughts. Fahid rubbed his face with his hand. He felt ready. He ran towards the farm where he was pregnant with okurai. All the children stroked him. This poor creature could barely hold on to its trembling legs. Its eyes were rheumy and it was making terrible noises. His huge belly looked like it was about to burst. The other animals kept in the stable snorted and whistled as loudly as if they were sympathetic and encouraging him. Fahid looked under the animal's back. It was evident that she was almost ready for delivery. His skin contracted just below his chest and spread to the sides, revealing an ellipse-shaped opening in his chest. Drops of sticky fluid dripped from the hole.

"The slot is too small," Fahid said.

"So what will happen now?" Adila asked worriedly and took her mother's hand.

"You have to cut," said father.

Rita sent her husband a scolding look. He quickly realized his mistake and sent the youngest children out of the farm. After all, they did not have to see it. Only Rita, Tamadur and Abdul remained. The younger siblings were basically focusing more on the fact that the poor okurai would be slashed in a moment, than on the fact that they had literally lost their sister moments earlier. Abdul handed his father a small, rounded pocket knife. Fahid has never done this before. He had seen such an operation carried out by his father several times. For a moment he thought that he would be willing to hand over the task to someone else. He looked at Abdul for support. The son just nodded as if to give him a bit of his strength. Yet he had so little of it. He was just a weak boy, barely a cleansing age and a half. Fahid felt that the boy gave him what was needed at that moment. With a single snip, he cut the animal's skin. Okurai kicked and roared in pain. Yellowish blood gushed out of the wound immediately. After a moment the elliptical opening opened more and the baby's head appeared in it. It squeezed through the opening and fell onto a tuft of straw from the dirshna stalks. Okurai glanced at the little boy and made a fondly sounding noise. After a while, another head peeked out of the hole. Rita smiled at her husband. She grabbed his hand and squeezed it tight. When Tamadur was wiping the first baby with a dry, soft cloth, more were coming out into the world. All identical. They looked like miniatures of okurai but had no pale brown hair yet.

After successfully giving birth to fourteen okurai, Fahid decided to go for a short walk. He did not want anyone accompanying him. Rita reluctantly let him out of her sight. She preferred him to discuss all his concerns with her. This time, however, he could not share them. When he came back he looked like a completely different person. She saw a power in him that had never been with him before. His strength was shared by Rita. She stroked his arm tenderly, always telling him that no matter what happened, she loved him and trusted him immeasurably. He smiled gently at her and summoned the eldest sons. Tamadur wondered for a moment what her father was going to do. Certainly, this was different from what he had done before. She decided to ask, but he quickly dismissed her. Fahid packed a lot of tools for a small two-wheeled cart. Meanwhile, Abdul harnessed the two fastest okurai to it, while Ragir tugged a large spool of yarn made from flying raidi animals.

***

The messenger who conveyed information about the successful completion of Haris' mission was royally received. Many priests were surprised by this fact, but no one was going to argue with him. After all, it was the decision of the High Priestess of the Omniearth. Not the only one that crazy. Just in case, she also sent a team of the bravest soldiers and some of the cleverest cardinals towards Pinati Falls. It was from there that they were supposed to escort the Inco visitors. They were given a clear order. No harm of anyone. When they were about to get to Patrix, Ae was anxious. Contradictory thoughts swirled in her head. On the one hand, she was disturbed by the visit of the rulers of the neighboring country, after all, they knew a lot, but on the other hand, she wanted to meet Haris again. In addition, she had to pretend to the Council that it was a necessary favor.

After a few days, the delegation arrived at the scene. A short welcome was arranged without undue delay. For Inco, only three officials attended: Prime Minister Clifford, Interior Minister Rubby, and Haris. On the other side of the big table were Ae, Kifor, Ali Ude, and some of the elders. Their attitude was not friendly. They looked rather interesting.

"Thank you, my lady, for your hospitality," Clifford began. "Our situation is quite complicated."

"How large is your delegation and how long are you going to stay here?" Ali Ude asked bluntly.

Ae looked at him reproachfully. He didn't do anything about it.

"We are thirty with our families," replied Clifford. "We believe that within two months we will deal with our problems and we will be able to return to Inco without any problems."

"You're going to live in the eastern quarter," Ae said. "Not far from Patrix and quite close to the border. There is a small settlement where you will be safe. You will get protection for the duration of your stay, as well as what you will need. Tell my brothers why you had to flee."

Clifford sighed deeply. He thought for a moment about what he could and should not say. He smirked and began his story to Ali Udego.

"The number of boys being born has been decreasing since many purifications. The public thinks it's the government's fault. We don't have that much power," he joked.

"It's the fault of your soulless technologies. Maybe it's time for you to put your trust in Patri?" Namali, one of the senior priests interrupted him.

"Let's not judge. Let everyone have a chance to decide what is best for them." Ae did not feel like a polemic, which would not come out anyway. She glanced at Haris.

He saw it. They exchanged glances for a moment.

"I would like to ask you to clarify what we can expect in return for our help." Kifor didn't seem interested, but he wanted to feel useful.

"Glad you ask," Clifford continued. "We have something very valuable for you. So far, you have used our machines or technologies to a very limited extent. We bring you some important inventions as well as the knowledge of how to use them. My brother Goeffrey is a respected engineer. He will join us later, because it took him longer to cross the border in a vehicle transporting the necessary tools and food supplies than it did for us. He should reach Patrix in two or three days. You will be able to count on his full help."

Overcoming the border between Inco and Floris in both directions was not such a great challenge for the average person. Nevertheless, apart from border trade, people basically did not do this. Since the dawn of history, the Inco Government has successfully advised the inhabitants of its country against foreign tourism due to the dangers that lurk there. The multitude of diseases, difficulty in finding food and the wildness of the inhabitants possessed by religion were sufficient arguments. It worked. Even when the GCO introduced abortion orders or new social privileges were taken away, no one thought about emigration. According to the people of Inco, the greatest punishment from the Government was nothing compared to the danger in Floris. There were those who wanted to see for themselves whether the Government was telling the truth. Those who returned, and it was only a handful, became followers of the truths proclaimed by the authorities until the end of their lives. They talked about how much evil lurks in a colorful land, ranging from insects, diseases, vermin, animals, deadly plants, terrifying shrines of various local deities, and the smell of food that caused a restless feeling of hunger. Not to mention the people who were, to say the least, strange in the eyes of the Inco inhabitant.

The exact opposite was done in Floris. The hierarchs of the Church became vigilant after the knowledge-seeking part of society separated from the Universe at the beginning of the world and chose the southern quarter as a place of new life, not very fertile, full of rocky steppes and rocks, surrounded by an intransigent mountain range stretching along the border. Church authorities then downplayed this fact, because who would like to live in such a remote area? After some time, it was noticed that the people living in the southern quarter did not return. Apparently, it was possible to live there, and perhaps it was even better. The very awareness that the next inhabitants may like a new, different life sparked an avalanche of ideas on how to tame an inquisitive nation. It was then that a set of rules was created, or rather prohibitions, which - as it turned out later - were created by Patri herself. A decalogue was also established, i.e. a list of mortal sins punishable by burning at the stake of the whole family. The heaviest of them were, among others: staying abroad without the consent of church authorities, joining in mixed pairs, i.e. with individuals from a neighboring country, taking unnatural medicines of foreign origin, practicing inappropriate, foreign sports disciplines, as well as heresy, i.e. glorifying science at the expense of faith. The role of priests was expanded. They were not only representatives of religion, but also began to control social moods and human life in accordance with the decalogue.

They became representatives of the executive power. The effect of introducing new rules has exceeded all expectations. Over time, they were only developed to adapt to current needs. During many purifications, both centers of power effectively discouraged people from migrating, although they maintained impeccable relations with each other at the highest level. Sometimes downright friendly.

It was quite different with the other living creatures. For many eras since the beginning of the world, despite the prohibition for humans, animals have wandered in both directions. When the Inco Government began to successfully get rid of them on its territory by concreting another not very fertile plant area, only insects, rodents and birds became the last bastion of fauna. They were dealt with chemically because they carried diseases. The problem of uncontrolled animal migration from Floris remained. That is why the Inco government decided to separate itself many times before. For this purpose, fine-meshed nets were installed in the River Ethne, through which even freshwater plankton could not pass. In addition, energy barriers were built in Inco, just before the mountain range. They easily blocked all species of insects, animals and birds from entering the country. The first trap was the energy fence two cubits high. He did not allow animals walking on the ground to pass, he was especially quick to deal with rodents and insects. The second, independent, a few cubits from the fence, was a far more effective form of protection, a luminous fence reaching to the clouds. It protected the birds' access, as they immediately burned to ashes after hitting its energy field. It was shaped like overlapping luminous walls. From above it looked like a makeshift maze, difficult for birds to cross, but easy for a human who would eventually have to cross it. It is thanks to these entanglements that Inco has become cleaner. However, if any of the human species wanted or had to cross the line, it would have no problem to overcome this specific obstacle course. It was enough to walk around the individual walls of the maze and go over the fence, for example using a folding ladder. After crossing the barbed wire, it was enough to pass the Ethne River unnoticed near the Pinati Falls. Of course, this place was guarded by the border guards of both countries, but they often turned a blind eye to single incidents involving local residents dealing in border trade. Smugglers were a bigger problem. They crossed the river one by one under the water. The Clifford Government delegation crossed the border in a completely different way, fearing a recognition. There was a hollow tunnel under the Pinati Falls through which spies could get through, and once all goods were smuggled out. Almost nobody in Floris knew about it. This is where the delegation of the Government and their families passed. Haris escorted them. He did it for the first time. He was very nervous about not being noticed. Goeffrey, the prime minister's brother, first had to disassemble the transport machine into several dozen smaller parts, overcoming the mountains, and after passing through the tunnel, reassemble it in the Floris area. Therefore, it took him more time.

***

Fahid's okurai, towing a fast-moving two-wheeled wagon, raced through the dirshna plantations toward Patrix. The coachman did not have to rush them. He fed them well before the trip, they burst forth with loads of unbridled energy. Anyway, they were still very agitated after giving birth to one of the individuals of the same species. A tender bond with him that only gave them wings. On the way to the capital, the first stop was the settlement of Litrijis. Here, Fahid intended to water the animals, but also to make sure that the escort of his daughter Sumi, Kadu, and the two male-like warriors, were passing this way. For this, he went to the center of the settlement. The sight of it aroused the interest of the local hawker who wandered in front of the inn serving the best tinghao in the area.

"Where are you going?" Asked the hawker, scanning the newcomer.

"I'm looking for Kadu. He was at my place, but he left something," Fahid said, pointing to a small load covered with a bedspread. "I have to deliver to him urgently."

"Can I see?" The hawker moved closer to the wagon.

Fahid hastily adjusted the bedspread as if he didn't want anyone to peek under it.

"Our good Kadu is very busy right now. He was coming this way, and he didn't even climb a single tinghao into the inn. He bought two barrels from me, ha ha. It will be enough for him for a few days of good fun. It's good that he had bodyguards, or he would get lost. They were taking the girl to Patrix."

"Yes?" Fahid pretended ineptly surprised.

As they passed, she looked at my stall and couldn't take her eyes off. It seems that something interested her. Unfortunately, she could not buy anything because she was handcuffed. Probably for resisting her parents who put her in Patri's service. After all, no one binds candidates for the priesthood."

"Interesting. What do you have to sell?" Fahid asked.

"Lots of useful stuff. Not only for fishermen, but also for farmers. Let me show you, my friend."

When Fahid walked over to the little stall, he saw a wonderful sight. The marketer had everything that every farmer would like to have in his handy workshop: many small, more or less precise tools made of metal or bone, boxes with pastes, sticky spreads, pieces of fabric of various textures, as well as screws, balls, nuts, plugs, springs. Whatever your heart desires. There was even a small pile of trinkets at the edge to decorate clothing and body. Fahid looked in her direction and was speechless. At the very top was a leather bracelet with unusual ornaments. He knew it very well. It was unique. It was this wonder that his father Mahmud used to wear. Even when the body of the deceased went to Asaran, the bracelet was worn around his ankle. At this point, several new, bad thoughts about the priest appeared in Fahid's head. Kadu not only kidnapped his daughter, but also robbed his father's body. This bracelet meant a lot to his family. It used to belong to Mahmud's brother Omar. It was the only memento of him. Mahmud wished her to accompany him on his last trek, so that, although symbolically, Omar would find himself in the Asaran Gorge and end up in Patri.

"Where did you get this?" Fahid asked.

"Ten gray stones and they could be yours," replied the hawker.

"I asked where did you get it!" Fahid did not want to waste time.

"It's a very valuable thing. A nimo shepherd sold it to me. Terrible drunk. He never remembers what just happened. Drunk all the time."

"I do not have enough. Sell me for two gray stones."

"Today I'm in no mood for jokes. Are you buying or not?"

"It belonged to my father!"

"He better quit tinghao," said the hawker and tapped his head.

"How dare you?"

Fahid pushed him away, but when he realized what he had done, he only looked down meekly. The incident was spotted by children playing nearby and a woman hanging laundry. Fahid returned to his wagon, avoiding the critical looks. He was ready to continue his journey but realized that he would be useless with farming implements. He needed a real weapon, not one made of a hoe or string. He wanted to be sure that at the most important moment, on which his daughter's life would depend, he would effectively protect her. From then on, he had a double incentive to hunt down Kadu before he reached the Patrix. He went back to the trader.

"Tell me, my friend, where can I buy a gun?" He asked.

"Friend? Now friend? Weapons are prohibited. Wasn't it enough that you pushed me and I nearly landed on the ground?"

"Do you have it or not?"

The hawker looked at Fahid as if to read his true intentions. He looked around to make sure no one was looking in his direction and reached under the quilt covering the neighboring stall. He took out a heavy bundle. As he unrolled the rag covering the hidden treasure, Fahid became very impatient. After a while, he saw the device, which surprised him strongly. He had seen one like this before, but that was a long time ago.

"Where did you get this?"

"Am I asking you what do you need this weapon for? This is called a crossbow."

"How much do you want?"

"You said you didn't have any money. This is a very scarce commodity."

"I'll give you a wagon. It is worth a lot."

"Why do I need a wagon if I don't have okurai."

"Okay. One okurai and a cart."

"Word up!"

"How to use it?"

The hawker just shrugged and smirked. He wrapped the crossbow back in a rag and handed it to the buyer. Then he added a small box of poison darts. Their supply was ample, but not for a novice crossbowman. Only now did Fahid make a scowl of surprise. A moment ago, he was sure that he can wield a freshly purchased weapon, and it turned out that it is used in a set with these small contraptions.

"On the edge of the hamlet, an elderly man lives in a house where the door is not locked. For a few gray stones, he will teach you how to use it. You just don't know this from me," said the hawker, patting Fahid on the shoulder.

***

Just before the émigré Government departed for Vatili Soll, Ae invited Clifford for a brief interview. He was surprised. Though they had had many difficult conversations in the past, they had never argued alone.

"Prime Minister, I do not know how to start neatly, you realize that I am not fluent in diplomacy."

Clifford smiled as if he knew that wasn't true. Ae has always built up the tension in a similar way.

"I am trying to remember all our meetings and do you know my conclusions?"

He shook his head.

"That we never spoke on an equal footing. This is our first meeting where you and I are on a similar level. You were always hidden under the mask of a lie."

"I do not want to offend you, but does everyone know where you came from in this position?"

"Thanks, Patri."

"Of course." He smiled discreetly, but sneeringly. "Well, as I understand it, we are still playing the game."

"The mockery is of no use."

"Sorry."

She thought for a moment.

"One question bothers me a lot... What was the purpose of introducing someone like me to the salons? Humiliation of the Church Council? You don't think I would have betrayed my people because of my commitment."

"I never thought that way."

"If so, why did you do it?"

"I had my reasons. Unfortunately, I cannot reveal them to you."

"So, grace again."

"Please don't exaggerate. Yesterday the lady was in a less privileged position, today I am in a similar position. Maybe even worse."

"But you still tower over me. You know very well that you are not here for your machines and technology."

"We have not made you a high priestess to help us through this difficult period. There are more important goals than you or mine."

"So, money and power."

Clifford shook his head in disbelief.

"We made a mistake in choosing you, lady," he said sadly.

"Audience over," Ae said, and turned her head.

Chapter 11 The plague

Irmina was surprised that her daughter received such a large amount of compensation. It was to her account that the three-month severance pay was transferred to her daughter. Thanks to such a ruse, nine thousand entitys, i.e. a more than three Jasmin's salaries, were not blocked against the future tax. It was the only reasonable option, prompted by Agness. It couldn't be arranged better. It was impossible for anyone to beg the removal of the system blockade. It could only be removed by a GCO officer based on an abortion performed and documented by one of the accredited gynecologists.

The mother felt sorry for her daughter. She was pleased that Jasmin had finally stopped insisting and decided to terminate the pregnancy. They talked about it for a long time, alternately hugging, tearing at each other and crying. Eventually, to help Jasmin in this extremely difficult moment, she agreed to go with her to Dr. Meilly, a respected physician. When mother and daughter approached the building, which housed the office of a famous gynecologist, they were surprised to see a queue stretching all the way to the outside.

"Only for registration," Jasmin said, trying to outsmart the furious young women standing in the line.

"We too!" One of them shouted.

"Is this the only office?" Mother asked in a whisper, astonishment combined with horror on her face.

"No, but this girl is really fine," replied her daughter confidently.

The line moved quickly and after a dozen or so minutes they entered the building. There, still in the corridor, they waited for a quarter of an hour and finally they could get to the waiting room that looked like a crowded cauldron. The young recorder, giving the impression of being a professional, was bustling with water. She made appointments, trying to shout over a dozen women of all ages. The sight irritated Jasmin. She hated chattering aimlessly, bored idiots. That was what she thought of them as she tried to politely label the phenomenon of gossip. Sometimes she thought worse, more indecent. After a while a young woman emerged from Dr. Meilly's office. Jasmin remembered he recognized her but wasn't sure where from. She didn't have to think long.

"Oh, Jasmin, you here?" Tarya asked.

"You haven't passed your due date?"

"The surgery was performed yesterday. Just at this lady doctor. I came for a checkup."

"You weren't supposed to," she said, but when she realized she shouldn't have interfered, she decided to be empathetic. "It hurt?"

"Why are you here?" Tarya asked.

"For control, too," Jasmin replied confidently.

Irmina looked surprised. She searched in vain for her daughter's gaze, as if to make sure she knew the real reasons for their visit to the esteemed doctor's office.

"When my husband found out that the new Government blocked the accounts of all pregnant women and sent wolf tickets to their workplaces, he left me no choice. Upper works wonders," Tarya said sadly.

"That's why there is such a line here. Motherfuckers."

"More like whores," Tarya said, though, noticing Irmina's scandalized expression, she blushed with embarrassment at the indecent judgment. "Every gynecologist who performs procedures is similar," she said, wanting to erase the bad impression.

Jasmin became concerned. It didn't sound good.

"I have to go, I'm sick. It's so stuffy in here. Take care, girl."

Tarya struggled through the crowd of women crowded together. After a while it was Jasmin's turn.

"Next!" The registrar said commandingly.

"Jasmin Kozllov, daughter of Irmina and Omar, née Manduarra," she introduced herself.

The recorder tapped the data into the computer module. She looked at Jasmin as if she were comparing the face of the original with the copy seen on the small screen projected under the desk.

"I can't make you an appointment," she said. "Next."

"What? But why?" Irmina was indignant, holding her daughter by the arm.

"We have another available date in eighty-nine days. This will be the middle of the second trimester for you. We cannot risk. These are the rules. Next please."

"What am I supposed to do?" Jasmin asked.

"There it is." The recorder pointed to the rack of leaflets. "Oh, already empty? I have just refilled groundbaits from other gynecologists. I have no more. You have to deal with it. Next one."

"So, what?" As they left the window, Irmina was clearly worried and confused.

"Ladies, I am asking for peace!" The recorder shouted. "I can't work here. And in general, if any of the ladies is at least four weeks pregnant, please get out of the line. The deadlines are distant."

"Now do you understand?" Jasmin didn't want to explain anything to her mother.

At that moment, all she thought was about her bed and the comfy sheets. She was fed up with the crowd of furious future mothers fighting for their lives.

***

Eva Noovack practically did not part with the public. From the time of the famous exposé, she appeared in theatremania almost every day and fed the nation with new information about the mistakes of the previous government and about the frauds that were alleged on the society. In the meantime, she banned both the Chemists Party and the Labor Party, arguing that differences were unnecessary in the country and that unity mattered. However, it was all nothing compared to the next bomb she was planning. For two and a half weeks, she prepared public opinion for another shock. The day has finally come for the presentation of demographics and healing ideas.

It was a warm, sunny morning. All members of the new government as well as heads and directors of major departments and state offices were invited to jointly watch the effects of the work of the marketing corporation. The audience gathered in the Meeting Room sat on the additional chairs that had been brought in earlier. Noovack stood by the door and watched everyone as they entered. At the end, she scanned the room, nodding as if counting. She looked at the time clock. The displayed digits began to approach zero. She glanced at the audience once more, smiled and turned on theatremania.

A streak of broad light projected an image on a large screen, with Prime Minister Noovack in the center of it. On the monitor, she was dressed like her own aunt: a heavy, dark suit and that horrible hairstyle. She looked sad. She stood in front of the blurred, gloomy view of the Inco center.

"Dear compatriots," she began pathetically. "Finally, I can share a difficult topic with you. It's been the one who keeps me awake at night. Barney Clifford and his government faked data. Many of you are aware that few boys are born, but it is only thanks to Luigi Pierone that we know why this happened and why the government allowed it. Because he was taking advantage of it. Throughout the purification we were told that medicines are healthy and that thanks to them we humans are healthy, look young and have energy. Do you know what the new Minister of Health, Mrs. Claire Gibbondy, discovered? That the famous drug called Ray almost two purifications ago was modified once again. The chemists say they have solved the Y chromosome problem that is causing all the misfortune, but that is definitely another lie for them. We also know that they added one more function to the drug, it was supposed to dull the public. Yes, my beloved countrymen. Lest you realize that we are heading towards destruction. That you would accept order. Their order funded by pharmaceutical cartels that made a fortune on every drug."

At this point, the picture darkened and after a while an idyllic picture appeared on the theatrical screen - a family consisting of dad, mother, son and daughter. The children played with each other and the proud parents watched them tenderly. The audience gathered in the Meeting Room reacted enthusiastically and with curiosity. There were even slight sighs.

"It used to be like that," the new prime minister sounded ominously. "Do any of you beloved countrymen remember those times? Because I don't. Even my grandmother, who has already undergone nine purifications, does not remember such a sight."

Another picture came out. It was easy to recognize the delivery room full of girls and the disappointed expressions of the fathers. Then there was a cut and the setting of the displayed story was changed to kindergarten, where the kindergarten teacher played at home with the children. They were all girls. Some of them pretended to be husbands, had boyish clothes, glued mustaches, and male-looking wigs on their heads. A chart with two axes appeared. One of them meant passing purifications, the other - percentages. You could clearly see that the downward trend - from more than fifty percent to less than five - began the twelve purifications backwards. After a while, the face of the famous, attractive, yellow-haired channel three editor, Martina Kuna, appeared in the background of the chart.

"Doctors are helpless. If it goes on like this, we will be doomed," she said in a sad voice.

"And it could have been otherwise." Prime Minister Noovack's face appeared on the screen again. "It was enough to find a solution. Instead of introducing penalties for women who wanted to give birth to a girl and rewards for those families who had a chance of a son, part of the profits had to be allocated to research. I omit that it was enough to turn off the production of the lethal drug. Dear compatriots, the situation is not interesting, but by joining forces, together with the new Minister of Health and her trusted specialists, we will save the world. We will save Inco!"

At this point, a joint photo of three people: Noovack, Gibbondy and Nakamuru was displayed on the theatremania screen with the caption in the bottom bar: "These people are fighting for our species. We trust them." Then successively individual data appeared in the form of slogans with unfriendly, squeaky sound effects: "Since twelve purifications, the number of men has decreased by 20%", "The current share of men in the entire population is 4.71%", "One purification ago was 5.89 %", "Nationwide 97 boys are born daily, but 420 men die", "At this rate, the world we know will end in four purifications!"

Immediately in the Meeting Room, one could hear a few sad-sounding whispers. The audience, especially the uninitiated, looked terrified. Claire Gibbondy was bursting with pride. The sight soothed her heart. She looked around the table where she sat with the rest of the Government, strutting like a winner. She noticed that her friends also had bad faces. Beside her, Eva Noovack beamed with delight.

"Now for the best," she said.

The eyes of all those gathered in the Hearing Room turned back to the theatremania screen, where Noovack's face appeared once again. This time it looked completely different than before when she presented the data. She was wearing a light, pale dress, her hair was tied up in two buns, and delicate makeup. The whole thing looked modern and tempting, even radiant. The prime minister radiated freshness.

"My Government has prepared for you, dear countrymen, several important decrees that will allow us to survive, and perhaps change the fate of the country quite quickly."

Eva Noovack, watching the broadcast, spoke simultaneously with the latter on the screen. It was evident that she had memorized the text and believed what she was saying.

"The first and most important decree changes the face of the Inco family," she continued. "We are introducing consent to polygyny throughout the country. One husband and one wife is a relic and a waste. You yourselves know how many single women live without any hope whatsoever. They also want happiness."

At this point, the screen was dimmed again, and after brightening, a board with a drawing labeled "Present Family" appeared. It showed a symbolically drawn father, mother and a few daughters, and next to it a group of sad women looking at them. The next board was signed with the slogan "Modern Family". It showed a dad who was kissed on the cheeks by several happy mothers, and a group of children of different sexes and ages stood next to it.

"The second decree is just as important," Noovack continued on the screen. "We have to protect our genetic treasure. From tomorrow, to protect the human species, I will ban working for men. They will also not be able to serve as border guards and play sports. Their role will be limited to procreation and rest. We women will support each one from birth to death. Robots will do the hardest work. Gentlemen today is your last day of work."

At this point, first the men, then a few women, and finally all the participants in the show held in the Meeting Room stood up and applauded. Eva Noovack bowed gently in approval. The applause lasted a moment, then she signaled for it to end and turned off the theatremania.

"We're going to work, friends," she said in a confident voice. "Colleagues, you are free. We will take care of your duties from tomorrow."

"I couldn't believe I would ever say that. Long live the women!" Kurt Schlagen shouted, Minister of Economy and Transport only until evening.

Noovack waved everyone away, except for the members of the Government seated at the meeting table. Then she looked carelessly at Schlagen and Donville. She smiled at them. Apparently, they understood that their role was over, because they left meekly and in no time. As Noovack made sure she was finally able to speak freely, a frustrated expression flashed across her face.

"Can anyone tell me why we haven't got Clifford so far?" She asked. "How long do I have to explain to the public that the country's number one enemy is free and is laughing right in our face?"

"We suspect he fled to Floris," Tatarczyna replied. "We've gone through every blade, every stone in the third and fourth districts. We have clues that he was hiding in the mine, but we can't find him."

"Did you question his closest associates who stayed in your ministry as I asked you?"

There was no trace of the successful theatremania charismatic leader on Noovack's face. Now she looked like a bloodthirsty predator. Tatarczyna swallowed hard.

"Of course. Clifford wasn't stupid. Rubby too. All the secret affairs of one or the other were cleverly disguised. None of the subordinates knew what project he was participating in and why he was doing it. Thanks to this - apart from the Prime Minister of the Government and the Minister of the Interior and several of those who fled the country with them - no one had a complete picture of the case. After its completion, all traces were always erased. The only thing I could figure out was that business was done with Floris. Their priestess, and not only she, was regularly visited. And before that, her predecessors."

"I don't understand," Nadine Bleur was surprised. "The villagers have nothing that could be of use to us."

"What are you saying, friend?" Harpy Duecklenbourg was surprised. "They have men."

At this point, all the women froze. This apparently obvious information fell on them like a thunderbolt that knocks them to the ground, and after plowing and defending, it creates a uniform surface, ready to sow a new idea, from which another change will sprout.

"Maybe it wasn't the pharmaceutical cartels that ruled this country, but the clever priestess."

Noovack was acting amok. She lost her heart. She looked like a person who did not believe her own thoughts.

"And we treated them like fools." Gibbondy just shook her head.

"Why would they do this? From the beginning of the world, our communities have lived in good with each other. You could say that in harmony. Who's interested in what's on the other side?" Asked Monssantoo.

"Then why both countries have an army?" answered the question Bassoon.

"We're holding it for defense. Just in case someone thinks of making us happy with religion. People who believe in fairy tales are incalculable. It is enough for someone wiser to convince them that some god wanted it so." Eva Noovack had been studying old books for some time and now wanted to boast about her conclusions.

"They say they don't have technology. Maybe this is why they want to destroy us from the inside?" Davis asked.

"I don't think so," Noovack said. "They don't care about our technology."

"One of the men who once worked for Rubby said the priestess was said to be greedy. That she is different from her predecessors," said Tatarczyna.

"But she is as old as long we grapple with our problem. It couldn't have been her idea to destroy our society." With her analytical mind, Duecklenbourg, as usual, deprived her colleagues of any illusions about trying to sanction another conspiracy theory.

"Why didn't Clifford try to get along with the priestess and create mixed pairs?" Noovack wondered.

"Because it would be against business," said Duecklenbourg.

"Not only. Religion does not allow them to do so," said Fagot.

"You had to bribe her to change the rules. Davis knew how to do it."

"Maybe Clifford knew more than we did, for example that pairing wouldn't help because the mutation was too advanced and could have more negative effects," Gibbondy said aloud.

"Maybe it's a good thing that Floris has a genetically pure society. Let's go see this priestess," Noovack suggested.

***

Jasmin didn't tell Addam that she was going to make an appointment. "Let him tire a little longer, selfish one," she thought. However, after visiting the office, or rather the waiting room, she realized that the so far difficult to make decision regarding the seemingly trivial procedure to be performed had gone too smoothly and was stopped by the miraculous possibility of abortion. Contrary to appearances, not because it was forbidden to perform. Simply from her favorite marketing point of view, the market equilibrium has been upset, that is, the demand has exceeded the supply. In such a situation, there was nothing else for her to do but to overtake her competitors. So she turned to another, supposedly recognized, gynecologist with a proposal to buy a closer date. The offer was concrete - a hundred entitys for his private working time. He did not accept. He was hiding his conscience. "Fucking conscience? Dogcatcher," she thought. "He will regret it." Two more doctors accredited to perform abortions to regulate gender also refused the offer, though Jasmin doubled the stakes. They did it for fear of losing the possibility of practicing their profession. After all, such a combination would have to be agreed with brown uniforms. Everything could be said about the GCO officers, but not that they would agree to confusion with the timing in the system, especially because of the financial gain. More than once, heads fell for this type of offense. It wasn't worth risking. On the other hand, an abortion performed by a gynecologist who did not have an accreditation was forbidden. Its execution could result in expulsion from the profession and a fine of the amount comparable to the annual income. Jasmin was apprehensive, but one thought pleased her. Good thing she didn't tell Addam that she had decided to undergo surgery after all. Now that she couldn't do it, at least she didn't look like an idiot. She decided that she would continue to look for a solution. She focused only on that goal. At one of the gynecologists she finally found a leaflet with the doctors' groundbaits. In one day, she visited everyone in the first district. Most of them had a full calendar and a few had their offices closed due to loss of accreditation or their being in custody. Apparently, they made a mistake and their ignorance of the law was not taken as a mitigating circumstance. For any offense, they were imprisoned for treason. Only a few doctors remained on the list Jasmin checked. They all had offices in the second district - the slums.

***

The poorer district of Inco looked like a forgotten, fallen city. The buildings were multi-story, but not as tall as downtown. Their facades were not made of glass or sheet metal, the standard building material used in the country. Most often they looked like a collage of whatever, various techniques and materials. It was important to be able to assemble a uniform surface in order to protect the household members against weather conditions and outside noise. And more than once it was really loud in this district. The promenades looked like chattering, sometimes shouting, human scribbles. The communication order that functioned in the first district - where the left side was moved there and the right side back - did not catch on here. Everyone walked as they wanted: from left to right, in a zigzag, in an arc. Keep going, among others. As long as you don't get your clothes on, especially your shoes. The promenades were more like gutters through which dirty, sticky sludge flowed quite often

- a peculiar mixture of sand taken from the third district, rubbish and used, dirty water, sometimes sprinkled with droppings. This has been the case since the people at Inco decided that slurry should be a job for robots. However, they were unable to cope with the service, so the sewage systems were often clogged. To unblock them, boreholes were made. It was an effective method. Unfortunately, instead of reaching the sewage treatment plant, the faeces escaped in small amounts onto the paved platforms. From there, straight to the feet of passers-by. The robots didn't mind the stench, and people got used to it over time.

Conveyor belts, which supported the elderly living in this district, were most often broken. As if someone was deliberately destroying these not very complicated drives by inserting pieces of sheet metal and metal rods between the spokes of their wheels. Clifford didn't like the second quarter. He treated the people living in it like cattle, mobs. As a punishment for being who they are, he did not invest in infrastructure or a more effective garbage or recycling corporation. He hoped that one day the slumers, as they were called, would kill each other.

During each election, none of the inhabitants of this district voted for the Chemist Party, but for a representative of the local community, most often a member of the Labor Party, despite the fact that there was no money behind him and he had no chance of winning. Clifford had no idea that several of the women hidden in the lower echelons of power came from the slums and were silent supporters of the opposition party. Instead, he was convinced that the party was under the control of Rubby and his Ministry of Home Affairs men. Occasionally someone was caught breaking the law and put in jail. Though it was always a show and it was about a hurdle, Clifford felt calmer.

Most of the slums were working-class families, outcasts, and social pathology. More and more often, packs of women living together as families were seen. That they could feel better in their loneliness. Most of them were high all the time, either due to excess medication or upper or cheaper counterfeit drugs. Homosexuality has become the norm among these communities. Besides, in the whole second district no one was surprised to see women walking by the hand or kissing. The fact that they wanted to be happy was appreciated. Nevertheless, when a man walking alone appeared, whether young or older, there was a great risk of being raped. Also, by women who had sex with a friend, sister or other representative of the same sex a moment earlier. Packs were rather grouped by age. If in any of them there were women of, say, two purification, then there was no room for the older one, suppose, one purification. It was an unwritten rule.

There was no symbolic transition from the first to the second district. It appeared to be fluid, although the garda' humaans could distinguish between them to control possible migration, which was customarily forbidden in both directions. However, people had to be careful when moving around, because the border was not easy for them to identify.

It was not known where the better world ended and the worse world began - not counting the difference in air purity that was felt from a distance.

From the first district to the slum, or vice versa, it was possible to enter only in two cases. Either to visit a documented family member or if social status has changed. There were no other options. Unless you were a government official, not even very important. Such someone could do anything. Jasmin knew she could only go on a trip to the second district in the presence of a government official. There was nothing for her to do but persuade Addam, who that day returned from work before noon.

"You must be crazy," he was indignant when he heard about her idea. "It's a dangerous place. Why do you want to go there?"

"To the doctor. There are distant deadlines in the first district. I want to get tested." Jasmin still preferred not to reveal the true purpose of the journey.

"Does anything hurt you?" He asked with concern.

"I met one girl, basically a woman who got tested because she wanted to see how her daughter was developing on the screen. Now this daughter is gone. I have a feeling..."

"Okay. Let's go. It sounds strange to say the least, but I read that pregnant women do like that."

Jasmin reacted with a soft smile. She knew what he meant. She herself felt that right now she was a perfect example of a lack of logic and an unnatural accumulation of mood swings that, to the accompaniment of furious hormones, raged again and again in different directions. After a while, she realized that Addam looked involved. She appreciated.

"Tell me, because it makes me tired, do you have any, even the slightest, affection for our daughters?" She asked in a sad voice.

Addam looked towards the wall as if he wanted to walk through it to the other side and stay outside. He looked distressed.

"I am asking because it bothers me a lot. I'm pregnant for the first time myself and I don't know what to do or what to make of my reactions. Once upon a time I didn't want children, remember?"

"Yes. I was trying to persuade you to have a baby. Then I was thinking about the boy. I was even convinced that you would insist on naming him after your father. I would agree."

"Really? That's nice. You know because I feel that I am carrying in my belly, hmm... that I am carrying a part of you."

"I don't feel anything."

He didn't seem to be telling the truth. He looked away again. She didn't notice it. She was focused on nurturing the feelings she had for him. She didn't want to get rid of them. At that moment, she wanted him to hug her and promised that everything would work out somehow.

"So, when are we going?" He asked, coming down to the ground.

"Tomorrow."

"Too late. Tomorrow I won't be able to go in there anymore. Today is the last time in my work."

"They kicked you out? What are we going to do now?"

"Calm down. All the guys in the whole country aren't allowed to overexert themselves. It's you women to support us, hi hi. Haven't you watched theatremania stuff?"

"No. I was busy. What are you talking about? All? Haenry won't work either?"

"Yes."

"That's good," Jasmin said, and thought of Luicey and her bragging about promotion. "Come on then."

***

Already in the vicinity of the imaginary border between the districts, a patrol of garda's humaans stopped Jasmin and Addam.

"Registration card," came a squeaky voice from one of the robots.

"Why? We don't look like slumers?" Addam joked and obeyed.

The robot read the card and extended a limb towards Jasmin. She slowly handed him the document, looking away.

"Addam Kozllov, age three and a half. You have a blocked account. Please go to the Gender Control Office.

"I remember," said Addam, glancing condescendingly at Jasmin, who just shook her head as if she didn't want him to remind her that it was her fault.

"What are you looking for here?"

"I wanted to show my wife the slums. I can't?"

Jasmin remembered hearing such an excuse before.

"It will be an unforgettable sight, for a lifetime," Addam joked again.

"Can we leave?" Jasmin was impatient.

"When is the return planned?"

"I don't know. Why do you care? Leave us alone." Jasmin turned into a walking bundle of nerves in no time.

"Put your hormones down, Mrs. Kozllov. Your pregnancy is no excuse."

Jasmin was surprised by the last sentence. She hadn't realized robots could bite back like that. "It's probably a newer generation", she thought. She remembered why she had never agreed to buy a robot to hang around her apartment. Precisely because she never trusted them. Addam did not mock her phobias, but felt that if she did not want a helper, she should do the cleaning herself. Humaan of garda wandered away without a word towards another group of passersby, but his words remained in her mind for a long time.

The slums were divided only into even sectors, easy to identify, well described. The name of the doctor they were going to was Dimai Caroliev, who lived in sector three hundred and forty-two. They walked over to the second quarter at the height of sector three hundred and forty-eight. It only took three sectors. Apparently not too far, but it could have ended in different ways. Addam took the paralyzing gas with him, which he did not account for when he said goodbye to his work. The basic equipment of every government official was used in case the public did not understand the power of the government. If that didn't work, Addam could still summon the garda on a communicator that was only active until the end of the day on the public network.

The stench of the slums was unbearable to the residents of the First District, especially to someone as sensitive as Jasmin. All the way she was holding her nose with two fingers of her left hand. She took careful steps. Walking along the dirty promenade, full of various rubbish, she tried not to damage her shoes. It was more the result of natural care for material goods than fear of losing shoes. Before leaving, she and her husband had assumed that all clothes would be thrown away after the trip. Addam walked beside her and held her hand. It was his second visit there. The first time - when he was given the trivial task of receiving questionnaires from one of the leaders of the group carrying out sociological research - while still an intern - he spent a short while there. He didn't even have time to get a look at the people living in the second district. So he was preoccupied with the task. Today he looked around as if he were visiting this place for the first time, as if he had moved to another world. Overturned water containers, overfilled garbage cans, graffiti on the walls and puddles so cloudy that no light was reflected in them made this place extremely hideous.

"That's what it was like when you were little?" He asked.

"I don't remember much," she lied.

Neither the sight nor the smell could be forgotten. Dirt, muck, stench. This is how you could describe the whole second district in three short words. Jasmin remembered very well what life was like there. That is why she fought with such determination never to return there. The slumers wore artificial clothing, had missing teeth, had greasy hair, and had dirty nails. He is rarely mistaken, for the water was there by the weight of the circonium. Their clothes were drenched with a mixture of the pedestrian smell and the passing sweat of several days. That was the norm. As in every community, the slumers also wanted to stand out and, contrary to appearances, it was not about keeping clean. On the contrary. If the smelly dirtiest guy had only a few woven labels on his body, he was treated like someone special. Since there was a fashion to tear a piece of leather and replace it with pieces of plastic, stones or metal plates - which over time grew to form a uniform coating - the word "bigwig" took on a completely different meaning. Twenty percent of the total population was slumers. For ten inhabitants of this giant ring-shaped neighborhood, sometimes affectionately known as the Inco filter, there was one humaan of garda, one emergency service, and two firefighters. There were frequent fires here. To prevent them from moving to the center, they were chemically extinguished with means that destroy the respiratory system. Containers, supplemented with this specificity on an ongoing basis, were present in every sector. They were not all airtight. Some gave off corrosive fumes. They blended in perfectly with the whole, creating a scent that cannot be found anywhere else. Despite the suffocating climate, the inhabitants were able to adapt. They learned to live with the stench in a kind of symbiosis. He did not even interfere with their sports. After all, the whole society, not only the richer first district, strove for health.

Jasmin and Addam went through two sectors. Every now and then, in the crowd of people they passed by, they noticed a funny looking, repetitive scene. Addam aroused undisturbed shame, pure lust among the passing women. It amused him, but Jasmin felt unnecessary jealousy. Though he probably wouldn't be interested in anyone anyway, she hurled thunders at the staring old bags. The women who passed the couple were so focused on Addam that they could see nothing but him. Every now and then one with his mouth open bumped into a lamp or another woman walking in front of him. It looked funny. But there were also pictures of a completely different nature. Every few hundred cubits they passed scrap yards with used androids, usually stored whole, sometimes taken apart. These humanoid-looking machines, when still operational, served in the household or as a substitute for a man. Now they looked like helpless, useless, metal corpses. An elderly woman was kneeling by one of the piles and hugging a broken copy. He had frayed varnish on the top of his head and shoulders, apparently from being petted repeatedly by the old lady. It was difficult to judge whether she treated him like a son or a lover. She must have had some affection for him. It was evident that her eyes were red from crying and she had spent more than an hour in this place.

Another unusual sight to be left in the minds of Jasmin and Addam were women living alone, homeless. Unwanted. Some of them looked frightened, others had maddened eyes. Most hid from strangers in nooks and crannies, or covered just anything to become invisible. They were all unnaturally thin and neglected. The pseudo-boys, or herms, looked similar. Only a handful of the third sex lived in the slums. Jasmin spotted one of them as he poked his head around the corner of the supermarket wall. She heard that the herms were injecting chemical substances under the skin of their faces, which were supposed to prevent anyone from recognizing them. Eventually, distorted, unnatural faces became their calling card. She tugged Addam to make him look, but it was too late. Herm managed to hide.

Word spread quickly about a couple from the first district walking down the promenade. Unwanted company appeared in the next sector as they passed. A dozen or so yards behind Jasmin and Addam were followed by a pack of twenty women, about one and a half purifications old. They looked mean - like slender, unkempt boys - one being the more repulsive. They were led by twin amazons. The one on the left had a shaved head covered with metal studs and a series of scars on a wiry body. In her hand she held a primitive weapon that looked like a piece of metal tube with welded bolts and pins sticking out of it. The second, the one on the right, looked almost identical, but instead of studs on its head, it had a piece of plastic bowl sewn in and covered with leather. It stretched from the forehead to the top of the head. You could recognize the manufacturer's name - "Gummin", although the plastic was already slightly faded. In her hand she carried a steel rebar with an unbonded piece of concrete. This weapon looked like a piece of reinforced concrete torn out alive from a demolished building.

Addam tugged Jasmin's hand and they quickened their pace. The group following them did the same. The pair started to walk even faster, but suddenly another pack appeared around the bend and stood in their way. She was less numerous, but the women looked more muscular and much older, around the age of four to five purifications. At their head stood a black-haired ruler with a sharpened metal file in his right hand. There were several cheap patches on her left forearm, securing a row of unhealed, unevenly shaped glass tabs. One of them was ulcerative, apparently due to inaccurate decontamination. Jasmin and Addam stopped. Terror combined with disorientation showed on their faces. They held hands tightly. They had only a few hundred cubits to their destination, but it seemed that this was where they would end their journey. Both groups looked like self-groomed, trained animals. Addam had read that discontinuing Ray, and especially its substitutes, could make some people more nervous. He didn't feel it himself, but it was clear that something non-obvious and terrifying was happening with these women.

"He's our guy," said the Amazon to the opponents with studs on her head, kissed her sister passionately on the lips and winked at her coquettishly.

"Let's find out," announced the chief of the older pack. "Shit muck," she added contemptuously.

"You wanna fight? There are more of us," replied the one with the plastic sewn in. "Better give up right now, old pus. The guy is ours, you can get this doll."

"Hello, can't you see me here?" Jasmin asked, who had just realized that a kind of market was taking place in front of her eyes.

"Shut up, bitch, no one cares," said the one with the studs.

"We take her, she has a pretty ass," said one of the older women.

"I'm pregnant."

"Fuck," a young Amazon with the insert said bluntly.

"I am this woman's husband and future father. Don't piss me off!" Addam finally tried to show that he had the balls.

"Ha, ha, ha," laughed the studded Amazon. "Like you, I eat for breakfast, and like her my sister picks up the remains from between her teeth."

Jasmin squeezed Addam's hand tighter. He looked at her knowingly, reached into his pocket, and unnoticed he took out his communicator. The Amazon with studs on her head took a few steps towards him. Her sister followed, and then the other members of the younger pack did the same, watching the rival from across the street. Jasmin noticed that Addam had activated a special button on the communicator.

It was a unique version for government officials with several amenities. She knew the feature. She knew the communicator had sent a radio signal to the nearest garda department. All that's left is to stall. Addam tucked the communicator away, but didn't take his hand back, kept it in his pocket.

"Close your eyes and don't breathe," he said in a whisper.

"What?" She was surprised.

"Do it."

When he was sure that his wife's eyelids were closed, he took a deep breath, clogged his mouth, and took out the paralyzing gas. The sight of the applicator brightened the young women. They lunged at him, but he had already released a great black cloud of discipline means. The women began to choke and tear. Then he corrected the destructive work, squirting straight into the faces of those closest to him. The head of the older pack watched with a sly smile as the young six were torn off by an apparently incapable of punching the guy. At this point, out of nowhere, three squads of humaans of guard and emergency services emerged. Several robots cordoned off Jasmin and Addam, the rest overpowered members of the younger pack and some of the older women. Those that managed to escape were hunted down and were quickly caught. All the participants of the incident were shackled with energetic shackles on their arms and legs. The robots unceremoniously tossed them into a glass cage as if they were dealing not with humans but with chunks of chained flesh.

"Thank you," said Addam, turning to one of the most scratched and corroded humaans he had ever seen.

"A registration card, please."

"Of course." Addam handed an identity document.

"You too."

"Again?" Jasmin was surprised, but carried out the order.

"You'll be escorted to the exit. You're not allowed here."

"I'm a government official. We have a business to do," said Addam.

"New directive. Men must not be put in any danger."

"Apparently they've already downloaded something to them." Addam said it in a tone that seemed to explain Jasmin how the new protection system works. He seemed pleased with this turn of events. He smiled and looked puffed up. His behavior only irritated her. She didn't like that trait about him.

"I insist we go where we planned," she said.

"Forbidden. We'll take you straight to the first district." The robot persisted.

"Do something!" Jasmin was furious.

"Forbidden," said Addam carelessly.

She gave up. If he didn't care, why should she care. She did not want to explain what the exact purpose of the visit to the gynecologist was. She looked at the handcuffed women locked in a glass cage. Several of them looked like mannequins smeared with black paint, motionless puppets in strange poses, often with a grimace of pain or rage frozen on their faces. She knew it was the effect of the paralyzing gas. She felt sorry for not only these, but all the women in the world. "It's not their fault," she thought. "It's the system's fault. Today are they, tomorrow me," she kept repeating herself.

"What will happen to them?" She wondered aloud.

"Disposal," the humaan squeaked voice replied.

***

The decision about plural marriage was met with ambiguous reactions. The men, most of them at least, displayed moderate joy combined with incredulity. Women who felt happily married were absolutely unhappy with this turn of events. However, they accounted for a low percentage. Everything else, from girls at the age of one and a half purification to mature women as young as five, exuded unimaginable happiness at the introduction of the new decree. They liked the idea of keeping men a tad less, but that was a detail. What mattered was the chance of a permanent relationship, and perhaps parenthood.

Due to the government decree, Professor Nakamuru should stop working, but Claire Gibbondy pleaded with Noovack for a few exceptions to the rule. Among other things, for him, thanks to which the outstanding geneticist built several project teams that worked on important inventions aimed at increasing the share of men in the entire population. By the way, they were to implement a number of ideas of the new Minister of Health. Nakamuru was ordered to control their progress and analyze the results. Nothing more. One of the experiments devised by Gibbondy was to improve, or actually accelerate, the method of gender recognition. In this way, the Minister of Health wanted to smuggle fertilization control. A team of several dozen people started working on a small handy device that could diagnose fertilization a dozen or so days after sexual intercourse, as well as recognize the child's gender and, if necessary, remove an unimplemented embryo in the uterus, i.e. an unwanted pregnancy. Until now, science has been able to cope with such challenges, but with three independent devices, none of them was portable. The work of a team of engineers and doctors, all women, got the lead out. Gibbondy gave all her ideas, drawings and suggestions. The device was called a "gibbonator" in honor of its originator. In just two weeks, it was ready for presentation in the form of a prototype. It was easy to find a patient who agreed to participate in the experiment.

"When was your last intercourse?" Gibbondy asked, feeling she was witnessing the birth of a new age.

"Two weeks ago, on evening."

"Excellent," said the Minister of Health. "I would like to remind you that you will receive one hundred entitys for participating in our study."

"Thank you."

"Please don't thank me. We will not spare on science and human health."

Gibbondy thought cheerfully. She realized that studying public relations was not in vain. She knew the girl would tell everyone that the Government was protective and that it was worth participating in scientific experiments. Even more so in a safe and successful way like this. Its success will encourage more people to take part in more courageous experiences.

***

The world known in Inco changed day by day. There were more men than women on the promenades at noon. They celebrated idleness. Some regret that they had something else to finish, achieve or prove. But there weren't many of them. Addam and Haenry spent their days in a large shopping mall. With no idea what to do, they even started trying on new clothes and pondering what they would do for the rest of their lives. They were afraid it would be boring, as they were not even allowed to play sports. Fortunately for them, most of the women spent their time at work at this time of the day, so they could feel safe, none of them harassed them.

Jasmin sat alone in the apartment and thought about her fate. She found it still quite bearable compared to the vegetation of slum women. All life in shit. No prospects. Supposedly there are schools in the slums, but what gives knowledge, since each of these women will end up on the production line like mother and grandmother. Even if they try to fight for something and they accidentally get caught, they are punished with death. "No wonder Ray has caught on so well," she assessed. She had already done morning gymnastics, ate a bar and washed it down with water, but still did not know what to do with herself. Her silly friend - that was what she called her when she was offended - was spending time at work. Jasmin didn't know the other women well enough to confide in them or just hang out with them. Loneliness was starting to kill her. She was even ready to go on gossip. At this point, the gong announced that someone was waiting outside the apartment door. It was Luicey. Jasmin was glad to see her this time.

"I quit my job. I have to change something in my life," said her friend.

"What are you talking about? Did you quit?"

"Well, not yet, but I asked for a day off. I think I'll quit tomorrow, for sure. I don't know what to do with myself."

"Welcome to the club. But I would like to work. What about Haenry?"

Luicey cried out. Jasmin walked over to her and stroked her arm tenderly.

"What happened?"

Haenry asked me what is my opinion if he had several wives."

"What? Haenry? Such a cu... clyde? I mean, not a clyde, just... Or maybe he fell in love?"

"He says no. But he sees it as a patriotic duty."

"All guys are the same."

"Addam wants several wives?"

"I would noty agreed."

"You're lucky. You don't have to share your man with other women." Luicey was sobbing like a girl. "I can not work. It all depresses me so much."

Jasmin wondered for a moment what if Addam had thought the same as Haenry. After all, he wouldn't even have to ask for permission. The new law made it possible to marry countless women. No. Addam would certainly not do this to her. Whatever the case, it was essential. By this time, Luicey had completely cried out and looked changed. She even smiled.

"I want a son," she announced. "I read that there are such new methods. A dozen or so days after sex, of course, the more fertile one you know, you go to the doctor. He investigates if there is a pregnancy. If so, it checks the sex of the baby. Do you imagine? From a regular cell. Shock, huh? If it's not the boy, you get rid of the problem right away. Can be done monthly. The study is funded by the state. What do you think about it? Good idea?"

"Is it safe?"

"Of course, everything is safe and legal. I signed up."

Jasmin did not share her friend's enthusiasm. She even felt sorry for the girl. For a moment she thought that Luicey might be her best friend. Although not very prudent. She chased the thought away quickly.

"Imagine my son and one of your daughters will be able to create a wonderful relationship. We'll be mother-in-law, ha, ha," Luicey chuckled, clapping her hands.

"I will have three daughters. Won't this little boy of yours take care all three? The new law allows it," Jasmin joked.

They were laughing hard, but only Luicey was genuinely happy.

***

The prohibition of men from performing any work was difficult to enforce. Many of them were still doing simple household tasks when they did not want to call the robot to, for example, replace a light bulb or a seal in the tap. But it was rare. Most decided that since this is the law, they should not be argued with. The first days were hard for their wives. They couldn't adapt to the new rules. It was even more difficult for women whose husbands immediately wanted another partner. Many male representatives misunderstood the intention in the decree approving polygamy. The government wanted to increase the chances of having boys, and men saw it as a privilege of having several servants with whom they could have sex as much as they wanted. The race for the prettier and younger ones has begun. It lasted for a short time, only to the point that news came out that a certain father of three sons wanted a thousand entitys for a deposit from his future parents-in-law. "If she wanted a husband, let her pay," was a headline in one of the newspapers. Since then, there have been wedding fairs.

Following the passed decrees, the Government introduced a new tariff. The allowance for each adult male was two thousand entitys a month, for a married man two thousand more. For the first son born, you were paid a thousand entitys a month, for the next one and a half thousand. This rate was valid until the boy reached sexual maturity. So if the family had three sons, it would receive four thousand a month for the father and another four thousand for the three boys. You could live a really luxurious life. In turn, the tax for each daughter - regardless of whether she was the first or fifth - was one thousand entitys a month. Due to the fact that families could consist of several wives, women's salaries were made equal. From then on, they could earn no more than two thousand entitys a month. Pregnant women were banned from working, but those bearing a boy in the womb continued to receive their salary, while those expecting girls received nothing. The blockades on future taxes have been lifted for men.

"This government is no different from the previous one. It's even worse," Jasmin judged when Addam communicated the new rules he had read about in the newspaper.

"Be objective. At least they don't lie to us that the drugs are fine. I believe the rules are fair. That we are in shit is another matter."

"Are you defending them?"

"It's not their fault. Do you realize we can't hold on?"

"Relax. Let's count. Ten thousand on your account, twenty-six on mine. Come on, don't say you didn't know. On my mother's account nine. That's forty-five thousand entitys altogether. For the next five months you will receive four thousand. When the girls are born, we'll have sixty-five thousand. Let's say three months after the birth, I'll be able to go back to work. This is..."

"What are you talking about?"

"I hope we have enough money for these fucking taxes. Seventy-seven thousand minus three times three thousand a month is nine. When I go to work, we'll have sixty-eight thousand to start," she said happily. "It's not that bad at all."

"Way to go. Your brain is already fucked up. Where are the costs?"

"What costs?"

"And who will pay for us for the apartment, water, energy and those shitty bars? What when something break?"

Jasmin turned pale. She didn't even notice that she was biting her nails. She had forgotten this involuntary habit long ago, because she felt like its slave. Today the hideous ritual returned with redoubled strength. Jasmin hid her face in her hands. A moment earlier, she was really convinced that it could be managed somehow. She was furious with herself. How could she, the analytical mind, forget the basic monthly fees or the food? And not only because Addam was paying for them. The rent itself, the tax for using Hello rays, water, sewage and all other payments related to the apartment amounted to an average of two thousand entitys per month. Food and drinking water for two almost another thousand. And yet pregnancy will require to increase the nutritional portions of up to four bars a day. It was at this point that Jasmin realized that there was no room in their apartment for three girls. Another shock. "What are we going to do now? Will we have to move to the slums? No. We have to work out something. The bedroom can be converted into a children's room. Great, but it can't be like that forever. And for the start you have to buy three cribs, three layettes" - she thought.

"Addam, where are we going to get the money for all this?" She asked.

"Abort, you stupid woman!"

Chapter 12 Penance

The knowledge that the priests in Floris gained was based on the canon established many generations earlier. It consisted of four main sciences: nature, social psychology, financial management and internal politics. When Ae graduated from the priesthood, she did not act like most of her peers. For some time she had felt uncomfortable as a student. Her exaggerated ego scolded her every time she had to descend to the level of her teachers. She has always despised them. She was just taking advantage of their calling.

When she finished school, the most important and respected teacher, and in fact also the head of the school, was Vishare. He was responsible for the quality of the new fry on behalf of the Church Council. He taught internal politics. He always made sure that each student had a proper view of all the most important matters in the state and that he had a good understanding of the interpretation of sins. He looked pretty good for a priest. Not touched by time, and the poisoning with the sacred venom left its mark on him minimal. He knew Ae's origins and her relationship to the world well. He knew that only through the priesthood could her recalcitrant nature be ensnared. The fusion of rebel and globetrotter genes. Nobody liked her at school. She always surpassed the others with beauty, knowledge and intelligence. She had an extraordinary passion. She liked to write beautifully, which often saved her from the unfavorable evaluation that made itself felt by her opponents. Vishare respected her very much. There were opinions here and there that they were too close to each other. Unjustified. She only diligently used her privileged position over the other students, and he admired her for her sharp mind. Her friends at first sent her to facilitate or arrange something. She didn't like it. She was not eager to help others, so over time they gave up humiliating requests. Even as a young person, she was enterprising.

That day, she sat alone in the break between classes on a medium-sized stone. A well-built but not very handsome young man, a little older than she was, approached her. Before he spoke, she thought it was another attempt to plead with Vishare for something.

"Don't expect a miracle," she said before he approached her.

"How do you know what I want to offer you?" He asked.

"I've heard that a thousand times."

"That you will one day be an important person in the country?"

"No one has called me that yet, but I understand your desperation," she grunted and turned her head.

"I'm not surprised you don't believe me, but I have good news for you." You are graduating soon. In ten Hello sunrise, the venom poisoning ceremony will end differently for you than it does for the others. Maybe then you want to talk to me. That's it."

He turned on his heel and walked away. Ae was completely unconcerned with his words, even belittled them. When the moment of the ceremony came, she was restless. That day, she did not seem like a proud, brave girl. Her whole boisterous demeanor was hidden deep under the penitential, scolding robe that, according to tradition, she donned especially for this occasion. She was walking very slowly towards the courtyard. There, the Church Council was assembled under the leadership of the then High Priest of the Omniearth, a certain Shamanui Ke. The members of the Council were seated on a slightly elevated platform, because from there all gathered, both teachers and students, who were to be poisoned, could be seen. Ae walked over to her seat, checked by eye to see if it fit in the perfect order of the ceremony - if she was standing well enough with everyone else. Vishare looked in her direction. She smiled insincerely at him, pretending to be charismatic at mocking the expected procedure. Everyone was waiting for her. Finally, clad in a bright yellow priestly garment, the Master of Ceremonies could begin to do the honors. One of the students assisting him brought a tray of syringes. There were exactly twenty of them, the same number of candidates for the priesthood. This student was the young man Ae had met a few days earlier. He smiled at her, bowed low to the crowd, and handed the tray to the Master of Ceremonies. The priest took the first syringe and motioned for the candidate first from the left. They stood facing each other. The Master of Ceremonies stuck the needle straight into his neck and squeezed out the entire contents of the syringe. The candidate immediately fainted. This incident caused only a slight stir, after all, everyone knew that the procedure always ended the same. Two lower-level priests, looking like soldiers, carried the body of the fainted candidate. Then the situation repeated itself with other students. Last was Ae. When the Master of Ceremonies took the syringe in his hand, the apprentice did not wait to be called. She went to the middle of the square herself and set her neck a bit closer than the others. The gesture amused the Council. The Master of Ceremonies quickly inserted the needle and squeezed all the contents out of the syringe. Ae fought her way out for a moment by squinting, but it didn't last long. Suddenly her head dropped to her left shoulder and stopped motionless. Ae fell to the ground.

They took her to a dark and cold room. Only because the cold helps with suffering. She lay motionless next to the others. They doubled up in pain. They cried, rubbed their skin, rubbed their bellies. After a while, one of the new priests began to defecate, screaming unbearably. Another felt like vomiting. He jerked as if someone wanted to tear a piece of his stomach out and expel it through an opening in his esophagus. After a while, almost all of them screamed out loud. It looked like a mass grave.

Ae didn't feel alike. She had chest pains but no other symptoms. When she saw that one of the priestesses was leaking blood mixed with mucus from her eyes, she looked away. She felt like she was under torture, but only for her eyes, not for her body. After a few days, the Master of Ceremonies entered the room. He was wearing a mask to protect against the foul stench. The priests who had been locked in the room for several days did not bother the stench at all, but for outsiders it was unbearable. The Master of Ceremonies made a cursory examination of the unfortunates. The first reaction to the poisoning of the sacred venom was behind them. Some even mentioned the need for food. As for the conditions in which they had to stay, it was quite a strange request. The next step was to wash the wounds. For this purpose, everyone was led to the great bathhouse. Only there - when the eyes got used to the light - could they see their new bodies. Flaky skin, abscesses all over her body, and her blurry eyes looked terrifying. A few days without water and food also did their job. Ae looked completely different. She was just hungry, emaciated, thirsty and cold. She was the only one to be released immediately after washing her body. As she ate her first meal - or, in fact, she stuffed herself - the Master of the Ceremonies was watching her. He was clearly surprised.

After a few days, she met this young man, who prophesied that only she would feel different poisoned by the sacred venom.

"What is this witchcraft?" She asked.

"It's not witchcraft, it's science," he replied.

"Can science change the composition of the sacred venom?"

"You can replace it with something that looks identical, works similarly, but the consequences are not so deplorable."

"Where did you learn it?"

"You won't believe me anyway. Just accept that you have friends to protect you and your future."

"You're talking about yourself?"

"Ha ha. No. I have no such authority. I am commissioned by someone much more powerful."

"Act for me and you will not regret it."

"I was just talking about you. My name is Jusif. I can help you achieve a lot. You just have to trust me."

"I don't need anything," she said.

After a while, however, she realized that she should take a closer look at this new friendship.

"My name is Ae."

She shook hands with him, feeling that she would never forget that day for the rest of her life.

***

The High Priestess of the Omniearth summoned Zenit. He was glad to meet his mistress, whom he did not see for several days.

"Tell me, my friend, how long have we known each other?" She asked.

"Why are you asking, lady? You know it. All right. I see. We know each other for two purifications. Back from the time when you were a fledgling priestess. You've been poisoned a few hello sunrises after me."

"Why does the chief of my guard, whom I know of two purifications and whom I trust, not inform me about what is happening in my country?"

"I don't understand, lady," said Zenit.

"A man disappears and no one knows what happened to him."

"Is this about that merchant, Jusif?"

Ae was gone to a burton when she heard what the ordinary - in her mind - guardian called her true friend. Until recently, this "merchant" was the only person she really trusted.

"Forgive me, lady, but it didn't seem so important to me. Of course, we will be happy to do your research. Give us some time."

"What else is keeping you here? You have a job. Do it. Find him!" She finally shouted.

Zenit, fearing the wrath of the High Priestess of the Omniearth, immediately departed. Haris was another person she planned to question about Jusif's disappearance. But she was going to have a completely different conversation with him. When he arrived at her chamber, he was surprised that she had received him while eating, with no witnesses at all.

"I would have offered you, but I know you will refuse anyway," she began the conversation.

"You know, my lady that I have tasted your food many times? It always ended up exactly the same. Still, I tried again. As if I were forgetting the pains that digestion of real food caused."

"What made you try again?"

"Smell. It's very tempting and... it causes a strange reaction in my body. When I smell your meals, not all of them, saliva rushes to my mouth. My stomach signals the need for satiety."

"Nothing unusual. The food is very enjoyable. What a pity you had switched to those bars of yours."

"It's healthier this way."

"Seriously? But if you changed your mind... Never mind. Tomorrow you are going to Vatili Soll. It's close to here. A day's journey towards the eastern quarter. I would like to ask if everything is as agreed. Did I deliver what you expected of me?"

"Not me. It was the Prime Minister's request. But yes. It couldn't have been better."

"So can you enlighten me how it happened that the High Priestess of the Omniearth did what the ordinary assistant asked for? Even for his superior."

The admission made him laugh. He sighed slightly and smiled at her.

"Maybe because she wanted to be seduced?"

"Nonsense!" She was indignant. "I am a woman of the cloth. I am replacing the goddess."

"Of course," he replied quickly with a slight irony in his voice. "Or maybe because this assistant knew the truth about your divinity and where it came from?"

"Apparently that's what Patri wanted."

"Of course. And did Patri also want your friend to buy votes or blackmail members of the Council to make an ordinary girl the High Priestess of the Omniearth?"

Ae looked proudly at him, though thoughts of disgraceful punishment flashed through her mind.

"Wasn't it a coincidence that you jumped one career level and became a high-level priest right after your military training?"

"There have been cases before when a priest had an outstanding talent for winning over elders."

"Of course. But if you add another incident to that, such as the death of your predecessor, a little Hello sunrises after being sworn in, would it still be a coincidence?"

"Vishare died of a sick heart," she said indignantly.

"Good one, ha, ha." A sneering smirk appeared on Haris's face.

Ae agreed with most of the accusations, but about the death of a respected priest like Vishare, she never knew the truth. She had so many questions for Jusif, and the ground swallowed him up. She wanted to ask Haris even more questions, but she lacked the courage. Fortunately for her, Haris was not your typical spy whose goal was to keep his mouth shut. He was a clever but still normal assistant. His strong need to dominate his interlocutor forced him to reveal new secrets. However, he preferred to draw down the information he had and slowly feed on her fears. She was teasing him on purpose. The deal suited her.

"Vishare was poisoned with a certain specificity. We prepared it for Jusif," he said. "It is nothing more than a chemical that can stop the heart and at the same time completely poisons the brain of the victim. Just in case. It does not cause other symptoms, so you diagnosed what we wanted. We were sure you wouldn't mess with his head."

"So Jusif worked for you?"

"I thought you already knew that."

"What happened to him?"

"I do not know. Here he lost face. He probably hid.

"He at least learned to eat our meals," she joked as she left, but Haris did not understand her mockery.

Again, Ae had no desire to argue any further with this hopelessly boastful bastard. What she wanted to find out, he told her himself. The conclusions only knocked her out. She trusted Jusif, treated him like her own man. Especially when she was sending him out to spy. Now it turned out that he was a double agent. When they started working together, she had the feeling that someone was watching over her and that is why they sent this man. She thought it was one of the council members, such as Vishare. Perhaps he helped her in her career because he saw her as an ally. In time, she forgot about this thought and believed that Jusif was actually only working for her. She never suspected him of treason. She was convinced many times that he even had a crush on her. Also when he brought her lovers. Secretly.

***

The old man's house was not actually closed. As Fahid got within a few steps, he already knew why. No bolts or anything to keep you safe and private. The door was swinging, but surely no potential thug would want to touch it. They looked like the door to a wretched outhouse. There was a suffocating, sewing stench from the house. "Who is the owner of this extraordinary house?" Fahid wondered. He did not want to go inside, but knew he could not take the crossbow out of its hiding place directly in the yard. Someone else would see and be in serious trouble. The need to learn to shoot quickly turned out to be stronger than the stench. He pushed one of the wings with his shoe, but unfortunately it quickly returned to its place. To slip inside, he had to hold the door to keep it from swinging. For this purpose, he used a piece of stick lying in front of the house.

It was even worse inside. Fahid was holding back the vomiting. He went through the various rooms, but found no one. He decided to go out immediately and wait outside. He approached the okurai, but the animal snorted in disapproval at the smell that had been brought on his clothes. After a long moment, Fahid saw in the distance his old man approaching him. He was completely bald and his face was scarred. He was walking with a heavy metal cane. In fact, he trotted as if every step hurt him. As he approached, Fahid noticed that the old man did not have a right hand. He also quickly felt that his dirty clothes were soaked with a stench. He had long fingernails and toenails black with dirt. His feet, clad in leather sandals, showed peeling layers of mud.

"What are you looking for?" The old man asked, casting an unpleasant look.

"I'm looking for someone who can teach me how to shoot a crossbow, but I don't know if I am at the right place," Fahid said, looking at the sleeve hanging down, empty from the shoulder.

"What is a crossbow?" He asked hesitantly, handless, although it was obvious that he could not lie.

"Show you?" Fahid began to remove a bundle casually attached to the okurai harness.

"Leave. You can get a hit for just watching. Why do you need this skill? Who has got into you?"

Fahid hesitated to answer. The old, smelly, armless man did not inspire confidence. Even his suspicious appearance promised trouble. But time passed relentlessly.

"My daughter has been kidnapped."

"That's what priests are for. Report this incident to Kadu. This is his districtm" said the old man. It was evident that just saying the priest's name had caused him a rather unfriendly memory.

"He wouldn't help."

"Kadu is an extremely inept idiot and drunk, but behind him is power."

Fahid felt that he had met an ally. That maybe he could confide in him, but he didn't have time to waste.

"Can you explain me how to use the crossbow? Please. I have to save my daughter."

"Show."

"Here? You just said..."

"I know what I was saying."

Fahid hastily removed the crossbow from the bundle and handed it to the old man. It was evident that the man knew the weapon well and knew how to handle it, even without one hand. He grabbed hold of it and glanced at Fahid urgently. Only after this glance did Fahid remind himself of the small contraptions that are inherent in this weapon. He took out poison darts. The older man put the crossbow between his legs, and with his hand placed one of the arrows in the grooved track and pulled the string. He grabbed the crossbow with his hand again. He aimed at the door of his house and fired confidently. Fahid was charmed.

"Now you," said the smelly man.

The student did the same as the teacher, using both hands, but missed the door and hit the wall.

"You gotta hold it tighter. The crossbow cannot move. Remember, the door is motionless and man can escape."

"How do you know I want to attack a human?"

The smelly man without an arm just snorted. Fahid shot again. This time he hit the door. He smiled as if waiting for applause. His teacher didn't budge.

"You have a talent. Five gray stones for learning," he said.

Fahid hesitated, but then paid. Overall, he was satisfied with the service, but decided that it was not right to end the acquaintanceship in this way.

"What do they call you?" He asked.

"I'm from the eastern quarter. On our site, such a question would be taken as a tactless question. I'm not asking you what your name is, anyway I'm not interested in it."

"From the east? You don't look edgy."

"Well, what's weird about that?"

Fahid had just realized that all the stories his father had been telling him, and then he was telling his children, could have been trumped up. Not only the one about edgy, savages or blowguns. He was ashamed. He put the crossbow in its wrapping bag, mounted the Okurai, and drove off towards the Patrix. For a long moment he could feel the remnants of the smell of the old man's house escaping from his clothes. Thanks to them, incomprehensible thoughts swirled in his head. He wondered what indiscretion he had shown to the old grandfather, who he was, why he didn't mind the stench, and why he didn't have a hand. The use of weapons in Floris was prohibited. Possession punished. Only the authorities, priests, in fact, were allowed to use it. Was the old man one of them? He had no hair or stubble, but he looked nothing like Kadu in appearance. He was much more neglected. He did not look like a calling card for the only righteous religion, but rather like a social outcast.

***

The settlement of Vatili Soll, where representatives of the Inco Government were to settle, looked poor. Due to the arrival of immigrants, Ae ordered the resettlement of the inhabitants living in it, as well as all from the area. She wanted as few people as possible to know about the guests' stay. Barney Clifford underestimated the help given. He felt like a prisoner sentenced to stay in the worst crap in the world. Despite the fact that the house where he lived with his wife, son and brother was quite well-kept, the Prime Minister of the Government of a country where cleanliness was a national obsession rated it as the worst pigsty. He had heard from Haris that the people of Floris were not using Hello rays. He understood that they did not need them for theater or robotics, but so as not to use them for obvious solutions, such as lighting the house at night? He couldn't comprehend that. He ordered to take from Inco several dozen portable power generators that generate and accumulate energy from Hello rays and simple light wells in batteries.

Rubby and his wife lived in a smaller house next door. They were not so picky, they even liked it. The other ministers and their families took over the next houses. Haris and several of the prime minister's bodyguards lived in a small hut on the edge of the settlement. The whole was surrounded by a cordon of guards guarding this place during the day and at night. Nobody could get outside or inside the settlement. Ae's command was clear cut. The guests had to be provided with the so-called comprehensive care. And by the way, collect the payment for their stay immediately. On the same evening, when a group of immigrants reached the settlement, the most technically gifted priests appeared. They set up a small camp consisting of several four-person yurts, where they arranged their lairs, as well as a handy workshop and a place to study. Goeffrey was slightly surprised by this turn of events. According to his brother's decision, he would rather not rush to pass on knowledge. In case Ae judged that there was no need for further education, and thus wanted to shorten the Government's stay in exile. The technical priests, however, were able to effectively force the training to begin immediately.

"Gentlemen," Goeffrey began the next morning. "We should start with the basics. Hello energy has great power. It can give life, but can also take it away if not handled properly. It moves thanks to the waves."

At that moment, he noticed that most of the priests' faces showed grimaces of mixed dullness with unimaginable surprise. As if they completely didn't understand what he was talking about. He just thought that his brother shouldn't be worried about the speed at which he learned. Apparently, it will take a long time to learn. Perhaps they will never be able to convey the promised knowledge and technology.

"Can you show us these waves?" The most inquisitive asked.

"Waves of energy cannot be shown without special devices, which we do not have here. At Inco, we have hundreds of thousands of different useful machines. I couldn't take them all. I am going to show you how these waves work. Practical learning is always the most effective."

Goeffrey launched one of the machines. It was a foundation drill rig. He set the energy intake panel towards the shining star and after a while you could see the device, drawing its power from Hello, accelerating the dry drill in the air. Finally he put them to the ground. A moment was enough. The drill rig drilled a hole almost one cubit in diameter and several cubits deep. The priests appreciated this thoroughly effective device. Until now, they had only seen a few agricultural machines in action. They acted slowly and inaccurately.

***

Contrary to what Goeffrey thought of them, the priests were by no means ignorant. They lacked the basics, but learned quickly. They were constantly hungry for her. What surprised him most was that they could explain all the truths he told them in a way they knew. Different, but not worse.

Also logical, albeit primitive. He appreciated the simplicity of their way of thinking. He decided to share his discovery with his brother during an evening family conversation.

"Don't be kidding," Barney replied. "They may be intelligent, but the knowledge they have has stuck to the fifth era."

"I would not underestimate their commitment and passion. In their own way, they are aware of the rules of life. This must not be underestimated," worried Goeffrey.

"Then why have they not even electrified the capital so far?"

"Because they see it all differently. According to their belief, Hello rays help plants and animals to grow, not to mention humans. But going back to plants, for example, the point is this: for a plant to grow, it needs Hello rays."

"Obvious."

"Wait, now it's more important. They explained to me that it was about movement, wandering, something like an energy exchange. Because these rays accumulate in plants. When animals or humans eat them, energy reaches them. When a plant dies, the Hello rays go with it to the ground and help other plants grow. If we burn such a plant, the energy contained in it will emit heat and light that will return to the star. That is why they burn torches and fires everywhere to give Hello, what is its. So Patri ordered them. Besides, according to the priests, since the flame is glowing and hot, it works like a mini-Hello, not in the sky, but on the Universe. Why waste the rays coming directly from the star, which are needed for cultivation or development, when the earth will sooner or later give up what it took?"

"It's too complicated. Why confuse so much?" Barney snapped.

At this point, Haris and Rubby arrived at the Clifford household. Barney was surprised at the late visit, but after a while he waved his wife, brother and son away, just in case.

"What's up, gentlemen?" He asked after making sure no one was interrupting the conversation.

"A new government has been formed in Inco. Eva Noovack became Prime Minister," Rubby said.

"What? She?" Clifford held his head. "How it's possible? Didn't you know he was up to something?" He turned to Rubby.

"Like every director, she was checked out many times. All I remember is that she got divorced and then remarried to the same man. I don't know anything else that might seem suspicious. We just found out that the day after the hackers' attack on theatremania, she left the Chemists Party, but that day came a lot of denunciations."

"Did she know about the Black Hands?" Clifford asked.

Rubby thought for a moment. He was obviously surprised by the question.

"I do not think so. No. Certainly not." Rubby writhed like an eel.

"It's good that we are quite close to the border." Haris had saved him, shrugging off Clifford's interest. "Here comes the messenger network. My trusted man told me that there was an award for our heads. Quite a lot. The return begins to fade away," he said.

"On the contrary. With each passing day, Noovack will grow stronger. We need to get back sooner than planned to pick up what's ours," Barney Clifford decided.

"Is that really a good idea? We're safe here," said Haris.

"What's this bullshit? It is only because we have the priestess in hand that we are still alive. This whole miserable Council of Fools would love to slaughter us."

"To be honest, sooner or later Ae will not forgive us that she had to bend. I believe her first visit here will be a wake-up call. Now she still feels insecure, but nothing lasts forever." Rubby looked sullen.

"Where did this conclusion come from?" Clifford asked anxiously.

"We know everything about her. We had several of ours in her palace."

"How did we have it? I guess not everyone hid like that coward Jusif? And what is this priest of ours called?" Clifford asked, surprised.

"His name is Rados, but he's completely useless. Ae doesn't trust him, he is in her's bad books regularly."

***

Zenit was exceptionally very concerned. Not like the boss of the Purple Watch. It was enough to look straight into his normally calm face to understand that he was worried about a problem of great importance. His eyes were wide that day. He did not walk very quickly to meet the High Priestess of the Omniearth. He delayed the transmission of uncomfortable information in time. Ae had been waiting for him for a long time. She wasn't even impatient anymore, her irritation was gone. Her head was busy with memories. He knocked timidly and briefly.

"Come on in."

"Hello, lady." Zenit bowed low and respectfully as usual.

"I've waited a long time so you don't have to rush to answer," she said with a slight irony, watching his nervous demeanor surreptitiously.

"Forgive me, my lady. I preferred to make sure that the information I had to give you could be true."

"So?"

"The unexpected death of Pirna led us to her relatives. It turned out that they were all dead. When they were burned alive in their own backyard, a man was spotted looking like a crafty merchant in the neighborhood. We have his assistant under guard. He knows a lot. He admitted it was Jusif's doing."

Ae froze. She licked her chapped lips and swallowed hard.

"Bring him."

"If you permit, my lady, I will do it the day after tomorrow. He is currently being questioned."

"Is this a mockery or a dream?" Ae said indignantly.

"No, my lady, we'll bring him back at the end of the procedure."

"I set the procedures!"

"I refuse. The procedure was established three eras ago. It is holy and no one can change it on their own. Only the Council can do that. This is what the canon says."

Ae took a deep breath and exhaled quickly.

"What's this man's name?" She asked in a calmer tone.

"And here's a curiosity. He claims Haris Sagavara."

"What?"

"He's not as wiry as that one. He is, you might say, stocky. He definitely comes from here, not from Inco. No, he doesn't look like he has anything to do with their eating."

"Is it the convergence of surname?"

"I do not think so. When he introduced himself, he watched my reaction. I tried not to show my surprise, but maybe my body betrayed me. I'm not sure."

"Can you at least tell me what you learned from him?"

"Yes. He said Jusif was an Inco spy."

Ae closed her eyes and began to breathe through her nose.

"He also said Jusif is dead. That he was killed on your behalf."

"What? This is ridiculous," Ae said indignantly.

"It seemed unbelievable to me too. We explain the revelations of the new Haris Sagavara."

"Who's in charge?"

"Me. I'm not admitting anyone."

"Okay. I'm curious about your report. Now get back to your duties."

Zenit nodded and left, unsteady, restless. When he left the room, he breathed a sigh of relief. He was aware that this was not the end of his troubles, but he felt glad that he had emerged unscathed from this difficult conversation. He passed Kifor just outside the door. The priest was nervous, he looked like he was eavesdropping. They exchanged cold looks.

"I report that recruitment is proceeding as planned, Lady," said Kifor, entering the priestess's chamber.

Ae didn't react. Her thoughts were elsewhere entirely. She wondered who the other Haris was, and if the former was real or was he just pretending to be someone. It was another person who knew too much. "In a moment, the whole country will rustle," thought the priestess.

***

Once Floris was well marked, but nobody cared for wooden, directional signs with images of specific cities, settlements or regions, so over time they faded or dried up in the wind. Fahid would have had no chance of chasing the soulless three priests escorting his daughter if he had relied only on them. At some crossroads, he had to be careful to decide which way to go. It was easier at night. It was enough to observe the sky, and more precisely the directions marked by the visible moons - this method was known even to the illiterate Florians. During the day, Fahid had to listen to his intuition sometimes. All he knew was that, after passing the village of Litrijis, he should head towards the spiritual capital of the country. Patrix was just below the summit of Mount Saandreal. He was tired of the journey, but he knew he couldn't waste a moment. Though he had no hunting experience, his determination to free his daughter from the clutches of the Church only gave him energy. Nor could he read the tracks. Besides, he was moving in unknown territory. Besides, he hadn't traveled anywhere all his life. He was farthest in Litrijis. And that's all. He knew the city of Hambarra a little, but only from his father's stories, which could turn out to be untrue. Every other corner was a completely new discovery for him. In the area where he lived, all the farmers cultivated dirshna for profit. Purple puke vegetables and several species of fruit grown only for their own needs grew in their home gardens. Not for trade. They diversified the diet. Fahid realized that the huge field full of shrubs he was just passing was growing a plant called mao. Its grains were used to make flour, so useful in every farm. He had never seen her live before. He was amazed by the vastness of the navy blue color of the stems and leaves, the wide webs of fine-meshed protective nets, and every bit stuck into the ground, the awkward-looking fear of kripi birds. These little creatures, although they looked like friendly butterflies, could be extremely mean. When whole herds covered a large part of the mao field, they would devour virtually any grain in the blink of an eye. They were caught in the net and stripped of the wings, which, after drying, served as a snack.

Fahid reached the great bay separating the individual plots. He noticed that the path he was taking had changed direction. As if it entangled farmland, it meandered between individual areas. What a waste of space, he thought, and then in the distance he saw the recently extinguished fire. He drove up quickly to see if it was a coincidence or a stroke of luck. A faint smoke was emanating from the still warm hearth. He did not have to be a seasoned investigator to find out that the crumbs and leftover food left behind signaled someone's stoppage. Fahid decided to take advantage of the decreasing distance between them and accelerated.

It didn't take him long to get close enough to recognize a familiar voice. It was Sumi. She sang a wistful Sundra song, and the echo between the hills only heightened her sad character.

"Shut up at last!" Hara shouted.

"Leave her alone," Kadu defended the girl.

Sumi continued to sing, as if on purpose her voice was getting louder. It pleased Fahid. He felt another burst of energy again. Now he was sure his daughter was a brave girl. It is even worth going to the end of the world for her. But don't get killed. "It must be done wisely", thought the farmer. He hoped that by using surprise he could incapacitate one of the people. But then any of the others would have hurt him immediately. Not only him, Sumi was also in danger. He didn't feel like a skilled crossbowman, so there was no question of overpowering all three of the hijackers. He decided to wait for another stop and kidnap his daughter under cover of night. Nothing else came to his mind. Several back-up plans appeared, but all of them seemed too naïve or impossible to implement. One thing was certain: the crossbow made him feel more confident. He followed them at a safe distance for hours. When he forgot what he was doing it for, he would sometimes pay attention to the passing landscape. Sometimes he was even delighted with something.

After passing the sea of navy blue fields with shrubs, Mao Kadu and his team reached the top of a great green plateau, from which the Asaran Gorge could be seen on the horizon. They were close to Patrix. Fortunately, too far to make it before dusk. As soon as they left Litrijis, the okurai Hara was riding hirpled and therefore they drove slower, making stops every now and then. Fahid, who was driving behind them, could no longer delay the action of retrieving his daughter. Fortunately for him, Kadu ordered the camp to be set up. Fahid hid in the bushes and put a hood over his head just in case. This was a proven way to keep the animal from making any noises.

It was not worth lighting the evening fire. This time, Kadu and the two women escorting Sumi decided that they would eat cold food and not pray in the presence of the girl. Before they could eat a piece of tine meat, bite it with a pie and wash it down with whatever you like, it turned gray. The clearing where they stopped was lit by the first of the visible moons, so there was no need to light a torch. Kadu hid under the cart and covered himself with the bedspread. He was tired and sleepy. Hara rested her back against the tree and closed her eyes. She knew she needed to sleep shortly and intensely. After midnight, which is two hours, Nate would wake her up. They will have to change on duty. The gentle sounds of the fauna put her to sleep quickly. She learned this from many of the battle practices that Ling Gui organized. After a while, Kadu began to snore. Nate just shook her head in disbelief and kicked him in the leg.

"Quieter, or you'll wake the sahadi," she said in a whisper.

Kadu kissed childishly and rolled over. Fahid did not anticipate that the group would put up a sentry. He thought he would just steal his daughter quietly while everyone was asleep. He struggled for a moment as to what to do. Slowly, almost noiselessly, he took the crossbow from the bundle, placed the arrow in a trembling hand and pulled the string. The weapon was ready to kill the sentry. It was enough to aim well. Wish it were that simple. After all, the crossbow was kept by a freshly baked shooter, an empathetic farmer with no criminal practice. A good man, not a murderer. Fahid glanced at his daughter. She sat curled up with her eyes fixed on the sky. At this point, three of the four visible moons have already formed one line, the so-called co-moon. It made it even brighter. The sky was cloudless. Windless weather. You might think it is idyllic. Fahid aimed straight at Nate's chest. He wanted to be sure he would hit. He knew he only had one shot. He took a deep breath and held the air in his lungs. He released the string and sighed. The dart glided towards the sentry, but missed her body. She slapped it right in the face, tearing her cheek. Nate gave a short groan and dropped quickly to the ground. Hara heard both the whistle and the soft sound of her companion's falling body. She stood up immediately, carefully looking around. She sent an evil glare in the direction of Sumi. The girl had just realized what had happened and put her hands over her eyes as if she did not want to see the carcass. Hara walked over to Nate's body to see if she was breathing. The poison dart did its job. There was a quick and painless death. Only the look of a torn cheek showed that something terrible had happened. Besides, there was nothing to be seen that was in the slightest suspicion. Kadu was still fast asleep. Fahid raised his eyes to the sky and prayed briefly in his mind. He forgot not to do it again, but his thoughts told him the solution itself. He did it instinctively, as he always did when he had to kill an animal and then cut its body into pieces of thoughtful size for consumption. He realized, however, that it was not an animal, but a man from whom he had just taken a precious life, in order to improve the existence of another man, his daughter. At this point, Hara crept up to Kadu. She tugged at his garment.

"Get up," she said in a whisper.

"It's morning already?" He was surprised.

Hara motioned for him not to speak. She pointed to Nate's lying body. Kadu rubbed his eyes as if he didn't believe what had happened. At that moment, Fahid's arrow hit Hara right in the broad back. She growled like a slaughtered animal and slumped to the ground. Kadu froze. He glanced at Sumi as if he thought it was a little girl who had done something so terrible. He hid deeper, bowed his head.

"Did you see who did this?" He asked.

"No."

"Get down."

Sumi, shivering, immediately lay flat on the wagon's landing. Kadu tilted his head slightly, but could see nothing. He became impatient.

"Who are you and what do you want from us?" He asked finally.

"Let Sumi out, and you'll survive."

"Dad, is that you?" The girl whispered.

The priest realized who had committed the crime. The only question was whether the murderer was alone or had any support. More like the latter, he thought. After all, Fahid was just a simple farmer. He had no weapons or skills.

"Fahid, don't be silly. Ae will never forgive you that," said Kadu. "Let's get along."

"I said, let my daughter go, you will be okay." Fahid's voice was very convincing. Different than usual.

Kadu slowly leaned out from under the cart and, with his head still hunched, stood behind one of the animals. He looked around nervously but alertly. He loosened the bonds with which Sumi's leg was attached to the goat.

"She is free," confirmed Kadu.

The girl stepped down from the wagon onto the carpet of radda herb growing in this place. She took a few steps in the direction of her father's voice. Fahid leaned out from behind the bushes, still holding his crossbow pointed straight at the priest's heart. Kadu was amazed at the sight.

"Sumi, come closer," father said.

At this point, Kadu grabbed the little girl and made her a living shield while pressing a small knife against her neck.

"She's not going anywhere. Give back the crossbow."

Fahid's face grimaced. He wondered what he should do. After a while, he took a few steps towards his daughter and the priest.

"Stop!" Kadu shouted. "Throw the crossbow. Over there." He nodded at a cluster of bushes.

Fahid hesitated, but eventually did what the priest expected, as instructed by him.

"Now turn around and walk away."

"Dad," Sumi said sadly, but Kadu pressed the blade tighter against her neck.

"You will answer to the High Priestess of the Omniearth. You killed two female warriors with a forbidden weapon."

"Does the priestess know what you did to my father's body?" Fahid asked.

Kadu swallowed hard. The words surprised him, taking away his confidence. His hand with the knife slipped slightly. After a while he corrected her, but then Sumi started singing a cheerful melody that sounded like an appeal.

"Be silent!" Kadu shouted.

She wasn't going to stop. The priest tugged at her and turned to face him, then covered her mouth with his open palm lightly tapping. She broke away. Fahid turned on his heel and ran as fast as he could towards them. During this time, Kadu managed to lightly scratch the knife in the girl's thigh. Fahid snatched the weapon from him and stabbed him in the throat with fierce determination several times. Streams of blood poured out immediately. The scream of a terrified girl scared the animals. They were restless - they gasped with dissatisfaction for a long moment. Sumi jumped aside and turned her head. After a while she realized what had happened. Her wonderful father, who never hurt anyone, had just killed three people, not to say a personage: a priest from their district and two female warriors. "What happens now?" - she wondered.

Fahid wasn't going to think too long.

"We have to burn them or bury them so that there are no traces."

"What are we going to do now?"

"I'll take you to Hambarra. I promised and I will keep my word."

Sumi was stunned and confused. She glanced at the wound on the leg. It was only a slight scratch, not worthy of a dressing. Fahid looked at the three dead bodies. He already knew that he would dream of seeing them for the rest of his life, but decided that he had done the right thing. Even if Kadu released his daughter, he would return well-armed and obey the orders of the High Priestess of the Omniearth. The problem had to be resolved promptly, definitively and without risk.

"Goodbye, Kadu. You don't deserve Asaran."

The farmer grasped Hara's swordfish with both hands and began to ineptly dig a hole with it. It was the only tool suitable for making a hole in the ground. Sumi could not find a place for a long time. All the time she could see the image of her father stabbing a priest right in the neck. There was blood everywhere. On the ground, on the body of the priest, and even on her clothes. It was a horrible sight, like from a bad dream. At this point, the farmer lifted the larger turf and a pit hidden beneath the ground appeared before his eyes. He quickly moved to a safe distance and with interest, stretching his hand as far as possible, tried to clear away individual clods of earth with his swordtopor. At this point, a small sahadi lizard jumped out of the cavity. He was irritable and confused. It was only three cubits long, six pairs of short, agile legs, and slick skin covered with fine scales. His teeth were quite small and sparse. Spade claws looked much more dangerous, as this creature was able to efficiently and quickly dig deep into the ground. Fahid had heard tales of these creatures many times, but had never seen them live. All he knew was that they were blind, had perfect hearing and smell, and had a hard, hard-to-cut spine. There was no need to mess with them. Sumi took two steps, not very cautious, and at that moment the lizard started sharply towards her. She jumped back nervously. Fahid, in defense of his daughter, hit him with his sword with all his strength, but the weapon only slipped on the skin. Dizzy reptile only for a moment. Father grabbed Sumi's hand and dragged her to his former hideout. Sahadi turned his head towards them and stood motionless. After a while, two more lizards emerged from the burrow. One almost twice the size of the former and one tiny. It looked as if it had just hatched from an egg. He was funny in his awkwardness and childish curiosity. He became interested in the Kadu blood, which had almost congealed. He began to lick her relishly, munching loudly. It was sticky like the liniment of a dirshna. Sumi felt a little disgusted. Fahid was not going to be devoured by predatory reptiles. In a hurry, he removed the hood from the okurai's head and adjusted the harness. At that moment, the animal felt the presence of lizards and began to behave restlessly. When her father helped Sumi up on his back, she was distracted. With apprehension and curiosity, she continued to glance at the sahadi family every now and then. But when the largest lizard bit off Kadu's hand, she groaned in fear and covered her eyes with her hands.

"Are you getting in or not?" Fahid was nervous.

The hitherto gentle tone of the father's speech, unbearable, frightened the girl. She quickly climbed onto the back of the okurai and glanced again at the lizards, who were now chewing off more pieces of Kadu's body. Sumi closed her eyes. Her father sat down behind her, then yanked the animal by the ears. It snickered slightly and began to slowly make its way back to Litrijis. The night was quite clear. The road, lit by the moons, made the journey easier. Fahid forgot that until recently he was terribly tired. He wanted to leave that place as soon as possible.

Chapter 13 Impasse

Noovack wondered for a long time who to send the message to Floris. The task seemed obvious: it was necessary to persuade the monarch of another country to come for a visit at the invitation of the newly appointed government. But it was difficult to achieve if you did not know the customs and rituals there, or did not feel comfortable in an unfamiliar, so different world. The woman who was ultimately elected a deputy had predisposing qualities, such as proficiency in negotiation techniques, diplomacy, as well as personal charm. He probably didn't count in winning over other women, like priestesses, but it was better than nothing. She was also able to defend herself, as she trained martial arts all her youth. She had fortitude, which could bring some benefits during a dangerous expedition, become a weapon. Noovack told her that the people of Floris generally do no harm to the fair sex. She believed. It only gave her a boost. In fact, she was chosen by Noovack because she was not related to the old system. If the prime minister sent one of the experienced agents of the former Ministry of the Interior, who was still trained by Petar Rubby, he might turn out to be faithful to his former bosses and, for example, would pass on secret information or join the fugitives. There was no place for risk or fiasco.

***

Nobody had the right to decide for Jasmin, much less give her orders, especially calling her a stupid woman. Even her husband. Over the past week, however, Addam had had time to rethink his words. He seemed to be mired in remorse that perhaps he had exaggerated. He walked around Jasmin like the Queen, but she wasn't going to forgive him. She completely ignored all attempts at reconciliation.

"Sorry," he finally said through his closed mouth. "I could have used other words."

She did not react. She just stared through the apartment windows at the landscape below. He has changed beyond recognition. The groundbait, related to the occupations traditionally performed by men, has disappeared and new ones have appeared in their place, promoting tools that facilitate the work of women or encourage the purchase of another robot. Addam took the slush out of the coolant and took a long bite. She thought she was doing it to make her ask him why he was eating again, even though it was not yet noon. And it just kind of rounded it up. He didn't look like him.

"Okay. You don't give a shit about me, please go ahead, but I would like to remind you that we are married and your decision has an impact on me as well," he almost shouted out.

"And that's why you eat and stop exercising?" She said finally.

"No. It's probably because of not taking any medications. My body won't listen to me. She is like my wife."

"Am I your wife or the executor of your orders?"

"You know what I mean. Don't tease me. We will starve."

"Yeah. If you eat so much, that's for sure."

"I wish we had children, but we cannot afford it. Let's abort them and start over. Maybe it will be possible with the boy."

"Let's abort? Are we pregnant together? I am the one who carries the babies in my stomach and bears the risks associated with the procedure. Anyway, it is already impossible."

"What do you mean? It's too late?"

Addam did seem interested, which encouraged her to tell an honest story.

"You could say that," she began. "All gynecologists who are accredited for legal abortions are crazy with work. None of them wanted to see me at a time that is, say, a guarantee of safety. I don't know what else to do!"

Addam thought about it. His demeanor indicated that he was sorry. Apparently he underestimated his wife. A gentle smile appeared on his face, which seemed to herald an uncovered ray of hope.

"Why didn't you tell me you were trying? Maybe there would be a solution."

"It's my pregnancy! My problem."

"What are you saying, honey? This is our pregnancy. Let me remind you that you didn't do it to yourself," he joked.

She wasn't laughing at all. She just snorted dismissively.

"I'll talk to Kimberly. Maybe she can do something. She is now a minister. She will ask someone in the Government and a free date will be found. How good you thought it over. I love you. You know?"

He walked over to her and hugged her tenderly. She reacted coldly. Her own reaction surprised her. Until now - even when they were arguing - when he was the one reaching out in agreement, she had always succumbed. This time she didn't feel like it. She had just confessed to Addam to weakness. That she had made the decision he expected of her, forced by everyone around her. In addition, she did not handle the matter effectively. She? So ambitious? With the possibilities? She couldn't handle the problem. He overwhelmed her. She felt muffled and weak. Her helplessness, accompanied by a slight self-loathing and fear of becoming a laughing stock, released the last remnants of pride. Probably unnecessary. Too bad, she thought. She believed that if he got the abortion, he would dominate. And she will have to obediently go wherever he directs her. Carry out the command. She hated her hormones. She blamed him for them. When he left to meet Kimberly, she lay back down on the bed. She cried for a long time. She relished her helplessness. She was winding a spiral of regret to herself, the world, the Government, and Addam. Even to mother and Luicey. Why wasn't Dad there with her? He would surely find a solution.

After relishing her own sorrow for two hours, she decided to exercise to chase away bad thoughts and prepare for her husband's return. She wanted to find the strength she had been missing for days. She had no intention of watching theatremania, where government materials were displayed over and over again, especially emphasizing the merits of the new prime minister and the Minister of Health, as well as the advantages of the new decrees. She exercised briefly, took a bath quickly, and started wearing a tight dress that worked best for difficult conversations with Addam. Jasmin always looked sexy in her, which made her husband distracted. She knew it and often pulled that ace out of her sleeve. This time something has changed. She was not able to fasten. How it's possible? Has the dress shrunken? After all, she did not eat as much as her husband. Well, maybe half more feed in the evening sometimes. Just enough. Is it possible that she has already gained weight? She went to the mirror and stood sideways. The dress was still loose. She stroked her hand over her stomach. It didn't look bloated. She stroked herself again, only this time she ran her hand from her breast over her stomach to below her belly button. It has become. She noticed a slight rounding. "Is it already?" - she rejoiced. And once again she ran her hand across her stomach, this time transversely. "Yes. It is rounding, I will be a mother "- she rejoiced.

***

Addam returned to the suite in good mood, but did not find his wife. He took out the communicator, the private one he hadn't used in a long time, and tried to connect to her. Unsuccessfully. Nothing worked. There were three options: either Jasmin was out of range, or the communicator was turned off on purpose, or, in the least likely, it broke. Another option was not to be expected. Communicators were simple devices, they probably shouldn't break. There was no need to charge them, because they took energy from the Hello rays. In turn, the lack of coverage meant that the user was far beyond the boundaries of Inco or underground. It was an unlikely scenario. Addam made contact with Luicey. She had no idea what was happening to his wife. Finally, out of boredom, waiting for Jasmin return, turned on the theatremania sports channel. The transmission of the competition that housekeeping robots took part in caught his mind. He smiled at the rivalry between four devices from different brands. Contrary to appearances, it is not only a sports discipline. The winning brand could count on greater purchases of customers. After the floor washing competition, the XTRO robot was driving, the second was Sky Robotics, the third was Freddy. The fourth MicroankO robot did not count at all. Another discipline was to determine the winner in cleaning windows. The unit of measure used in the competition was the square cubit divided by a unit of time equal to one-thousandth of a day. Emotions really grew.

***

Irmina was not thrilled with her daughter's idea, but tried to show her support. It was her that Jasmin moved in when she realized that she ultimately wanted to give birth to girls and that nothing would force her to resign from her decision. She even considered divorcing Addam. The law allowed for this type of solution in case of pregnancy, but in this case it only protected the mother. A husband who wished to divorce his pregnant woman could not file a lawsuit. Wife, if she had had enough of her husband, she could do it.

Jasmin only took a few essentials from the apartment where she and Addam lived. Mother's apartment was smaller, so there was no point in cluttering it up. In case the girl assumed she would borrow something from Irmina; she was even moved when she thought that she might be walking in maternal clothes. The more advanced the pregnancy was, the more the daughter felt the bond with her mother. She was becoming more and more sentimental. She gladly returned to old stories. She felt good in her company. They made up for all the times when they saw each other less often. Now they could talk about any outstanding topic. In order not to waste energy on a pointless conversation with Addam or Luicey, who would probably defend him, Jasmin turned off her communicator. She could focus on the conversations, on herself and on her mother, and basically on the entire female line of her bloodline: grandmother, mother and three daughters she was expecting.

"Are your parents alive?" She asked, though the question puzzled her. "I meant Grandma and Grandpa." She smiled at the thought of how she called them.

"No," replied Irmina. "I also had a sister, Kualarisa, the elder. In my youth, two daughters were not a problem as they are today. I haven't had contact with her for many purifications. She stayed in the slums. She preferred women, so it is unlikely that she would have children. He's definitely dead, anyway," she finished in a sad voice.

"Then tell me what you know about Dad's origins," Jasmin suggested, bringing a slight animation to mother's face.

"I don't know much. He came from the so-called western quarter. This is the equivalent of our district. He had a brother, Mahmud, and a sister, Sumi, but she died when Omar was still very young. He didn't remember her very well. She was then in the age of one purification."

Jasmin regretted bringing it up. She was counting on a chat with her mother about family topics, but each started evoking unpleasant memories.

"It's sad," she concluded.

"No. They were very religious, and for the people of Floris, death is rather good. If anyone was dying, it meant that the goddess Patri wanted it that way. She was calling him to her place. Omar wasn't sad about it. He also had a brother. They grew up together, but they were different. The other loved farming, and your dad loved the technical stuff, the machines. He liked to learn. I admired him. Certainly it was very difficult for him to fight alone for knowledge."

"And it was hard for him to leave his family," said Jasmin, who had just realized how much her father had suffered and what choices he faced in his life.

"That's true. When he left home to go to Inco, he couldn't tell anyone where he was going as his family would suffer."

"Why?"

"I do not know. So he explained to me. He didn't talk much about customs because he knew I wouldn't understand them anyway. We are completely different communities. They definitely don't understand our life goals, rituals, money, science, nothing. We will not appreciate why they choose to live in such conditions. Omar never spoke badly of them. He just wanted to study and that was it. That's why he emigrated. Sometimes he recalled that he could not watch his family work from dawn to dusk because he had obligations to the state. They gave up a tenth of the crop."

" Wow. Ten percent? What would they say about the three times greater tax that we have to leave to these bloodsuckers?"

"He saw it differently. When he finished college and we got married, he urged me to move there. My family cursed us, then we didn't see any prospects in Inco."

"You must be kidding. Did you want to move to the rump?"

"He never stopped missing."

"Why didn't you do it?"

"Because I got pregnant with you, and he was finally appreciated, he got a great job. All our lives we have wondered if we made the right choice. I really wanted to go with him to see family. I wanted to meet them. Your grandparents are long dead, but there are certainly other members of the Manduarra family."

"I'll take you there." Jasmin was pleased with the new idea. "When the situation normalizes. Maybe they won't kill us there," she joked.

"I'm too old to travel, but you could visit your uncle someday. From what I can remember, he was younger, probably still alive. Rather, he has a family. Maybe they would help you in your difficult situation. And take Addam. He really does have a lot of virtues," she said, smiling fondly.

Jasmin didn't know what to say. On the one hand, she was furious with her husband and did not want to see him anymore, on the other hand, she still felt a bond with him. If she had anywhere to go, it would be with him. She wasn't that much independent. Anyway, triplets were to appear on the horizon. Besides, what is the idea to move to another country. Was it really so bad in Inco that emigration should be considered? Although Floris is definitely a better place than the slums. Would she ever find a family in such a great country? What would they think of her? Is it allowed to travel there at all?

"I won't bow to any gods," she said to close the case.

In this way, she manifested her disapproval of the feelings that she had for Addam, and from which she was defending herself in some way. He was the symbolic god she listened to, sometimes she had to manipulate him, got mad at him, believed him or lost her trust in him. She had just realized that the word "god" had also become a metaphor for her relationship to Floris. She felt pleased that her mother could follow this line of reasoning. That she does not want to live in a land where she would have to make false obeisances to gods in whom she does not believe.

***

Addam quickly realized where his wife was hiding. He only asked once if he was going to come back. She refused with a sneer. He asked no more. He realized that if she did come back that was fine, and if she did not, life was opening up entirely new perspectives for him. He finally understood what his father had been trying to tell him once, before his marriage to Jasmin. It was about reaping the benefits of a life that is so short. "Isn't my father happy with my mother?" He thought, but not for long. He immediately started implementing his father's idea, which is using his freedom to the fullest.

He lived alone in a large apartment. His account has been unlocked, which should be credited with a large amount monthly. For himself, it was perfectly sufficient. He convinced everyone that Jasmin and he were in the past, that he was waiting for a divorce. A few wealthy women quickly appeared next to him. Finally, he didn't have to explain that he was cheating her with one of them. It was always like that in Jasmin's time. Finally, this ordeal is over. He liked the new life. He felt free, quite young and independent.

"You can marry whoever you want," said Ksaverius, the new neighbor who had just moved downstairs and dropped by with three young wives for the introductory evening.

"I can, but I want a break from women. I spend a little while and that's it. My ex gave me so much trouble that I don't want any obligations. Fuck, I'm not gonna pay any more for girlish humor!" Addam shouted stoned.

"If you don't care, you can take a pretty good dime for it," suggested Ginger, Xaverius's first wife.

"Awesome patent!" Addam shouted. "I'll give you a discount for that."

"Let's go." Ksaverius apparently thought the party was slightly extended.

Addam was not going to end the play. He left the apartment for a short walk. He came back not alone, but in the company of three beauties. They accosted him themselves. The first time he did not refuse, and even entered into small negotiations. Upper worked great. It gave him the spirit that had been missing since he had set Ray down. The women were formful, slim and well-groomed. He offered a rate of one hundred entitys for each. They agreed without hesitation. He regretted whether he had sold himself too cheaply. He took it like study. When they entered the suite, all three undressed and headed for the recovery room. Addam turned on the flush module. A light, warm rain falling from the ceiling washed away the remnants of shame from all four of them. They landed in the bed Jasmin had been lounging in lately. They had fun until the host fell asleep from exhaustion. Before they left, one of them had left a note with the signature of Jenny Pillow, a drawing of a fancy heart and two sequences of numbers. One was her messenger number and the other was her bank account number. He needed it in order to retrieve the promised three hundred entitys. Women could deceive him, but surprisingly they paid. Perhaps in case Addam ever wanted to serve them so cheaply.

The next day, he slept until noon. He was awakened by Haenry's pre-planned visit.

"How's Jasmin?" Asked his cousin, seeing Addam sleepy.

"I have a new idea for life. I can earn money as a prostitute."

"I can see that Upper is still in you. When you leave the house, remember not to get too close to the humaan."

"I'm not joking. Look." Addam pointed to a note from Jenny. "I guess that's legal, do you think?"

"What does Jasmin say?"

"She will definitely not be happy, but only in this way we will quickly get out of debt."

"And you agree to the triplets?"

Addam thought about it. He didn't seem to know what he wanted. He actually missed her already, just didn't want to admit it to himself. This pregnancy, however, did not suit him very well. He wished Jasmin had decided to have an abortion sooner. It would be over. Now they were in trouble. Will there be a day when he might like girls? Nothing by force, just like that?

"If she agrees that I will have sex with other women, I'll accept her whim. In such a situation, we will be able to afford it."

"We can't have children," Haenry replied, ruining the host's mood. "I mean, I can't. We were at the examination yesterday and..."

"Luicey mad?"

"She doesn't react like Jasmin. She is broken and cries all the time. She laughed once when she realized that no one else would want me. She once said she would not marry me, but later called it off. What should I do?"

Addam smiled at his thoughts.

"Cheap sperm. Cheap. Little used. Who want it, who?" He joked, although Haenry didn't look amused.

***

Jasmin's communicator was still off. She knew that if Luicey cared about her, she should have figured out where to find her. She did not count on Addam, although she mentally hoped he would visit her someday. She wondered how he could get along without her, whether he missed her, or at least thought. Why did he only come once? For too long she had been tormented by pesky questions. She decided to check who was trying to connect with her. She clicked on the pink communicator and flashed a list of recent calls on the wall. There haven't been many of them from Addam. Literally six. There was more from Luicey, twelve. However, most of the missed calls were from the restricted number. "Who was looking for me?" - she wondered. She checked the message list as well, and then everything became clear. She guessed who was trying to communicate with her. She had received fourteen short notes from the Gender Control Office about the compulsory follow-up visit she should have done the previous week. She got scared. She dialed the GCO number immediately.

"Hello, helpline of the Gender Control Office, I'm listening." She heard a voice coming out of the micro-speaker.

"Hello, my name is Jasmin Kozllov, daughter of Irmina and Omar. I was supposed to come for a control visit, but I felt bad," she lied.

"Wait a minute, I'll check. Really. We called on you many times. Is your communicator working properly?"

"Yes. I turned off because I didn't want to be disturbed."

"It must not be turned off. It's forbidden when you are pregnant. We must be in constant contact with you."

"I did not know. Sorry."

"Please do not do this again, because we will have to disconnect you from the national program."

"What program?" Irmina, overhearing the conversation, was surprised.

"What program?" Jasmin repeated the question.

"Governmental. You are on the list of happy mothers who will be looked after by the state. When can you come for a follow-up visit to the Ministry of Health? I have two available dates: tomorrow or in three days. Only morning hours."

"Maybe tomorrow," Jasmin replied in surprise.

"I'm booking. Room number three thousand and three G. Goodbye."

"Goodbye," she replied to herself.

"What list?" Irmina was surprised when Jasmin finished the conversation.

"I do not know. I was just on the worse one, now I'm on the better one. Do you understand any of this? How can you trust them?"

"You should be happy, not complaining all the time."

"Right," Jasmin admitted silently. "Was there any light in the tunnel? What happened to them? Maybe Addam did something or Haenry," she mused. She thought again that she missed her husband. And even behind his boring, red-haired cousin and his fiancée Luicey.

***

Even for such a seasoned, analytical mind as Jasmin was, finding room three thousand and three G in the maze of corridors of the great edifice of the Ministry of Health was not easy. The command from the young girl in the registration office seemed simple: down the corridor to the left, then to the end, to the second floor, there to the right, then left again, all the way to the letter T and then straight ahead, but more to the right. Jasmin is lost. When she found the room in question, an unusual commission was waiting for her inside, consisting of a woman who looked like a gynecologist and dressed in a modern suit of a famous person.

"Mrs. minister?" Jasmin asked.

"Who did you expect?" Gibbondy was surprised.

"I thought it was going to be research."

"Talk to me first. See, cute girl, I like to be sure everything is going my way."

"What are we going to talk about?"

Gibbondy launched the computer module. Data flashed on a screen projected on the wall. Jasmin recognized her first name, surname, account balance with information about the blockade, as well as all the data related to health, past work and current pregnancy. She was disturbed by the excess of exclamation marks that could indicate that the heroine of the report was treated as a special case.

"Why was I called?" Jasmin asked anxiously in her voice.

"I created a new project. I call it, perhaps too modestly, the protection of women... It's a working name. Does not matter. The idea is to provide special care to women who have multiple female pregnancies. We currently have over a dozen such cases across the country."

"Why were we awarded?" Jasmin was surprised.

"Such a case is associated with a completely different hormonal balance than in a single pregnancy."

"I did not know. And what's next?"

"We want to use this fact to perform a series of specialized tests. What do you say? Research will be paid. I mean, you won't pay, but we will. A hundred entitys for each weekly visit. We want to observe how the hormonal economy changes over time."

"I don't understand something here. Haven't you tested it?" she asked the gynecologist.

"We do," she replied. "We want to check how the fetus will behave under the influence of injecting testosterone into the amniotic fluid."

Gibbondy gave the doctor a disciplining look. She was clearly dissatisfied that the gynecologist had revealed the intentions that had been discussed in secret too quickly.

"Is it safe?" Jasmin asked.

"Absolutely," Gibbondy replied. "It'll only make the girls stronger. Already in their mother's womb they will experience their eternal struggle for existence. Then they will be unbeatable."

"We think so," finished the gynecologist, not caring about the potential service consequences.

"Then I'll think about it," Jasmin replied.

"There is nothing to think about here. Now we encourage you voluntarily. Do you understand me? We'll take your lock off!"

"Still, I have to discuss it with my husband. Anything else? Can I go now?"

Gibbondy scowled, sighed heavily, stood up sharply, and made her way to the back of the office without a word. The gynecologist shrugged and looked meekly down.

"Will you prescribe some vitamins or something?" Jasmin asked.

The gynecologist's thoughts were elsewhere.

***

Haenry's apartment was not very well located. First of all, on the lower level, from where there was no such awesome view of the city center as from the Kozllov windows. It was also smaller and more audible were the sounds of human bustling from the boardwalk. According to the owner, the only advantage it had was the proximity of a gigantic shopping mall. In addition to the multitude of shops, service outlets, small rooms where theatricality was displayed all the time, there were also rooms for group exercises. Before the introduction of the second decree, both sexes used them. Currently, only women who need a change. The boredom of exercising alone in private regeneration rooms in their apartments could be excruciating.

The swimming pool was the most crowded in the gallery. There was no water in it, but condensed air enriched with lufflin, a dense gas of organic origin imitating the impression of a liquid. You used to swim in it in special, skimpy clothes, consisting of several tight straps. Lufflin offered resistance, just as you would feel in a pool full of water, but it was more economical. Breathing was difficult, which was treated as another challenge. By using any of the swimming styles, it was possible to move at practically any height at low speed, both above the bottom and under the ceiling. The swimming pool, which was entered through a special lock, was located in a glass extension. From the outside you could see who was swimming, what he looked like in funny clothes and what style he was using. Haenry liked to come here, but since sports were banned, he only looked longingly at swimming women. Sometimes they would come with Luicey to cheer on the swimmers. They pretended to be commentators. Luicey most often bet on the victory of the middle-aged ladies, and her fiancé to the younger ones. Over time, they liked their ritual.

Haenry was aware that the fiancée had a crush on his slightly younger cousin. They have talked about it many times since she moved in with him. However, this fact did not prevent him from proposing Addam as a donor. "Everything will remain in the family," he said. Luicey was delighted, but a bit embarrassed. She also felt a little guilty about stealing something precious from her friend. She also knew she was the jealous type. She suggested to Addam that they never reveal their secret. He readily agreed that it would be better for everyone.

There were several methods of settling the matter, but it was Haenry who suggested that Luicey should be fertilized in a natural way while she was not yet his wife. He decided that for Addam, who was increasingly making extra money as a prostitute, it would not matter, and that his beloved would at least fulfill her dream, this one time. He loved her sincerely and dearly. He wanted to please her. It was the only way to repay her for her sacrifice. This is what he called her loyalty to him in a gesture of despair, when they learned that he was sterile and that he was of no value in this country.

Sex with Addam did not live up to Luicey's expectations. It was average, fast, but professional. No passion, no tenderness, only technique. She felt like she was making love to a robot in a child manufacturing company. As if she were one of the many women on the breeding belt that ran along the long factory. After cooling down and thinking, she didn't feel disappointed. In her opinion, it was just an innocent gesture of help. "Jasmin shouldn't be jealous", she thought.

***

Jasmin felt uneasy that day. She didn't know why. The previous short night she had dreamed about her father and told her he would do it tomorrow. "Just what? What was he talking about? " - she wondered. She was walking nervously around her mother's apartment. Every now and then she turned on and off the theatremania. She ate two bars, unnecessarily. She wasn't hungry. Irmina decided to deal with her on some topic significant to her.

"What are you going to do with these Ministry of Health funded tests? Will you agree?" She asked.

"Did you have to remind me? Now I have another fear on the back of my neck. Soon their excess will overwhelm me. There are so many of them. I don't know what's happening to me. I have no contact with Addam, Luicey pisses me off, I'm always hungry, soon the money will run out. I dream of removing the blockade, but a hundred entitys for a visit is not much. What am I going to buy for this? Everything is getting more expensive. In two weeks, the price of the bars increased by twelve percent. Pearl costs almost twice as much as a month ago. Where is all this going?"

"Everything will surely work out somehow," said Irmina, and tenderly stroked her daughter's white hair that had not been trimmed for a long time.

At that moment, they heard a soft knock. Irmina was surprised because she was not expecting any visitor.

"Will you open?" She asked.

Jasmin went to the door and when she opened it slightly, Luicey strode into the apartment with a cheerful expression. She was exuded with unimaginable happiness.

"She remembered," Jasmin said sarcastically, deliberately speaking in the third person.

"I am pregnant, I will have a son!" The friend shouted.

"This is great news," said Irmina, when she saw that her daughter had not reacted with the proper courtesy for such a moment.

"Wonderfully." Jasmin smirked and hugged Luicey. "When did you find out?"

"Day before yesterday."

"And you're telling me about it now?"

"Iwill go to bed for a moment," said Irmina, allowing her daughter and her friend to talk freely.

"I was not sure. Haenry says that this device invented by Gibbondy is not worth trusting. Today I checked on a different device, in the second office. Managed to. I will be a mom."

"I'm glad. How's father doing? Happy?"

Luicey looked away, but quickly reflected.

"Yes. I don't know anyone happier in the world. And how are you?"

"I'm resting. I'm catching up on theatremania. There has been a lot going on lately," she said ironic.

"I didn't have a moment for this nonsense, but now I have a lot of free time. We will be able to watch together. I won't have to work," she said, chirping.

"How's Addam? How is he doing?" Jasmin asked, pretending she didn't really care.

"We have no contact with each other," she lied. "I have to go. We'll talk later. I will communicate with you. Don't walk me out."

Luicey left. Jasmin could stop pretending to be pleased at last. She was furious. For herself, for her reaction. At her friend that she is happy and that she will give birth to a son. At her husband, he did not support her in this difficult moment. At her father, he foresaw the worst-case scenario in her dream.

"She's gone now," she said aloud so that Irmina could return.

There was no reaction. Jasmin was surprised, but thought that her mother might have fallen asleep. She went to her bedroom. The mother was lying with her back, wrapped in quite thick, for Inco, duvet. Her face was not visible. The daughter slipped under the covers and hugged her mother. Irmina, even in her sleep, always returned such a gesture. This time she did not react. "She is fast asleep", Jasmin thought, but after a while she opened the covers and rolled her mother's body onto her back. It was a difficult operation to perform, although Irmina was not a heavy one. Her body was just limp. Jasmin checked the pulse. She didn't sense it. She put her ear closer to her mouth, but none of it, not even the shallowest, stray breath came out. So that's what her father was talking about in her dream. She cried.

***

The funeral at Inco looked modest compared to the ceremony at Floris for generations. After securing the most important organs, which, according to the decree in force for many purifications, could be useful in transplantation, the body of the deceased was cremated. The ashes were sent for recycling, i.e. they were used in the pharmaceutical and food industries. This supposedly devoid of feeling ritual surprised no one. It was common knowledge that the body is just a shell.

The situation with the memory of the dead was completely different. People in Inco - despite an absolutely atheistic approach to life - believed that there is no such thing as soul, but the human mind should not be forgotten. It was in him that the emotional sphere was perceived as difficult to assess, and emotions were treated as its attributes. It was difficult to part with a man with whom feelings were attached. For many purifications, there was a mourning, through which the relatives said goodbye to the deceased family member. For ten days after the symbolic funeral, each related person was dressed completely in blue, including dyeing their hair in this color for this time, sometimes also the face. The mourners stood out from the crowd. The rest of Inco citizens used a modest range of colors for their clothes, regardless of the time of day. White, gray and black have become a guarantee of unity, purity and order. Men, usually no older than the four purifications, wore transparent shirts and pants, but only during the day.

In the first quarter, there was a strange fashion for dyeing any part of the body any of the metallic colors. The most common decorations were fingernails or toenails, less often the eyelids or ears, sometimes the entire face, in which case gold or copper. Hair was dyed least often, because it was treated as a showcase. However, if someone was not satisfied with them, they dyed them most often diamond silver. Very rarely for one of the natural colors, such as black-haired, brown-haired or yellow-haired. Older ladies, whose natural hair had lost its density, wore wigs. Jasmin loved her hair and its rare color. When she was a girl, the other children laughed that they were white. They treated her like a misfit. She fell ill many times, crying late in shame. Her father, who was also white-haired, told her to find an interesting explanation and then the children would stop mocking her. She figured only a select few had white hair in honor of the Inco flag. They treated this information as something unexpected and thus won their favor. Her hairstyle was never mocked again, although she attracted attention, not only in color. Only once - when Omar left - Jasmin dyed her hair. On the blue. She chose this shade for the time of mourning. Now she had to do the same, in fact she wanted to, as a sign of respect for her mother. And she was not embarrassed, as in the last time, that she drew attention to herself.

Despite their loss, she was relieved that they had had so much time to talk about it. The flat after my mother was paid for by the company where father used to work. They had asked for them, so shortly after Jasmin's funeral, she had to move out and hand them over to the attorneys sent by the owner. Before doing so, however, she decided to search all nooks and crannies. And it wasn't easy. Each room in Irmina's small apartment had two floors. The lower one was the actual ceiling between the floors. The top floor, almost a cubit higher, was removable. It consisted of platforms based on scaffolding, i.e. the top layer on which people walked. Between them there were decks of additional space for storing various things. Throughout their lives, Jasmin's parents collected a lot of more or less needed items. Among them, she found a few treasures that she took with her as a souvenir. Among other things, a collection of mom's toys, some of her clothes, beloved old-fashioned knick-knacks and a few dad's notebooks. They were written in the old language, but this was not an obstacle for her.

***

She went back to Addam. Ashamed, crying, all blue. He didn't ask, he didn't judge for anything. He knew perfectly well what that color meant. It was chilly between them at first. Jasmin avoided his gaze, often surreptitiously crying for her mother when she realized that she would never really see her again. Addam disappeared for days and returned late. They will sleep separately. She is on the bed, he is on a pile of blankets and a few warmer, soft pillows. She noticed he looked good. He was often in a good mood and every now and then brought new clothes, dressed for hours and smelled different too. She wondered if he would fall in love with someone, but even at the thought of asking him, she scolded herself. Not so long ago, she had wanted to divorce him, and now she knew she could not do so. After all, she was at his mercy.

Addam never once asked how she felt, what was happening to her, and how she was doing. The gestures are over, they have not touched each other for a long time. Once he asked if she had managed to get the money back from her mother's account. She just shrugged. Sometimes he said something like that the weather is nice or a joke heard in male company about the stupidity of women. Neither made her laugh. When he didn't see it, she looked at him, more and more contemptuously. She wanted to crush him with the unspoken insults that had accumulated since her return. Contradictory thoughts swirled around her. The remnants of the feeling she had once felt for him were hidden deep in her. But it is more because of the fruit of their union carried in the womb. When he left one day, she finally decided to dispel her doubts about where Addam spent her days.

He looked great and looked confident. In the mall he went to, he stopped at a candy vending machine. He didn't buy any. He was leaning against its casing as if he was waiting for someone. Jasmin, dressed in a colorful mother dress, with a hat on her head, was hidden behind the entrance door to a spare parts store for household robots. She feigned interest, but was really looking at Addam.

"What can I do for you?" The the robot salesman asked.

"I'm watching, get out of here," she replied harshly.

Addam noticed this incident and met his wife. Nevertheless, he intended to continue with his plan. After a while, an elderly woman, aged five and a half of purification, approached him. She inspected him like an item she was interested in buying.

"How much?" She asked.

"Five hundred," he replied.

"Four hundred."

"Five hundred," repeated Addam.

"Can we go to your place?"

"I have a renovation."

The woman nodded at him, motioning for him to follow her. He did so. Following his client, he sent a brief glance at his passing wife. She was surprised and indignant. She could not control herself for a long time. When she got back to the apartment, she was mad with jealousy mixed with the desire to kill both her husband and that hussy. She wondered what she should do. Walk away with dignity, divorce him, or come to terms with his fate. She had no idea what to do next. She knew she was dependent only on him now. Her stomach was reminding her of her needs. She ate another bar, nibbling on a huge male furious bite. She went to freshen up. She wanted to wash away all her anger at the man she had had feelings for until recently. He came back in the evening. Before she could speak, he turned on his communicator and flashed his account balance on the wall. It showed the amount of twenty two thousand three hundred entitiys.

"Why are you showing me this?" She asked.

"You can think of me what you want, but I do it for us. Thanks to this, we will be able to live in dignity. Until they realize it's a job too."

"Addam, what happened to us?" She asked to take a moment to think.

"I do not know. I want to save us."

"You didn't seem like a man who wouldn't like it."

"Custom. A few days ago, I had doubts, but a day later came a further twenty percent increase in electricity, water and rent."

"I wished I had listened to you. At the beginning. But now I don't regret it. When you leave me, and I know you will, I will remember you in the form of our children. But where are we gonna live?"

Jasmin lowered her head and stroked her stomach.

"I will not leave you. I love you all the time. The next half of the purification will be the worst, then downhill."

"Can't you see what's going on in Inco? Did you know a hundred days ago how this will turn out?"

Addam shook his head.

"So what, should I stop it? How are we going to live?" He asked.

Jasmin slowly began to calm down. The last few sentences made her puzzled. Did she understand correctly that Addam was prostituting her and the children? To help them? She could not trust her feelings or a superficial assessment of the situation. She needed more time. She certainly didn't like the fact that a man who had come so close to her recently cheated on her with so many other women. It didn't matter to her that it was just sex or that he did it for girls. The mere fact that anyone could have her husband was unbearable. "I'm not jealous, the mere thought that they think they've taken something away from me makes me angry. They must be mocking me", she deceived herself mentally. She even wondered if she wished Addam had one true lover instead of a hundred clients. Besides, there was always a risk that one of them would infect him with some nasty stuff or betray him that she was working as a prostitute. It is true that he would not be punished for the protection of the male sex, but perhaps he would become the subject of scientific experiments, which had been quite loud for the past three weeks.

It was then that she realized that his last job was very risky. Life in Inco was becoming unbearable. For everything, penalties, prohibitions, blockades, prison. In addition, the raging inflation deprived any illusions that they would be able to survive this situation as a family or its substitute. At this point, she had a completely crazy idea. She hadn't thought it over, decided to share it with Addam right away.

"You have to marry another woman who will give our family a son, if it needed two. Not more."

Adam was speechless.

"That way you won't have to sell yourself like a whore," she continued. "The law permits it. There is talk of wedding fairs. I agree that you marry a girl from a wealthy house. What do you think? We're gonna get a lot of money from her family. They will give everything to make their child happy."

"Are you sure?"

She was not. She knew there was no other way.

***

Addam knew Jasmin very well, but he did not suspect that she would be capable of such a heroic, albeit clever, move. "Beautiful and wise, my white-haired," he thought of her as before. When he cooled down, he eagerly set about planning a multi-stage knockout casting. Jasmin told him it was a waste of time, that all you had to do was set the rules and go to the mall, and all you had to do was walk down the hall and they will go to him. He did so. He conducted an initial selection and invited the more attractive candidates to his apartment at the agreed time of the next day. He ordered each of them to bring an up-to-date health report. Jasmin hardly slept the second consecutive night. She looked like a living dead in the morning. She didn't even have the strength to pretend to be rested, she hadn't adorned her face. The women entering the apartment, some with their families, passed by her, giving her dismissive glances. They didn't seem surprised why Addam was looking for a younger one.

Despite her exhaustion, Jasmin had no intention of assuming the victim's position. She wanted to feel like the mistress of this place and situation until the end. She decided that it would be better if he did not show weakness, but only a devastated commitment.

"Hello, ladies," she began. "First, I need to discuss the rules that will apply today. First: we decide together. Both my husband's voice and mine have the same weight. Ultimately, we are to be a family, so there can be no disputes between the first and second wife. There should be chemistry between us. Second: if we choose one of the ladies, most likely you will have tomorrow," she stuttered, but no one noticed, "intercourse with my husband. After a few days, thanks to modern technology, we will check whether fertilization has occurred and whether it is a boy. Only in this case will the wedding take place. Third: every child in the family will be treated the same. Regardless of whether it will be a son or a daughter, regardless of which mother it will be and when it will be born. Fourth and last: I would like to remind you that women who do not successfully pass the casting will not receive a refund. Two hundred entitys paid will be treated as the cost of participation in the casting. Is everything understandable?"

"Yes," replied the candidates in a chorus.

"Please introduce yourself," she suggested to the first of the ten who had been invited for the day.

"My name is Constance Ciccone. My body ratio is one to four tenths to one to one and three tenths. I have two and a half purifications and three and a half cubits of height," said shapely yellow-haired girl with large breasts.

"Will you undress, Constance?" Addam asked, looking at her curves.

Jasmin gasped. She worked out all the details with her husband, but it was out of the question. She wanted to shoot him in the face, but remembered why they were doing it. Constance was a bit ashamed of the onlookers, but in the end the desire to marry won. Slowly she took off her dress and stood completely naked in front of Addam, then twisted around like a robot presenting new fashion in a clothing showroom. She looked healthy. She had a few moles on her stomach and a gray mark on her ass. Addam scowled at the blemish. Jasmin noticed his reaction and cheered silently.

"Thank you for coming. Please get dressed," she said.

"My family gives for the wedding..."

"Yes. We know, but we want to meet another candidate now."

Jasmin did not care at all about following the rules, but about quickly covering the girl so that Addam wouldn't stare at her. At the moment, the whole casting idea felt like an own goal. She hoped to postpone the verdict as soon as possible. "One of the competitors has been shot", she thought. She looked at another and invited her with a gesture. A young girl came out into the middle of the living room, followed by an older man, a small, gray-haired, thin mustache. At that time, Constance managed to dress in panic and hide in the corner of the living room. Only now did she look ashamed and scared.

"My name is Ivvard Morgoruth. My daughter's name is Vicky," said the mustachioed, presenting the comic beauty. "Her proportions are one and five tenths to one to one and forty-five. It is true that the ideal? She has two purifications and an ideal body made for birthing. Undress," he turned to his daughter. "See what wonderful, firm breasts, narrow waist and wide hips she has. I'm paying twenty thousand entitys for the wedding. When my son is born, I'll give for layette."

Vicky, without hesitation, undressed and proudly presented her body.

"Tempting," Jasmin said. "We'll think. Now another candidate."

"I'd like to ask a few questions," said Addam.

"Oh please." Jasmin knew his look.

The husband looked excited by the intuitive choice he had just made on behalf of both of them.

"Tell us something about yourself," he suggested.

"I finished pharmacy," Vicky said pleasantly. "I know that in the current political situation it is not a very popular profession, but sooner or later it will return to favor. People cannot live without medicines. Diseases are already spreading."

"Right. Thinking. Good," said Addam briskly and smiled at his first wife.

"Do you have any more questions to this lady, husband?" She reminded of her position.

"I don't have any more questions," he replied, smiling at Vicky.

"It's all right, I need to write down your name." Jasmin decided to remind the rules again.

"What does it matter? Soon I'll be Mrs. Kozllov," Vicky replied confidently in her voice and started getting dressed. She did so slowly, keeping Addam's gaze on her for a long time.

***

Although the casting lasted until late in the evening, the next candidates were basically dismissed. Jasmin was furious at Addam's choice, but couldn't make any other options. She had the idea of casting herself and knew that she should not withdraw from it. It would plunge her into her husband's eyes. She only had him left. She preferred to beat off one competitor than a whole herd of customers. She was convinced that even if the attempt at sex was successful and her husband just married Vicky, sooner or later he would get bored with her. The girl wasn't his type. Everyone knew it. Jasmin took the deposit from the mustachioed's father and dismissed him.

The procreation attempt was to take place the next day, but, according to Addam, it was a pity to waste time on unnecessary delay. He suggested that Vicky stay the night immediately. Jasmin was furious in her mind. He did something again without making any arrangements with her. Where was she supposed to be at this hour? If it had been during the day, she would have wandered around the neighborhood. But at night? Vicky suggested that the three of them could sleep in the same bed, that she didn't mind. "Come on!" Jasmin said indignantly. "Punk will be inviting me to my own bed. No way. She will not do me a favor", she thought, offended. She did not agree. She preferred to sit alone. She was just wondering where to find such a place, since this class apartment had hardly any corridor or partition walls. It was one big open space. The bedroom area was separated from the large living room only by a portable partition, something like a screen. The coolant and wardrobe resembled built-in wardrobes. Only the regeneration room was a separate apartment. Jasmin thought it was the perfect place. At least she won't hear anything.

She was wrong. She heard everything. How they giggled, how they gasped, how Vicky was moaning with pleasure, and Addam was breathing hard. She heard every word. They talked fondly. She hadn't heard such words from her husband's lips for a long time, and that night the bastard gave the freshly learned nymphet with whole series of compliments. "What a fucking romantic," she cursed silently. Clogging your ears didn't help to drown out the mumbling of that dung, the chatter of the idiot, and all the intrusive thoughts. And these hurt her the most. They took out on her. For her wrong decisions and the delayed ones. For being too lenient to Addam, too abrasive, and sometimes senselessly jealous. If she hadn't confronted him for any reason and had been more a partner than a rival, he wouldn't have even thought of another. He would never have agreed to an idea as crazy as polygamy. Though he has always liked to be adored by women, she knew him well and knew he wouldn't go that far. However, everything has changed. She owed herself. She missed her mother.

She didn't like Vicky very much as a human. She looked saucy and cheeky. One who didn't care for rules, morals, or respect for elders; as to his goal he goes over the dead. Her long eyelashes, big eyes and really impeccable figure must have aroused envy in every, even very attractive representative of the fair sex. The only thing she was missing was height. Black-haired Vicky was only three cubits tall, half a cubit shorter than Jasmin. Addam's first wife could look down on her.

Jasmin fell asleep on the floor, exhausted after a quiet and lonely struggle with her own fears. However, her sleep did not last very long. Addam woke her up, joyfully announcing that he and Vicky were going to refresh themselves. He asked that - if she didn't want to do this with them - she left the recovery room and waited in the living room. Her heart broke.

Chapter 14 The Secret

"We need to rest," Fahid said. "Hello will be up in a moment. Okurai is barely walking."

"Are there no lizards here?" Sumi asked with concern in her voice.

Fahid looked around. The place they were just passing looked quite similar to the one they were escaping from the sahadi late yesterday evening. What should he say his daughter? That they are definitely not here? How could he know? He wasn't at all sure the neighborhood was free of any dangers. Until recently, he was an ordinary farmer, not sticking his nose beyond the hole where he lived. Now he has become a traveler, adventurer and murderer together. He just realized again that he had killed three people, and in front of his own daughter. With this shameful act, he destroyed all his achievements. Throughout his life, he has been working on the image of a righteous man. One evening everything changed. He became a moral principle violator, the opposite of his own being. What answer was Sumi to give? That he had become a thug and being with him was more dangerous than the company of lizards? He felt a great deal of regret and powerlessness. This was not how he had imagined it all.

"Dad, are we stopping or not?" The tired girl asked.

"Yes. Let's get some sleep for a while. In hiding. Maybe there."

Fahid pointed to a large boulder that might obscure the resting place. He got off the okurai and helped his daughter do the same. They came closer. It was actually a good choice. They walked around the boulder. Sumi treaded quite carefully, examining the roughness with her foot. He seemed stable. Father unfastened the animal's harness and tied it to a nearby bush. He spread the quilt out as bedding for his daughter. He himself lay down directly on the ground. His garment was resistant to dirt and sharp edges, so he was not worried about damaging it as he was about Sumi's delicate dress. The girl wanted to hug him and thank him for saving her, but then she flinched. She saw her father stabbing a knife in the neck of Kadu again in her mind's eye, and then the little lizard would lick the blood off it. It was too much at once. She curled up in the fetal position and closed her eyes. Fahid was terribly tired and fell asleep quickly. In fact, after a while he was snoring heavily. After a while, he also began to kick his legs nervously, as if he had dreamed a nightmare in which he was running away. Sumi turned to her father and watched him. She focused more on him than on herself. He looked poor. She dismissed all bad thoughts, only remembered the good times. At dad's lap, with mum at the table, with siblings at play or fooling around. She clung to those memories. She could not sleep because of them for a long time. Anyway, she was a bit hungry and thirsty. She was tired until late at night. She finally fell asleep, but only in the morning.

When she woke up, her father was bustling around the small fire. It smelled quite nice. She was surprised. She didn't know Dad cooked well and could make anything out of nothing. At home, the meals were always prepared by the mother, this time by the father, and that was strange for the daughter. He was tending a long shashlik of plants found nearby on the fire. It was possible to recognize the thick red caps of anake mushrooms interspersed with pieces of edible mohair tree bark impaled on the stems of the wild mao. Sumi was looking forward to breakfast.

"Have you had enough sleep?" Fahid asked.

"I prefer my bed. Do we have anything to drink?"

Fahid shook his head, but then smiled as if an excellent thought had occurred to him.

"We can look for fruit," he reported happily. "I saw wild moree birds. Where they are, there should be clumps of turlin."

"I'd rather water. Do you know how to get to Hambarra, Papa?"

"We'll get there somehow. I'm more concerned that we only have one okurai. Why didn't I take more animals? I'm a fool. I hope no one finds out what happened and they won't pursue us. Okurai with two on his back will not be able to run from the chase."

Sumi looked sad. Fahid glanced pleadingly at his daughter as if asking for forgiveness.

"Who will be our priest now?" She asked.

"I do not know. I'm sure they'll send someone, but I wouldn't worry about that. Before you leave school, things can change."

"It doesn't comfort me at all," she replied maturely.

She glanced at a few morea birds that flew overhead. Their interest in human food was clearly evident. After all, Fahid was preparing a dish flavored with Radda herb.

"Look over there."

Fahid pointed to a hill with many windmills lined up by tens in rows. Despite the considerable distance, every spinning propeller was clearly recognizable. It was a monumental sight, never seen anywhere else. Sumi was not at all interested. Apparently she thought it was something ordinary in those parts, or maybe she was just too busy with her own hunger.

***

According to beliefs cultivated even before the beginning of the world, i.e. when there was no division into two lands, Patri was always treated as the embodiment of Mother Nature. Before becoming a goddess, she lived like a human.

When she was born from the pure energy of Hello, she absorbed its best rays and thus gained enormous power to create. It was known that she had exhausted most of the star's strength, and since then its rays have never been so essential again, and with time they have started to lose their power. In the beginning, Patri was all alone on the earth covered planet. She was bored with the sight, so she decided to create a company for herself. First, by her touch, she triggered the appearance of the first plants. She was not satisfied with all of them. The ones that were not very successful grew quickly like weeds. Others, the more beautiful ones, grew very slowly and rather as the only representatives of their species. However, all flora developed too slowly for the dynamic nature of the vigorous goddess. Patri decided to create something that will have more life in it. And that's when the first animals were created.

Strolling through the lush garden, she invented more and more interesting creatures and endowed them with different qualities. Most often, two individuals in case one of them fails. Sometimes one at a time. She planned to feed on vegetation that was starting to cause more and more trouble with their growth. After some time, she was bored with monotony again and invented the first predators. She endowed them with a fighting instinct and external carnivore attributes such as claws, fangs, and an agile body. Finally, things started to get quite interesting. Predatory animals killed and ate the boring herbivores. The planet has become one huge battlefield. But Patri realized that if she did this, soon there would be only carnivores and a lot of vegetation left. It would be a disaster. To remedy this, she gave the world disease, natural death, and regular renewal. It helped.

Subsequent, bolder ideas only improved her work. Birds, rodents, insects, fungi, molds appeared. And when she decided that her world was ready, she noticed that she could not boast of the result obtained to anyone. There was no one to appreciate her work. She decided to bring to life someone similar to herself, so that she could talk to them, commune with them, experience together, rejoice and grieve. She created man in her image and endowed him with divine qualities. Other than she had; you can say that they complemented it. However, he underestimated the gift. When he felt strong, he decided to take away her power to rule the world. She should have gotten rid of him, but she couldn't. She loved him. It was for him that she created the abyss, made him an eternal prisoner. Lest self-annihilation should occur to him, he would be taken over by the reverse world. She took his eyes off him, limiting his powers to work only in the dark, only there. From then on, he did not interfere with her creation. Even so, Patri knew all the time that he was out there somewhere. Occasionally, she thought about him, wondered what he was doing, and even secretly mourned him.

In order not to lose herself in longing, she created another human, but this time she did not endow him with the qualities of a god. He died quickly. "Why did I invent disease and death?" - she was furious with herself. She had barely called someone into the world and had become friends with him, that someone was going away. It was then that she decided to create a great human race and teach it to live independently. Without her control. But people also began to die, this time en masse. She had to renew this species from time to time. Before she could form one group, the other was leaving. Over and over again.

Patri was tired of recreating her world over and over again. And then she had the idea that someone could replace her in a great creation. Only who? Certainly not the god of evil hidden in the abyss. However, none of the animals, plants or humans had even the tiniest particle of energy that could create. All species could grow, even develop, but did not give another life. The only option turned out to be the transfer of all her power.

Patri loved the world she created very much and would not be able to part with it. If she gave her energy over to someone, that someone could get rid of the creator. She would have passed away like the creatures she created for her own amusement. She realized that she had to make a sacrifice and give herself entirely. To unite with all the Universe. Only then would no one destroy the work or the work itself. She did so. Patri's last will was to convert her body into the many particles of energy she was made of and bestow them to the entire world. She breathed every particle into all creatures and plants. From then on, everything that lived gained the ability to reproduce. The creation of new life happened in different ways, but always thanks to the transferred energy that was in the cells. They looked like micro-seeds.

After Patri, only her spirit remained - her consciousness. When people realized that thanks to it they lived and reproduced, they decided to give thanks to build a sanctuary on top of Mount Saandreal. Those who fell in love with their goddess so much that they decided to put themselves in her possession, or in service, became priests of her Church. This was the only way they could repay her for her sacrifice. Patri appreciated this gesture and let them rule the world she had created. She watched in advance if everything was going according to the order she had set. She communicated her decisions through visions experienced by the holy sages, known as the High Priests of the Omniearth. That's what the holy old scripts said. They contained the words of the goddess, and it was not allowed to argue with them. The first of the sages wrote them down. In the first era, right after the division of the Universe into two realms, religion became the symbol of Floris statehood. Over time, more old scripts were found explaining how to interpret the creator's words. Only then did people learn about the abyss, or the inverted world, and that people without faith go there. Also about the commandments that Patri herself gave, including those about mortal sins.

***

This morning, Ae did not show up for the daily morning prayer. Kifor led it instead. He experienced this customary ritual very personally. He felt like someone really important. Many times he imagined that he was the High Priest of the Omniearth, and today for a short moment he could feel a substitute for divinity. As he left the Golden Temple, he was eager to celebrate a replacement, but was disciplined by a backbone of false morality. He called to find out why the priestess had not appeared. When he knocked on her door, he had to wait a long time for permission.

"Are you all right, my lady?" He asked as she finally opened it.

"I only fell asleep in the morning. I fell asleep. I don't remember the last time that happened to me."

Kifor felt strong again as he saw his rival faint in his eyes. Even Zenit did not respect her anymore. Where is this strong woman who so ruthlessly rose to the top of power and settled there for good?

"How is the recruitment?" She asked to show interest.

"Okay." Kifor was disgusted with the point that Ae hadn't been listening to him lately. "I remembered something. Yesterday I met Ling Gui. He said he was worried about Kadu."

"Exactly. Has the good Kadu completed the task?" Ae really looked committed this time.

"He should be here a long time ago. You might think he was overdoing the tinghao as usual, but this time two low-ranking priestesses went with him to protect him. The best fighters from the military school."

"That's too much. This Kadu is making me furious."

"What if something happened to them and it's not his fault?"

"Does not matter. There has been no degradation for a long time. When he returns, he will be assigned a new assignment. Another priest will have to be sent to his quarter."

"Good idea. I even have someone who's good," said Kifor, and smiled like a child.

"I already have a candidate. What was the name of the rebellious one, the one in the mask?"

"Taarida. Her?"

"Kadu has spoiled his district. We have to bring order. Call her, please, but not too soon. Just don't tell her anything."

"Okay," he replied, though he did not seem to believe in the success of this change.

Ae liked to pray alone. Sometimes she did it in her chamber, and sometimes, especially on days like this, in the only place where no one was allowed to enter, which was the Patri Shrine. It was there that she intended to go now for a brief conversation with the goddess. This place was above the Golden Temple at the very top of Saandreal Mountain. It was shaped like a regular pyramid. From the inside, it was lined with precious stones and colored glass. They were called diamond, although there was not a single piece of this precious stone there. This secret was known to the High Priests of the Omniearth, because only they could stay there. The rest of the Floris population knew the version that the sanctuary was made of all diamonds. Despite the lack of these specifically precious stones, the place was magical in its own way. The rays of Hello came through the colored glass, creating an unprecedented phenomenon. The mirage of colorful rays dancing together resembled a colorful mass of energy trapped at the top of the pyramid, similar to the aurora. If anyone has tried to visualize the Patri spirit, it is this way. The High Priests of the Omniearth prayed here often. Here they received visions, decisions or ideas communicated by the goddess. Ae's prayer was very different from that of her predecessors.

The entrance was from below, directly from the Golden Temple. One had to climb a few stone steps and open a not too heavy cover resembling a small horizontal door. Ae went inside and closed the partition located in the floor behind her, after a while she stripped naked. She lay down and looked up. She admired the colorful sky that could be seen through the individual glasses.

"Patri, only you know the truth," she said in a shaky voice. "You never betrayed me. I could always count on you. I am asking you for help again. Let it all be cleared up and all right."

She sat up and shed a single tear. It took her a long moment to calm down her thoughts. When she returned to her chamber, a veil was thrown over her face. None of the priests passed by was surprised by this sight - it was frequent. Taarida was waiting for her there. She was standing in the middle with her head bowed. She wore a mask on her face because of the sacred venom that touched her more than the others. She looked haggard and modest, as if all her rebelliousness had been killed by waiting too long for the desired district.

"Taarida."

"Lady."

"I have an interesting task for you. I'd like you to unravel a few mysteries."

"Kifor said I would have my own district."

"If you pass the test?"

Ae knew the deputy would not listen to her. He will want to personally convey the good news to buy an ally and feel a substitute for power.

"I will do whatever you want, Lady," Taarida said with palpable gratitude.

"First you'll find Kadu. If he's alive, kill him."

The masked priestess twitched as if the command had surprised her, but nodded her head to show that she understood.

"Find out in advance why he did not comply with my request. There may be two low-ranking priestesses who have traveled with him to the western quarter around him. I don't know what they are called. Learn at Ling Gui school. It would be good for them to see this death. You show them my letter, so you'll be explained. In any case, they should know it's my decision. They are to bring his embalmed body to the gorge of Asaran. Everything according to the ritual. During this time, you will complete the quest for Kadu. It will be slightly modified compared to what he was supposed to do, but don't tell him when you meet him. If you do it, you'll get your quarters."

Ae basked in a perfect mood. She immediately started writing the letter.

***

The outskirts of Hambarra itself were announcing that the city belonged to a small group of particularly gloomy places for Floris. It did not show the colors that beat the eyes in the agricultural parts of the country. Apparently, art and culture were associated rather with the gray stone streets and dirty beige houses. Most of them looked alike. The central part of the city was occupied by a large square with stalls, in the center of which stood a pyramid-shaped temple, a miniature of the Patri sanctuary from Mount Saandreal. Not only prayers were held there, but also chamber concerts. Every few sunrise of Hello, the stalls were dismantled and the square hosted theatrical performances, orchestral parades or jugglers' parades. Everyone who came to this city and managed to feel its atmosphere, usually stayed there for life. It was a magical place that was hard to leave.

Fahid and Sumi arrived quite late, but soon realized that Hambarra never sleeps. Despite the dusk, tinghao games were held in the small streets lit by rows of torches. In one place the sound of drums was heard, in another, a young girl sang a Sundra song to the accompaniment of a lute, in another, a chorus of young men pounded with a harmonious bass. In addition, musicians could be found on almost every corner. Most often they played on just anything, ranging from various types of hummingbirds, binoculars, pimples, through multi-bells, trumpets and krales, and ending with tarantulas and transverse flavors broken twice. You felt that music was the most important thing in this city. The passing people seemed quite close to each other. Everyone was friendly and welcoming. They were happy to invite an unfamiliar-looking couple. Although Sumi was curious to meet new people, her father did not want to get involved in new acquaintances, the more so because they had an uninteresting adventure behind them and he preferred that no one would remember him. But when he saw that his daughter was finally smiling, his soul felt lighter. The whole trip to Hambarra looked sad, so now even the smallest glimmer of her happiness made him very happy.

"Where can we find a singing school?" Fahid asked one of the passersby.

"Which one?"

"There are more of them?" Sumi was surprised.

"Girl, there are ten schools here," replied a passer-by with a disarming smile, his height suggesting a cleansing age and a half, but a younger face.

"Which one is the best?" Fahid asked, looking away.

"I am studying at Manius Drey," a passer-by sang, arousing admiration and considerable surprise of the girl and disgust of her father.

"I want there too," she replied.

The father did not like the way the daughter stared at the slightly tipsy young man. He was unlike anyone worth trusting. Fahid heard from his father that artists can be crazy. Nevertheless, singing in public was incomprehensible to him.

"We need to take a nap, goodbye, good man," he said, pulling Sumi aside.

"Go around the corner. There is such a tall building there, an inexpensive night shelter for visitors."

"Thank you," Sumi replied and smiled sincerely at the passerby. "We'll definitely meet again."

"Call me Adalberto," the passer-by singsong said.

"Su..." The girl did not have time to finish, because her father gagged her mouth and sent a scolding look.

The lodging house looked very friendly. The lowest level, i.e. the deep basement, was intended for protection and sleep during the short season, called renewal. There was a welcome room in the basement, something like a reception desk, and the guest bedrooms started from the first level up. The doors to each of them were perpendicular to the winding staircase, curving in both directions like streamers. Fahid had never seen such a tall building. He was terrified by its monstrous size. He entered rather cautiously, as if he were afraid that the structure of the four-story tenement house would collapse under his heavy feet.

"I have to write your names down," said the not-so-handsome man in the night shelter.

"S... a strict father and his disobedient daughter," Sumi joked.

"If that's your name, I don't mind. I wrote down. Two gray stones are due," he replied and gave the girl a trained smile.

Fahid handed over the payment, avoiding exchanging glances. He was dissatisfied again. Not because his daughter taunted him. On the contrary, he appreciated that she quickly got out of a difficult situation and gave nicknames. He was more worried about another grown man who smiled at a young girl, and she stupidly reciprocated. "What will happen when she is alone here? Who will she grow up to be? Will no one want to deceive her?" He wondered. As they went up the stairs to the room on the top floor, he struggled with his thoughts as to whether he had made the right choice. Having made the decision to hide his daughter in this city, he was convinced that it was the perfect solution. The priests rarely visited them. Anyone could hide here. It was enough that he pretended to be a freak and he blended in with his surroundings. Sumi had a beautiful voice, so she didn't have to pretend to be anyone. From Fahid's point of view, the prospect of his daughter pursuing a profession of singer, even the worst one, sounded far better than the most dazzling career of a priestess. The view from the window opening on the fourth level bricked him up. He felt like a moree bird that looks down from the sky at tiny people and looks for easy prey. Sumi was also charmed, but as is usually the case with children, she downplayed the height. She felt that she was in a place made especially for her. She thought of herself to be like the goddess Patri looking down on her world. She knew that she would not forget this sight for the rest of her life.

The next day, when Fahid met Manius, he breathed a sigh of relief. The teacher looked quite normal. He did not speak like an artist, but like a craftsman, the best in his trade. He was to the point and to the point.

"Sing something, girl," he suggested. "Not everyone can be my student."

"I'll pay if I have to," Fahid interjected, but quickly realized it wasn't the way to go.

Sumi sang a few simple scales and a favorite country song. Manius said nothing. He was watching the girl like an animal bought at a market. He was close to looking into her mouth to see if her teeth were healthy. He didn't have to do this. He looked into her mouth imperceptibly as she sang. He couldn't afford to admit a girl who was not very pretty, without teeth, or lame. He had a reputation. The most talented and attractive singers in Floris graduated from his academy. Sumi was even pretty for a farmer's daughter.

Manius's gaze began to embarrass her. Fahid cleared his throat and sent him an urgent look.

"Learning takes about one purification. The total cost is only five hundred gray stones. Including food and washing. Paid in Advance."

"How much?" Fahid said indignantly. "I have only thirty."

Manius shrugged his shoulders simultaneously and made a mocking noise.

"Why are you bothering me?" He asked. "Learning costs money. Even if she only studied with me in the morning and then worked somewhere, I suppose she could earn no more than one gray stone in ten Hello sunrise. It is still not enough."

"Where can you work here?" Fahid wondered aloud, after all, he associated work only with farming.

"What can you do?" Manius asked, looking straight into the little girl's eyes.

"I can clean."

"Unless so. You could earn. There are more slobs in this town than cleaners."

Sumi looked at her father pleadingly. Various unpleasant thoughts flashed through his mind, most of them related to Kadu and his task. Then he made a face as if he were counting in his mind. It took a while.

"Today I can give you thirty gray stones," he finally stammered out. "I have another ten at home. If everything goes as planned, I can collect the missing four hundred and sixty gray stones by the end of the studies. I will be bringing in batches every few collections. That's all I can do. Please accept her. Please."

Manius scratched his perfectly trimmed beard. For Sumi, this customary short gesture lasted forever. She heard the slightest brush of a fingernail on each individual hair.

"I agree, but on my terms. The girl will work every day until the end of her studies. I will find her job myself, but all the earnings will go to me as interest on your debt. Today I'll take thirty gray stones, but you must give me back six hundred in twelve installments. If you fail to deliver even one installment of fifty gray stones on time, the girl will be expelled from school. He has to learn, make progress, and finally pass the exam. Otherwise..."

"She will be kicked off," Fahid finished. "I agree."

Sumi threw herself happily on her father's neck. She hugged him as tightly as she could. She was overjoyed. Her innermost dream came true. She had always wanted to sing, but she never thought that anyone in her family, based on a reasonable upbringing, could practice such a profession, which was not very practical in the opinion of her parents. Fahid was convinced that he was doing well, though not very wise. Even if the cost of studying was only a hundred gray stones, such an investment would never pay off, in his opinion. How wrong he was.

"A good singer can earn a few gray stones a day. Not in Hambarra. Not even in Patrix. There are places where talent is highly valued," Manius said, and shook his hand to seal the deal.

***

Zenit felt he could no longer stall and irritate the High Priestess of the Omniearth. His act will certainly be treated as insubordination anyway, although he acted in accordance with the applicable canon. The revelations told by the prisoner no longer follow logic, so it is high time to hand him over to a more severe authority.

"Leave us alone, Zenit," said the priestess.

She didn't even notice when he left. She focused on the prisoner. She looked at him searchingly. He looked perfectly normal, not like Haris. He was short and indeed stocky, as the chief of watch described him. His hands looked strong. He certainly did not have to use any tools to split the shells of the nimo, one of the hardest materials used as a building material.

"What is your name?" She asked.

"So it worked. I told your boys that my name is..."

"I know what you said," she cut him off, as if to imply that he didn't tolerate lying. "Did you hear my question?"

"Yes. My name is Xami. Although I don't look, I am from Inco. That's better?"

Ae sighed heavily. "Another man who probably knew a lot. How many such are wandering around my country?" - she wondered.

"Why did you want to meet me? Because I understand that mentioning the name I know had just such a purpose."

"A fair argument. I'll get straight to the point. I would like to offer you my services."

"Why would I use them? I happen to know what's going on at Inco. You probably won't be returning to your home country. With us, sooner or later you will die. Have I forgotten anything?"

"Believe me. You need me. Only I can track down Jusif."

"Apparently I have already given you such an assignment. Yeah." She smiled at her thoughts. "That was another catch to get me interested in you."

Ae looked away. How did Xami know that this was the man the Queen of Floris was looking for? She thought for a moment. The fact that they supposedly worked together and didn't make it true didn't have to be an excuse.

"If you give me a contract, I'll do it for free," he continued. "I'll bring you his head. You have to set me free, of course, and tell your pink boys that this isn't their league. They are not to follow me or they will finish..."

"Enough. How can I be sure you won't run away?"

"You're right. There is no life for me in Inco. The government I worked for doesn't exist. I have nowhere to go back. My country is now ruled by crazy women. They would like to see me as a food supplement."

The priestess made a scowl that looked like a combination of surprise and disgust.

"The new government has new ideas," he continued. "All who oppose must first work off their faults under humiliating conditions. When they no longer have the strength, they end up as a secret ingredient in recovery bars."

"So the bars are healthy after all," she joked. "You and Jusif know each other well?"

"Too good," he replied sarcastically. "We were sent here together. At the same time. Unfortunately, he was the first to get closer to you and he was given the most important task. I got only support and a few more important liquidations. Let's be precise: murders. Vishare is actually not his, but my doing. And not only him."

Ae made sure the door was closed.

"Go on."

"Nothing else to add. Give me a task and you'll find that you need me very much."

"Why do you think I'd like to get rid of Jusif?"

"Because he wasn't honest with you."

"Maybe I could forgive him?"

"And why did he disappear when Haris Sagavara appeared in Patrix?"

Ae thought for a moment.

"I want to question him first."

"You think Jusif will tell the truth?"

"How long will it take you?"

"How much will you give me?"

"Two Hello sunrises, sly dog." Ae smiled triumphantly.

"One is enough."

***

Jusif's head did not look freshly cut. It was covered with dried blood mixed with dirt, but it was definitely him. Ae would identified him anytime, anywhere. They knew each other for a long time. As she looked straight into his bulging eyes, she swallowed and narrowed her eyes.

"I don't know if I would like to be your enemy," she said.

"You've been for almost two purifications, but you've been safe," replied Xami.

"Because I liked Jusif?"

"He's gone."

"You didn't wait for my commission. You killed him before."

"I see that nothing will escape your attention. Who's next on your list? I take a hundred gray stones for one head," Xami said, lifting his nose in a gesture of triumph.

"I have some ideas, but this time you won't get it done that quickly."

"Jusif couldn't do it either."

"But I knew him."

'Really?"

Conflicting thoughts fought in Ae's head. On the one hand, she felt the need to strangle the thief alive, on the other, she felt that he might be a godsend.

***

The next day, right after the morning prayers, Ae asked Zenit to be accompanied by a group of cardinals on the way to the settlement of Vatili Soll. On the pretext of visiting Clifford, she was going to meet Haris first and foremost. The road passed quite quickly, as the High Priestess of the Omniearth did not exceptionally ask for any stop. First she met with priests who learned technical matters from Goeffrey Clifford. Then she pretended to be interested in the life of a former prime minister in exile. She entered the house where he lived with a group of cardinals. It looked like a spectacular parade.

"Hello Ae," Barney Clifford said in surprise. "What an honor is this?"

"I wanted to see how science is going. Poorly."

"I don't mean to offend anyone, but it's not my brother's fault. Your level of knowledge is, to put it mildly, backward. I think you understand, lady," he said.

"Yes. I know. You are delaying."

"Not completely. I was just about to go to Patrix."

"Something happened?" She asked with mock concern.

"I wanted to thank you personally for your hospitality, but we must be back now. The country needs us."

"What? Everyone?" Ae asked, though she wanted to ask about a specific member of Clifford's team. "You said it was dangerous out there now," she said, looking Haris straight in the eye.

"If we stay longer, we'll never have to go back. Revolutionaries take power," Rubby told her.

"I don't remember the debt being paid." Ae huffed in displeasure and took a few nervous steps.

"We live here shorter, we teach you shorter. It's fair, isn't it? We'll leave all the machines to you. There is no debt."

"Do you value your family's safety so cheaply? Interesting."

Clifford swallowed and looked at Haris as if seeking support.

"You'll be able to return when my tech priests confirm that they have learned all the knowledge they were about to acquire. If you want to leave faster, try harder."

"But, lady..."

"I wish you a nice afternoon. Can I ask you to leave? All. You stay." Ae pointed at Haris.

Her decision was met with slight indignation. Clifford hesitated for a moment whether he should comply with her request. She looked at him flatly, penetratingly and coldly. He realized that his position was no longer privileged. He left slowly, his gloomy eyes running across the floor. The others did the same after him. One of the purple guards looked at the priestess. He waited for confirmation as to whether he should go away as well. She nodded.

"What do you want from me?" Haris asked when they stayed together.

"Who is Xami? Just tell the truth."

"A shrimp? So he came out. Idiot."

"What do you mean?" Ae clearly liked Haris's tone of insulting others. In her perception of the world, it was the most appealing attitude of men.

"You would never catch him. He is losing the ground."

"Or he has other intentions."

"That's possible. It is certainly a perfect complement to Jusif."

The High Priestess of the Omniearth smiled gently. This ordinary, seemingly insignificant little thing pleased her. She had just realized that for the first time she knew a little more than Haris. It was a small but important victory that gave her strength. It turned the tide of her inner struggle that had been fought for some time. She no longer resented Haris for blackmailing her once. At that moment, all she thought was how to convince him to stay in Floris. As she stepped outside, she saw an unusual sight. Several Inco notables, including Clifford and Rubby, stood nearby and watched the exit of the house as they whispered like little boys. Their plotting looked grotesque. That picture made her laugh.

"High Priestess, let me and my family at least go home," Clifford stuttered uncertainly.

"No way. The family must stay here. I can finally agree that you go alone, without bodyguards. You will definitely hit the place, the road is straight. If you're afraid, I can send one man to help."

Clifford lowered his head. His companions became sad. Apparently, they realized that the situation was getting out of hand. Interestingly, until recently they had the impression that they were in control of everything. But really, that was a long time ago.

"You'll stay here. Make sure he leaves alone. The day after tomorrow at the earliest," she whispered to one of the guards.

He nodded, accepting the order.

"If the others rebel, kill someone for an example."

***

Back at Patrix, Ae was surprised to find a messenger waiting for her. It was a woman. She was tasked with inviting a priestess to Inco to familiarize herself with the new Government. Ae listened to her but did not give a specific answer. Admittedly, she was curious about the new prime minister and what the consequences of her appointment would be, but for the moment she refused gently, covering herself with a health indisposition. She didn't want to meet with any official until a few things were cleared up. To this end, she asked Kifor to summon a prisoner named Xami. He was surprised, because such orders were only given to Zenit, but he quickly realized that there were two possible scenarios. The High Priestess of the Omniearth is simply disappointed with the attitude of the chief of cardinals, or worse, she was mortally offended by him. He was right in that regard. She forbade Zenit to approach her chamber.

When Xami appeared, she politely asked Kifor. He wasn't going to go too far. He was interested in who the prisoner was and what Zenit had earned. He hid behind the door and began eavesdropping.

"I'm going to ask you a tough question, Xami," she said after making sure the door was locked. "How many people do you think know my past?"

"This type of information is rather not publicized, so I am convinced that there are not too many of them. As for now living in this land, I think only twenty. In Inco a maximum of five. It will be more difficult with them, but if I was given such an assignment, I have someone who could help."

"Do you give any discounts for the bulk order?" She asked in a cheerful voice, as if it were meant to be a delicious joke. "Let's say twenty-seven heads?"

"And those two heads are who?" Xami was surprised.

"Who said two? Maybe three," she continued in a bubbly mood.

"If there is a chief of guard on this list, you will save money on this assignment. I will make it for free. Let it be this discount."

"Try harder. I like to negotiate."

Ae smiled gently. Xami smiled back, but in a sly way. He felt like a friend of an important person. Kifor, standing outside the door to the chamber, opened his eyes wide with terror. He had always known Ae was warmblooded in his own way, but this was the first time he had heard such words from her lips. She has passed judgment on many people and it is as if she was making a decision about what to eat for dinner. Kifor also knew that Zenit's life was doomed. "Should he report it to someone? Will anybody believe him? Shouldn't he get some evidence? Who else was on the bloody list of the priestess?" He wondered.

Chapter 15 Competition

The agenda of the next meeting of the Government contained only one point. His name was Wierra Slippnot. The members of the prime minister's cabinet waited with great excitement for the moment when a woman with this name would happily return with the envoy from Floris and give the good news.

"Hello, friends," Noovack began. "Slippnot arrived at night. Tired, but alive. We'll be able to talk to her in a moment. I gave her some time to rest after a tiring journey. Before she gets to us, I have a few questions for you. Most importantly: how does society respond to change? Natalie?" She looked in the direction of Tatarczyna.

"Almost perfect," she replied uncertainly. "We had a few incidents recently, but they were nipped in the bud."

"Nonsense," Davis said indignantly. "You have no idea what's going on. Society is divided."

"What do you mean, my friend?" Noovack asked.

"Second district is raging."

"Don't be defeatist, Kimberly," Tatarczyna commented. "This is nothing new. This has been happening for many months. I would even be tempted to say that it is getting calmer."

"It must be because of the new procreative solutions," Gibbondy reminded of herself in her unique style.

"Are we then ready to introduce further decrees? Asked the prime minister.

There was an awkward silence. Noovack glanced at the heads of ministries one by one.

"Kimberly? Just answer honestly."

"In my opinion, nothing stands in the way," Tatarczyna replied, cutting herself in front of a thoughtful Davis.

"The revolution requires casualties," said Monssantoo. "I think it's time to introduce the X Directive."

"Already?" Noovack was surprised.

"What's this?" Duecklenbourg asked.

"Stay awake in our meetings, my friend," Noovack admonished her. "It was mentioned. It's still Clifford's idea. Even noble."

"Ah, this one. I didn't remember its name." Duecklenbourg pretended to know what was going on, though no one fell for her play.

At this point, the door to the Meeting Room was opened, and Wierra Slippnot appeared. She actually looked tired and sleepy. Her face was tanned, as if she had wandered many days in the hot sun.

"Sit down, my friend," Noovack gestured. "Tell me. We are very interesting."

"Thank you," answered the black-haired Slippnot and sat down in the place of honor designated by the Prime Minister who conducted the meeting.

"Introduce yourself first," Duecklenbourg said, trying to make a good impression with the manners of the house.

"All right. My name is Wierra Slippnot. I have four purifications. My father was an engineer in an armaments plant, and my mother was a food technologist. Both are dead. I have two brothers. Terrible idiots." She laughed. "Maybe this is enough for a start."

"Did you manage to meet the priestess?" Davis asked.

"Yes. Ae is a beautiful woman, not like the others in her church. She looks young but experienced. She is sparing in words."

"Did you get along easily? In terms, is our language very different from their gibberish?"

"No. We say exactly the same. Maybe they use phrases that we do not know, because they refer to animals, plants or objects that do not exist in our country, but they use the same language. They only write differently. These are not letters like ours, but something like signs. I saw on the scrolls that lay in her chamber."

"When will she come to us?" Noovack asked.

"I do not know. Rather not soon. She said she would meet, but in a while. She did not confirm when. She said she was sick..."

"Sick? Better not to come here, because shewill infect us. They don't care about health."

"They care, just differently, and she didn't look sick." Rather, she was acting like she wanted to dismiss me.

"Do you think she was hiding something?" Noovack asked.

"Hard to say. I don't know her, but she certainly didn't seem open to making new friends. She was quite artificial when she pretended to be nice. I certainly wouldn't trust her."

"I knew. They're up to something," said Davis.

Noovack was cooking from the inside, but not wanting to show that she was troubled by the priestess's nonchalance, she decided to change the subject.

"Tell us about this land. What did you see? Did you like something?"

"Have you met Clifford?" With this important question, Tatarczyna attracted the attention of the other participants of the meeting.

"I did not see him. Nobody knows anything. Floris is an interesting country. There is a lot of colorful vegetation. You can meet real living creatures. There are tons of them. And this is a bird, and this is an insect, and this is some rodent."

"And the people?"

"They are too, of course. White hair dominates. They dress weird, they have different habits, they are not as thin as we are. But... they don't look bad. I've never seen so many men at once. I guess there are even more of them than women. Or at least it would seem."

"Impossible," Davis said indignantly.

"Really. And their wives, mothers, sisters, daughters look happy."

"In our place will also be wonderful. We just need to rearrange our world." Noovack couldn't hide her jealous phobias.

"Exactly. Our world is better," Gibbondy chimed in.

"Slobs," Davis said.

"They're not slobs. I mean, not that they were perfectly clean. They just don't stink. Some even smell good. Herbs, food, flowers."

"Wonderful," she commented with a hint of irony in Gibbondy's voice, encouraging Noovack.

"And religion? Is it ubiquitous?" Duecklenbourg asked.

"It was the worst. Everywhere these statues of their goddess. People pray like they don't have brains."

Noovack finally felt better. If Slippnot went too far in its assessment by pointing to only positive aspects, Floris would be an idyllic country, towering over Inco.

"How do you think?" She asked Wierry. "Could these men cultivating plants be able to live in our world? No religion, no job, no nature..."

"I think so. They are simple people. It is enough to convince them that they will have the status of gods with us, and that they will be convinced with flattery," she replied.

"Since there are so many of them, no one will notice if some of them move to us," Duecklenbourg suggested.

"You hit the nail on the head, friend. I already like it. Let's steal some for test. We'll see if they find themselves," "Noovack suggested.

"Great idea," assessed Tatarczyna.

"Bravo Prime Minister," Davis echoed.

After a while there was a thunderous applause. Only Gibbondy didn't seem very pleased with her boss's new idea. She smiled fixedly, the way she always did when she had other view.

***

Just a week and a half. It was enough to wait to make sure painlessly that the embryo would one day be a boy. Jasmin didn't want Addam to go alone with Vicky. They were about to go to the office of Dr. Meilly, the doctor with the best hands and the most efficient handling of the device invented by the present Minister of Health. She decided to go with them. They were supposed to be a family, so under the pretext of far-reaching commitment, she invited herself down to the company. She washed the blue dye off her hair as a sign of the end of the mourning. She threw away all the blue outfits, deciding that she would no longer need them. She dressed differently than usual - she put on a loose, gray dress over which she threw a long, thin scarf masking the slight roundness of her stomach. She knew Dr. Meilly's waiting room, but had never thought that she would ever show up other than as a patient. Vicky came in first to get ready. After a while, the doctor who looked like five purifications invited Addam. Jasmin slipped inside after him. When she saw Vicky, half-naked, lying on the couch, she decided that this young bitch had a brazenly perfect body.

"Please spread your legs," Dr. Meilly said to the patient.

Before Vicky complied with her request, she glanced fondly at Addam. He was excited. He could barely hide his emotions. His mouth was wide open, he was short of breath, and his eyes were running wild. Jasmin noticed it. She had seen her husband like this several times. She decided it was a shame to be like this with strangers. She decided to distract him. She walked around the couch and crouched on the other side. She grabbed Vicky's hand affectionately, which surprised both her husband and, probably, his future second wife. It seemed to be an exemplary act of empathy devoid of all atoms of jealousy. Managed to. Addam stopped shaking idiotically.

"You are a nice family," said Dr. Meilly. "Are you a mom?"

"I am this gentleman's first wife," Jasmin replied harshly.

Dr. Meilly looked surprised, but it was only for a short time. Apparently, that's not what she had seen. She tugged the fanciful looking gray handle two steps to the left and pressed the square button that activated the gibbonator.

Something clicked and clicked in the small portable device, and after a while a rattling sound began to come out. Vicky glanced in horror at the device, then toward Addam.

"That's nothing. They still have to work on it," said Meilly, embarrassed. "It actually works too loud. But it really works."

Meilly grabbed the tube protruding from the device with a sensor that looked like a glass eye with micro-cameras. She wiped it dry with a cloth and smeared it with fresh gel.

"It's gonna be cold, but only for a moment. Mr. and Mrs....," she turned to Jasmin and Addam. "Look over there now. On the screen."

Vicky hissed to confirm that the gel was indeed cold. A screen projected on one wall, near the corner, showed an image of the inside of her uterus. Addam made a face of disgust. Jasmin frowned slightly and stared at him. Meanwhile, Dr. Meilly was changing the settings on the device. The image came closer and further away, sometimes slightly rotating. The adjustment took a while.

"My leg is numb," Jasmin said, and extended her hand toward Addam, hoping he would act like a gentleman.

He did not react. He had gotten bored with the waiting, unconsciously staring at the gynecologist's desk as if reading her prescriptions upside down. Jasmin shook her head in disapproval, released Vicky's hand and struggled to lean against the bed as she rose, exposing her tight stomach. Meilly saw it.

"Which week is it?"

"Eleventh," she replied and walked aside.

"It grows fast," commented doctor.

Addam twitched nervously, as if the information had brought him down to earth. He looked towards Jasmin's stomach and sighed deeply. At that moment another image appeared, projected on the other wall close to the same angle. There was nothing there, everything was blurry. Dr. Meilly turned up the contrast and the image began to resemble the former, but from a different perspective. Addam became interested. After a while, a third image appeared, this time superimposed on the previous two, creating a three-dimensional projection. Now not only was Addam stunned, but so was Jasmin.

"Why does the theatremania not work like that?" She asked.

"Because state funds go only to the development of medicine," replied Addam, still shaking his head in disbelief.

Dr. Meilly turned more knobs, simultaneously switching all the synchronized images creating a three-dimensional whole.

"Got you," she said excitedly. "There it is. See?"

Addam, Vicky, and Jasmin looked at the screen. Their expressions were confused, and their eyes darted between the folds of Vicky's internal organs in disarray as if they were looking for a needle in a haystack.

"Come on over."

"Where? Here?" Addam asked, frightened.

"No. Over there. To the screen. Put your hand out."

Addam did what the doctor asked him to do, but he still looked not so much confused as more disgusted that Vicky had to enter the virtual uterus. Jasmin was having a lot of fun.

"Now to the left and a bit up. It's the dot," said Meilly.

"You can't see anything here. Can you enlarge?"

"You have everything at hand. Anyway, it couldn't be more. You want to nest here, one kid."

"Boy?" Vicky asked hopefully.

"I do not know yet. I just wanted to show you. We'll find out in a moment, but at this point we'll thank the audience."

Jasmin didn't have to be asked twice. Limping on a numb leg, she walked over to the door, grabbed the handle, and scurried to the waiting room. Addam smiled at Vicky to cheer her up and left the office as well.

The man with mustache was already waiting in the corridor, he looked restless. He paced back and forth with his eyes fixed on the floor as if he were counting the individual triangles it was made of. Those leaving did not pay attention to him. They stood to the side. They only noticed him when he reacted nervously to the sounds coming from the office. It was an even louder mechanical rumble, this time coupled with a rhythmic gurgling sound. It didn't sound very good. Jasmin and Addam exchanged glances. "What are you doing to me?" She thought, looking straight into his absent eyes. It looked as if his soul had stayed there in the study. They continued for a while, until finally Addam looked away towards the door. And that's when it opened. Vicky appeared in them. Dressed, joyful, with a print in hand.

"I'm glad you were here with me," she said.

"Boy?" Asked the man with mustache.

"Yes!" She screamed and shed a few tears of unimaginable happiness.

"Wonderfully!" Addam responded. "You will be my wife."

"I know. Dad, meet my fiance," she joked.

"Beloved, I adore you." Mustachioed couldn't contain his emotions.

"Congratulations," Jasmin said dryly.

Nobody noticed her bitter reaction. Addam was kissing Vicky, and his father, staring at the happy couple, was wiping tears from his cheeks.

"Now you must propose to her in the Glass Dome," Jasmin tried to remember, postponing the wedding in the process.

"Yeah. This is the tradition," reacted mustachioed.

"I don't give a shit on conventions," said Addam.

"You're so strong and so smart," Vicky replied proudly. "You impress me. I love you. Whack these superstitions."

"Damn it. What an emotion. So what, wedding tomorrow?" Addam's future father-in-law asked with delight.

Jasmin stood like a pillar of salt. Nothing was reaching her. In her mind, she repeated the words of the bride and groom all the time. "Wonderfully? I love you? Idiot. And this one? Motherfucker. Also fell in love at first sight? Into the uterus, I think." Jasmin was mentally speculating on what the world stands for. After a while, her marketing spirit spoke. She realized that she couldn't show morbid-looking envy, even if it came out of her own accord and wanted to puke everyone around.

"Yes," she replied for her husband. "We will prepare a modest but original ceremony. I'll take care of everything."

She finished with mock glee and hugged the mustachioed. Addam patted her shoulder several times. More like a friend. That's how she perceived it.

***

The day has finally come for which Eva Noovack and her closest family have been waiting for quite a long time. Her husband, Rinno, until recently worked as director of one of Ray's factories. Eva delayed the next major decrees until their joint account was credited with his last tranche of high severance pay. As Prime Minister of the Government, she did not intend to starve, although she had deliberately set for herself and her colleagues in the cabinet, the same salary as for all women in the entire Inco, equal to two thousand entitys. "Just like everybody," she would say to her daughter, who tapped her head with her finger as she tried to talk her mother out of a cardinal error. Unsuccessfully.

"My dear," Eva began her daily theatremania performance with Mrs. Duddlemayer by the arm. "Yesterday afternoon, two more decrees were signed and we implemented them on the same day. The first was simple. The time has come to liquidate the unnecessary Council of Advisors. Following the introduction of the decree banning male activities, the Council was too slimmed down. It is difficult to continue the activity alone."

At this point, Noovack smiled fondly at the old woman.

"Our dear Mrs. Duddlemayer has promised that, whenever there is any doubt, I will be able to ask her for advice at any time. Don't go away yet, dear," Noovack told Duddlemayer fondly, though it didn't seem sincere. "The second decree I signed yesterday was definitely more important. It is about the long-awaited crackdown on murderers who have destroyed our community. They wanted to deprive our children of the future. I am thinking, of course, of the families to which the pharmaceutical industry and the cartels belong. Their deed cannot go unpunished. My friends and I thought for a long time what we should do and it was then that our adviser, Mrs. Duddlemayer, came in handy."

At that moment the old woman looked surprised, as if she did not know what it was about.

"How not to love her. Right?" Noovack continued. "She suggested a bold, but very wise and fair solution. Thank you, dear," she said to the old lady who had just been led aside, though she still looked completely confused.

From that moment on, only the prime minister flashed on the theatremania screen.

"As suggested by the Council of Advisors in force until yesterday, the cartels should be taken away from their owners. Therefore they will be nationalized. We will combine all of them into one body with the State Treasury as its dominant shareholder. The name of the united pharmaceutical concern will be easy to remember, "Inco Pharma". Isn't it nice? I would like to introduce you to a person who, like no one else, is suitable for the extremely difficult function of the president of the newly established company. This is Monya Kirsch. Please do not be deceived by her young age. She is experienced and has extensive chemical and management knowledge."

A brown-haired woman, aged three purifications, appeared on the screen. Noovack theatrically shook her hand. It was evident that the hug had been practiced beforehand. The Prime Minister's daily talk ended with this nice accent. After the broadcast, Noovack hugged Monya. She knew both of them made the difficult choice. The new president of Inco Pharma faced serious challenges. "Can she handle it?" The head of the Government inquired. From now on, the eyes of all residents will be focused on this young manager. Many women will envy her, more than one will become her enemy. "Besides, will she reconcile the role of wife and new mother with the role of president? She has to. If necessary, we'll help her," Noovack thought. She knew all the advantages that predispose a girl to success, especially courage in the heart, as well as the inexhaustible layers of ambition. After all, Monya Kirsch née Noovack, the only daughter of Eva and Rinno, inherited a talent for pharmacy from her father, and a talent for governance from her mother. It had to work.

***

Information about the nationalization of the pharmaceutical industry went virtually unnoticed. Eva Noovack deliberately made the news at a time when the public was focused on a completely different topic. For a week in the first district, it was hard to find a humaan guard. Most of them implemented the implementation of Directive X.

That morning, as most of the women in District 2 had gone to work as usual, glass cages of guards began to roll up to their homes. They were accompanied by humaans, but in much larger groups than had been seen before. In the blink of an eye, sectors hundred and forty-six were filled. Sectors from the Top Hundred were omitted as no men lived in them anymore. An old teacher with a long family lived in one of the lower buildings in Sector 212. Everyone was ordered to go outside the building. The children were still asleep, and the old people were not very lively.

"Giro Anttca?" One of the robots said in the direction of a black-haired man about four purifications.

"Yes, it's me."

"In accordance with the X directive, please take only the most essential personal items and get into the vehicle."

"What have I done? You didn't even read my card to confirm, sheet-thing!"

At that moment, a balding old man, holding a little boy by the hand, trod out of the building, followed by an old woman and two girls.

"Please don't make it difficult." Humaan was adamant.

"What's going on here?" Asked the old gentleman.

"Professor Jullo Anttca?"

"Yes. It's me, although no one has called me that for a long time."

"In accordance with the X directive, please take only the most essential personal items and get into the vehicle."

The old man frowned and scratched his head.

"Mirosli Anttca?" The robot turned to the little boy clutching his grandfather's hand.

"Can you tell me, sir, what's going on here? What are we arrested for?" The professor asked.

"Father, don't call it sir," his son admonished him.

"A mistake," said humaan. "It's not an arrest, it's an eviction. Due to the protection of male sex, resettlement to the first district of all men living in this sector was implemented."

"What about families?" Asked the old gentleman.

"All females stay."

"I'm not leaving anyone!" Giro shouted, pushing his way towards his daughters as he pushed the humaan away.

At this point, the robot hit an elderly woman in the nose in retaliation. She immediately fell over, her face flooded with blood. The old gentleman froze.

"Why did you hit her, bastard?" Giro asked, helping the woman to get up. "Dad! Probably broke," he turned to the old man.

"Certainly," he replied, holding back tears of helplessness. "This is a mistake. We need to explain this."

"Make no mistake. I repeat the last time, please take your personal belongings and get on."

The little boy jerked nervously and gripped his grandfather's hand tighter. The old lady had already stood up, took out a handkerchief and started wiping the blood off her mouth. The girls approached her and hugged her. They looked scared and lost. The old gentleman looked around. Only now did he notice that there were similar Dantesque scenes taking place at each of the surrounding buildings. One of the more quarrelsome men, two houses away, hid behind his mother and daughter. He was shouting insults at the humaan dealing with the eviction in that building. The robot stood in prison, then removed its automatic weapon and fired two precise shots. The woman and her granddaughter fell to the ground. Shocking. The man rushed to rescue, but it was too late. At that moment there was a slight panic. The whole sector came to life. People were running in amok. The men started packing up, the women hugging each other and trembling for the future.

"What happened to the decree on the superiority of the human race over cybernetics?" The professor asked in an indignant, though trembling voice.

"Canceled," replied the humaan coldly.

"Where are you taking us?"

"To a better place."

"But I'm old, I'm no use anymore," said the old gentleman.

"Exactly. Let father stay at least. Look at him," said Giro irritated.

Humaan turned his head towards the old man.

"Such a grandpa would deal with procreation?" Giro continued. "Are you kidding?"

"There are no exceptions. Just like everybody."

The old man gestured to his son and grandson that they should surrender. It was evident that he had respect in the family. Each of them took some of the most important things and, accompanied by the lamentation of the old lady and the girls, got into the glass cage. The teacher smiled at his wife as if to show her that nothing disturbing was happening.

"Do not worry. We will try to come back as soon as possible. Tell mom I love her very much," Giro said to the crying girls hugging Grandma.

Not only the second district lived in similar tragedies, but also the first district, from where women began to be evicted. Men from poorer families who previously lived in slums were forcibly dragged to their apartments. Until a marked improvement in demographic statistics, they were to abandon their families and live in a more secure neighborhood. Only those who at least one of the wives were actually carrying the boy in their womb were released. The rest, according to the Government's decision, had to move. At the same time, reports glorifying the "Cascade of Eviction" appeared on all channels in theatremania. With these words, more in terms of marketing, Noovack redefined Directive X, the resettlement process introduced to protect the human species. First, there were interviews with women who seemed happy to give their apartment in the first district as housing for the men in the second. Then, similar interviews were shown, with men who were glad to live clean, in a new place, away from the cramped slums and the dangers lurking there. As a matter of fact, every moderately intelligent inhabitant of both the first and second district knew that it was embarrassing, staged propaganda. Evictions took place in front of the families, and their feelings about the brutality of the humaans quickly spread throughout the country.

The Cascade of Eviction was a well-planned logistics project, and Clifford had figured it out. The Noovack government only took advantage of his dissolution. First, in the first district, entire skyscrapers full of women living alone, sometimes well off, were displaced. They found new places to live in barracks, erected at an express pace in the third district, far from the factories. No running water or energy. It was supposed to be temporary, but it didn't work. More difficult was the resettlement of men torn from wives, daughters, mothers or lovers to abandoned skyscrapers. It was not without bloodshed. In this way, nearly a million men from the second district were to find their new place. The grand operation was divided into many stages. Two and a half to three thousand slumers were relocated daily. It was assumed that the entire process would take no more than twelve months. Each of the displaced persons had a special microchip sewn into the wrist for control purposes. He hurt badly if the host came too close to the border between the districts. At the same time, the construction of wire entanglements began.

***

Noovack liked to shift the interest of the Inco society from one scandal to the next. Another topic that arose at practically the same time was reheating Luigi Pierone. Since the outbreak of the scandal with Ray, the journalist's topic has not been forgotten, but sidelined. After all, people were bothered by matters of much greater importance than the insignificant scammer and what happened to him.

"Luigi, my friend, we're finally seeing each other," Noovack greeted him, pretending to be nice, and dismissed the assistant.

"Why did it take so long? Why did you imprison me?" Pierone asked indignantly when he noticed they were alone in her office.

"We? I don't understand. As far as I know, it was the Black Hands protecting you from getting to Mr. Clifford. As I understand it is safe, so you could finally come out of hiding."

"Don't be kidding. Black Hands? And who is behind them? Just don't tell me that Ana Mariya. I've heard that answer before."

Eva Noovack started shaking her head to gain time. She thought for a moment. She wasn't sure what else this slimy guy knew. Could this time the journalist discovered a scandal for the first time on his own? She decided to test his knowledge. She felt that this lousy journalist wouldn't keep his mouth shut for a long time.

"To my knowledge, Ana Mariya stole data from Metachem about the effects of Ray's actions and gave them to the Black Hands, and these clever women made them available to you."

"Don't lie, woman! The data was stolen by your husband. I know he worked in one of the factories under his mother's maiden name so no one would find out about his connection to you. Why did you pretend to be divorced for half the purification? I have evidence that you were driving the Black Hands. Ana Mariya is you!"

Noovack's lower lip twitched nervously and dropped to his left side, revealing a clenched jaw. As if the prime minister was going to bite looking five purifications a copper-haired freckle-face.

"Let's get along," she answered through her teeth, but in a calmer voice. "How can I make it up to you?"

"I was promised to be the head of the Media Council. I hid for a long time and now I'm not going to give up my honors. I will not hide like other guys! I have balls! I'm a national hero, damn it!"

"I have no doubts, but how do I explain the exception to the decree? Just like everybody. You can't work."

"I'm not interested! Why are you looking at me?" Pierone asked, seeing the madness growing in Noovack's eyes, she looked like a predator again. "Listen, if you accidentally get the idea to get rid of me, one of the lawyers has the relevant documents waiting to be published."

"Ha, ha, you must be kidding," Noovack chuckled. "You think I'll let myself be blackmailed? Are you sure any attorney will want to mess with me and print anything negative about me in the newspaper? You clearly underestimate me. I'll tell you because it won't matter anymore. On the day of the coup d'état, we launched censorship. We are currently in control of everything. Not only theatremania and newspapers. Even messages across the messaging network. The national hero is found. You owe shit, you dumb idiot."

After a week in theatremania on channel one, there was an extensive report of the burial of a journalist who discovered the biggest scandal in the history of Inco, but unfortunately the Clifford's services caught up with him. This unprecedented death was remembered for a long time.

Pierone was found completely naked. While still alive, his body was bolted to a platform made of highly conductive, rapidly heating metal. In turn, the landing was left in a small rocky desert in the fourth quarter. There, a border guard unit patrolling the area found him. It took only a few hot days and Hello rays to practically fry Pierone's body. He was hailed a hero, and in honor of his martyrdom, the new School of Controlled Motherhood planned for construction in three months was named. It was to be built on the site of the Glass Dome planned to be demolished. Thus, the age-old custom of proposal was to be forgotten. After all, the model of building a family was just changing - first procreation, then marriage, without further ado.

***

Addam's wedding to Vicky Morgoruth, who chose to stay with her maiden name, was quick and to the point. That's what Jasmin had planned. The bride and groom did not object. In accordance with applicable law, it was granted by an elderly brown-haired judge dressed in a black robe in a festively decorated room on the first floor of the building of the Ministry of Law and Justice. No artificial black flowers, as was the custom, no rituals. The very essence. The ceremony was attended by Addam's parents, his brother with his wife and sons, Haenra, Luicey, and the large family of Vicky. Of course, Jasmin was there as well, though being there, especially under such circumstances, caused her great pain. Even the memory of her own wedding, which she had with Addam, did not give any relief, quite the contrary.

In order to somehow survive the disgrace planned and implemented by herself, she used the golden upper case earlier. This particular version gave a feeling of bliss comparable only to the effect of backbreaking training, as a moment later the brain was releasing endorphins in unbelievable amounts. Thanks to them, everything around looked almost perfect. Only the golden upper, among all those available in the underground circulation, was delayed. Jasmin took it in the apartment for fear that later she might not be able to. She was a little worried that humaans of garda might sense it on the way. Success. None of the passed by on the way came close enough to the retinue for its sensors to detect the drug.

Jasmin calculated that it should work at the beginning of the wedding. But something went wrong. Upper did not release anything throughout the ceremony. Each passing second was mercilessly prolonged. As Jasmin looked contemptuously at the joyful faces of the guests, she felt doubly lonely. Useless. Like an intruder. Addam's wedding to Vicky was for Jasmin a torment almost comparable to her horrible experience before. Back then, she had to accompany, admittedly through the wall, but the thin future young couple during test sex. She mentally scolded herself for every wrong and delayed decision she made in life. Just when she thought it couldn't get any worse, Luicey walked over to her.

"They look beautiful, don't they?" The friend asked, watching the couple receive their first congratulations after a short ceremony.

"You've always been a master of diplomacy. Let me remind you that this is my husband."

"And I will remind you that it was your idea."

"Thank you darling. You can always be counted on."

"You're welcome. I think I'll be friends with her. We'll both have sons, won't we?"

"What a stupid argument," Jasmin said indignantly. "Why don't you become friends with every woman who will have a boy? There aren't many of them."

Luicey held back for a long time. She even smirked, which made her friend slightly anxious.

"Anything I should know?" Jasmin asked distrustfully.

"I just thought that someday we can be a nice patchwork family."

Jasmin didn't feel like commenting on that anymore. At this point, the upper finally started working. Immediately hard, as if making up for lost time. She was grateful to it. She felt blissful and happy. It freed her from meaningless conversation with her friend, silly Luicey, who never understood anything the way she should. Jasmin looked carelessly at the thirty-person group of happy-looking people lined up for wishes. "And what was the point of complaining like this? I am happy. I have an excellent life that everyone envies me," she admitted to herself in an emotional way. In her eyes, Addam looked like the most handsome theatremania star again, and Vicky, standing at his side, was the goddess of one of the female sports. "There will be no shame in showing up with her. My family," she thought warmly. Even the mustachioed at that moment seemed to her a good old uncle whom she had never known. "If my parents would see Vicky and Addam look beautiful, they would definitely be happy too and love the couple. Just like me," she thought.

Meanwhile, Luicey was constantly saying something to her, but not a single word reached its destination. As if the upper barrier formed just in front of Jasmin's ears prevented access to any inappropriate words in these wonderful circumstances.

Chapter 16 Pandemonium

If okurai had wings, it could be said that Fahid had almost flown to his homeland. When he said goodbye to his beloved daughter Sumi in Hambarra and made sure that she was safe, that she had a place to sleep and what to eat, he rushed his pet towards the house. He thought all the way about when he would manage to pay back the debt he owed the singing teacher. By the way, he tried to avoid the worst thoughts, but they pushed themselves into his head, usually in groups, even in whole hosts. Both those about escaping from the decision of the High Priestess of the Omniearth, as well as those invoking the silence of the priest. It didn't matter that Fahid had killed three people to keep his daughter calm. He had done wrong and remorse crushed his liver, and the walls of his shrunken stomach rubbed against each other, forming more ulcers. He also returned his thoughts to Kadu many times. They didn't know each other very well, but the priest had been associated with his district for several purifications. Everyone knew him, some liked him, not everyone respected him. Especially those who knew about his age-old relationship with the tinghao drink, they thought he was a drunk. Sumi shouldn't have known something so horrible had happened, much less witness it. After all, Kadu, Hara, and Nate were just doing their chores. Never mind that it was not in line with the plans of a caring father. She shouldn't have seen it, and it was over.

Aside from Mahmud's death, so much has happened recently. Fahid has come a long way, both literally and figuratively. In defense of his daughter, he first reached Litrijis, then almost to the Asaran gorge, then by side roads to Hambarra and back home. His okurai looked very tired. "When I get home, the animal will never have to work again," thought the poor farmer. "He deserved a long rest. He saved me from oppression more than once and took me through such a large part of the world," - he continued his thoughts.

Fahid had no intention of wasting a single day more. He knew his role was to cultivate the dirshna. The eldest sons must have reclaimed the plantation, but they were unable to plant new plants. Everything was waiting for their father. This was a waste of time for the earth. Almost thirty Hello sunrises. It will all have to be made up for. Were it not for the journey, the stalks of the plants would be planted in and perhaps some of them would already be sticking out of the water. It didn't matter anyway. When Fahid remembered that he had saved his child from the tormentors, his heart felt lighter. Then he thought of the interesting places he had seen during the journey. He was going to tell his wife Rita and the whole bunch of kids about everything. About what the mao cultivation fields looked like, about the highlands near the ravine, about the sahadi lizards, and about the funny city of Hambarra, where buildings reach up to the clouds. Some have as many as four levels sticking out of the ground.

The wide copper plate separating the individual fields between the neighbors greeted him with an unexpected image. He hoped that he would see the flowers fully collected and the stalks cut by his sons, and also reclaimed soil in favorable winds. There was hardly a trace of the flowers, but the stems were still sticking out, let alone the next stages. The sight surprised him but did not worry him. "Apparently, Abdul and Ragir had failed," he thought. "They still have time to learn." As he drove towards the homestead, he wondered what he would teach them and what they would do together. He imagined that when they were exhausted, Tamadur would bring them one pot of Keeffi per head. He also dreamed of changing his clothes, bathing and trimming his beard. It was high time to come back.

The closer he got to the house, the more uneasy he felt. One of the children should have spotted him from afar. He should hear them chirping by now. He himself should see them waving hello to him. It was always the case when he returned from the market in Litrijis. "Or maybe they went on a little trip or to visit their in-laws who live not too far away?" - he thought. Sometimes they did it together, only on holy days. It is true that they had a long way to go then, but for the hygiene of the relationship it was worth going to someone. Sometimes they would visit each other with Rita's parents just to speak to someone other than the householders. It helped for a while. But there was no holiday that day.

As he approached, all Fahid could hear was a slight breeze playing on the dried-up stems of a purple plant. Apart from that, you couldn't hear anything. Not even the sound of a squeaking windmill. For a moment he thought maybe he should rush the okurai to get to the yard faster. However, something told him not to be in such a hurry. After all, the animal was very tired. When he got in front of the house, he first took them to the backyard waterhole, which he used sometimes during his break from work. Okurai sipped water as if he hadn't been drinking since the day before. At that time, Fahid went towards the stable to see how the little ones were doing. The day before departure, one of the okurai, younger than the one he came on, gave birth. Fahid wanted to see if the children were taking good care of the new family.

When he got inside the stable, he froze. Four of the tine animals were missing, while the hydapi and okurai lay passed out in their faeces. Some of them were dead - all young and one adult. Fahid covered his mouth with his hands, his eyes wide open screamed out in terror. He walked over to one of the babies. His skin was cold and stiff, covered with a fuzzy substitute for a child's hair. The sight terrified him. He immediately ran out of the stables towards the house. Already in the yard he noticed traces of blood. He noticed a red streak on the steps, as if someone injured was crawling into the house. In the kitchen, his wife Rita was lying on her back in a dried pool of blood. She was exhausted, bruised and bloodied. She was breathing, but with difficulty. Her mouth was chapped and it hadn't been in the water for several days. Fahid approached her and kissed her cheeks. She did not recognize him. She was staring absentmindedly in his direction as if he were transparent.

"Where are the kids?" He asked.

She didn't speak. He checked all the rooms in a flash and returned to the kitchen.

"Ta-ma-dur, Kha-lid, A-di-la," he syllained, looking Rita straight in the face. The other names just shouted out. "Nadir, Fatima, Hassan, Malik, Abdul, Ragir!"

As he listed the last two, Rita howled like a wounded animal. He hugged her tenderly and wept with her.

***

Six Hello sunrises earlier, when noon had passed, Rita called the children playing in the backyard into the kitchen. She prepared only their favorite delicacies for her toddlers. In addition to the traditional mao flour pancakes with dirshna liniment, sandi fruit and pieces of tine meat, this time she made shuri brew, a favorite by Adila and Nadir, sweetened with raspberry flowers. The children obediently sat down on the floor. Only Tamadur stood next to her mother. She took individual pieces of food from her and gave it to her siblings. The pancakes were not too hot, rather warm, pleasant to the touch, and did not sting the children's hands. Rita introduced this way of eating when she noticed that the little ones were bored of ritual eating on the terrace. A bit of madness had never hurt anyone, she thought. However, she could not carry out this plan when Fahid was at home. He always kept order and rules. Children liked her crazy improvisations. Since Fahid left to save Sumi, the rest of the family had eaten in this way almost every day. Freshly prepared dishes in person or with the help of Tamadur, the mother fed the family, sometimes putting the food straight into the mouths of her children. Then she sat down on the floor with them. No plates, no wooden cutlery. "Like savages in the northern quarter," she joked. After such a meal, she had a lot of cleaning work to do, but the moments were worth every amount of gray stones.

"Guys," she said to Abdul and Ragir. "When are you going to cut the stalks? You promise the third day."

"We'll make it before the father comes back," answered the eldest son. "Not much left."

"We wouldn't want to disappoint him," she said in her husband's mock, gruff voice, and after a while she sighed slightly disappointedly.

"And when will he be back?" Khalid asked.

"Certainly soon," she replied, hiding her concern.

At this point, bustling sounds began to come from the yard. Joy appeared on the faces of the kids.

"Dadi?" Malik said, what in his childish language was supposed to mean father.

Abdul glanced at Ragir with apprehension, as if he had realized they were going to get hit. They haven't had time to clean up the dirshna harvest, and they eat in the kitchen with their fingers. Rita looked as if she was afraid of her husband's reaction to such an unusual sight for him. She felt like a little thief caught stealing something worthless. "Too bad," she thought. "At most I will get hit. The important thing is that he came back. Is Sumi with him?" A sad thought crossed her mind at once, but she was not going to wait in the kitchen any longer. She wanted to see it visually.

"Come on, get up. Go to the yard. Then we'll finish," she encouraged the children.

Nadir was the first to walk outside the hut. An unexpected sight appeared before his eyes. He saw a group of a dozen or so low-level priests. The thugs themselves, well-armed. The next two children, who ran out to the yard with a smile on their lips, grew serious at the sight of this bunch and returned at the same pace. Rita planned to be the last to come out, but the startled and surprised expressions of the three hiding under her skirt chilled her enthusiasm. She walked to the door and looked apprehensively.

"Rita Manduarra?" One of the priests asked.

"Yes," she replied, folded her arms and leaned against the doorframe, pretending to be more confident than she was.

"Get your husband."

"He's not here. He went to Litrijis. What do you want?" Rita asked.

"And his father, Mahmud Manduarra?"

"You don't know? Dead. Kadu took him to Asaran. There will be forty Hello sunrises when we said goodbye."

Rita wasn't going to go outside. In her opinion, she defended access to home and offspring. At this point, the front row of priests parted, and Taarida emerged, hiding behind them so far. Okurai, whose crests she was sitting on, walked a few steps closer. The priestess took the lead of the group. She looked to be the leader of a gang of the worst filth that had come with evil intentions into the backyard of ordinary, quiet people. The hostess shuddered slightly at the sight of the mask covering the woman's face.

"Sorry, Rita," Taarida began. "Can I say that? We have shortcomings in the documents and we came here to straighten everything out. Before I get to the most important thing, I have a simple question. Do you know where a certain Omar Manduarra, your father-in-law's brother is?"

"He was missing a long time ago," Rita replied. "My husband never met him."

Taarida thought about it and after a while she took out a neat roll. She put it at arm's length towards Rita, as if to encourage her to take a few steps.

"I can't read," replied the hostess, still standing in a boisterous posture.

"That's okay."

Taarida pushed the roll closer to her and slowly began to unwind.

"Beloved friend Fahid and you, his wonderful wife Rita," she began to read, over-emphasizing her pretend nice tone. "We are facing a difficult period. For the sake of Floris, I am building an additional base of priests who will guard our land when the time of trial comes. Apparently we got it wrong about your eldest daughter Sumi. Probably because of the wrong reception of my pure intentions. I am asking you to hand over another daughter, Tamadur, this time. Blah blah blah. I would not like to experience my profession again and waste my time on unnecessary animosities. I kiss you warmly and greet you, in the name of me, Patri, and our whole congregation."

Taarida looked up and looked at Rita as if to enjoy her fear. An unease began to build up on the landlady's face, which quickly turned to horror. She lowered her head meekly. Meanwhile, from the house one could hear single voices of disbelief, and finally the crying of a small child.

"I was supposed to read this letter in case Kadu brings Sumi to Patrix." But so far has not arrived.

Rita glanced at the priestess with a spark of hope in her eyes.

"Where is your husband?" Taarida continued.

"I really do not know. He followed Kadu to plead for Sumi's return, but did not come back. Please don't take my next daughter from me."

Taarida looked at Rita from a position of strength.

"Until Sumi is found, I have a duty to find a replacement. I am taking all the children so that Ae can choose as many candidates as she needs."

"What?" Rita was almost mad with despair.

"Now I will name the names. I am asking everyone to appear in the yard. Abdul..."

"He's just past the age of one purification," Rita interrupted.

"Well, so what? He's got to go out! Ragir. Come on."

Abdul appeared in the doorway. Rita grabbed his hand, then released him, groaning painfully. The boy went out into the yard and stood in front of Taarida, shaking nervously all over his body. He did not meet her eyes. She scanned him, then sent a urgent glare to Rita. Ragir also came out, stood next to his older brother.

"I want to see a large cart or two small animals tied to them in a minute. The best you have. Understand?" She asked the boys.

They nodded humbly and ran towards the stables. Rita hid her face in her hands out of helplessness.

"I understand that the other children have not yet reached the age of one purification. There are seven of them. That's right?"

Rita nodded.

"I read from the oldest and invite you to the middle. Tamadur, Khalid, Adila, Nadir, Fatima, Hassan, Malik."

Children with tears in their eyes took turns leaving the house into the yard and positioning themselves according to their age. When the youngest, tearful and snotty boys, Hassan and Malik, holding hands, passed Rita, she gripped them tightly and hugged them. She knew that it was no use trying to defend them. Before that, her husband had failed with three priests. Meanwhile, what was she to do? Should she face a dozen trained well-armed soldiers? At that moment, all hope left her.

"Come on. Enough of these tenderness," said Taarida. "What about this car?!" She screamed.

"One more moment. Ragir's voice was trembling, and after a while the boys brought the largest, six-wheeled dirshna transport cart harnessed to four tine animals.

"Get in. Bind them," the commanding officer said, addressing the two closest priests.

They got off the okurai and began to place the kids on the cart, tying them with one raidi rope to the railing. Rita began to lament loudly. It was evident that one of the slim priests was measured by her reaction. He finished the binding and walked towards her. He made a gesture, but she still didn't stop. He hit her face with all his strength with the hilt of his sirius. She covered herself with blood and passed out immediately. At this point, Abdul and Ragir set off to save their mother. The children tied to the wagon started screaming.

"Calm down, carcass!" Taarida shouted.

They froze in the blink of an eye. The priest who had hit Rita a moment ago, lightly waved his sword and cut Ragir's left hand off with one stroke.

"Aaaaaaa!"

Rita was awakened by her son's scream of despair. Before she realized what had happened, the priest managed to stab the boy with his sword straight into the torso, fatally wounding him. Meanwhile, the stocky second cut Abdul with his sword-taper.

The boys' bodies fell to the ground. The children in the wagon started crying loudly. Rita launched her fists towards the torturers.

"Shut her up," Taarida said.

Khalid started to pull away as if to come to the rescue, but the ties were too tight. At this point, another priest hit the wagon with a double whip. The raidi cord with pokuna scales split in two. Each of them lashed the heads of innocent babies, wounding them to the blood. During this time, Rita took a few blows to the stomach and back.

"Enough!" Taarida shouted, stopping not only the beatings of the mother, but the crying of the children as well. "She must survive. Collect the body and throw it on the way to Asaran. Holy rituals above all, ha ha!" She joked and showed with a gesture that one of the intentional ones peek into the house.

One of the priests entered the house, the other began throwing the bodies into the cart, first Abdul, then Ragir. The younger children stood motionless, frightened, tied to the railings. Next to the whole group were the bodies of their older brothers. Adila was trying to move closer to one of them as if she wanted a hug. She couldn't reach it.

"Tell your husband that he is not messing with the High Priestess of the Omniearth. I would forget the tithing would be doubled. Someone has to feed these mouths."

Rita didn't even react. She was staring at the children. Huddled on the wagon, tied with a hard rope, the raidi looked like the essence of misfortune. After a while the priest came out of the house carrying a purse. He shook as if checking weight, but looked disappointed.

"This is for the burial of these two," Taarida said, and drove off first.

The other priests followed. The one who had hit Abdul wanted to play coachman, got off his Okurai and tied him behind the wagon. He himself sat down on the trestle and signaled the four tine to depart.

"Why did you leave her alive?" The priest on her right whispered to Taarida.

"Make the kids think the mother is alive. They will be more obedient."

"She won't live to see tomorrow."

"But they won't see it," she said dryly.

"I was convinced that father would suddenly jump out of some hiding place and would want to save them. Pity it would be funnier."

"Remember what the people in Litrijis said? He was seen asking about Kadu," Taarida recalled.

"Do you believe that a peasant like this would have so much insolence that he would like to rescue his daughter?"

"Everything is possible."

"Kadu is too smart. He would definitely defend himself. He probably sobered up in the end and made his way to the top of Saandreal somehow. Now he drinks again and laughs at us that we're wasting our time looking for him in these holes."

Taarida remembered Ae's words about the future of Kadu. A sly smirk appeared on her face.

***

Jusif got Ae used to frequent reports. Even if he did not have the opportunity to personally convey the progress of the commissioned work, he sent an encrypted letter - he knew the old language. She loved them. They were short and full of funny phrases. When he wanted to convey that he killed the delinquent, he wrote, for example, that he was adorned with a dirshna. When the case dragged on, he described such information as a time paradox. Xami departed with a considerable advance eight Hello sunrise and did not provide any, even the shortest information, what was happening to him. Ae began to worry. She wondered if the new Jusif knew the old language, or if she had been fooled this time. He seemed to know all about her and she knew little about him. In order not to get paranoid, she looked for a job. She decided to personally check what the recruitment looks like. So she went to school, without Kifor and even less Zenit. The sight of the High Priestess of the Omniearth walking alone astonished the passing priests. Some even wondered if it was really her. She never walked without bodyguards.

To reach the priesthood school on the other side of Saandreal, Ae had to travel through a small maze of tunnels. Few knew this abbreviation. Most walked around the mountain, making it seem like a remote place. Nothing could be more wrong. Anyway, high-level priests had their own proven paths that quickly moved around the Patrix. After all, the city hidden inside the mountain was vast. You had to manage somehow when there was no communication.

"Good morning, my friend Mi-tu," Ae said to the head of the school, a member of the Council.

He was surprised no less than the others. Usually, the arrival of the most important person in the country was announced. This time she came without even bodyguards. Mi-tu appreciated her, even though she had the name of a harpy at school.

"Hello, lady," he replied.

"I gave you a lot of work.

"I don't take it that way. It's a matter of reorganizing your timetable."

"Can we see the new fry?"

"Of course, please."

Mi-tu went ahead. In fact, he trotted off. As Ae walked two steps behind him, she remembered Vishare, her first teacher, head of the school, and then the High Priest of the Omniearth. Mi-tu looked very much like him. It also emanated from him with kindness, commitment and passion. He was one of the few very conscious priests. One with a calling. She did not feel threatened with him. He wasn't plotting behind her back, he probably never thought that anything disturbing would happen to him from her side. He was focused on his chores, and she liked him for that.

"I was wondering why there are almost only girls in the next recruitment."

"You know the signals coming from Inco. We cannot underestimate them."

"Truth. They are to blame themselves. Nothing artificial is good. And our neighbors seem to have gone astray in this artificiality. Are additional recruitment related to preparations for war?"

"I hope that the new Inco authority is not stupid enough, but such a scenario is possible. I think the borders will have to be strengthened to keep our men safe."

"And that is why we will teach girls?"

"Why tempt fate?"

"Now I understand. Clever."

Ae smiled gently. She didn't take it as an empty compliment. Mi-tu's tone was sincere, she noticed. They took a dozen steps and heard the sound of a chase coming from a distance. Ae turned back. These were the two of her guards who should normally be with her.

"Now you're awake, bastard," she joked when they ran over.

"Forgive me, my lady. We didn't notice when you left," one of them explained.

"Come back. I feel safe here," she said, smiling fondly at Mi-tu.

"Lady, don't do this to us. Zenit will punish us for not fulfilling our duty."

Ae looked at Mi-tu again. His paternal gaze only amused her.

"Okay. Nobody will know. Follow ten steps behind us. These corridors are too tight to walk in fours."

"Yes, my lady."

One of the guards lunged at her hand and pursed his lips as if he were getting ready to kiss her.

"Come on. No caresses," she joked.

They came to a large cave where the division of the newly arrived candidates into smaller groups was taking place. They were selected according to the territories they came from. It was easier. The method gave a sense of belonging as many cleansing bonds were formed at that point. It has always worked. The girls looked scared, but when they found out that they could live in the room with their friends or neighbors' daughters known from stories, they immediately felt safer.

***

A few days later, the last group, very late, arrived at the priesthood school. It wasn't just girls. The seven children who had not yet reached the age of one purification were walking with one rope. Taarida escorted them. The wagon in which they had arrived was left in front of the Patrix entrance, next to one of the small taverns, tied to a mohair tree.

"Why do we need such little boys?" Asked the priest, whose task was to pick up the children and assign them to a specific group.

"Ae's decision," Taarida replied, dismounting her okurai.

"Do you have documents?" He asked.

"They weren't needed. I have a letter from the High Priestess of the Omniearth."

Taarida handed over the roll. The priest skimmed its contents briefly.

"Tamadur, Adila and Fatima, you will line up there."

The priest indicated the place under the "wailing wall". This was the jokingly name of the corner where the children said goodbye to their old life. There was a pile of clothes on the stone floor. You had to strip naked, throw away your clothes and wait for your turn. Sometimes a long time. It was humiliating. There was no one strong to hold back tears. Especially children at the age of one purification or younger. Especially girls. The sisters went to the appointed place. The priest standing there explained to them what to do.

"Khalid, Nadir, Hassan, Malik," he turned to the boys. "You'll stand on the other side until I find out what the plans are for you."

Khalid followed his twin sister Adila for a moment, then grabbed the hands of Hassan and Malik. Nadir felt lonely. He grabbed Hassan by the other hand. The little brother didn't even feel that his grip was too tight. They were walking as four in the indicated direction. They looked scared, hungry, and tired. The last few days of these boys weren't the most pleasant ones. They witnessed the murder and burial in the Asaran Gorge of their two eldest brothers. They saw their mother beaten so badly that she passed out. They did not know if their father was alive or what happened to Sumi, their eldest sister. Now, in addition, they were separated from the other sisters and it was not known what their fate was. Will they be prepared to be priests? Will they also look as repulsive as Kadu? Will they ever meet their parents?" - they wondered.

***

Barney Clifford was released at Ae's decision only after a few days. He didn't know the way to Pinati Falls very well, but he had been given a map made by Haris. It was very accurate, with an intact scale, and a lot of important places marked with small stars, with comments described on the back. Nevertheless, the Prime Minister of the Inco government in exile felt insecure. He has never traveled alone, especially in a foreign country. His wife packed him a lot of food for the road. He didn't take too much water, as Haris had told him where to drink directly from the spring. It was a shame to waste energy carrying around. As he left, the family said goodbye to him fondly, but the members of the Government were afraid he would be able to handle it. After all, their common fate will depend on the success of his journey. The High Priestess of the Omniearth looked tired of the alien presence, and each day could bring a change in her attitude. It was similar with the changes in their homeland, which they left with the intention of waiting a short while. It was getting more and more dangerous with each passing day. The incoming signals did not sound optimistic. Inco appeared to be undergoing a dynamic metamorphosis. The longer the revolution lasts, the less likely it will be to return to the old system. Some events cannot be undone.

On the first day, Clifford traveled quite a distance. He was walking rather fast, driven by fear of wild animals. He did not reckon with fatigue. His first stop was only planned in the middle of the distance. In that direction, the road was a bit longer for him. Then they went in a larger group and from time to time someone needed a break for physiological needs. Besides, children who were delaying their arrival traveled with them. Now Clifford dragged no ballast behind him, he could walk at his own pace. As befits an Inco resident, he had a stamina that was practiced on many fitness machines. He was an almost perfect walker.

Hello was on the horizon. It was high time to find the right hiding place. Clifford had picked up a small hill a moment before that might be a stopping place. He could see them from a distance and appreciated the location from a strategic point of view. He decided that the whole area would probably be seen from above. He was convinced that he would see any impending danger. It was only when he climbed to the top that he noticed that at the very top of the hill there was a treasure. There was a relic there, a little temple of Patri. Clifford had no interest in religion, but the place was quite intriguing. Between the rocks, individual stages in the life of the goddess were carved. He did not know her history, but the find, like an artifact, immediately interested him, even fascinated him. On one of the carvings, which looked as if it had been carved at least ten years earlier, he noticed a beautiful woman surrounded by animals. On another, with a chipped piece missing, he noticed a part of her body that was hugging a small child. It was a touching and romantic picture. Clifford took a green bar from a small purse, took a bite, and began studying more of the finds. He enjoyed a monument he had never seen before. He walked towards another bas-relief. It showed Patri sitting on the riverside. She looked worried. A tear was running down her cheek. In her hands she held the symbol of her power, hidden inside the inverted ancient bell of the Gondolu, like in a chalice, a miniature of the Universe, a planet divided into four unequal quarters. On the other side of the relief, Clifford saw an old man with a blindfold covering his eyes. Was Patri suffering from this old man?

The prime minister was unsure how to interpret this find. He thought for a moment. He would have given much to know what the Florians saw in this deity.

Like every inhabitant of Inco, Clifford was an atheist, or more precisely, a follower of the only right religion called science. Exactly at the age of two, he graduated from two schools in parallel, pharmacy and state administration, both financed by the Metachemie group founded by his great-grandfather, the creator of Ray. On that fateful day, he definitely gave himself up to politics because he had already realized that the world was overrun by evil. He was convinced that there was no goddess behind him, but always a man. Clifford thought again. He remembered a lecture by his favorite subject teacher with a rather brazen name: The Mirage of Humanism. He then wrote down each word and then repeated it over and over. Whole sentences came in handy during tough negotiations or summit talks, though some sounded too blunt. He learned them over time. He loved to quote them from memory, although he didn't quite believe them. This time he recreated the larger passages in his mind. And they sounded like this:

"Man is the most rational creature who usurped the right to rule over all things. He has subjected vegetation, animals and science to his ego. Not any god, but man could manage the world. Among individuals of this species, there was always someone better - a ruler, a chosen one - endowed with a greater portion of ambition and greed than others. If there was no need for possession, there would be no development, no science."

"Man invented and took three inventions by storm: law, religion and politics."

"What would religion be? Bondage served in white gloves and on a golden tray? Paid in blood, no matter whose - faithful or unbelieving. For development? No. For power. Power over other people, nature, health, and mind, often out of convenience. And also for wealth. For these two purposes man succumbed without planning it to involuntary development. He looked for better and better ways to get to the top, but a development called evolution came suddenly, by the way. Such a bonus."

"Keep going, more generously, faster and easier. It was not allowed to go back. If anything, fall from the very top to the bottom, smashing your body to pieces. So that there is nothing to collect."

"If you are kind, generous, friendly, faithful or honest, that is, more like an obedient animal, the stronger your humanity is. And the more you are greedy, dishonest, unworthy, hostile, that is, behave like most people, the less humanity you have. This is the paradox."

Clifford smiled to himself. He just realized he could remember the most important sentences from the lecture, but couldn't remember the teacher's name. Before he began his studies, his senior students called him Antt. His yearbook only picked up the nickname and it stayed that way. Antt was like a guru. Everyone respected him, teachers, students, management. He marched daily from the second district, where he lived with his family, to work at a school in the city center. Then he went back the same way. He had permission to move between districts, because his position was state-owned. "I should have taken care of him, he must be dead by now," Clifford thought.

In his opinion, Antt's lecture was great, but it contained errors. He could name them and separate them from the whole. Eliminating his flaws, he came up with his own, better vision of humanity. He leaned it against the people of the first district, especially when they were easy to control, and the men in the second. He detested the slumers, or more precisely, the women living in this district, treated them as subhumans. He did not envisage a place for them in his ideal world. He was once a co-creator of the system of effective penalties for minor offenses. He hoped the slumers would crumble, or at least get rid of scum, thanks to him. As for the inhabitants, Floris had a long-held, not very critical opinion. He modified them slightly when he moved in between them. Then he additionally appreciated their interesting social habits, which he did not know about before. He mentally connected both lands many times, but on almost utopian terms. After cutting unhealthy tissue unworthy of being part of an ideal community.

The New Universe could only be home to the best. He had dreamed about it since he became involved in politics. It was the day he found out where Ray came from and what his real effects were. He felt co-responsible for all the evil that has spilled over the world as a result of the development of the business started by his ancestors. He denied his roots, but when the opportunity arose to fix everything, he took advantage of family connections and ruthlessly entered the leadership of the Chemist Party, assuming first the role of treasurer. When he was elected party leader - before he was even offered the position of Prime Minister - he ordered a modification of the drug. In the end, the Y chromosome was brought under control, but the effects of previous generations of the drug could no longer be stopped. Then the GCO was founded. At the same time, he worked on connecting the two lands. He thought that only a priest who owed him could be dealt with. Therefore, he planned and successfully implemented the infiltration. He managed. Ae - a man by his hand - became the most important person in a neighboring country. He gave time for her position to become steadfast. He also had to clean up on a regular basis, because as it turned out, religious priests were plotting all the time. He planned to ultimately mix communities to - as he called it - dilute the infected society with a healthier one. How wrong he was. All his plans, like dominoes, turned over in turn, creating one big mess. They were getting out of his control, and he himself became a prisoner of his ideas.

At that moment, he felt that someone was standing behind him, breathing heavily. He focused so much on the memories that he lost his alertness. Shivers ran through him. He turned slowly and carefully. It was Xami.

***

By the time Fahid had groomed the animals that had miraculously survived the fast for several days, Rita was already awake. Dressed only in a nightgown, she went out into the yard. She was weak, but the first rays of Hello gave her the necessary energy. There was a strange calm on her face. After a while, Fahid appeared.

"What are you doing? You shouldn't go out," he said anxiously in his voice.

"Look, what a beautiful day. Come for a walk with me, my love."

"Let's eat something first. I'm terribly hungry."

"What to do to you?"

"No kidding. Lie down."

Fahid helped his wife reach a comfortable bed. He covered her with a linen bedspread and set to preparing a simple meal. She watched him fondly as when they met and had no children yet. Today they were alone again, only to themselves. It had only been a few days since his return from Hambarra. He dedicated them only to his wife and animals. He did not care about the next dirshna crops. He also did not mention the subject of children, as if he did not want to hear the truth. He could feel what could have happened and guessed who might have done it. Until recently, he had not realized that only Church officials had such insolence. When Mahmoud Fahid traveled to Litrijis during his lifetime to exchange crops for gray stones, he heard some uninteresting stories about priests, but then he did not believe any of them. Now he was pretty sure they could all be real.

He humbly waited until Rita was ready to tell him what had happened. He didn't rush her, he knew it would happen sooner or later. She felt better day by day, among other things because of his travel stories. He didn't talk about what happened to Kadu and his guards. He focused on the positive passages. He talked for a long time about Sumi who started studying at Hambarra. He also described all the plants he had never seen before. He did not forget about the sahadi lizards and the hills full of windmills. She was most interested in the story of a smelly man without a hand who lives in a house on the outskirts of Litrijis. She laughed, and he just turned up the more spicy flavors. That's what he occupied her. That's why she didn't think about pain and loss. Probably thanks to his stories there was an improvement.

Fahid placed a tray with several wooden saucers in front of her. They were packed with food. Some finely chopped meat, one pie, fruit and herbs. Plus a small pot of keeffi. She burst into tears when she saw the food.

"We were eating in the kitchen when they came," she said, sobbing. "They had terrible faces. They looked and acted differently from our Kadu. He's pretty docile compared to that gang."

Fahid focused only on the emotions that accompanied her during the story. He didn't want to interrupt with unnecessary questions.

"They knew no mercy," she continued. "If they had to kill all the children in the world, they would have done it without hesitation. I don't know why Patri liked them. They are not worthy of her."

At this point, Fahid couldn't hold back.

"Because they're bandits, love. Pokuna droppings." That insult to the filthy scaly creature sounded like the worst, unexpected curse in his mouth. "They are only interested in power over the world, over the fear of people like us. In the priesthood school, all their humanity is stripped away.'

"Will our children take it too?"

Fahid looked down.

"I don't know," he said. "I hope they stick together and remember what house they came from."

Rita howled like a wounded animal. He dropped the tray in her lap and hugged her tenderly.

"It's my fault," she said vaguely.

"No. My. I was the one who messed with the Church."

"Abdul and Ragir are dead."

Fahid's eyes immediately burst into tears.

"They wanted to save me. They were defenseless, innocent." Rita's last sentence sounded like incomprehensible gibberish.

"Repeat it."

"They were innocent..."

Fahid noticed her enlarged pupils and not very rhythmic twitching. His wife's head slumped to the right side, and the eyelids slowly drooped.

"Rita, Rita, love. What's wrong? It was okay now."

He grabbed her hand. She was inert and not as warm as usual. He tried to warm her up by rubbing his hand, but the desperate gesture did not produce the desired effect. Fahid did not know much about treatment. He didn't know what he should do. He only looked at his beloved with tears in his eyes, which he wiped with his sleeve from time to time so as not to wet the sheets. Rita resembled the girl he had met for the first time in the neighbors' dirshna field. Hasn't changed much. Warm, friendly, slightly rounded face and sincere smile as usual. When Fahid realized that his wife did not look as for her three and a half purifications, he smiled heartily at her and stroked her hair tenderly. She looked cute. As if she was taking an innocent nap. However, her breathing grew shallower. Until after a while it definitely disappeared. She was gone.

Chapter 17 The hunger

From day to day, Jasmin's position decreased until it was practically marginalized. Addam began to treat her no longer like his wife, much less the former, but the servant of the three.

"Why didn't you want a robot to clean your apartment?" Vicky asked, ostentatiously wiping the dust off the theatremania display with her finger.

"Because she likes to clean up," sneered Addam. "She wanted it so, she has it that way."

Jasmin was fifteen weeks pregnant, she had felt a surge of power for several days, a slight swelling appeared on her face. It was difficult to judge whether the lack of reaction to Addam's malice was due to her sincere desire to clean the apartment or because of the excess body water and her inability to clearly display her dissatisfaction in the form of a grimace. Addam glanced at her as if to remind himself that she was to blame for herself. Not only because she had planned three girls. After all, she also made him swear that he would not engage in prostitution. Therefore, they could not afford a cleaning person.

"I'm leaving. I'm sick of these female hormones," he said, and slammed the door.

Vicky was surprised by his behavior. She went to the window and looked at the city skyline, then down to the bottom. She followed Addam with her eyes as he left the skyscraper and then as he walked towards the gallery. Finally he disappeared around a bend. She became sad, for a moment she was spinning aimlessly. It was obvious she wanted to talk to Jasmin, but she was missing the right words.

"What time do you think he'll be back?" She asked finally, instead of addressing the most proven subject of the permanence of the weather.

"When he buys something, dandy. He always reacts like this when he doesn't know what to do with himself."

"I don't remember the last time I bought myself clothes. My papa transfered me a lot. I didn't have to ask. Addam gives me nothing. Yes, I have nothing to complain about. What I ask him for, he brings me, but I have no entitys, even for small things."

"Get used to. It will be worse." Jasmin didn't feel like talking to the person who had been pointing her finger at the dirt a moment ago.

"That's not how I imagined it," Vicky said, looking for an ally.

Jasmin wiped all the dust from the walls and appliances. She cleared the coolant. She lay down on the small, uncomfortable mattress that became her bed after the owner's second wife moved into the apartment.

"You have a lot of nice clothes," Vicky said.

"Old times. Most of them are unfashionable."

"I don't have any."

Vicky looked sad. It was evident that the hormones were beginning to bubble up. Jasmin knew why this young woman was acting this way. She felt a bit sorry for the girl who was at the end of the fourth week of pregnancy.

"I have an idea what to do so that we can buy ourselves some nice clothes."

"Can you convince Addam?"

"You gotta do it. He won't listen to me. This is about your baby."

"Are there any maternity allowances? Just don't talk to me about participating in an experiment. Papa will never agree."

"Papa? Not husband? Idiot." Jasmin judged critically in her mind.

"No. I have a completely different plan," she said, trying to get involved. "You will give birth to a boy, he will be able to marry in about one and a half purification. Why wait so long before getting married? We could offer it to potential in-laws right now."

"I have not heard of anyone paying for the wedding of a child who has not yet been born."

"Because it's a new solution. Just popped into my head. There's no harm in trying."

"Only if Addam will agree," Vicky worried.

Jasmin smiled inwardly. "I wonder what Papa will say about that. A moron," she thought of her lousy.

"I'll tell you how to convince him," she said.

"Brilliant," said Vicky enthusiastically. "We will find a wealthy family, who are expecting a daughter, and arrange a wedding. It will take place in more than one and a half purifications, and we will get the entitys now."

"Why one?" Jasmin interrupted. "Let's arrange a few weddings like this. Decree on polygamy, remember?"

"Unbelievable. Addam's been saying all the wrong things about you, and you're not all that stupid."

This time Jasmin didn't react, she was focused too much on quietly celebrating her creativity.

***

The idea of developing the idea of the wedding market turned out to be a bull's eye. Convincing Addam was easier than Jasmin had realized. When he threw the subject of a new casting to his friends, a lot of suggestions popped up within hours. In order not to waste time analyzing each case, the first wife offered a shakeout. From thirty-one offers, it quickly turned into the final eleven. Some risky but ultimately effective criteria helped. First of all, a deposit of five hundred entitys scared away ten families at once, because the child's potential mother-in-law did not intend to pay blindly. Second, another ten families gave up when Addam announced that the wedding was due fifty percent in advance. It took almost half a day for all three of them to determine the next rules for conducting the auction. Most of the contentious issues arose when Jasmin proposed that Vicky and Addam's son should have eight wives. Addam thought five, Vicky refused to agree to more than three. Ultimately, she agreed to the father's proposal. Jasmin was pleased with the negotiations. She had purposely raised the bar to that level, knowing that Addam as a typical guy - even on behalf of another, admittedly unborn guy - would strive for more wives. Another difficult topic was the admission of the Aratunia family, who had emigrated from Floris several generations earlier and did not hide it at all, although this did not turn out to be unacceptable to Vicky.

"All the potential wives for my son are still in their bellies," she explained. "Only the Aratunia family wants to squeeze us a girl who has already had more than half of the purification. Not too old?"

"And I think it's even better when the wife is older," said Addam authoritatively. "What will he know about the world when he is in the age of one and a half purification. What sexual experience will he have? None. A competent wife will teach him this and that."

"Would you like her to be trained in these matters?" Jasmin said indignantly.

"Exactly! They must be virgins," Vicky demanded flatly.

"Exactly," Jasmin defended second wife. "One more thing. I believe that each wife should have a different status in marriage."

"I know what's on your mind, smarty," Addam joked, shaking his finger at her.

"It's not what you think. How are you going to justify the demand that they pay more?" She asked. "If there's a single wage for being a wife? Come on, think about it. It is difficult to judge what the children will look like in more than one and a half purification and whether they will like them. I believe that the selection of future wives should be carried out in the form of an auction. Hearing the offers of the competition, rich families will overcome each other. The one who pays the most should get the most privileges.

Jasmin remembered the market principle of supply and demand again. Vicky didn't understand anything. The complexities were explained to her by Addam, who quickly grasped the sly plan of his first wife. The two also persuaded Vicky to agree to the Aratunia family on the condition that the girl's father would pay a higher bid bond. She agreed to it. When the auction day arrived, the younger wife was very worried about whether she would be able to handle it. Addam asked Jasmin to replace her. It didn't take long to ask her - she liked such challenges. In addition, the bothersome symptoms associated with carrying three babies in the stomach disappeared and she felt a new boost of energy.

Papa with the mustache also appeared at the auction. Vicky was not happy about it. She asked him not to interfere under any circumstances. Jasmin proposed that only the dads enter the bid competition. It will be this way more transparently - with no other family members who could only make it difficult. Addam recalled the guiding principle of choosing wives. He said mothers still had to be looked at. "If you want to know what your wife will look like in old age, take a look at your mother-in-law," he joked. Both Vicky and the more experienced Jasmin were unfamiliar with this maxim, but the man with mustache confirmed it. A four-person committee, because Vicky's father was allowed to vote this time, rejected one of the women because of her ugliness. The rest of the mothers and other family members were asked to leave. Only ten fathers remained. They were lined up in a row and were given plaques with the names of the families they represented.

"Hello. My name is Jasmin Kozllov née Manduarra, I am Addam's first wife."

When she mentioned her last name, the eldest father, the white-haired Mr. Aratunia, glanced at her and frowned as if he associated something with something.

"His second wife, Vicky Morgoruth, is expecting a boy," Jasmin continued. "He will probably be as strong as his father, grandfather, uncles and cousins. These are good genes. We are looking for five wives for him who will give him sons..."

"What if one of the wives doesn't give him a son, only a daughter?" Aratunia interrupted her. "Will you hand over your bid security?"

"I see you're uninitiated on new solutions," she replied, though she didn't seem pleased to be interrupted. "Now it is possible to determine the specific sex of the child at the stage of procreation. A simple study is enough. However, I will come back to the rules, if you will allow me. First wife status will be paramount. She will be able to give her husband three sons, and she will also sleep with him two nights a week. The second wife will be able to give her husband two sons, she will sleep with him only one night a week. Each successive of the three wives will be able to give their husband one son and will sleep with him only one night a week."

"And the other two days?" Aratunia asked stubbornly.

"Let him decide for himself whether he will want to sleep with one of the wives, or, for example, he will prefer to rest and sleep alone."

"If you wants to rebuild the human race and you need men, why do you want to limit the number of children?" Asked the brown-haired man from the Chikoon family.

"That father would have time for them, to feel loved and to raise them to be decent people." Jasmin was clearly irritated by the lack of understanding.

"What if daughter appear?" Aratunia did not let go.

"No."

"But if so, what than?"

"My son will love her as much as boys," Vicky replied, glancing knowingly at the mustachioed.

He nodded, showing his overwhelming pride at his daughter's responsible attitude.

"The state allows a man to marry a woman at the age of one and a half purification. When Vicky and Addam's son reach this age, there will be the first wedding, followed by each wedding every thirty-two Hello sunrise. So," here Jasmin turned to the inquisitive Aratunia to forestall his question, "that his wife could enjoy her husband for so many days. During this time, none of the predecessors will have any rights to him in the bed. Let at least one co-moon be just for them. Are there any questions?"

All the fathers looked as if their thoughts were already in the process of the auction, watching each other. Mustachioed was slightly excited. Vicky asked him to sit a little further away, and he turned around as if he was being chosen his wife.

"Since there are no questions, let's get started. The rule is: win the one who will give more. For the first five wives, we have prepared a reward in the form of the son of this beauty."

All eyes turned to the embarrassed second wife of Addam.

"I have a question," said the man from the Dee family. "What will Mrs. Vicky's son be called?"

There was consternation. Addam shrugged. Jasmin glanced at Vicky, but she looked away at her father.

"Victor," the mustachioed said.

Jasmin scowled, as if she didn't like the choice of name. She looked first at Addam, who just shook his head idiotically, then at the beaming Vicky.

"Victor," Jasmin repeated. "After my mother. His surname is after his father, Kozllov."

Vicky smiled warmly at her, like a friend, maybe even a sister. Addam made a silly face, but it was obvious at this stage that he didn't care.

"Now that everything is known, let's get started," Jasmin announced. "The starting price for the wedding is two thousand entitys."

Aratunia immediately picked up his nameplate.

"We have two thousand," Jasmin confirmed. "Will anyone raise? Two thousand one hundred?"

Chikoon raised his.

"Great, we have two thousand one hundred. Who gives more?"

After a while, the fathers, holding plates with the names of their families, began to outdo each other in picking them up. Jasmin didn't have time to confirm who was in which place. It got a bit of a mess. Mustachioed got lost at the beginning and looked confused. Only Addam was as happy as a child to see his interest in his genes.

"Stop," Jasmin said. "Let's put it in order. Mr. Chikoona gave eight thousand one hundred entitys."

"No, I gave eight thousand one hundred." Kviaat said. "He only gave seven."

"Eight thousand and two hundred," said Chikoona, and picked up his sign.

"Eight thousand and two hundred and twenty," said Aratunia.

"Eight thousand and three hundred!" Kviaat shouted.

"Eight thousand and four hundred," Dee said calmly.

"Eight thousand and five hundred," Texani said.

"Eight thousand and eight hundred," said Rabului.

"Nine thousand" said Chikoona.

The fathers started rolling their eyes nervously.

"Nine thousand and five hundred!" Texani shouted.

"Twelve thousand," Chikoon announced proudly.

Shocking. Jasmin was speechless, and she raised her eyebrows in surprise. Vicky smiled gently. Aratunia looked down, he looked disappointed.

"Does anyone wish to go higher?" Asked the auctioneer. "Mr. Texani? Mr. Aratunia?" she addressed the individual fathers in turn.

"I don't have enough," replied Aratunia. "I care. Please agree to six wives," he turned to Vicky. "I'm begging you."

Vicky glanced at Addam, nodded, then at her father, he blinked his eyes in approval. She thought for a moment. Everyone held their breath. The atmosphere was so dense that the air molecules practically stopped moving.

"Okay. Let there be six wives," she said, releasing Mr. Aratunia's euphoria.

Jasmin winked at Addam. It was obvious that she couldn't contain her emotions. Even when she wanted to show seriousness, there was a bright smile on her face.

"So the first wife will be Chikoona, the second Texani, the third Rabului, the fourth Dee, the fifth Kviaat, and the sixth... Aratunia." Please prepare money transfers and sign the contract.

Jasmin was proud of how she carried out the entire operation. It was the most interesting and spectacular project that she had realized in her life, both private and professional.

Just a few days later, Vicky acquired a lot of new clothes for herself and Victor. She spent most of her half of the entitys obtained from bid bonds and auctions. Addam took the other half. Jasmin got nothing.

"He's our baby," said Vicky. "Why did you expect me to share with you?"

Jasmin's went to hell. She was furious with herself for getting so easily approached by this bastard. "I'm stupid", she thought, and promised herself that she would never say a word with that bitch again.

***

Noovack began experimenting with the theatremania message. One day she praised everything, the other day she had reports on how people live after the change. She called the new strategy the Power of Realism. She realized that the public was not satisfied. Things weren't going well in the country, so you couldn't pretend that everything was going in the right direction. It was necessary to prevent the public from knowing what was good and what was bad. As proof of this, she most often said that for it to be better, it had to be worse first. The new decree prohibiting male activities has had unplanned consequences. It started with the fact that women were not able to cope with responsibilities previously dominated by men. In these areas, quality, efficiency and effectiveness have deteriorated. Production costs have risen, and so have prices. Inflation began to gallop at an alarming pace. Humaans, focused on the efficient execution of the evictions, could not properly deal with the packs of furious women from the slums. They were seen more and more often as they obstructed the Cascade, as well as when they caused brawls in the first district. They easily overcame the barbed wire in search of the men who had been taken from them. It was getting dangerous. The packs began to grow with new members. Recycling containers, shops, and even garda and fire vehicles were set on fire. On the other hand, no one touched the vehicles and humaans of the emergency services.

***

Theatremania was on almost all the time. Most often, Vicky watched it with her nose almost at the screen, although she did not understand most of the information presented about the state of the country. That day, Addam decided to accompany the inexperienced spouse to the viewing and explain her intricacies of politics. He even turned up the sound, a little to spite Jasmin, who was hiding her nose under the covers to keep out of the crooks. Martina Kuna, once a modest editor of the third channel, now a journalistic star, host the most important journalistic programs on all channels, appeared on the screen.

"More male professions are dying," she said in her favorite, sad voice. "Poverty begins to appear in previously well-to-do farms. Product prices are rising. There is also a fight for our dignity, for increasing the participation of men. Let's check what's up with the fearless heroine fighting for our species. Let's move to the Ministry of Health."

Gibbondy appeared on the screen, she had a fake smile, casually and not very evenly to her face.

"Lady minister," Kuna said to her. "Please tell us about the next experiments you are working on."

"I can't tell you too much, but we are testing the masculinism-based method, among other things," Gibbondy replied. "There are also attempts to change the gender of women into men, but at this stage they are unsatisfactory. Even if a woman, under the influence of surgery and taking hormonal drugs, begins to look like a man, she still has no value," Gibbondy said.

"That is?" Inquired Kuna.

"So such specimens cannot be breeders," Gibbondy finished in her style.

The image from the ministry disappeared from the screen, and a picture of several men with male physique and facial features appeared. They looked more like failed robot models than humans.

"We keep our fingers crossed, Minister," said Kuna enthusiastically. "We're changing the subject. The first wedding show took place a few days ago. It would not be surprising, if not for the fact that it concerned children who were not yet born. The government decided that it was an excellent social initiative."

"Oh, it's about us, it's about us," said Addam. "It's our idea."

"It's Jasmin's idea. Thanks, sister," Vicky said, but the white-haired girl did not poke her nose out from under the covers, but listened.

"On this model I will try to explain to you how it works." On the theatremania screen, Kuna started commenting on the picture that was displayed behind her back. "We see the family walking: the husband, and next to them a few wives staring at him. To their left, a few single daughters walking. They have sad faces, but well... Maybe someday they'll get lucky. And on the right side of the father, his happy son is walking, followed by a dozen girls, future wives. It doesn't look that bad anymore, does it? Our society is so progressive and creative. So many changes are created thanks to the civic initiative. Now the government has to work out a few directives and a new family model will be approved soon. According to its assumptions, married girls will be able to serve their future husband together. This would strengthen their love for him, and they could become friends with each other."

"It's sick," commented Jasmin, still tucked under the covers.

Addam and Vicky reacted by sneering smirks. At this point, the image on the theatremania screen was changed into the image of a monumental building with a logo in the shape of a huge machine with wings.

"And now good news," said Kuna. "The state-owned company operating until recently under the name "Flysky", dealing with the production of unmanned smog-dispersing machines, was divided into four smaller companies. Its previous president, Ms. Angelicc Nerible, became president of the largest of them, "Flyboot". This company, let's call it a daughter company, will only produce machine bodies. The second, Flyengine, will be managed by Ms. Amanda Nerible, the third, Flyenergy, by Ms. Ana Viler, and the fourth, Flyelectro, by Hermegione Lumb. The new CEOs received from Jerone Martinez, the newly appointed Minister of Economy, not only symbolic keys to governance of businesses, but also real keys to state-funded apartments recovered through the Cascade of Eviction. Congratulations on your promotions."

"What a spongers," said Addam.

"What happened?" Vicky was surprised.

"I just know these women. Everything was left in the family. The one who got the second company was the sister of the former, the third was her cousin, and the fourth was her paternal aunt."

"Well, so what?" Vicky was surprised.

Jasmin uncovered the covers and started laughing out loud. Vicky was confused. Addam just sighed.

"Better not ask questions anymore, darling. I'll explain everything to you later," he said in almost a whisper.

***

Noovack, using the rules of the Cascade of Eviction, annexed the highest skyscraper in the country, as well as eight directly adjacent buildings. Just in case some disgruntled inhabitant of the country decided to take advantage of the close distance between the skyscrapers and express dissatisfaction with the decision of the new government, the neighboring buildings were to be left empty. The whole complex was fenced off, four humaans of garda and one border guard guarded it day and night. Nobody was allowed to slip through. Anyone wishing to visit Noovack or her family in private apartments had to go through several sieves to obtain approval. In fact, people who were honored could be counted on the fingers of two hands.

Eva Noovack's bedroom was on the top floor of the building. Just for her. Rinno had his own, smaller one, located a few floors below. In the center of the Prime Minister's great bedroom was a six-person bed and some antique furniture. In addition, there were smaller rooms on the same floor for new fiancés, as she called lovers. They were to wait for one of them to call to see if he was fit for a husband. Lovers were served by butlers, only men. The prime minister did not want any of the new fiancé to become interested in the beautiful maid by accident and to show indecision about their feelings towards the hostess. That is why the lackeys were the least aggressive political prisoners. Their ranks were bolstered by Clifford's loyalists, members of the pharmaceutical cartels, and physicians who resisted the GCO.

They all wore energetic hoops, different from the ones used by humaans of garda beings to bind villains. The street variant would not work well in rooms, as it would certainly make it difficult for men to move around. That is why on both of their wrists, on their legs, just above the foot, and on their heads, the valets had metal hoops tightened, unconnected by any energetic link. They looked humanely enough, as if their purpose was merely to symbolize enslavement.

On the lower floor there was a meditation room. It looked like one huge maze. So that the prime minister would not feel lonely, they were filled with several animarobots on a scale of one to one. The two adult hydapi, one tine and three okurai looked alive, even with the hair almost identical to those moving in the natural habitat of Floris. The floor and the lower parts of the walls of the room were covered with permanent, artificial vegetation. In two places, for the time being, monoflora, artificial organisms imitating vines, developed. They were based on interconnected microbots evolving through nanotechnology, so far rather clumsily and slowly. Their artificial branches grew at a rate of only a quarter of a cubit a month. Nevertheless, they looked interesting. On a person who was able to see the effect with his imagination, they must have made a stunning impression. Especially in combination with four-dimensional painting, several works leased at the expense of the state from one of the most eminent art galleries. They were to support the prime minister spiritually to make the right decisions.

It was to this room that Noovack invited the members of her office for a semi-private meeting. She wanted to show off new technological achievements. It was evident that the invited friends had recently improved their social status, and they were no strangers to the splendor and enormity of the Prime Minister's apartments. They also looked more neat than they had been when they were planning a coup with her.

"Now look at this." Noovack clapped her hands, and immediately the first theatremania program was displayed on the great wall. "If I clap twice, it will be a sport."

She clapped twice and turned on her heel as the theatremania screen swiveled with her, onto another plant-free wall. This time it presented female martial arts.

"Oh, how progressive it is," Gibbondy remarked, and began to watch the sweaty players as they pounded each other's faces, splashing blood left and right.

At that moment, three footmen dressed in anthracite-colored, festive uniforms with short white sleeves appeared. Each of them wore beige-metallic hoops. They looked like unusual jewelry. The one on the head, at the height of the forehead, was three fingers wide, the ones on the wrists and hanging just above the ankles had two fingers. The first butler carried a tray of Pearl brand water, the second a tray of nutritious yellow bars, and the third an armful of disposable towels. Everyone smiled artificially.

"What are you feeding them to keep them smiling, upper?" Davis asked, smiling.

"Mind you, upper is forbidden," said Tatarczyna, winking.

"It's the hoops," Noovack explained.

Gibbondy noticed one of the footmen - the one who brought the water. She sniffed him at the insolent, then looked him straight in the eye as if she were searching for an answer. He didn't budge.

"You recognize me, Steavans? I know you do. Do you think that when you sprinkle yourself with cheap perfume, I won't smell the smell from your office?"

The footman, Dr. Steavans to be exact, remained motionless, devoid of the slightest hint of emotion, like a robot.

"Roar like okurai," she said.

"I don't understand," Steavans replied.

"Come on, roar. Like an animal. Now." Gibbondy was staring at him, eyes narrowed.

The other butler, the black-haired, the one who brought the bars, looked anxiously at Steavans and Gibbond.

"I don't know how okurai roars. I haven't seen it live," Steavans said stoically.

"Here it comes, did you not have such a toy in your childhood? Well, you were playing doctor," she said sarcastically.

At that moment the black-haired butler glanced in their direction again and began to shake slightly, drops of sweat trickled down his forehead. It was evident that he was fighting with himself. Suddenly, in a split second, all four collars on his wrists and above his feet were at the height of his head, right next to the rim on his forehead. His body, curled into a ball, limbs badly wounded, crashed to the floor. Bars from the tray scattered across the floor. The butler had torn ligaments and damaged knee joints. The members of the Government froze. Steavans were still unmoved, as was the third butler. They stood in prison and waited for orders.

"He was so cool, I was getting used to him, really," Noovack said with mock sadness.

"What happened to him?" Bassot was surprised, so far bewildered.

"Apparently he couldn't take the pressure. The headband is equipped with sensors to detect bad intentions in the brain," Gibbondy explained, still staring at Steavans. "When one of the footmen only thinks of hurting someone, all other collars are pulled to the forehead in a split second by powerful electromagnets. You could say that his hands and feet are punishing his stupid head. This is my idea, it was enough to add a little technique."

"Isn't that dangerous?" Davis asked.

"Some people get their spine injured, but a maximum of ten percent die, which is safe."

"Well, it's actually a small percentage. Maybe we could equip all people with the hoops of discipline?" Duecklenbourg asked quite seriously.

"We don't have that many humaans. Who would clean them? Ha ha!" Tatarczyna joked.

At this point, two robots appeared. One of them picked up the bars and after a while he left with a full tray, the other carried the body of the poor man.

"Was it just me that the bars were yellow? What do they taste like? I wanted to try it," Fagot was sad.

"We won't eat off the floor, we'll get fresh in a moment. Meanwhile, Julia, tell your friends about your new success," Noovack asked, peering at the floor as if looking for blood stains after an action with the butler.

"We stole five men from Floris," Fagot reported proudly. "It wasn't difficult. The border is practically unguarded. Even a large branch, probably fifteen people, easily crossed the border."

"Where are you keeping these men?" Davis asked anxiously.

"They are in my apartment with the consent of the Prime Minister."

"They should go to the Ministry of the Interior," Tatarczyna said indignantly.

"No. Men should be monitored by the Public Opinion Research Bureau. It's in my ministry," Davis fumed.

"This is not about a sociological experiment. Nobody forces them to do anything or checks how they shit on our bars. They're going to feel better than at home," Noovack said, her voice unbearable. "Julia Fagot has no husband, she has beautiful maids. It is a real paradise for these young men."

"Do they like it?" She asked with sincere curiosity in Duecklenbourg's voice.

"At first they were scared, now they are delighted."

"How are these things? Have you tasted them?" Tatarczyna asked, smiling lasciviously.

"Don't be vulgar, Natalia," said Gibbondy.

"If that's what you mean, then no, but if any of you wanted..."

It was evident that the mere thought of what she could do with them made Bassoon drool like a snot.

"How does the conversion of flying machines work?" Noovack asked.

"Excellent," Tatarczyna replied. "Image recording devices have been tested on our territory. The only problem is the length of the record, but we have an idea. Within a month, I think we'll be ready to ship them on their maiden flight. The only question is what we will use to spread the smog in Inco."

"Penetrating the enemy's country is an absolute priority," Noovack said, and stroked the animarobot walking along the back.

"Oh, I would have forgotten. I think Clifford is dead," Nadine Bleur said.

"What? How do you know?" Tatarczyna was surprised.

"Someone used the communicator right on the border, on the other side. We checked this connection. It was a male voice that conveyed information to another man in the Inco area."

"Who received?" Tatarczyna asked.

"Unfortunately not detectable. It was an unregistered device. One of the ones Clifford's people used. The signal came only once, then not."

"You should have notified us right away," Tatarczyn said furiously.

"Relax, friends. This is not the time to argue. You have to make sure it's true Clifford is dead. If so, we'll declare a public holiday," Noovack said. "And now I suggest that we move to Julia's apartment and look at these Florinians closely. Then we'll give them what they want and... let them go free. Let them tell their friends that rich Inco offers a paradise for young men."

"They will be our ambassadors," rejoiced Fagot.

"Yes. And if they do good work and they come back to us, we'll give them whatever they want," Noovack said, and winked at the two butlers standing still.

***

Jasmin returned from a walk. A startling sight appeared before her eyes. Luicey and Vicky sat in the bed gossiping like best friends.

"Oh, you are back," Luicey replied enthusiastically. "We're all three pregnant. We can support each other."

"It's good that you are back. Get me some water," Vicky said.

Luicey looked towards Addam's first, then second, wife.

"If so, I'll ask you too," she said.

Jasmin just snorted. She entered the recovery room. After a while, the rustling of the water was heard, like a light rain.

Luicey struggled to her feet, like she was in the end of her third trimester, not the middle of her first. She went to the coolant, picked up two bottles of Pearl brand water, and returned to the bed. Vicky handed one of the bottles. They drank almost at the same time it amused them.

Suddenly Addam entered.

"Oh, hi, Luicey. Vicky, honey, how are you feeling?"

"So-so," she replied sadly.

"Do not worry everything will be fine. I read that in the fifth week, all anxiety is perfectly normal."

"Oh, he's cute. He's so worried about you," Luicey judged.

"Well," Vicky said blissfully. "Come hug," she said to Addam.

"So we're not going to the gallery?" He was surprised.

"Yeah. I forgot. I'm getting ready," Vicky chattered, and there was no trace of her hitherto sad expression.

By the time Jasmin finished regenerating, Addam and Vicky had time to leave the suite. Luicey sat alone on the bed watching theatremania stuff.

"Finally. How much can you rinse off?"

"And what happened to you?" Jasmin was surprised, running her hand through her hair and making her head even more messy. "Have they gone?"

"Addam is gonna be a great father."

"We will see."

"I don't understand why you're complaining about him so much. No wonder he ghosts you. You walk sour, you look as if you were hurt. Look at Vicky. She bursts with happiness."

"There's a slight difference between us. I was the first, she took my place. Have a right to be pissed off?"

"That's the difference. She's not pissed off about anyone at all. And who is wise here?"

"What else," she snapped. "About me? Angry? I was first."

"I didn't mean you."

"Who?"

Luicey bit her tongue.

"You know something? Admit it, Addam has someone and she knows it, right?"

Luicey rolled her eyes.

"I wasn't supposed to tell you, but I don't care anymore," she began. "You never treated me like a friend. What else, Vicky. I can trust her. After all, we'll be like a family soon."

"Can you tell me about this game? Because I'm going to be damned in a moment. You mean you had a baby with Addam's cousin, right? Is this the family you mean?"

"You don't understand. Haenry cannot have children. It was Addam who helped us."

Jasmin's eyes widened in surprise.

"And what? Did you sleep with him?" She asked, though she still had the impression that she was dreaming it all.

"Only once."

Jasmin turned and stood still. She felt the blood rush to her head. It was as if someone had hit her with a blunt instrument a moment ago.

"Get the fuck out," she said softly.

"Take it, take it easy," Luicey downplayed. "Do not be a child. See what's happening around you. Everyone does it with everyone."

Jasmin turned and looked directly into Luicey's eyes.

"Get the fuck out! Should I spell it for you?!"

"Fine," Luicey said casually. "You'll come to me."

"Get out of my house, out of my life! Get out!"

Luicey got up and walked slowly towards the door. Jasmin dropped to her knees, covered her face with her hands and cried.

Chapter 18 Insubordination

Nothing has pleased Ae more than the return of the shrimp in a long time. She quickly adopted Haris's contemptuous nickname for the swashbuckler Xami. She accepted him like Jusif once, pretending to be seeing a merchant. The shrimp had indeed brought the news she had been waiting for, and just in case someone had spied on it, a sack of stem fiber filled with Inco smuggled goods.

"You got it quickly," she asked when they were alone.

"The most important thing is that I did what you expected from me. No witnesses."

"Excellent. I understand I can check off the Clifford case. Who else?"

"Better not know. These five names won't tell you anything, and you'll have a better sleep."

Ae wondered at the mysterious posture of the court cleanser. She didn't want to be tricked into paying for five heads that didn't exist.

"Okay. Write their names on a piece of paper and put them in a sealed envelope. When I feel like a restless sleep, I will reach for it."

"As you wish," he said, and thought for a moment. "I think you will find it interesting. Haris has come to Patrix."

"Yes?" She reacted happily, then made a face as if the information did not matter to her. "He recognized you?"

"No, but I heard him talking to the chief of your guards. He begged for an audience."

"Interesting what for?" Ae couldn't hide her interest anymore.

"I don't know, but maybe it was better that he came here and not stayed in Vatili Soll. You told me to do it last. I would have to pretend not to see him."

"Right." Ae was already thoughts elsewhere.

"I have something for you," he said.

Xami took a transparent Inco-style women's pannier from the sack. It was handed over by Ae. It was easy to see the contents. There was a communicator, an animarobot on a scale of one to twenty imitating a hydapi, latex gloves with fingernails that looked like living hands, a medicine vial, and a brown box. Ae started with him first. She opened the lid, but quickly closed it with distaste, as if expecting the contents. At the sight of the gloves, she made a face as if to say that her hands did not require camouflage. Then she focused on animarobot.

"I've seen this thing before," she said, playing with the micro hydapy. "And what is this item for?"

"To communicate. It won't work here because it's too far from the border."

"And these drugs?" She asked suspiciously, especially staring at the well-known logotype.

"I thought you might need it."

"I don't understand." She was clearly embarrassed.

"Let me remind you that not only Jusif knew your secrets. We both brought these guys in, then disguised as priests, took their bodies to Asaran, and took turns smuggling you medicine that would take away any trouble you might have."

She blushed. After a while, a frustrated grimace appeared on her face.

"Don't worry. Only Jusif and I knew this secret. No one more."

"I won't need this drug anymore. Take it. When are you going to Vatili Soll?"

"Tomorrow at dawn."

"Be careful," she said with sincere concern, handing over the usual payment, a purse of gray stones.

Xami bowed low and walked away. Ae noticed that he hadn't taken the medicine vial with him. At first she considered this gesture insubordination. She should have called him back and scolded him so he wouldn't think he might mock her. After a while, she only smiled at her thoughts.

***

The tree of dew, next to which a pile of stones was piled up in memory of the dead, began to grow spontaneously for the first time in many Hello sunrises. Juices appeared on its curled, tubular leaves. They dripped like tears from the dead Rita. Fahid thought so. He knew that the tree grew regularly, usually every month, a day or two after its moon. This time it was only two weeks after the night where three of the four visible moons formed a single line in the sky. It must be a sign, Fahid thought as he noticed the anomaly. His faith in Patri was shattered and he sought solace in the signs of nature. He decided that no priest should mummify Rita's corpse or take it to Asaran. She should rest underground, next to the stone grave, in their yard, shielded from the claws of the underground sahadi lizards by several layers of clothing made of raidi fabrics. So he decided and did.

When he buried her body, he cried. He remembered the last breath of his beloved when she was practically dying in his hands. But he didn't kill her. It was done by ruthless priests whom he swore to take revenge. He was going to find each and personally stab their knife right through the heart. He intended to do the same to the High Priestess of the Omniearth, as soon as she freed her children from her hands.

Before leaving for Patrix, he visited Rita's parents. They were neighbors, although in Floris it was difficult to call the hosts who had their cultivated fields even a few days of tiring journey. The in-laws, Roh and Kitta, as well as Gira, Rita's sister, who stayed with her parents on the farm, were surprised to see him. From the yard, they watched him ride a young, crippled okurai for a long hike.

"What brings you to us alone, Fahid?" Asked Roh anxiously, as if he were airing misfortune.

"My Rita is dead. Abdul and Ragir too. The rest of the children taken," Fahid stammered and made a mock boisterous face, as if he wanted to look like an emotionless, immune to misfortune man.

With every word he spoke, Kitta shed another great, unstoppable tear. Her husband stood still, made an unimaginable grimace of pain, and gripped the handle of the cane he was propping up in his hand. Gira, Rita's twin sister, fell to her knees and began to beat her hands on the ground, mumbling incomprehensible syllables. It looked like a prayer for the dead.

"Be silent, stupid!" Fahid shouted at her. "It won't help her. The priests killed her."

"What are you saying, Fahid?" Asked Roh. "What is my poor daughter's fault?"

"Not her. It's me. I didn't want to turn Sumi over to the priesthood," he replied.

"You drew the wrath of Patri. Oh, not good," Kitta whimpered. "You had to take it easy and allow Sumi. She would be a priestess, not some singer. You wasted her life. Could be closer to Patri."

"You don't understand anything!" Fahid shouted.

Roh walked over to him, propped his cane on his right hip, and stretched out his broad arms, expecting them to hug each other. In vain.

"Fahid, what happened to you? Do not challenge the most loving lady, or you will attract more misfortunes," he said.

"And that's unheard of, after all Mahmud has just passed away. Oh, sorry Fahid we were unable to come to the mummification. We found out too late. When are you planning the ceremony? This time we will be on time," declared the sister of the deceased.

"I already buried her, in the ground near the house. Her body will not go to any Asaran."

"What are you saying?! He's mad!" Roh said indignantly, seeking support from his wife and daughter.

"Probably exhausted and needs rest. Gira, get him some food," Kitta suggested.

"I'm not hungry. I'm going to Patrix. I will not come back here anymore. If you want, ask a new priest to give you my land. I set the animals free so that they would not starve to death. Here is my last will."

Fahid handed Roh a rolled papyrus.

"What new priest? Where is Kadu? Fahid, don't be silly!" Kitta worried.

Fahid adjusted the bundles attached to the okurai, checked the crossbow hidden under the coverlet, and raced towards the Litrijis. His deceased wife's family could not recover from the news he gave them for a long time. Each of the godly three remembered his visit differently. Roh was furious that Fahid had probably drank his tinghao, released the animals, and refused to engage in the cultivation of dirsna, as was the custom of neighboring families for generations. Kitta wondered what had happened to Kadu and whether Rita would find a way to Patri since her body had not ended up in Asaran. Only Gira noticed that her two nephews, Abdul and Ragir, had gone to Patri, and that, according to her, was a great injustice. Neither of the three inquired about Fahid's last will, though they should have. After all, they could not read papyri.

***

Before going to Patrix, Fahid hesitated to check in on Hambarra first and see how Sumi was doing. Ultimately, he decided that he would not do so. He wasn't going to worry her. She was curious, she would have asked him about her mother, how the youngest brothers were doing. He couldn't lie. She would even realize that something more terrible had happened than what he had done to Kadu. He decided to stop by when he returned from the capital. Driving through Litrijis, he decided to visit a stinky man without an arm. Only him could trust - he could understand and support him with a kind word. Perhaps only this wise man could advise on how to persuade Ae to give him back the children. He thought so.

"You have nothing to count on," the smelly man replied to the infantile question. "This woman is ruthless. If she has already made a decision, she will certainly not change it at the request of an ordinary farmer."

"Then I'll kill her!" Fahid shouted.

"Of course. She is definitely possible to kill. She is waiting for you to come for her," replied the old man ironically.

"I'll find a way. I have a crossbow. Help me. She killed my wife, two sons, took the rest of my children from me!"

"Fool. You don't know who you're dealing with. Ae is not an ordinary priestess like Kadu. She's a furious pokun, only pretending to be the head of the Church."

"How do you know that? You were among them, weren't you?" Fahid looked pleased, as if he had discovered the greatest secret.

"Yes. I was a priest, one of the most important, a member of the Council. My name is Ghaideng Ru. You probably heard about my brother Visharem. Nobody talked about him Ru, just Vishare. We were recruited together when we had less than one purge. He was the High Priest of the Omniearth before Ae. She killed him."

Fahid looked at the stinky man in disbelief.

"I know it sounds unbelievable, but that's what I'm sure of. Together with Vishare we made a career in the Church. I was the more impatient, more inclined to fight, to duels, he devoted himself to prayer, he was the wiser. When I spent most of my time practicing martial arts, he read old books. That is why he was elected first the head of the school, then the High Priest of the Omniearth. Vishare, my older brother, called me to the Council a few days before his death."

"Why do you think she killed him?"

"Not alone. Ever since she emerged at the top of power, strange things have started to happen. I don't remember any of the priests having been murdered before. If one of them argued with the other, and it happened that they fought each other, even in duels, no one was killing anyone. Of course, I'm not talking about what happened with the wayward subjects. If there was a need to calm them down, some would get burned or skinned. Sometimes we cut off their limbs, took their kids, or threw them alive into Asaran, bound and gagged. But these were still exceptions. Never on a scale like this. The church in Ae's time was completely broken. I'm sure she was behind every murder in Patrix."

"I believe you. The priestess uses her power to kill at a distance. My Rita was first painfully mutilated, then - as she began to recover - she died suddenly."

"Nonsense. It's not witchcraft, but probably a head bang effect. Sometimes it happens like this, the disease seems to regress, and then it strikes with redoubled force."

"Such things did not happen with us. It's a quiet neighborhood. Once, in Litrijis, a trader said that the closer he got to Patrix, the more people were intimidated. That it wasn't like that before."

"That's true. Formerly, faith was enough. Asaran fills up faster and faster after several cleanings. It started with a priest who got in the way of Ae when she was still a student."

"What happened to him?"

"He was found nailed to a pole with his hands above his head. He was naked. He had a truncated genitalia. He bled to death."

"For what?"

"Apparently, before poisoning, at school, he used it many times. She never officially confessed, but Vishare knew the truth. As Ae began her career, the priests began to disappear. There were corpses without a head, eyes, hands or tongue."

Fahid was disgusted and terrified.

"She cut your arm off?" He asked.

Ghaideng Ru held his breath.

"No," he replied calmly. "When Vishare died of a heart condition under strange circumstances, I knew that I would be another. I hacked it off myself and started pretending to be crazy. The remaining stump began to purge and had to be cut off. It took a long time to heal, but that was the only way I could survive. I managed to. They expelled me from the priesthood because Ali Ude, one of the elders, had interceded for me."

"And that stench from your house?" Fahid realized that nothing would surprise him anymore, but he absolutely wanted to know.

"Practical proof of my insanity. Nobody is touching me. I can do my own thing. And I do. Would you like to join us?"

***

Zenit came to Ae to ask Haris for permission for an audience. The High Priestess of the Omniearth teased a little, but eventually agreed. She asked for some time. She bathed in the milk that the maid brought, let herself be smeared with fragrant oleum, and pinned her hair into a clever hairstyle that was a combination of a bun and a braid. She was wearing a silvery gown embroidered with blue thread. She almost looked like a Patri. That's what she thought of herself.

Haris was stunned to see her. He stared at her for a good few moments, forgotten what to say. She was pleased that she impressed him. She flared. Eventually she became impatient.

"Why did you want to meet me?" She asked coquettishly.

Haris shook his head back and forth as if to wake up, to get back from where he was now in his mind.

"I was sent by my compatriots who live in Vatili Soll. They are worried why you treated the prime minister this way."

"I don't understand," Ae said.

"That you made him go unguarded. You gave him the order like a shaver."

"What do you think?"

"You probably think he was trying to cheat you. Unnecessarily. He has good intentions, although few know about it. He is a good man."

"Good? Blackmailer."

"He had no other choice. This wasn't how he planned it all. If it weren't for him, you'd be an ordinary, poisoned priestess in some crap."

"Nobody told him to make such decisions."

"True, but I think he deserves respect. He is the head of state. He did it for his country, to save people. Not everything is as it seems."

The High Priestess of the Omniearth was getting bored with this conversation. She didn't want to waste time listening to Clifford's merits list. She had completely different plans for this evening."

"What I should do now? It's too late," she said, but quickly bit her tongue.

"Not yet. Send a small squad of intentional after him. Just in case. The road to the border is easy, but anything could have happened. Clifford might just be lost."

Ae realized that Haris probably had interpreted her last sentence differently. She held him in suspense to put her decision right into words.

"I can do that," she said after a moment. "You're right. Blackmailer or not, he will be more useful as a living debtor than a dead, insignificant neighbor."

Haris was pleased with her decision. He walked over to the table on which stood a carved tinghao casserole and, to his hostess's surprise, filled two copper goblets with alcohol. He handed one to the priestess, the other he took in his hand and made a toast.

"For the success of his mission."

"I hope you don't regret it." She smiled and gulped down the contents.

Haris winked at her and drank tinghao, choking twice.

***

Kifor eavesdropped outside the door, but when he realized what was happening in the chamber of the High Priestess of the Omniearth, he asked Zenit for help.

"They're completely drunk," he whispered to the chief of the watch.

"And what. It happened that she drank with guests from abroad," Zenit replied.

"I know, but is it right that she should share a bed with someone?"

"What?" Zenit was surprised.

"Listen yourself."

Zenit put his ear closer to the door. Haris's voice was clearly recognizable as he was regaling the priestess with some indiscriminate joke, and she responded with a dissolute laugh. It didn't sound right. Zenit looked at Kifor and pointed to a place from which they could see something. They went a few cubits down the corridor. There was a small hole between the planks that covered the inside of the walls. It was clogged with a piece of mohair tree. Zenit took it out slowly and noiselessly. He peered through the buttonhole, but made a face as if nothing could be seen. The interior of

Ae's chamber was not lit by a torch. When Zenit's eyes grew accustomed to the dim light there, he noticed that the only source of light, quite warm, was a forged metal candle holder with eight oil lamps filled with sirra oleum. Only three wicks smoldered slender flames, the rest were burnt out. Apart from the candlestick, Zenit saw only a Sundra jug, its shadow falling on a small wooden statue of Patri. There was nothing else to see. With his eye pressed almost to the center of the buttonhole, he shook his head a little, first to the left, then to the right. Finally he saw two naked butts lying in the purple sheets: a bony male and a female heart-shaped.

***

"We all benefited when Jusif chose you," Haris joked, scanning Ae's naked body with a lascivious gaze.

"He chose me?" She was surprised.

"He was tasked with finding a person who stands out and is wise."

"Either Jusif was smart or you're a professional liar now, Haris," she said coquettishly, and finally embellished her statement with a mocking smile.

"I knew you weren't poisoned, but I didn't think you were capable of making love because of a faith that doesn't allow you to do so."

"And you see someone here with whom I could do it so far? Ha ha!"

"Yeah, fact. Ha ha! Only lousy faces, bald ones. Probably none of them. And Jusif? Didn't you feel attracted to?"

"He was a professional," she said fondly.

Haris thought about it. Ae stroked his hair tenderly, as if the gesture were a memory of a loved one.

"But it's a waste," he said. "There are so many women in Inco who will never have sex in their life. You have so many priests who live a celibate life. If only they had known the charms of carnal enjoyment, they would not have decided to poison, ha ha!"

"And here you are wrong," she said. "The priests know this feeling."

"Really? How it's possible? When? They're recruited for a kid, after all."

"And what? School takes all one purification. During this time, they all mature slowly."

"Yeah. And what, can they do it?" He showed a lascivious gesture. "Nobody's keeping an eye on them?"

She shook her head.

"That's why you are skilled in these things," he said excitedly, as if he had discovered her secret.

"Such an age-old custom. Until the time of poisoning, the students of the school, until they are still priests, can do whatever they like. They are supposed to have fun for the rest of their lives. Doesn't matter who with whom and how. Individually or collectively. Boys and girls, girls and girls, and even boys among themselves."

"People think you're so decent, they feel sorry for you. And here is such debauchery. Ha ha!"

Ae became sad.

"Unfortunately, there are also dark sides to this habit," she said.

"I guess what one of them becomes pregnant?"

"Rarely. I mean so-called sacrifice. The older ones take advantage of the younger ones. And it's not just about forcing you to work. Sometimes children, even at the age of one purification, are invited to bed by the stronger. It doesn't matter if you are a boy or a girl. If someone older wants you, you must give yourself up. Nobody can protect you. It is an unwritten law." Ae, finishing the last sentence, she thought. It was obvious that she had no good memories.

Haris stood up abruptly. He looked at her reproachfully. He dressed in a hurry, as if he was ashamed of all the bad deeds she had told him about, or as if he was about to be raped.

"Because Patri wants to?! What a fucking cowardice!" He shouted.

"First, don't use words that I don't know."

"Which?!"

"Fuck. Do I pronounce it right? What does it mean?" She was surprised.

"Well, in your country women do not sell themselves for a vain few gray stones! You are such an ideal society. But you do tolerate that adults rape children! Secondly?!" He shouted louder and louder.

"You're not indulging in too much?"

"If you think it's wrong, put it in order. Are you the goddamn High Priestess of the Omniearth or not?" He shouted, gesturing.

Ae threw on her gown, put on her sandals, and listened, airing the immediate rescue of the guards. It was strange, but no one showed up to defend her, though surely someone heard her visitor's screams. But after a while, right behind the wall, you could hear a few creaks. Ae began to straighten her hair. Meanwhile, Haris took a few staggering steps, still agitated and drunk. Suddenly he started rolling his eyes and staggering on his feet. He fell down and began to vomit. It was evident that his body had not had time to get used to real food. And from what he expelled, you could guess that he had eaten a few Florian snacks earlier. She looked at him with disgust and called Zenit. He appeared immediately. She thought he was standing outside the door and was most likely eavesdropping, but she wasn't going to give him any satisfaction. She had everything cleaned up, including the guy who got sick. She ordered him to be severely punished. She wasn't even going to explain herself.

***

Zenit carried out Ae's command with the utmost care. Haris, still heavily influenced by tinghao, was locked in a grotto with a checkered chamber, but this time no one tortured him as lightly as when he was there the first time. He was tightly tied with a raidi cord to grids made of sahadi backbones. Their sharp ends of individual vertebrae pierced his back, cutting the skin to blood. But that was not the most severe punishment he had ever received. This time, instead of flogging and beating with a wooden stick, the priest honoring the executioner abused him in a completely different way. He was force-fed. Plain food has become Haris's most burdensome torture. After each bite, he choked and from time to time vomited, and the executioner opened his mouth with one hand, and with the other hand stained with food, he stuffed more portions of various food straight down his throat. From pancakes to fruit to pieces of meat, and every now and then, before gagging his mouth, the priest would put a lump of black lard into it. Haris had not expected such a punishment for making Ae an accomplice in the monstrous procedure. Once he tried to bite the torturer, but this ended in a severe warning that he should not do so again. In return, the executioner stuck a sharp pin in his ear, it worked.

This time Haris gave up without a fight. He was drunk, hungover, wanted to vomit, and the inside of his digestive system was ravaged by a slurry that was a mixture of leftover food with stomach acid and enzymes to digest the bars.

"Plea-se, ma-n. I am dy-ing."

Haris was unable to utter a word fluently. He continued with syllables as the executioner took a break and prepared another batch of food.

Hidden in the depths of the grotto, Kifor and Zenit watched the torture, hidden under a shadow. Just looking at them was also drawn to vomiting.

"Enough!" Zenit shouted. "We will spare you, but on the condition that you tell us the whole truth."

Haris nodded that he understood and agreed.

"If we find your information interesting, you can keep talking until you say everything you know. If we believe that you are lying or postpone the sentence, the executioner will resume his work. Understand?"

"Yes," Haris said, spitting the contents out of his mouth.

"Why could the priestess share the bed with you? How is it possible?"

Haris scowled in surprise. He thought.

"Does she know what you're asking me?" He wondered, as if he were convinced that the torture was carried out on the orders of the most important person in the country.

"Speak!" Zenit shouted.

The executioner just brought his food-dirty hand to his mouth, and Haris reacted immediately with a gag reflex.

"Because she's not poisoned," he said through his almost closed mouth, turned his head as far as he could and took a deep breath.

Zenit and Kifor exchanged glances.

"Next. You were supposed to be talking all the time!" The executioner yelled and pointed to a table with food that looked like a pigsty with his dirty hand.

"I'll tell you everything, but I don't want to eat any more." Haris took a few more deep breaths. "Our Government helped her get to the top. She had our spy, the saboteur. He worked for her and murdered on commission."

"Xami?" Kifor asked.

"No, Jusif."

"Jusif, that loathsome trader," Zenit said. "Go on!"

"It was he who caused that Vishara was first elected the High Priest of the Omniearth. Then he killed him and some of the more important priests. Some he bribed to vote for Ae when there were elections. Earlier, he forged documents, he signed for Shamanui Ke, among others. For example, he signed a consent that she would not have to manage the district as a middle-ranking priest and immediately after a short military service she became a member of the Council."

"Jusif didn't work for Ae?" Zenit was surprised. "She wanted me to find him," he whispered to Kifor.

"He did too, but he actually worked for Clifford."

"She was the one who ordered the murders, right?" Kifor asked.

"And Xami? Who is Xami?" Zenit interjected.

"He's an insignificant asshole, Jusif's sidekick. He must have escaped to Inco."

"You know he used your last name?"

"I'm not surprised he went so far as to go back to the old methods. If he could come up with a creative solution himself, he would impress me," said Haris.

"Why do you think Ae gave him the liquidation list?" Kifor asked.

Haris sobered up in no time. He focused on the last question and repeated it, narrowing his eyes.

"Has she handed over the list of people for liquidation? To be liquidated? Liquidation? So kills? Kills? Whom?" He slowly asked himself more questions aloud, which looked like a fight against his own insanity.

"All of Inco. Mr. Prime Minister, his family and others who are hiding with us," said Kifor.

Zenit looked anxiously at Kifor. The latter nodded as a sign that he was not kidding.

"I do not believe. Why would she kill them? She owed them so much," Haris whimpered.

"You are also on this list," the Deputy High Priestess of the Omniearth interrupted in a calm voice.

***

Kifor realized that he would not get Haris out any more. Nor could he use him as a witness if the Council asked for it, for the slender bastard had already fallen upon the elders once, knocking the wagon down to Asaran. The important priest needed more evidence of Ae's criminal activities. He felt that this was the moment when there was a chance to remove her from power. Too much has changed since she became the High Priestess of the Omniearth. He decided to go to Vatili Soll. He had two reasons. First, he wanted to warn the townspeople about Xami. Second, he needed to call one of the Inco officials as a witness. He didn't have to ask Ae for permission to go to Vatili Soll. He was her deputy and a respected member of the Council. However, just in case, he took the Sirius and hung it on his back.

When he got there, he saw a cordon of guards guarding the settlement. It pleased him to see it. He thought that with the bravest warriors guarding it, no rodent would pass.

"Let me through. I'm going with a message from Ae."

"Hello, Kifor," said one of the guards.

"The lady ordered me to check the progress in science."

"Our technical priests live in that yurt." The guard gestured to a distant spot. "What's up at Patrix? We haven't been home for a long time."

"As usual," answered Kifor, and went in the direction indicated.

As he got closer to his goal, his unease grew. After all, the settlement should have been teeming with life. "Where is everybody? They hid around the houses? Or maybe they are up to something?" He wondered. Just in case, he took the Sirius out of its scabbard and gripped the hilt firmly in his right hand. When he came to one of the houses, he saw bloody tracks on the stairs. He knocked on the door with his sword. His hands trembled and his breathing quickened. He hadn't fought anyone for a long time, and he hadn't wanted to die in the final straight, just before punishing Ae. However, curiosity pushed him to the next steps. He opened the door and stepped inside. The interior did not resemble a typical Floris homestead. There were all kinds of technological devices of foreign origin everywhere. After a while he entered the sleeping chamber. A terrifying sight appeared before his eyes. On the large bed, on a slightly dried blood stain, lay the massacred corpses of Rubby, his wife and son. All three had their throats slashed, gouged eyes, and striped skin. It looked as if someone was playing with the corpse long after it was killed. Kifor couldn't catch his breath for a moment. He was horrified by the sight. He ran outside.

"How did you guard the settlement, dorks?!" He yelled at the top of his throat in a style that was reserved for Ae.

***

Returning towards Patrix, Kifor passed a group of several dozen men walking with bundles. At first he did not pay attention to them, as if the sight was familiar to him. Contrary. It was not normal in Floris for young people to travel in such great numbers. Kifor was simply completely lost in the world. All the time he had a sight of the bloody corpse, not only of Rubby's family, but of other officials as well. When the guards, assisted by incredulous guards, discovered more bodies of brutally murdered people from Vatili Soll, his faith in humanity was shattered. "Could it be Xami's doing? Was the murder on behalf of Ae? Why weren't all these unfortunates just killed? Why were their eyes torn out, their bellies slit, their skin sliced into strips? Who could have done such a wicked deed, and why were Clifford and his family not among those killed? Could they have escaped?" He pondered, multiplying the questions.

But as Kifor passed the third group of wandering young men, he wondered if there was anything he needed to know. He turned the okurai he was driving towards the Patrix.

"Who are you and why are you going in this direction?" He asked.

"And who are you that you ask us?" A man of two purifications answered with a question that was not unfounded. For riding on horseback, Kifor wore a comfortable outfit that did not resemble a priestly garment.

"My name is Kifor. I am a member of the Supreme Council."

"We don't have to answer you. You don't have power over us anymore, ha ha ha!"

The rest of the group laughed loudly. Kifor thought it would be no use frightening this country rabble with Sirius. There were too many men. Nothing would do, and he could get quite a hit. They were young farmers with muscular shoulders and an idiotic faces. So he rushed the animal, although he was not pleased with the way it was treated by ordinary peasants.

***

When Ae found out that Kifor had called the Council, she reacted furiously.

"Who let him?" Zenit asked in a raised tone as he led her towards the Golden Temple.

"Each member of the Council may do so in accordance with the applicable canon."

"You don't teach me, Zenit. You showed me where my place is once. You know I'll never forgive you for this. After the council meeting, report to me for your resignation."

Zenit bowed low as usual, with the only difference that this time there was no customary submissive gaze in his eyes.

The members of the council waited in the temple, anxiously wondering what would happen. After a while, Ae entered. Zenit who had brought her closed the door on the outside behind her, for, according to custom, he was not allowed to stay in this holy place during the deliberations.

"What happened, Kifor, that you called the Council?" She asked, hiding her displeasure.

"Sorry, Ae, I made some matter serious. Two, in fact", said Kifor in a slightly shaky voice.

"So don't keep us in suspense," she sneered, grinning at Ali Ude.

Kifor hesitated for a moment. It was obvious that she couldn't start. He chose the right words for a long time. Finally, stuttering, he pulled out a sentence.

"Our statehood, which we have been proud of for many generations, is in ruins."

"What are you talking about?" Ae said indignantly. "Stop talking nonsense."

"High Priestess, let's give Kifor a chance to explain what's on his mind," Ali Ude suggested.

"Ae said it was very bad in neighboring Inco," Kifor continued in a less nervous-sounding voice. "Boys are not born, their Government has changed. A group of women has come to power who do not care about our customs and our dignity."

The priestess just shook her head critically. There was an image of disdain for Kifor's revelations on her face.

"Until a few days ago, if someone had told me that the Florinians could recognize Inco's superiority, I wouldn't have believed a word of it. However, I saw with my own eyes huge groups of young men who decided to leave our country encouraged by living in a quasi-luxury abroad."

"What is this nonsense? When did you see them?" Ae asked nervously.

She looked as if she had become a bundle of nerves. She wasn't hiding her anger anymore. The madness that the members of the Council noticed filled her eyes.

"Back then, when you shared the bed with that spy Haris, I was checking out what was going on in Vatili Soll," he blurted out the entire sentence in one breath, as if afraid Ae would interrupt him.

There were whispers in the Golden Temple. The High Priestess of the Omniearth got up and slowly walked over to Kifor. She gave him a superior, contemptuous look.

"Zenit! Zenit! Guards!" She screamed, but no one showed up.

"Sit down, lady. The council should find out the whole truth," said Kifor calmly.

Ae returned to her seat without a word. She didn't look terrified. She flared. Her ego and unimaginable pride told her not to show fear. She calmed her breathing, looked up, and studied the faces of the Council Members as if she were counting individual traitors.

"Ae was never poisoned," said Kifor.

The priests froze. Their stony faces only looked as if they were searching for an answer. They looked surprised as if the message they had just heard was unimaginable to them.

"Can't you see what she looks like?" Kifor continued. "Not like us. She is in the service of Inco, admittedly of the previous Clifford Government, but she is behind the murder of Vishara and many other people. Floris rules a juggler!"

The council priests glanced at Ae in disbelief, some with embarrassed eyes as if they were scolding themselves for not making a clear judgment.

"I request her immediate appeal. She should not be a member of the Council," suggested Kifor.

"The Canon does not allow an appeal. At most, suspension until the matter is resolved. There is even a special procedure for this."

"There is nothing to explain here. Because of her, our country is plunged into ruin, and Inco is ruling at home. They take away our dignity."

"Is that true, lady?" Rados asked.

Ae looked in his direction. She wasn't sure if it was reaching out or trying to finish it off. It certainly did not sound like the clownery he was habitually regaled her. She had never liked this priest because he was talking nonsense. Sometimes it felt as if he was deliberately laying on. This time he asked quite credibly. She looked at one of the burning torches. She kept her eyes on her, took a deep breath.

"If I was, as Kifor claims, at the request of the Inco Government, why can its members and their families hidden in Vatili Soll no longer do us any harm?"

All eyes turned to Kifor.

"I can't explain it," he replied. He was surprised by the question. "They are indeed dead, I don't know why, but I'm sure it was you, lady, who ordered them to be killed!"

"I don't understand anything," said Rados. "Why do you think Ae was in the service of the Inco Government when she later ordered its members to be killed?" Rados turned to the priest sitting next to him. "The very thought of murder gives me chills," he whispered to him.

"We have witnesses! Zenit, the chief of the watch, heard the same as me!"

"Don't scream, it's not right," Ali Ude reassured.

"Who did he hear from? From Haris?" Ae exclaimed. "Please, he is a liar, the smartest of all. That is why I am the High Priestess of the Omniearth, not you, Kifor. Come back to the children's games," she sneered.

"It is not right to mock a Council Member," said Ali Ude with concern.

"It is not right to undermine the words of the High Priestess of the Omniearth!" She replied, almost screaming.

"Forgive me, my lady. Just tell us, are you poisoned or not?" Ali Ude asked. "If not, it means that you are not even an ordinary low-level priest, but rather a student."

The priests froze. The words sounded like an ax hanging over their Church, almost like a death sentence. If they turned out to be true, its foundations would be crushed.

"You all witnessed my poisoning. Don't make me explain why the pin spared my body."

"Are you or not?"

Ae held her breath.

"Yes," she replied confidently.

The members of the Council breathed a sigh of relief. There was moderate satisfaction on their faces. What a decision they would have to make if it turned out that the High Priestess of the Omniearth, who has been in charge of the whole country for two purifications, mocked their faith without even receiving priestly ordination, and is a simple trickster. How would the Florian people react if they found out that their beloved ruler was not a saint?

"It's a lie!" Kifor shouted.

"We will not seek the truth of either of you now," Ali Ude turned to Ae and Kifor.

"You are of weak faith. I'm disappointed in you," she said in a calm voice, scowling at one of the oldest priests.

The High Priestess of the Omniearth reached behind her right ear and unhooked the hairpin hidden behind it. Then she did likewise with the other ear. She closed her eyes and tugged the lock from her forehead down her face. The hair began to slide down, covering the priestess's face and revealing the skin on top of her head. They turned out to be a wig. After a while, Ae associated with a beautiful, brown-haired haircut discovered the rest of her shaved head. She put the wig aside and stroked her bald head with her hand, as if the gesture she had just made tickled her and her skin itched. She opened her eyes and looked at the stunned mouths of the priests who had never seen their ruler without hair. In fact, they did not know that you can spice up an artificial hairstyle, much less what is a wig. Ae enjoyed their surprise. Only Kifor looked as if he hadn't noticed anything unexpected, still gasping with rage.

"Please send some troops towards the border. All women. No man is allowed to leave Floris anymore. I announce the full mobilization of the entire army," she decided, and left with her head held high, the wig in her hand.

***

Ghaideng Ru asked Fahid for an oath of confidentiality. Only in this way could he assure himself and others of the fraternity that a newly met man would not hand them over to the priests. The oath was aimed at the psychological aspect. The people in Floris were reluctant to break the word. Besides, the man didn't look like a liar. They went - or rather, Ghaideng Ru limped, and Fahid followed - to the fraternity's secret meeting on the banks of the Ethne River. When they got there, a few distrustful glances wandered towards the alien-looking farmer. The gathered people lit a night bonfire.

"Don't worry, brothers," said the smelly man, grabbed a piece of wood and tossed it over the fire. "Do the same," he said to his companion.

Fahid grabbed a larger log and threw it right in the middle of the fire.

"It's a symbol of our unity," said the black-haired man of five purifications.

"My name is Fahid. Who are you?"

"My name is Sande. Me and my brother Karini are fishermen. Muott is a carpenter. Jimii a nimo shepherd. You already know Ghaidenga Ru."

"Me too," replied the trader Fahid had once bought a crossbow from. He appeared practically out of nowhere. "My name is Kaaratu."

"Can you help me kill Ae?" Fahid asked carelessly.

The members of the fraternity only smiled.

"Hardy," said Kaaratu. "He will be useful to us."

"Our brotherhood doesn't kill if it doesn't have to," said Ghaideng Ru. "We're a secret group, part of a larger network dotted around Floris."

"There are more of you?" Fahid was surprised.

"Yes. Many people do not like what is going on in our country. Behind everything is a hypocritical hag, priestess of Ae," said Muott.

"Are you a believer?" Fahid asked, causing consternation.

"What is that question?" Karini said indignantly. "We all believe in the goddess Patri, the power of Mount Saandreal, and the Diamond Sanctuary. We just want this crazy pokun in a woman's body to be lost forever."

"I understand our new brother's doubts. We have all lost faith in the Church as it is today," said Ghaideng Ru and gestured to Fahid not to rush with difficult questions.

Until the end of the meeting, the farmer didn't say a word but listened. He learned of the plan to provoke a revolt, and that in the northern quarter - long considered less disciplined and more wayward - several priests had quietly joined the ranks of the brotherhood. He remembered his father's stories about savages living in those areas. He thought again that his knowledge of the world was extremely meager. As they returned at night, finally without company, Fahid returned with a question to Ghaideng Ru.

"Do you believe?"

The stinky handless man smiled gently and considered the answer for a moment.

"Depends on what you ask. I believe in Patri, but not everything the Church says, if that's what you mean. But it's better not to flaunt this view. People who have trusted all their lives that there is a driving force cannot imagine any other possibility. For example, that perhaps no one is watching over us," Ghaideng Ru said in a calm voice.

"What are you going to do?" Fahid asked.

"You know. I want to restore the old order from before Ae."

"I don't understand. Why are you doing nothing to get people to know the truth?"

"There is no objective truth. The only thing that is known is that we will all die one day. Until we find out what is the reason for our presence in this place, it is not worth killing their faith in people. Let everyone answer the questions bothering him for himself."

"What if he's not smart enough to imagine that there is another possibility at all?"

"You're right, Fahid. But we can't do anything alone. There are only a handful of people like you and me. Change requires work and time. Probably many generations. All hope in the young."

Fahid thought about it. In his mind, he saw his children. First suffering alone away from their family, then as adult priests forced to preach superstition. He became sad.

"I'm moving on tomorrow," Fahid announced. "Thank you for your hospitality and kindness, but I cannot sit still..."

"You do as you think. Just consider what will be better for your children."

"I'd rather die than give them to those mendacious bandits!"

"Do not shout." Ghaideng Ru looked around as if checking to see if his companion had heard. "If you die, and that is more than certain, who will protect them?"

"Should I wait for the brotherhood? How long have you been debating instead of acting?"

"You don't understand anything. Anyway, go. Let yourself be killed, and it is best to jump into Asaran immediately."

Fahid grew sad. It was obvious that he was fighting with his own thoughts.

***

The life of a girl studying to be a singer was neither easy nor pleasant. Despite this, Sumi felt happy. Manius Drey, the most eminent singing teacher, gave her a job in addition to tutoring. So that she could start her chores early in the morning, she did not live in the dormitory like the other students, but in an outbuilding, a small wooden house made available only to her. None of the students had the right to accuse the school of not caring for the vocal cords, so Manius attached great importance to order. Sumi got up earlier than the household members, prayed briefly and immediately took to sweeping the school yard. Then she washed the floors in the hall and individual exercise rooms. Despite the fact that she did the same activities at the end of each day, it was important to expect that in the morning she would have something to do again. It was, in fact, thanks to the constant breeze called the prankster. He accompanied the people who had lived in Hambarra for many generations, applying successive layers of dust.

Manius Drey had perfect hearing, so only with him the lessons looked different than with other teachers. There was one student in each practice room, sometimes two. He listened to everyone, gave directions or ordered an exercise to be performed. Then he did the same with the next student in the next room. He had a brief consultation, but listened to the exercises in other rooms out of the corner of his ear. When he heard even the slightest falsehood, he would go back to the person who made the mistake and reprimand him. Sometimes in all the rooms, and there were eight of them, you could hear different melodies, one fast and one slow. It all sounded like a mess. It didn't bother him. He could separate every note from every melody. Therefore, Manius Drey was treated as a guru among the disciples. Jealous competitors, owners of other schools, could not count on what Drey was getting.

Sumi was very teachable. Manius rarely needed to correct it. She always performed her tasks reliably and with great commitment, as well as with a noticeable passion. They liked each other pretty quickly. The teacher saw in her an ambitious, country girl from a poor home, fighting for survival. She treated him like a strict but fair uncle. She mentally called him Omar, like the brother of a grandfather she had never met. He impressed her. He had a backbone woven from the principles he followed. When it was necessary, he found the right one for every situation in no time. Its rules gave a sense of professionalism and security.

That day, Sumi and Adalberto had lessons in two adjoining rooms. Manius was furious because the young man - because of his tall stature looking more grown up than he really was - could not concentrate. He lost the rhythm, and every few phrases, in the exact same place each time, an unbearably sounding falsehood crept into the melody he was singing.

"We're finishing today," the teacher decided.

"Forgive me, master, but I hear a different rhythm in the next room."

"I told you a thousand times. During the exercises, you hear voices coming from the neighboring room so that you can learn not to hear them. You will thank me in the future. At each concert, you can meet a spectator who during our performance, even the most important one, at the least appropriate moment will feel like talking, laughing, stomping or singing his favorite melodies. And what? Are we supposed to stop our singing because we can't concentrate? Admit that this girl has turned your head."

"But, master..."

At this point, they both heard that Sumi had falsified.

"And yet," Manius thought aloud, and smiled. "We're really done for today."

Adalberto lowered his head meekly as a sign of thanks for the lesson. As he was leaving school, he saw Sumi sweeping the yard. He walked over to her.

"Today you sang out of tune," he said.

"No more than you. You howled like okurai in childbirth," she laughed.

"I forgot you were a farmer. I've never heard an okurai howling."

"You'd better go away, because your silvery-haired vocal cords will be covered with dust and you'll be choking like a hydapi, ha, ha!"

"Just because you're a girl will I spare you any more flattery," he joked in return.

Adalberto walked towards the dormitory. Sumi wondered for a moment if she had done the right thing to insult the artist. That's what she called him. "Not what we, farmers," she would say to herself when no one heard her. And then she remembered her father again, his tired hands and the animal's resilience as he carried out superhuman tasks with virtually effortlessness. How little he spoke and worked a lot. How he did not waste time having fun or meaningless conversations about just anything. He was always so prudent and orderly. Tough, but sensitive in its own way. He was sensitive, but not an artist. Just a good man. The fond memory only lasted a moment. Again, the unbearable thought of what Fahid had done to the Kadu and the two warriors came back. No. Her father was not sensitive. He was able to kill a man. She didn't know him like that two months before. In time, she decided that Manius Drey would never kill anyone. Conflicting thoughts about her father and teacher confused her mind. The longer she lived away from her family home, the less often she returned to the terrible moments she had witnessed. Sometimes she remembered her home, siblings and her mother. In her memories there was also a father that caused malaise, which was transferred to her singing art. When she realized this, she decided not to think about him at all. In order for her to succeed, she began to talk to strangers about herself as an orphan.

***

"What happened to Rados?" Ae asked, nervously scratching her head through an unstable wig that moved with her nails.

"As you say, he's gone to Patri," Xami replied with a smile on his face.

"Seriously?" She sneered. "I am asking for what reason."

"He was on the list of those who knew."

The High Priestess of the Omniearth was surprised by this information, but decided not to show anything that she cared about.

"I sent Zenit and Kifor to the river under the pretext of guarding the border," she said, handing over the money purse.

"I understand, lady. I know what to do," he replied, bowed, and began shaking the pouch as if checking weight. "Heavier than usual."

"It's for the wig idea. I appreciate."

"Thank you. I would recommend for the future."

Xami left. Ae looked in the mirror, took off her wig, and scratched her skin furiously. When she finished, she calmed her breathing and studied her reflection. She noticed that she didn't look bad at all. "It's good that Xami has replaced Jusif," she thought. Maybe he was the brain all this time. Jusif would never have come up with such a crazy and unexpected idea as the one with a fake haircut. Besides, he wasn't that forward-looking. She opened the brown box and looked inside. It was lightly crammed with a few strands of carelessly cut hair, kept as a souvenir. She sighed in exasperation at the sight of them. She stuffed them in the box so that the wig would also fit, tucked it inside, and covered the lid.

***

Taarida, riding a three-wheeled wagon pulled by a pair of rather lively hydapis, was heading towards Rita's parents' house. She was in an excellent mood, feeling confident and competent, as befits a new priestess in charge of the district in which she was now located. Kifor handed her the nomination without agreeing with Ae. According to the canon, he shouldn't have done this, but he felt strong. It had happened a few days earlier, in the morning. Just before the High Priestess of the Omniearth was about to appear before the Council. Kifor was sure that Ae would be punished and locked in a grotto with a checkered chamber. He saw himself as her successor, not Ali Udego, the senior priest.

"Hello, God-fearing. I am the new priestess in charge of this district," Taarida told Roh and his wife.

Both lowered their heads, but not as to bow. They avoided eye contact, as if they did not want to embarrass the priestess hiding her face under the mask.

"What happened to Kadu?" Kitta asked concerned.

"He's given a new assignment. He did not have time to say goodbye to everyone."

"Then welcome to our humble doors, lady. What do they call you," Roh asked.

"Taarida. I have a few questions for you."

'Gira, one more place setting!" He shouted. "We were already sitting down to our meal," he said to Taarida. "We also have tinghao. Kadu liked it very much."

"I'm not Kadu," Taarida said, but when she noticed how awkward she was, she cleared her throat. "I would love to try your favorite family delicacies, but I always eat alone," she added.

"Obviously," Roh said, sniffing that it was a mask she did not want to reveal.

He led her to an unusual looking room. A branch of a dew-tree, almost an elbow thick, ran through its center.

Rolled letters with bows were attached to the smaller twigs sticking out of it. Their colors, in particular, made it easy to identify the senders - the last few High Priests of the Omniearth.

"A miracle, right?" Roh boasted. "The tree from the yard has grown so much. The branch pressed in by itself, went through the wall and came out with the other one. It grows both inside and out, so that the bowls need to be put on top."

"And?" Taarida asked as if she were completely uninterested in the revelation.

"It's Patri's doing, that's why we made a little shrine here. Do you want to pray?"

"Maybe another time."

After a while, everyone was sitting at a table covered with several plates and a large tray full of snacks. Among them were pancakes made of mao flour, but wrapped not like in Fahid's house in rolls with dirshna liniment, but in the form of dumplings stuffed with fat, salty stuffing. Apart from them, you could see colander eggs, small anake mushrooms stuck on twigs of turlin, pieces of roasted tine cheeks, smoked okurai ears and slices of cheese roulades with the aftertaste of pokuna horseradish, the hottest spice available only in the western quarter. There is a keeffi cocktail to drink with shuri shoots, sandi fruit, sweetened with raspberry flowers.

"I'll get to the point," Taarida offered.

"Ask then," Roh said with a slight click.

Taarida took out a rolled parchment and began leafing through its contents.

"Your daughter Rita lives next door," she said. “She married a certain Manduarra, Fahid. That's right?"

Kitta and Roh exchanged glances. It was obvious that the question troubled them. There was not even a trace of their good moods. They nodded, though Taarida quickly realized that they couldn't lie.

"I'm looking for them right now, Rita and her husband. I was with them a few days ago, but I didn't find anyone. The animals were running around on their own. I understand this is the property of the Manduarra. Do you know where they went?"

"Our daughter Rita is dead. Her husband Fahid told us so."

"Really? It's sad. What happened to her?" She sneered, but they didn't see it.

"Patri took her."

"Sure," Taarida said, though that wasn't the answer she had expected. "Then where is her husband?"

"We would like to ask for your consent on this very issue. If he doesn't do the dirishna anymore, we will gladly take the whole field after him."

"How will he not do?"

"Well, that's what he said. That he is leaving. Probably like his uncle, Omar."

"Omar, you say... And that's interesting. You know a lot." Taarida noticed that it was enough to provoke the poor peasants, there was no need to frighten them.

"How are we not to know? Omar was promised me, but because he decided to go to Inco, my father married me to Roha," Kitta reported proudly.

"And that's a story, ha ha!" Taarida laughed. "So everything is like in the family. Your daughter then married another Manduarra."

"We are all as one family here," said Gira happily.

"We just can't find her man," Roh joked, embarrassing his daughter. "Maybe if your priestess found out somewhere in the city for a working man, we would give her. And there would be a field..."

"We'll see. So Fahid left for Inco. Interesting."

Roh nodded. Taarida made some ritual gestures to sacrifice the house and thank them for the meal they had packed for her journey. She walked away towards the yard. She approached the wagon. Kitta and Roh stepped out onto the steps of the house to bid her farewell to the road. When they realized that the priestess had unfastened the large curved cleaver from her harness and, holding it in her hand, she walked back towards them, only making terrified faces. Without a word, Taarida made two precise cuts. The severed heads slid down the necks and the bodies fell limp. Roh's head rolled at Taarida's feet, leaving a trail of blood on her right shoe.

"Your souls are in my hands," she said and walked home to finish the work.

Gira didn't even defend herself. She had the same fate as her parents. Taarida stuffed the three heads into a sack of stem fiber and threw the body along with the corpse onto the wagon. The whole thing was covered with a soft, patterned bedspread found at home. She led three healthiest looking animals out of the stables. She fastened them with a raidi cord at the back of the car. She left the rest inside. From the stove on which the infusion of raspberry flowers was boiling, she scooped a burning log with a poker and before she ran out of the house, she kicked it on the tablecloths arranged in a pile. They caught fire quickly. In a split second, the fire spread to the wooden walls and roof, then spread faster and faster. Taarida had only gone a few hundred cubits, and the fire was now spreading to the windmill and the stable. The only sound was the terrifying roar of trapped animals. After a while, the entire farm was burning, including valuables, documents and family heirlooms, including Fahid's last will written on parchment - all traces of life. You could see the smoke from a distance, but not so much that the neighbors could see it.

***

Kifor and Zenit were reaching the border. They led a unit of 40 low-ranking priestesses tasked with stopping male migration to a neighboring country. The women were riding the hydapi, with equal spacing between the foursome. The commanders mounted the okurai. They had a gallows mood. They hadn't spoken a word with each other for hours. The High Priestess of the Omniearth punished them by exile for insubordination. This is how they assessed the new mission. Kifor felt that his career in the Church Council was hung by the thin hair of her wig. He made his appearance in front of the most important people in the country, and from now on no one will believe him in the next revelations. In addition, Ae put it in one bag with Zenit, which has been under censorship for some time. Kifor looked critically at the head of the purple guard, who was riding next to him. Zenit felt his gaze on him and turned his head towards him.

"We let ourselves be approached like children," he said.

Kifor looked around as if he was checking the distance of the top four behind them and if she had heard anything. Probably not, the warriors stared straight ahead, with no trace of emotion on their faces.

"Ae is smarter than we thought," he said quietly to Zenit.

"Are you gonna leave it like that?"

"We have to wait until it all calms down. You heard what happened to Rados."

"I just don't know what he deserved. For some time he has been exceptionally not questioning her ideas, and even getting into her ass."

"In any case, there are matters of more importance. The fact that we have been given a task allows us to believe that there is an opportunity for us."

The first challenges appeared before the border. Half a day's drive to the Pinati Waterfall, the detachment traveled along a wide road crossing a great forest full of mohair trees. He was approaching a group of twenty walkers who looked to be those in the eastern quarter. Their plans could be easily recognized. They had light bundles hung on sticks for defense. Kifor knew it wouldn't be easy to turn them back. Most likely, they would have to use force to stop the determined men from reaching Paradise. Zenit first wanted to know how it was all organized. This information could come in handy when planning a strategy to turn back groups. Kifor agreed with him, but did not feel up to engaging in a personal polemic with the peasants. He was careful, he wasn't going to lose his teeth in a stupid skirmish. He hid behind the last four priestesses.

"Where are you going?" Zenit asked.

"We are not looking for a strife," answered the person who walked at the end, the white-haired ginger at the age of two and a half purification.

Zenit realized that the man did not seem to be an obedient Patri follower. This attitude surprised him. "What has happened to this nation that they have nothing to do with the representatives of the Church?" - he wondered.

"Just asking. You know that border crossing is a mortal sin."

"Sins don't concern us anymore. Where we're going, nobody cares about them."

"What about your family?" Zenit asked.

"Parents are old, brothers and sister took the church. Nothing keeps me here."

"Yes? This is interesting," Zenit feigned surprise and almost caught up with the marching white-haired man. "How do you know what's in there?"

"My neighbor Derdui's cousin said he heard from Trinus, who in turn heard from Barchun, who has a brother, Barshal, and he lives near the border. And he was there in the city of great houses. He said it was the most wonderful place in the Universe. Every man has as many women as he wants, and a household so large that fifteen large families can live there. You don't have to work."

"Do you know how to get to this city? Maybe I would go there too."

"You don't have to walk far. Half a day's journey south, there are transport machines waiting for us, which take us straight to the place. They will accept every man, because there are only women living there. Come, sir, with us. Just don't take them," he finished in an almost whisper, nodding towards the priestesses following Zenit.

"I will consider," Zenit replied, and turned the animal around.

He drove up to Kifor.

"They don't think about consequences. I do not understand this. After all, it is known that their families will suffer," he said. "If we hold them back here, they'll scatter in the woods and we'll only waste time catching them."

"What do you suggest?" Kifor asked.

"Let's get ahead of them and set up an ambush. More troops will also have to be called in."

"There are three more behind us."

"It is not enough."

Chapter 19 The seedbed

Three months have passed. Vicky was in her twentieth week of pregnancy. Her hormones were crazy. Not only did she not feel like having sex, but her husband did not even let her be touched. Luckily for him, she was quite tolerant. She saw nothing wrong with the fact that new friends of the master of the house had started to appear in Addam's apartment; that was what they were called. It is important that he does not plan a wedding with any of them.

The first regular visitor to their house was the brown-haired Madelleine. She came from a slum, had an insert under her left eye, a delicate piece of pink glass. In combination with an impeccable figure, long braids and golden makeup all over her face, she looked phenomenal. Then the redheaded Kadina, the owner of an unnaturally sized breast and many moles, began to appear. He quickly got bored with her. Another one that kept me entertained was Appolomea, a black-haired, crippled beauty. Her left leg was shorter, not much, just three fingers. She explained that the twin brother had the left leg longer and that they complemented each other, but no one believed the story. In time, Appolomea and Madelleine, both less than two years of purification, took up residence in Kozllov's apartment. Addam bought another bed so that Vicky could get enough sleep. From then on, she was sleeping alone, comfortably, and he was frolicking in fresh sheets with his new friends. Jasmin, who was in her thirtieth week, though she looked like she was about to give birth, was still asleep on the mattress. Everything was indifferent to her. So she said.

One day, Vicky and Addam went for a routine checkup. The two new friends of the master of the house and Jasmin stayed in the apartment for the first time. She wasn't going to talk to them. She turned on the theatremania. Not to watch it, but to drown out the depressing silence. She didn't even look at the screen. At that moment, a report on the Florinians who lived in Inco was being broadcast. This particular group was given accommodation in an apartment building overlooking the Glass Dome. Martina Kuna interviewed them in the spacious living room.

"How is it for you to live in our country?" The famous editress asked.

"Your? This is our home now," replied the white-haired man, aged almost three purifications.

"Where you come from?"

"We lived in the western quarter."

At this point, Jasmin looked up at the screen. Madelleine noticed her revival.

"He's white-haired like you, too," she said.

"Well, so what?" Jasmin snapped, as if to distract from the real reason.

"We live here wonderfully," continued the white-haired man on the screen. "We are getting used to your food yet, but how clean it is, unbelievable. And finally, this terrible nature is gone."

"It's safer," added the second.

"Few Inco Natives have that color on their heads," said Madelleine. "You won't be special anymore."

"I'll be. The white-haired imbeciles from Floris are men," Jasmin said.

"And we don't have to pray anymore," the white-haired man from the screen continued, the first one.

"A moron," commented Jasmin.

"Why are you talking about them like that?" Madelleine's question didn't sound appraising, rather as if she didn't understand the intention.

"They speak with learned texts. You can see that they are lying. They don't have an opinion?" Jasmin started to wind up.

"Fact. The country hunk talks like our queen, Vicky. Ha ha!" Madelleine joked.

Jasmin saw a friend of the master of the house as an ally, yet she did not intend to trust her.

"Thanks to the good nature of the government, our society already has nearly a thousand satisfied men from a neighboring country. Thank you, Prime Minister," said Kuna on the screen.

"Today I'm going to have a migraine. I can't take the drug because it will hurt Victor. You guys have to be quiet, okay?" Appolomea mocked Vicky amusingly, bringing smiles to Jasmin and Madelleine's faces.

"Fucked Queen Vicky," commented the other friend. "When she will born the kid, I'm moving out."

"Jasmin, tell me, do you not mind that we came to live with you?" Appolomea asked.

"What does it matter?"

"You know, we support you a lot."

'I don't know in what area."

"That you are, you know, brave," said Madelleine honestly, although it sounded pathetic to Jasmin.

"And smart. We're on your side," finished Appolomea.

"Should I thank you?"

Jasmin was not at all pleased with the fact that her husband had brought two young girls into the apartment. "What did he do this for? Fool. They'll trick him and we'll all lose," she thought. Instead, she knew why they had done it. He wasn't good in bed at all, but he was a man. In addition, he kept these pics at the expense of his family. It would be foolish if they refused the invitation. Many single women would give a lot to have sex almost every night. It's good that Vicky regularly reminded them to be quiet because sometimes they totally forgot that they weren't alone. Jasmin slept badly at night; not only because the mattress was uncomfortable. She had frequent muscle spasms in her legs and her skin was itchy. She counted the days to the end of her ordeal, and the company of Madelleine and Appolomea was not helping.

***

"It's already the thirty-third corpse." A squeaking little voice came from the humaan of garda.

The woman in the officer's uniform sighed heavily and pulled out her communicator. She dialed the number, rubbed her hand over her face as if to cheer herself, twitched her jaw nervously, and stiffened as if she was about to speak to a higher authority and wasn't going to stutter.

"Good morning, I report that another Florian did not make it. We found him all vomitty. His hands were folded over his stomach as if he were clinging to him in pain," she reported.

"Please don't panic," came a female voice from the communicator. “We'll start to worry when twenty, maybe fifteen percent die from a diet change. Are there those who respond well to change?"

"Yes," the officer reported.

"Please focus on the pluses. Dispose of the corpse as usual. Nobody can find out."

"Yes, lady."

***

At that time, several small packs of women from the other district appeared near the border on the Inco side. A little out of curiosity, and also to take matters into your own hands. Neither of them, they argued, wished to wait their turn until the Government had graciously assigned them the desired Florian, only for the purpose of procreation. They decided to choose men for their needs just after they crossed the river that separates the two countries. They had set up a small camp at Pinati Falls and waited for further developments.

At this point, the two communities saw each other. Between them was only the broad Ethne River, guarded by the guards of both lands. The women waiting on the Inco side watched the struggle on the other side between the young men and the priestesses guarding the border. They hoped that the Florinians would be able to break the cordon, they cheered for them fiercely. They saw how the priestesses disciplined men, how they punished them, flogged them, and even the most determined ones took their precious lives. They suffered with him. They wanted to help somehow, but had no idea what to do. A few rushed into the stream to set an example for the rest of the passive observers, but were quickly shot with a crossbow. The corpses floating on the surface of the water scared more desperate women.

On the Floris side, the situation began to clear up. Twelve divisions of low-ranking priestesses guarded the border around the clock. In the clashes - in fact, only in minor skirmishes at the end - only three priestesses died, but also almost half a thousand young men who wanted to leave the country without the consent of the Church Council. They were not trained and did not have the appropriate weapons, so they did not stand a chance. It was not known how many men returned to their families, but there were thousands of them. About a hundred of the most obstinate ringleaders were shackled and escorted to the capital, whipped with whips all the way. They were escorted by a military unit, which was tasked with publicizing the case in such a way that the whole country would talk about it.

When the situation began to seem calm, Ae called on Zenit and Kifor to return to the Patrix. They were pleased with this news. The handwritten invitation by the High Priestess of the Omniearth sounded like praise for the excellent results. They left at dawn, hoping for a blessing. They took a small group of priestesses trained in sabotage and unusual espionage tasks for protection. Their help was of no avail. Kifor and Zenit did not reach the capital. All hearing from them was lost. Ae sent two troops of soldiers to search piece by piece all the way. They found nothing, there were no traces.

"Patri called them over. We should enjoy their happiness, but this time Asaran is crying," Ae said at a Church Council meeting. Her voice sounded pathetic. "How are we supposed to bury them when there are no bodies?"

"Maybe they're still alive," Namali said, swallowing nervously.

"Then where are they? They escaped to Inco?" She reacted nervously and scratched her wig.

"Maybe they were kidnapped," Mi-tu said in a calm voice.

"Where do these assumptions come from?" She was indignant.

"Forgive me, my daring." Ali Ude looked like he was about to be executed. "We are hearing that the situation in our country is bad. People blame the Church, they are not satisfied..."

"For what reason? That you forbade them from crossing the border?"

"Me?"

"Including you. Church Council. Are you a member of it?"

Ali Ude smiled, pretending it was a delicious joke.

"We can't let everyone do what they want," Ae continued. "People are too stupid to make their own decisions. We tell them what is good and what is bad for them. Nothing organizes human thoughts like surrender."

"The problem is that it is not only about the prohibition of migration. Residents are starting to talk about strange disappearances of entire families, setting fire to houses, unfounded, inhuman punishment. That Patri was merciful and the priests are the opposite."

"Because it is required by the good of the Church!" She screamed, but then realized she was not reacting properly. "How do you know that?" She asked in a completely different tone.

"Eighth paragraph of the canon. People themselves say what they know. You don't even have to press them down too hard."

"Oh, that's great. So the eighth paragraph works. Those who complain should be thrown into Asaran. They will definitely have a different outlook on how they interact with mummies."

"Then no one will tell us anything."

"Ungrateful," she sobbed theatrically. "The goddess has done so much for them, sacrificed herself for the people."

The high-level priests exchanged glances. After a moment, Ae cleared her throat and an irreconcilable grimace appeared on her face. There was no trace of the drama due to the disappearance of Zenit and Kifor.

"We have to start getting stronger," she said in a cold voice. "Mi-tu!" she asked the head of the school. "We shorten the priestly education to the necessary minimum. Then we poison the candidates, without any ceremony. Ling Gui takes them over and trains them to become soldiers. We now have two enemies. Outside and inside the country. Ali Ude, see that each council member meets with subordinate middle-level priests and has a disciplinary conversation. Those who have troublemakers in their territories will lose their privileges. I will not tolerate lack of vigilance."

There was silence. Ae looked towards Mi-tu, thought for a moment.

"And what about the matter I asked you for?" She asked.

"Everything is ready. A group of twelve of the bravest, ready to poison students await your orders."

"Okay," she said and gestured for him not to talk. "Their initiation is delayed a little. They must first acquire additional skills."

"Another thing. What are we doing with the families of those who went to Inco?" Namali asked.

"If we punish them too, the revolt will grow stronger," Mi-tu assessed.

"Patri will decide on them. After all, she is fair and merciful," Ae said in a calm tone.

***

Meanwhile, in the first district of Inco, the situation was slowly returning to normal. People got used to the Cascade of Eviction, no one mentioned the brutality of the guards anymore. The hardships of life were sweetened with the first good news, not only announced in theatromania, but also passed from mouth to mouth. Counting began in the hundreds, then in the thousands, of women expecting boys. They all became pregnant as a result of fertilization by immigrants from Floris - a process fully controlled by the GCO. Successive hosts of men assimilated with society on constantly evolving principles. Those who first appeared in Inco were buried from women. It was supposed to look like a quarantine. During this time, they were to completely adapt to the new conditions. They underwent a drastic change in their diet, which, if carried out too quickly, resulted in excruciating pains and, in extreme cases, death. Subsequent groups of newcomers from a foreign country were allowed to contact the women on the march, and the bars were introduced in stages. First as a snack, then as a dietary supplement, and finally as a dietary habit. This method has worked brilliantly. Over time, their bodies supported by supplements began to produce other types of enzymes, their bodies began to become slimmer, and constant sex made life easier. Florians, mostly white-haired, were seen more and more often without protection. The Inco people approved them, they became stars. When immigrants discovered the existence of the Glass Dome, they began to visit it more and more often to commune with nature. They said so.

***

Noovack called the cabinet for a brief meeting. During this type of weekly meetings, each head of a given ministry presented the achievements of her ministry, as well as plans for the next days. All the ministers were to be privy to every important project of their colleagues, what is more, they should know the same line of the Government. If any of the journalists were to accidentally ask an uncomfortable question - it doesn't matter that all the media at the time were state-owned - the members of the Noovack cabinet should know the only correct answer.

"What is the situation in the health service?" Asked the prime minister.

"The breeders are going on strike," Gibbondy replied.

"Don't call them that. The Florians are people, too," Davis said indignantly.

"What do they not like? Are they tired of frequent sex? Ha ha!" Duecklenbourg joked.

"They found out about the plan to demolish the Glass Dome, bits," Gibbondy said.

"Childish." Davis shook her head in disgust.

"Put yourself in their shoes," Martinez said. "They are far from their families, from their world, and this place reminds them very much of their home."

"I heard they pray there. The Glass Dome is like a temple for them," said Tatarczyna.

"All the more so to demolish this place," Noovack said. "Someone else will see."

"What are we going to do with the animals that live there?" Martinez asked.

"Simple, recycling," Gibbondy replied.

"And the lake? After all, there is a huge lake, as far as I can remember," Martinez said.

"That's why this investment is so expensive and will take more than half a purification," Noovack replied. "The water will be pumped out. We will flood the inactive bidrite mines with it."

"Isn't it better to leave this lake and put a school next to it, a smaller one?" Martinez asked timidly.

"You know why the lakes in the third district are dead? The same will happen here. When we dismantle the roof deck and dispose of the animals, the Hello rays will cause smelly algae to start growing. They will have to be chemically removed. Do you want to discuss with science?" Tatarczyna explained.

"Then why don't we leave this dome. Why it bothers us?" Martinez wasn't going to give up.

Noovack smirked, as if she had just decided to change the Minister of Economy and Transport.

"We conducted a survey. Eighty percent of the population wants the dome to be demolished," reported Davis proudly.

"Yeah. Nobody will accuse us of not consulting. Everything is going in the right direction," concluded Noovack.

***

After visiting Dr. Meilly, Addam and Vicky were focused on each other all day again. Madelleine and Appolomea made jealous faces but still had no plans to move out. They disappeared for days and returned in the evening. Jasmin practically wasn't going anywhere. Her breathing was shallower and she was getting tired quickly. Her stomach looked like a guard vehicle, and the contractions that appeared more and more regularly heralded that this day was inexorably coming. Her hair grew so she could pin it into a five-finger long ponytail.

"Honey, do you want a candy bar?" Asked Addam anxiously as the three of them stayed, as usual.

"Oh, give me. Yellow one," Vicky replied.

Jasmin snorted contemptuously. For some time now, she has stopped hiding with true intentions. She lived in a so-called happy family where none of the members was even aware of what she was going through. She became a curmudgeon. They treated her that way too. "Will someone ask me if I want a candy bar?" She asked the question in her mind. "A bunch of egoists. What are you staring at? Fucking sissy and dumb shit. They have made a wonderful nest for themselves and they will grin to each other so much at my hurt. I hate you and that brat of yours. Victor and Victor. Let him die. Nobody is interested in my daughters," she thought.

"How does it taste?" Addam asked.

"Delicious and I feel so alive. Jasmin, do you want?" Vicky asked. "Addam, get your first wife a candy bar," she said sarcastically.

"I don't want it."

Jasmin was bursting with venom and did not feel like trying the new thing in the market. Her pleasant was spoiled by that little shit, Vicky. According to the producers, the recently introduced bar of this color was designed to improve thinking and concentration. "Nothing's going to help her," Jasmin sneered in her mind.

***

Fahid slept in a small yurt near the house of a smelly man without an arm. He had announced several times that he intended to move towards Patrix to the rescue, but his grandfather had successfully talked him out of his suicidal expeditions to the pokuna cave. For days they talked about religion and ethics, they also touched upon social and existential topics. Ghaideng Ru was vastly knowledgeable compared to the poor farmer, so his apprentice absorbed every piece of information. The more he learned, the more he asked, and his doubts were intertwined and they would not leave him. If all his life he was convinced that the inhabitants of the eastern quarter did not have teeth - and it turned out to be untrue or perhaps half-true - then nothing is as it seems. Everything else can also be a lie. He stated that he no longer believed in anything.

Every few days, the apprentice and the master went to the evening fraternity meetings. Usually they were organized by the river, in a secluded place. Fahid liked to go there and watch a fisherman, a shepherd, or a hawker, lighting the Patri's evening campfire, plotting a coup. "Naive," he thought. “The priestess will never allow the villagers to overcome her. He cannot take her power away." Heard from Ghaideng Ru what Ae can do with people who stand in her way. Despite his doubts, he willingly accompanied the master. He even acknowledged that the fraternity had become his new family, and he became a little closer to them over the months. Although he missed the children kidnapped by Taarida, he unwittingly postponed his trip to Patrix.

One day, as they were on their way to their weekly meeting, Fahid noticed that one tree was inhabited by moree birds. They hung upside down, clawed on a branch. He had seen individual cases before, but never that the entire bird family would hang like this. And then he remembered Rita and the children who had been pulled out by force. Also about Abdul and Ragir, the poor people who paid for their mother's defense with their lives. About Sumi who had to hide in Hambarra. He remembered how much he hated the High Priestess of the Omniearth and all this religion with so much misfortune.

"What's wrong with bad people? Are they going to Patri too?" He asked as they arrived at the meeting place and tossed his piece of wood into the fire.

Ghaideng Ru reprimanded him with a scolding look, as if to remind him that he had repeatedly forbidden him to talk about the faith in front of godly peasants. This question, however, surprised everyone. The stinking man without a hand knew the answer, both official and obscene, but he was not sure what the other members of the brotherhood thought about it.

"Exactly, how do you think?" He asked, turning towards Sande and Muott.

They just made silly faces. Kaaratu reacted similarly, frowning and scratching his head.

"They are going to the abyss, to the opposite world," he replied hesitantly.

"My grandmother said that the body of a bad man should be burned and then all his sins would be forgiven him," Karini explained. "His ashes are being taken to Asaran."

"Yes, but only when he is burned alive," Ghaideng Ru said in a calm voice and lowered his head.

Everyone, including Fahid, froze. This information chilled their hot hearts. They looked at each other as if they were looking for answers to new questions that were arising in their heads.

"There is a prophecy written in old scripts," continued Ghaideng Ru, head bowed. "When Asaran is full, the world will end. Before this happens, however, a descendant of the god of evil will visit the Universe. In the form of a pokuna, born of a strange woman. He will wreak havoc and death. His appearance will be heralded by birds so large that their shadow might obscure the entire Universe. And Patri..."

"What, Patri? Where will it be then?" Muott asked shakily.

"I don't know. The rest of the script is missing."

Ghaideng Ru looked up at each of his companions in turn. This moment lasted for all eternity. The members of the fraternity looked terrified, absent-minded, and short of breath. Their hearts pounded in harmony with the sounds of crackling sparks coming from the fire. To summon such terrible things could tame the bravest warrior, let alone cowardly, poor artisans. After all, they, like every adult resident of Floris, knew the tale of the origins of pokuns. It was derived from one of the oldest scripts, written before the beginning of the world. Already then, they learned to ascribe to the gods the characteristics of animals and humans. If there was any mention of Patri on any of the old cards, she was described as a mature, beautiful woman. In turn, the evil god managing the abyss, or, if you prefer, the lord of the inverted world, was personified with an old man with bulging eyes. He was associated with the place where the souls of people without faith, sinners or doubters go. It is believed that many eras ago this old man was unable to cope with the crowds of wayward souls of evil people. That is why he created to help the pokuna, creatures that looked so terrifying and had such mean characters that no evil soul would dare to mess with them. One day a blind old man released from the abyss a whole army of these horrible monsters to destroy humanity. He did it out of spite of his creator - he knew that Patri liked these creatures best. People resisted for a long time. Many of them fell, but in the end it was them, with the help of the goddess, who managed to win the war. Individual pokunas are hidden in the forests and are still looking for an opportunity to redeem themselves. One thing that was certain was that there would be a day of playthrough.

"How good that I didn't learn to read," said Kaaratu, which amused his companions, distracting them in no time from the thought of the catastrophe.

"You don't even know how to tell, ha ha!" Karini chuckled.

"And good. At least I don't fray like you do," Kaaratu snapped. "I can count for it."

"Then count on yourself," joked Muott.

"Why did you need to learn to read?" Fahid asked, amused Jimi.

"Father convinced me. He taught me, and he was taught by my uncle."

"But you took the bait, ha ha!" Sande summed up.

The fraternity members have long joked about the benefits of not having a variety of skills. Fahid realized his previous ignorance had also been a blessing. He would give a lot to keep everything as it used to be.

At this point, out of nowhere, Taarida appeared. She stood behind Fahid and held the knife to his throat.

"Fahid Manduarra?" She asked, enjoying the terror of her companions.

"Yes," he replied.

"You'll come with me."

The members of the fraternity were speechless. Their expressions said it all. Kaaratu remembered that he had sold Fahid the crossbow, and he would probably hand him over. In his mind's eye, he saw the guillotine cut off his head. Ghaideng Ru sighed sadly. He silently said goodbye to a man he could call his friend. As he cooled down, he remembered that Taarida had probably been hidden for some time. How much did she hear?

***

The news about the closure of the border by the priestess of Floris spread to Inco in the blink of an eye. Many of the women who had been waiting in line for the desired man so far had their plans for procreation and even getting married. The devastating news, tinged with rumors, made the nation nervous. Until recently, everything seemed to be going in the right direction, which is why Ae's decision was treated in the media as an attack on democracy. Feelings were mixed and society was divided. Some Inco residents blamed the priestess of Floris for everything, and assessed the activities of the government exemplary. Others - and this group was as numerous as the first - criticized Eva Noovack's cabinet for diplomatic mistakes and lies despite strong propaganda. The third and smallest group were conspiracy theorists who believed that Noovack and Ae were one person.

***

Meanwhile, things were getting hot in Floris. The news of the men killed at Pinati Falls spread throughout the country, and rumors fueled by jugglers about Ae's dark nature sowed seeds of anxiety in society. One company in particular, managed by a puppet woman with a tattoo on her face, was acting eminently brazenly. Wherever they appeared, they aroused unhealthy sensation and applause. The spice was added by the fact that each time her corpse escaped justice. How much fun it was to chat with the clumsy, belated actions of a local priest to catch the enemies of the nation. "Chuckle of fate" - whispered. With time, the word of mouth to mouth about a spectacle wandering around the country, telling the story of an ugly puppet played by an ugly puppet, reached Patrix and angered Ae. The priestess ordered the company to be silenced and the puppeteer to be brought to her presence. Alive. It seemed to be easy to do, but not at this particular time. It was then that successive brotherhoods began to crawl out of hiding and wind each other up against the authorities. With the support of the enraged nation, feeling the power of solidarity with the families of the fallen, they unceremoniously criticized the Church.

"We will retrieve Fahid!" Kaaratu shouted during the brothers meeting, exceptionally organized not under the cover of night, but at noon.

"Yes. Give us back Fahid!" Sande replied defiantly.

The other members of the brotherhood also looked determined. Only Ghaideng Ru watched their eagerness in cold blood.

Then the unexpected happened. Large birds appeared in the sky on the Floris side. Flying machines with wings powered by Hello rays, which crossed the energetic labyrinth at a high ceiling, broke into the country from Inco. God-fearing brothers who had not had any contact with technology so far perceived this event as an announcement of calamity.

"You were talking about that?" He turned to the man without Kaaratu's hand. "Big birds herald the birth of an evil god?"

Ghaideng Ru looked up at the sky and made a face as if he didn't believe his eyes.

"See what shadows they cast. They are huge. Woe to us," lamented Jimmii.

"Patri, save me!" Muott shouted.

"Let's go to the temple," Sande suggested.

"Only the High Priestess of the Omniearth can help us," Kaarat chattered over and over.

Flying machines - previously used to disperse smog in the first and second Inco districts - were designed to record an image of the border between countries, as well as cities, settlements and population centers. After the modifications that were introduced, their range was multiplied, mainly through intelligent control programs. The appearance of great birds in various regions of the religious country silenced public discontent. The temples were filling up with people again. Faith has become society's only hope. Even those doubters humbled themselves before Patri.

***

In Inco, interviews with the Florians were broadcast on all four theatremania channels. They were interspersed with shots from the border.

"Priestess Ae does not agree that Floris men donate their semen to unbelieving women," one of the white-haired men said on the screen. "Many of our brothers lost their lives for wanting to come to your aid."

At this point, the image from the camera in the flying machine appeared on the screen. It was a sight of hundreds of women from the second district huddled together by Pinati Falls. After a while, the image was zoomed in and moved towards the river. Several dead bodies were floating on its surface. The next shots showed close-ups of the priestesses guarding the border. They were armed, and their implacable, horrible mouths would scare the bravest man away. They looked downright disgusting. Then, against their background, Martina Kuna's sad comment was heard.

"The priestess of Floris thinks our country should die out, because we live against the guidelines given by the goddess Patri. According to their sacred canon, each man can only have one woman," she said.

"There are many prohibitions in our religion." The white-haired Florian appeared on the screen again. "We call it mortal sins, because if someone does not obey the restrictions, he will die."

At this point, Eva Noovack appeared on the screen. She looked modest.

"Dear compatriots," she began pathetically as usual. "Perhaps the world we know will never be the same again. The neighboring country wants to hit our freedom and democracy. They wants to humiliate our society. We are to bow, kneel before their lord, as did the vain Clifford Government. The priestess sent an army of Florian women against her men who wanted happiness alongside our women. We should not interfere in their internal affairs, but they begin to affect us as well. I promise you I will find a solution. Long live Inco! Long live love!"

Chapter 20 The spectrum

"I think something's starting," said Vicky in the morning. "I'm having contractions."

"But it can't be," said Addam. He sprang up from the bed he had slept in with Madelleine and Appolomea. "You're only in the twenty-fifth week."

Jasmin looked anxiously at the young girl, then at Addam, then at his sleepy friends. She hadn't slept in an hour. She heard Vicky spinning, looking for a more comfortable position, but ignored it.

"I'm calling the emergency services," he said. "You're not gonna walk to the hospital."

Everything happened very quickly. Before they could get dressed, a doctor rang the doorbell with two humaans. Their green uniforms - unlike the guardians - resembled nurses' gowns. As she left, Vicky looked towards the other pregnant woman as if seeking support; she looked terrified and lost. Jasmin looked away, though she regretted it later. After all, she would not lose anything if she encouraged this heaven.

After leaving the apartment, Vicky was taken by elevator to the ground floor, and from there by emergency vehicles transported to the hospital. Addam ran after them.

Jasmin was having troubled thoughts. "Has something bad happened to the baby?" She remembered cursing the boy silently. "It wasn't smart," she thought. "The boy wasn't guilty of anything. What if Vicky also thought badly of her? And about her daughters? It shouldn't be like this. Let it just end well," she mused. "I forgive her everything as long as the children are not hurt." At this point, she realized that her pregnancy was much more advanced. Jasmin was in the thirty-fifth week, and she had three in her belly, which was usually associated with premature babies. She decided that she would start packing. She didn't want to be surprised how Vicky was.

***

Childbirth was complicated. Addam was sitting in the waiting room, texting everyone he knew informing him that he was going to be the boy's father at any moment. Congratulations came back from Addam's parents, his brothers, and even from the future parents-in-law of the yet unborn child. All the fathers of the boy's future wives, including Aratunia, promised to visit.

"Mr. Kozllov, please," Dr. Meilly said, entering the waiting room.

"Is there a boy?" Addam asked.

"Please come in." Dr. Meilly gave way to Addam as he crossed the threshold of the delivery room.

Vicky was lying on a hospital bed covered with a transparent, warm duvet. It was evident that she was dressed in loose body-covering garments, slightly stained with blood in the area of the still puckered lower abdomen. She looked happy. She smiled at her husband. After a while, humaan brought an incubator with a sleeping baby on the deck. Victor was wrapped in a thermal blanket. Only his puffy, closed eyes were visible.

"Little," Addam said, rubbing his eye, pretending he had caught something.

"Will you tell him or should I do it?" Dr. Meilly asked.

"What is he going to tell me?" Addam reacted with a nervous tic, anxiety spread across his face.

Vicky turned her head. Dr. Meilly sighed, mentally rebuking the new mom for cowardice.

"Please sit down," she said to Addam, pointing to the edge of his wife's bed.

He did what he was asked to do, but made a face as if he still didn't understand the seriousness of the situation. He was smiling stupidly.

"Your son is premature. This has many consequences."

"Whew, I'm relieved. I thought it was worse. So much is said about these mutants now."

"That's not all," said Vicky.

"Your son has hypohydrotic ectodermal dysplasia," Dr. Meilly continued. "Autosomal recessive mode. It means an invalid gene from both parents."

"What? What the hell is that?" Addam aired the worst.

"A very rare disease. It manifests itself as a complete or partial lack of some glands and quite often facial deformation."

Addam sprang to the incubator and began panicking to open it. His fingers touched what seemed to be something like door handles.

"Please don't open it."

"I need to see."

"You can kill him. The disease has no visible symptoms yet. They will appear only with time. If he survives."

"What? If he survive it?! What the fuck is a hospital or a funeral home?!"

Addam ran up to Vicky and hugged her affectionately.

"Honey, what did they do to you?"

"It's not them," she replied.

"But you can spot the disease in time," he was hysterical. "Why was it not possible to do this?"

"Your wife knew from the very beginning what we were struggling with. We injected the EDA-1 protein as soon as we discovered that the fetus was not producing it."

"Did you know about this? Why didn't you tell me anything? You made me always wait in the corridor. Everything's fine, everything's fine," he mimicked his younger wife's voice ironically. "It was not good at all! Whore!"

Vicky closed her eyes. She looked ashamed.

"Leave her alone. It's not her fault. She counted, just like us, that it would be successful. Now I need your support."

Addam got up. He took a few quick steps. Finally, he stopped and thought.

"What does facial deformity mean?" He asked.

***

Addam warned the whole family that everything was fine with the baby, but like any premature baby, he had to stay in the incubator for some time. Vicky would be back in two days, and then visit the baby every day until he was of the right weight and developed a sucking reflex. Everyone, however, was very curious what the descendant of Addam looks like. None of my friends and relatives was going to wait until the whole family was together. They visited the boy in the hospital without invitation. Only Jasmin wasn't going anywhere. She couldn't. The only thing that surprised her was her husband's behavior. She watched him anxiously. He didn't look happy, and she knew him well. Even if he was talking about what his firstborn looked like, his face showed no wonder, but something like a disguised fear. Three days after leaving the hospital, Vicky and Addam went there to see the baby. Then they were to buy a crib, a baby carrier, a stroller - more for the sake of the mustache, so that he wouldn't bother with carrying the baby - and a few necessary trinkets. They did not do it earlier, because Papa the mustachioed decided that it should not be combed. However, Addam did not return alone from the hospital until late in the evening.

"What happened?" Jasmin asked at the sight of his tearful eyes.

"We were together at Victor's in a small room, in the hospital. She said she had to go to the toilet. I asked if he could handle it. She answered yes. I heard a few screams, as if someone was yelling at someone: "Give me your money, thief." Then other voices, bustle. I figured they'd found a place to argue too. I wanted to go there, but I didn't want to leave the boy alone. I know he would be okay in the incubator, but that's what I thought then. Then I heard a woman cry, the sounds of rescue workers, doctors and midwives. Then Dr. Meilly came in and looked at me."

"What happened?" Madelleine asked.

"Vicky was murdered."

"What? How is that? Why?" Jasmin asked.

Addam shook his head as if to say he had no idea.

"And the garda? What are they saying?" she threw up more questions that bombarded her husband with worse and worse memories.

"They're investigating."

"What about the baby?"

"I put him in the adoption program. I can't handle his upbringing."

"Are you crazy?!" Jasmin screamed. "And what will happen to us? We were to get an allowance for him."

***

Addam told about the boy's illness, which caused quite a shock to the household members. As it turned out, Victor had a life in hiding, not only from the world that would treat him like a freak, but also from Hello's rays. The disease he experienced made his sweat glands malformed, preventing the body from sweating and thus cooling the body down, even producing tears. Such children, and there were only fifteen of them in Inco, were nearly bald, with dry skin, and conical teeth, if any. They looked like little monsters, they were more frightening than herms. Madelleine and Appolomea moved out the same evening. It got unbearable in the house. Addam was using an upper day in and day out. He said life didn't make sense to him. At night, he mourned loudly for his second wife, keeping his neighbors awake. Jasmin couldn't find a place for herself. On the one hand, she felt guilty about thinking badly about Vicky and her child. On the other hand, her life was turned upside down once again.

Mustachioed was unable to cope with the loss of his beloved daughter. He blamed Addam and Jasmin for everything, especially their greed. When he realized that he had lost not only Vicky, but also the money invested in the relationship, he was sure that the killings were made by the families of Victor's future wives. They probably ordered someone to murder. The garda could not handle the investigation at all, as they had much more important matters of state importance. Therefore, the mustache decided to find the perpetrators and administer justice. In the end, he assumed that he was adopting the child himself. After all, Addam, insensitive in his eyes, wanted to get rid of the problem. When Jasmin found out about this, she suggested to her husband not to turn the boy off, that she would take care of the upbringing. She knew that only when they kept Victor in the family would they have a chance for benefits. She was not glad that her fate had deprived her of her rival.

"I disagree," replied Addam. "These will be four brats wandering around the house."

"Do you want to give your baby to strangers?"

"It's all your fault. If you hadn't talked Vicky into that fucking wedding fair, she'd be alive. You're the one who cranked up the dads to make more money. You were especially on the side of this Florian. I hate these villagers. I hope there will be a war and we will eradicate this plague."

Jasmin saw a completely different man. He was not like the one he had once proposed to her in the Glass Dome.

Addam in her eyes became a cold motherfucker, without feeling selfish. Even his analytical mind ceased to interest her.

"It's enough that I can't get rid of you," he said suddenly. "If you agree to the divorce, you can get it."

Jamin didn't think too long. She agreed. They agreed that she would live in the apartment until the girls were three months old. Then he has - as the spouse put it - to get the fuck out. During this time, he will live with his parents so that no one will get used to anyone. She decided that after three months she would go to work and could afford to rent a small apartment in the slums. Finally she saw a light at the end of the tunnel.

Due to the advanced, troublesome pregnancy, the adoption and divorce took place without leaving the apartment, in electronic form, only in the presence of witnesses. They were neighbors Ginger and Ksaverius.

***

Early in the morning, a faint chime was heard in Addam's apartment, where Jasmin had been living alone for several days. The pregnant white-haired girl slept in the bed, until recently occupied by Madelleine and Appolomea. She hadn't cleaned since Addam moved out. There was a mess that showed that it was a temporary apartment, and the landlady had all the chores somewhere except taking care of her own butt and, above all, her stomach. She stood up slowly and moved even slower towards the door. The gong, more insistent this time, reminded that someone was waiting outside, but she couldn't go any faster. She finally caught up, and when she opened the door a crack, Aratunia entered uninvited.

"You have a mess here. Where's your husband?" He asked.

"Addam doesn't live with me," she replied. "How can I help you?"

"I came for the money. You have taken a down payment for the wedding, and there will be no wedding. You persuaded me."

"I didn't take anything. Please ask my ex-husband. You signed the contract with him. I was just a witness."

"Yes, but this guy, Victor is a monster. I will not give my daughter to waste."

"What are you talking about? It's just a premature baby."

"I read what grows out of them. Give the money back!" Aratunia shouted and he slapped Jasmin in the face with all his might, so that she fell to the floor.

He looked at her contemptuously and took a knife from his pocket. Jasmin grabbed her stomach and made a scowl of pain.

"Don't pretend," he said, waving his knife menacingly. "You have a week to pay a double down payment. Otherwise you'll end up like that black-haired shit. Did you hear what I'm saying to you, Florian? You thought I didn't know. Are you ashamed of the roots, white-haired cunt?"

Jasmin slowly started to get up, but her body refused to obey. It was evident that this breakneck art caused her not so much difficulty as pain. Finally she got up, but her head was spinning. At that time, Aratunia entered the coolant.

"You still have a lot of water. I take everything," he said.

Then he began to rummage through the cupboards. He was throwing out their contents, making a mess that was even more impossible for a pregnant woman to comprehend than before. Meanwhile, Jasmin was walking towards the bed. He saw it and overtook her.

"You must be hiding something here," he said, and uncovered the quilt.

His disappointed expression said it all. All snotty handkerchiefs, communicator and crumpled candy bar wrappers.

"Mucky pup. What a family," he drawled through his teeth.

Jasmin managed to get closer. At that moment, Aratunia was looking around the living room as if looking for something.

"This is for a white-haired cunt!" She screamed and hit him on the head with the portable air humidifier on the nightstand. "And this is for Vicky!" She corrected.

Aratunia lost consciousness immediately and fell over. Then Jasmin fell, not on the bed, but next to the torturer. They both lay motionless. Jasmin's eyes were flooded with tears, but she wasn't crying. She started blinking as if she wanted to dry every drop. She was losing consciousness.

After a while, she heard footsteps and familiar voices, male and female, but they were like in another dimension.

***

Jasmin awoke in a dingy recovery room. She was alone in it. The flickering fluorescent lamp hummed unbearably and the cameras it was attached to beeped unevenly. She felt her belly. It was smaller, not much, but there was no life in it. She might have thought she was dreaming all of this, but she realized that nothing hurts when she sleeps. The fresh, deep wounds from the operation burned her with living fire, and her abdomen reminded her that it was time for her uterus to shrink to its normal size. Jasmin couldn't remember how she ended up in the hospital. She remembered that thug, of Florian origin, who had come to get his money back. She also remembered that they were struggling. Nothing else.

At that moment a black-haired midwife entered the room. She had about four cleansing and a nice appearance.

"Is it over?" Jasmin asked.

"Please be careful. You lost a lot of blood."

"Can I see my children?"

The midwife looked at her as if pretending not to hear the question.

"Did something happen?" Jasmin asked.

"We fought for your life. You had serious injuries."

"Where are the girls?"

The midwife looked down.

"What did you do to them?" She asked, her voice still calm, full of doubts.

"It was impossible to save them."

Jasmin froze.

"It's good that the neighbors showed up on time, because there would be nothing to collect. Luckily the garda caught this bandit."

The midwife was talking to herself, but the patient's thoughts were elsewhere.

***

Pain and emptiness. Nothing more. No desires, no yearning, no want to cry. Jasmin looked like a corpse, as if her oxygen supply had been cut off along with the umbilical cord. All femininity in the form of three girls was torn from her body by force and thrown into the garbage.

"What happened to them?" She asked the midwife as she came in to check the drip. "With my little daughters?"

"Baby, they were dead," she replied with palpable empathy.

"I do not believe. I need to see."

"What? But this is impossible. Procedures prohibit."

"I have to. You fucking understand?! I have to!" She screamed.

The midwife thought for a moment, bit her lip.

"You don't want to watch this," she said.

"Check me."

They showed. It mean Jasmin had to visit the basement herself. She was walking slowly, even twitching attached to the drip, which was held by the emergency services personnel walking alongside. The girls, or basically three blue-eyed babies drowned in a mixture of amniotic fluid and blood, lay in a transparent bag labeled "X, Y, Z. Offspring of Jasmin and Addam Kozllov. Intended use: for recycling".

This sight would knock down the strongest. She swayed, but humaan held her hand.

"Fuck off, scrap of metal!" She screamed.

"Take it easy, kid." The midwife took the patient from the hands of the humaan and gave her a firm hold.

"X, Y, Z?" Jasmin was surprised.

"We didn't know the names." The midwife sighed and looked down.

"Irmina, Jona and... Vicky," Jasmin said sadly.

"Nicely. They sure fit. Speaking of Vicky, there is information in the GCO system that you have adopted her son. Do you want to see him?"

"No."

"I understand, nothing by force. We'll wait until you get better."

"You don't understand anything. Where I'm going, I won't need it."

"You are stupid. Just please without any suicide attempts on my shift," the midwife joked, though she bit her tongue after a while.

***

When they returned to the ward and Jasmin was left alone in the recovery room, she was shocked. The body began to tremble by itself, the heart was pounding, and the brain in a frenzy spewed out only depressing thoughts. As if all the worst emotions, both the old, entrenched, not thoroughly healed, and the fresh, smelling new, wanted to cause a downpour of tears. Eventually she exploded. She was crying with bitter tears. She howled, gasped, beat her fists on the bed frame. She screamed at herself, the world, Addam, even in her eyes that she didn't want to stop producing tears. She wiped her nose, snotty in a moment, with her sleeve on a regular basis. She didn't care that she smeared her underwear with sludge. Everything that was bad, slimy and terrible came out of her. Nobody interrupted her, nobody came in for a moment to comfort her. The whole world gave her time to complain. As if all the people in and around the hospital where she had been heard had allowed her to throw out this devastating tragedy. When three hours later her eyes took pity on her and stopped producing tears, she felt nothing. She only sniffed unconsciously from time to time, though he was now clean.

***

Two weeks have passed. The scar healed. The one on the stomach; the one in the heart not. Despite the painful loss, Jasmin continued to feed her breast every day. She took it through the breast pump straight into the glass vessel and passed it on to the midwife. It was she who persuaded her to do this, despite appearances, a heroic act. Jasmin's first reaction was a flat refusal, but she finally agreed when she heard that most women weren't as lucky as she was. "Honorary donor" - that's what she thought of herself.

She was supposed to leave that day, but she was still waiting for the electronic discharge. She could get it only after being examined by a gynecologist. The excerpt was very important, it guaranteed the removal of the blockade in the GCO system, i.e. the longed-for access to the saved twenty-six thousand entitys.

Jasmin was already impatient, it was past noon, and still waiting for the doctor to check her in the morning. Such a delay could be assessed as reprehensible, but not in this particular case, as the patient was exceptionally ill at surgery. A few days after she saw the bag marked "X, Y, Z", she asked to be moved to another floor. She preferred to rehabilitate among patients with broken legs, arms or with wounds cut as a result of street fighting, and there were more and more of these, than in the company of happy mothers or listening to the unbearable crying of their children.

She did not intend to wait until evening and finally went to the gynecology and obstetrics ward herself. Halfway to the doctor's office there was a room for premature babies. Jasmin stopped and looked inside curiously. Most of the little ones were girls. Victor, like a chosen one, was lying in the incubator located in the very center. As if even in a maternity hospital, gender priority played a colossal role. Jasmin sneaked in silently. She just wanted to see what Vicky's son looks like. She didn't know what to expect. Addam told only terrible things about the boy, so she approached him carefully. The baby didn't look like a monster. Almost all of it was covered with a special suit protecting the body against temperature surges. She saw only the eyes - beautiful, after her mother.

“He put on weight quickly, actually,” said the midwife, who followed her unnoticed and approached the incubator.

The woman slipped her hand through the sterile sleeve up to the elbow. She put her finger to the mask that obscured the boy's face. She pushed it back. Mouth didn't look weird, something was wrong with her, but it was definitely no monster. His lips began to respond to touch.

"He has a suckling reflex," said the midwife.

At that moment, Jasmin felt food flooding into her breasts. She grabbed her left breast with her right hand and felt for it, staring instinctively in her direction.

"I can feel it," she said.

"You could feed him," suggested the midwife.

"I don't want."

"As you think. Your choice."

Jasmin thought for a moment. She looked at the little boy.

"Or I want to. But how are we going to do it?"

"Wait."

The midwife began to carefully pull her hand from her sleeve, but it was to no avail and the boy immediately began to cry. Jasmin's heart was beating like crazy.

"Faster," she said.

"Wait a minute, we have to equilibrate the temperature," answered the midwife and clicked the button on the incubator.

The LEDs started flashing, followed by the sound of exhaled air with high pressure. Something squealed, something scraped, and the lid opened. Wiktorek cried all the time. The midwife carefully removed it from the device and handed it to Jasmin, who was unsure how to hold such a small child. With her right hand she grasped her butt and placed her head in the left bend of the elbow. The boy was still crying. It was obvious that Jasmin did not know how to go on. The midwife helped her tilt her blouse and pulled out her swollen breast. The baby's crying ceased when a nipple with life-giving food was placed in his mouth. Jasmin made a scowl as if something had started to hurt her.

"I can feel my stomach. Is it because it's a foreign child?"

"You're talking nonsense. It's normal. During feeding, oxytocin is released, which causes the uterus to contract faster. Besides, Victor knows the taste of your food." The midwife smiled triumphantly, as if she had just revealed a great secret.

Jasmin returned a hearty grimace that looked like a half-smile and focused on the boy. After feeding, under the pretext of severe exhaustion, she returned to her room. She decided to wait for the doctor there. She had to quiet down.

After the examination, she made sure that the blockage was removed, dressed quickly and, holding her stomach, left the building. She was convinced that she could not take Victor with her. Wherever she was going, she no longer needed him. Nobody paid boy's allowance there. She decided to fulfill her mother's dream and find the Manduarra family, and then she would see each other. At most she will come back. She had the money to start. As far as she knew, they lived in the western quarter of Floris. It was in this direction that she intended to go.

When she got to Addam's apartment, she cleaned up all the mess she had left behind, including evidence of Aratunia's struggle. Eventually she could start packing. This activity turned out to be enjoyable. Jasmin felt inspired and excited. She quickly got a few essentials ready, including a generous supply of candy bars, a change of clothes and shoes, a dozen bottles of water, and all of my father's notebooks.

It was only when she was packing, or actually stuffing between the only empty gaps, red and green bars that she realized that she shouldn't have to carry that much. The luggage was quite heavy, although she only took the most necessary things. Then she remembered that somewhere she had such a funny device for drawing water from humid air. It was called a condenser or something like that. It was neat and light, just right for such a trip. It was working on Hello rays. When she bought them, they quarreled with Addam. He then said that he would never use it and that these were lost beings. Still it will come in handy, she thought. She found it easily. She unpacked most of the heavy glass bottles and it grew lighter straight away. Just in case, she left two smaller ones. She decided to divide the rest of the things so that she could distribute the weight on both sides of her body. She didn't have two of the same panniers, so she took one white and one transparent. She packed them equally with all the necessary luggage. She made an attempt to see if she could. It was not bad. She left Addam a farewell letter in which she decided to let him know about the girls. "He should know," she thought.

She looked at the city skyline one last time through the apartment window. In it, she spent the last one and a half purifications, so she felt she had to do it. The Inco Center looked like it was getting ready for another shift. Prime Minister Noovack's talking head was visible on all the screens where the groundbaits were presented until recently. She encouraged me to do something over and over again, but none of the passers-by paid attention to her. Jasmin amused the sight. She entered the recovery room, looked around, and smiled at her thoughts. Then she returned to the living room, made the bedding, and sat on the edge of it. She looked at a few more places so as not to forget about them for the rest of her life. She sighed, got up, picked up the panniers, and left.

***

"Lady, let us advise you what to do," said Ali Ude concerned, as another extraordinary Council of Priests began.

"I was convinced that not in my lifetime we will face the end of the world," Mi-tu said.

"t is up to us whether it will be the end of the world. Do not demonize," the priestess reassured.

"But the birds... The prophecy is coming true," lamented Namali. "Only you, my lady, can protect us. And blessed Patri."

"Shut him up or I'll puke. I should forbid studying old books. They take your mind away. Ling Gui," asked the head of the military school. "Tell us about the situation."

"At school, we have about five thousand low-level priests of all ages. There are almost twice as many in a standing army. Border guards and purple guards are basically a handful, you can't count on them. I do not recommend that priests who are responsible for our security in the territories should be reappointed. We sent some spies. We know that the enemy army is overrun by women who have no military experience. The men were eliminated from the command. This gives us an advantage."

"It equalizes the chances, I would say," Ae concluded.

"But Inco has machines. They don't have to shed the blood of their inhabitants."

"Have our priests of technology recorded any successes in converting agricultural machines into war machines?" She asked.

"There is progress, but it can hardly be called a success. Mr. Clifford's brother could use it," said Ling Gui.

Ali Ude glanced at the High Priestess of the Omniearth. He was counting on the emergence of an emotion that would confirm Kifor's words that Ae had ordered everyone killed. She pretended not to see it.

"I can't accept the loss of Zenit all the time. Whatever you say about him, he was effective. It is thanks to him and Kifor that we know what is happening at the border. It's good that they managed to send a full report on the situation. Many important priests have given their lives to defend the Patri. You also lost your cousin, good Kadu," she told Ling Gui. "Their deaths cannot be wasted."

"Maybe we should go back to talks with their new government? Maybe nothing is lost yet?" Ali Ude shyly suggested.

"Maybe," she said, in a tone that suggested she wasn't interested in his opinion.

She looked around. Each of the hierarchs looked terrified. "A bunch of cowards," she thought.

"Most importantly, the internal problems have stopped," said Ling Gui, trying to defuse the atmosphere. "The checkered chambers are filled to the brim. If the protests continued, we would have nowhere to close."

"Anyone who can lift a Sirius counts now. We will teach wayward peasants how to use it. They should all be sent to the border," Ae decided. "On the first line."

"And if they stand against us?"

"No time to taunt. You don't know what to do in such cases?" Ae did not hide her emotions.

"In one of the checkered chambers there is also a man from Inco, Haris Sagavara. We also have to send him to the Pinati Falls?" One of the elders asked.

Ae was surprised by this information. She was convinced that Haris did not survive the tortures that Kifor and Zenit gave him.

"No. We'll find another job for him," she replied.

***

"I'm sure this is the last chance to send a group of twelve daredevils," Xami said.

He waited in hiding behind a curtain in the chamber of the High Priestess of the Omniearth.

"Are they ready?" She asked. "Of course. You wouldn't report me if you weren't sure."

"They got to know the taste of the bars. They have a complete set of information. They know names, strategic places, including those that no one knows about. We just need to make it easier for them to break through."

"It's already taken care of. I wrote a letter. When they cross the border, they will be fired upon, but none of the priestesses will hit."

"What about the women who wander on the other side? Won't they eat them alive?"

"They have to cope somehow."

"You know they won't come back from this mission, don't you?"

"Since when have you been interested in whether someone will survive?" She asked and scowled. "Mi-tu chose the best students. The most valuable. They have very important tasks to do. However, if they do get caught..."

"The new prime minister will know it's us. We'll give her an excuse," he finished.

"Speaking between us, I welcome any war that will eradicate evil," she said.

Xami looked down as if to avoid exchanging glances.

***

In less than half a day, Jasmin had already passed through the first district. Only three guard controls disrupted the march. Unknowingly, she handed over the card, and after reading it, put it in her pocket. Apart from these incidents, she did not record anything that seemed significant. All the way she thought about her mother's life, her own, Addam's, even Vicky's, and what would happen to Victor. Punishing thoughts cut her legs and raised obstacles higher and higher. When she reached the barbed wire separating the slums, she stopped. She noticed a little girl, quite similar to her when she was the same age, but brown-haired. She was playing at home with a rag doll resembling a boy - pretending they were walking together. The girl turned the doll's head towards her face and spoke to herself in a childish voice, then kind of answering, but in a more serious, almost adult voice. It looked like a conversation between mother and child. Jasmin stopped. She stood still as if she were wondering something, then suddenly turned back. She started going in the opposite direction faster and faster. Then she was almost running, forgetting the crutch in the form of the two half-full panniers hanging from both shoulders. When she got to the hospital, she sat down in the waiting room. She evened her breath and rested for a moment.

Victor was in the incubator. Jasmin felt her breasts come back with milk when she sees him. She felt unimaginable happiness. She wanted to hug him as hard as she could.

The midwife was nice. She was surprised to see the panniers, but tactfully pretended it was normal. She gave Jasmin many instructions on how to deal with a child affected by this heartless disease, what to avoid and what she must not do under any circumstances. They were basically just prohibitions. As if the child was allowed to do almost nothing. Jasmin wrote down everything, though after a while she felt furious that this particular boy must have had such an ungrateful ailment. Then she realized that if it weren't for the disease, his mother would be alive and she would be in her place. "Poor Vicky," she thought. And then she remembered the little girls again. She wanted to croak to the top of her throat, but the sight of Victor asleep held her back. She couldn't do this to him. She retained every emotion, even the most effective one that wished to reveal her suffering. She was already skilled in such battles. The last eight months of her life were like that. Either she was defending herself against the world or against herself, and the sea of tears she had cried two weeks earlier had shed a cup of bitterness forever. It was only going to be good from now on, she thought.

They made an appointment with the midwife in a few days. Then Victor will be able to install a mask for vaccines, vitamins and microelements. After all, he is a boy, and the state financed healthy rearing of children under the national program. Jasmin promised that that day she would give the midwife the carrier she had just borrowed from her. It was pale gray and worn but intact. Perfect for hiking. Jasmin knew she would not show up on the scheduled date, but she couldn't reveal the reason. Certainly the midwife would not let her carry out the plan, and perhaps call in some services. It would be unnecessary trouble. At least, thanks to the sling and mask, she had an alibi. She could move.

***

The inhabitants of the settlement of Litrijis were ordered to participate in a supposedly daily ritual, carried out in unusual circumstances. Taarida - the new priestess in charge of this district - invited everyone to the river, where it was customary to burn fires in honor of Patri. This time the hearth looked different than usual. A thick pile was dug into the center, and around it lay piles of dry wood and bundles of stems of various shrubs. On a wagon to which two hydapi were tied, there was something like a human body covered with a bedspread. Taarida greeted each of the inhabitants with respect - even those who were brazenly staring at her wooden, slightly mossy mask. And there was a lot to see. The mask was rotten yellow due to the occasional soaking of sirra oleum. Thanks to this treatment, she did not dry out or the tooth of time bit her. It covered almost the entire face, except for the not very symmetrically cut openings for the eyes, the right one being larger than the left one and running slightly obliquely from the bald eyebrows to the cheek. In the center of the mask, roughly below the nose, there was a small ornament in the shape of a withered dirsna flower. The two tight metal clasps around the head looked unfastened only during a meal. They had already carved furrow-like scars into the wrinkled skin of the back of the head. When they were fastened, they looked as if they had been permanently eaten on the head like a monolith. Masks were not a common phenomenon in Floris, but as a rule they did not attract attention. The one Taarida was wearing could evoke unhealthy fascination or even anxiety because it looked unholy.

When a fairly large crowd of fishermen, nimo shepherds, carpenters and other trades in Litrijis had gathered, as well as their entire families, Taarida discovered the body. It was difficult to recognize who this man was. His face was bruised, and the cuts on his legs and arms were stained with dried blood. He was breathing, though slowly. He was bound with a rope of raidi. The sight of the massacred body caused a stir.

"This poor fellow's name is Fahid Manduarra," Taarida began, looking each one in the eye. "He's a farmer. He confessed to the murder. He killed the priest of Patri. He killed Kadu!"

Still in complete silence, Taarida walked over to the wagon and took the crossbow in her hand.

"He used that forbidden weapon!" She shouted ominously.

Kaaratu swallowed and his eyes widened, but no one noted his terror. There were whispers among the assembled. In some you could feel a hint of criticism, in others incredulity. All eyes were on Fahid, who didn't even flinch. Kaaratu lamented silently. He thanked the farmer that he had not released it to Taarida. After all, it was he who sold him the crossbow. Such sins were punishable by severe punishment. And then he remembered that he still had that bracelet, the memento of his father that Fahid wanted back.

"I could have given it to him," he thought, and quietly prayed to Patri to forgive him. The other members of the brotherhood no longer looked like brazen opponents. They all stood courteously by their families and watched what happened, pretending they didn't know each other.

"Anyone who raises a hand against the Church will raise it against the Floris. There is no consent to break God's laws. This is a mortal sin, and for it is due death! Have you seen the big birds?"

"Yes." There were a few engaged but scared voices.

Patri signaled that she would not tolerate human stupidity. We must be one. We must defend our borders. We must care for our holiness. The enemy is everywhere. Sometimes in the form of people from a strange land. Sometimes in the form of loved ones who are confused, like this unfortunate one. Sometimes in the form of a pokuna!

The inhabitants of the settlement reacted nervously. As if the summoned animal signified the most horrible things they had ever heard of in their miserable lives.

"Now this man is a murderer to us," Taarida continued. "But merciful Patri gives him a chance to redeem him. Burning in sacrifice according to the teaching of the Church, in the presence of each of you, is missionary. Until the body is completely burnt, no one can leave. We will all pray that his soul will go to the Diamond Sanctuary. Then I will take his ashes to Asaran so that he can rest in a mass grave. With this he will redeem his sins, and for us he will be a symbol that everyone, even the worst man, can atone for mortal sins. He can be saved. Isn't Patri just and merciful?"

Nobody reacted. Taarida tossed the crossbow back onto the cart and pushed Fahid to the ground. He just groaned. Someone from the gathered rushed to help, but she signaled that she would be able to handle it. She grabbed the prisoner by the hair with one hand and the other by the shoulder. One tug brought Fahid to his feet. She led him closer to the pile and tied it tightly to the pile that had been stuck in it. He did not resist. He looked like a man who didn't care. His eyes were absent, as if his eyes were fixed on some distant, invisible target, reaching far beyond this place and time. Taarida crouched down, took two small flints and rubbed them together. Sparks fell on the driest bundle of dirsna stalks, but the fire would not catch fire. The priestesses shook hands with subsequent attempts. She gasped as if patience wasn't her forte. A bead of sweat ran down her forehead towards her face, apparently making it itchy as she furiously rubbed the mask across her face. At this point, one of the sparks began to smolder and after a while it turned into a flame. The fire quickly spread to the entire bundle, then to the pile of wood. Taarida stood up and sighed with relief. Fahid was still motionless. In his mind's eye he saw his children playing in the yard, then Father Mahmud and his wife Rita. Everyone looked happy. When the tongue of the fire reached his calf, he hissed briefly in pain.

"Children, I love you. Sumi, little daughter, forgive me!" He shouted, then cried, releasing the hitherto suppressed lament of the concerned women who watched the execution.

After a while, his clothes caught fire - he looked like a torch.

"Oh Patri merciful!" Taarida sang, though it sounded more like a chimeric caricature.

People stood dead. She gestured for them to join in prayer.

"Oh Patri merciful!" A few voices repeated after her.

"Oh fair Patri!" She continued even more macabrely.

"Oh fair Patri!" More voices repeated.

Taarida exchanged further qualities of the goddess, and the crowd repeated after her. Ghaideng Ru, standing in the back, watched without saying a word. He was calmly leaning on his cane, but his hand was trembling. He felt as if his tongue had been paralyzed. As if someone powerful had tied a knot in the middle and made it not untangled. The day before, Ghaideng Ru had received a letter from Ae, written as usual so that only a priest - at least an intermediate level, and preferably only he - could understand it. She used, as always in such cases, a sublime, mysterious language. He knew this handwriting and unique style. The letter read: "Man is alone. He has the blood of Litrijis on his hand."

The former priest clearly understood what the High Priestess of the Omniearth wanted to convey to him. If she wrote "on his hands," it could be anyone. Since the addressee of the letter was the only man in the area who had only one hand, the clue, or rather the threat, was about him. It meant that if he continued to do the wrong things, such as upset, he wouldn't be hit for it, but the whole village of Litrijis instead. He would be able to watch them die in solitude. He will be to blame.

The stench of Fahid's burning body and the suffocating, unfriendly smoke scared off the surrounding birds and caused many inhabitants of the settlement to cover their noses with their hands. Pursuant to the decision of the new priestess responsible for this district, they waited as for punishment until the end for the corpse of her predecessor's murderer to burn. They were to remember that day for the rest of their lives.

***

It took Jasmin very little time to move from District One to the slums. She was prepared for the worst, especially since Victor was in her carrier. She hid in the vicinity of the barbed wire between the districts and was looking for opportunities. This one appeared quickly. Regular fights between the packs, who were not bothered by the prohibition of movement, have reached this place. Humaans of garda did not keep up with fixing the symbol of the border between better and worse Inco.

She slipped quickly. She was helped by a pretty red-haired girl. It was she who pushed back the tangled coils of barbed wire so that Jasmin and the baby could cross the border. Then it was easier, though not without nerves. Jasmin was on the alert all the time. When the women approached her, she pretended Victor was a girl. In fear of losing him, she called him "Victoria" fondly. None of the nosy women got it. On the same day, Jasmin arrived at the edge of civilization, or, if you prefer, the Abyss, the Third District. She wasn't going to rest yet. She marched on, although she knew that Hello would soon hide behind the horizon and total darkness would ensue. She wanted to be sure that she could find a suitable hiding place where she could refresh the boy's body. She couldn't let the skin in her sealed suit scald him. For this occasion, she had a thermal blanket that could be used as an insulating screen. However, she could not use it, so as not to arouse suspicion, so she went a little further into the country.

After feeding Victor and washing him with the rest of the water, she fell asleep. She slept briefly. In the morning she was awakened by the voices of women marching nearby. It was a group of six people from the first district. They looked wealthy, were nicely dressed and well cared for. As she moved, Victor woke up and began to whine. The women took notice of the incident but did not stop. They wandered on. Jasmin fed the boy, ate the bar herself and headed in the same direction as them. She could not drink water, because the fancy condenser for her production refused to obey - it did not work in a dry climate. She was a little disappointed, but decided that she would be able to find water quickly.

The road through the third district turned out to be a hard work. It was hot, the air was dry, and Victor reminded of himself crying regularly. There was still no water. Yet Addam was right about the condenser. "What idiot invented the device operating on the Hello rays? After all, humid air only appears at night, and then Hello doesn't shine," she was pissed off. A day later, in the morning, she noticed that there had been some dew on the purse during the night. She used every drop to wet the baby's mouth and licked the rest. That same day, in the evening, she put out a thermal blanket overnight to get more water. She managed to. The next morning, she saw a swarm of wet drops all over its surface. She was as happy as if she had seen a million creatures on her account or at least discovered a new planet. As she ate the bar, she noticed that she needed to save because they were over soon. After feeding Victor, she went on enthusiastically. On the same day, she reached the shore of a dead lake. A group of women rested with him. This time they looked quite similar to the older pack who had their teeth sharpened at the sight of her and Addam in the slums. Jasmin walked cautiously closer to the shore. She took the container out of the condenser to get some fresh water from the lake.

"You better not do it," said the yellow-haired girl at the age of five purifications and indicated with a gesture the vomiting women hidden behind a large boulder.

Jasmin fluttered helplessly on the rather soft surface of the stone lying just off the shore.

"I can't do it anymore," she said.

"Why are you going alone?" Asked the yellow-haired girl and handed over a half-drunk bottle of Pearl water.

Jasmin took a long sip, greedily, then licked her lips so as not to waste a drop.

"Don't worry, I have a few more." She showed the full pannier. "I worked in a water factory."

"The factory? She is not imported?" Jasmin was surprised.

The yellow-haired girl just smiled and nodded her head.

"I'm Luka," the yellow-haired girl said.

"Jasmin. And this is Victoria." She looked fondly towards Victor.

"What's wrong with her?" Luka asked, showing the unusual suit with which he was covered.

"She has hypohydrotic ectodermal dysplasia. It's too rare a disease to be worthwhile devising a cure."

Luka looked away and shook her head as if resisting her urge to scold the younger woman. Jasmin shouldn't have complained. After all, many women will never know the charms of motherhood.

"You can come with us if you want," Luka suggested.

"No way!" Another slumer who was looking at Jasmin reacted. "She will delay us, and the brat will yell."

"Go alone," Jasmin said.

"Get lost, you dumb ass," Luka said. "Don't listen to her," she said to Jasmin.

After a short rest, the women moved on. Jasmin was walking several dozen steps behind the group. From time to time, Luka looked with concern if the mother and the child were not lost.

The rocky steppe of the fourth district, hard as concrete, gave everyone a hard time. None of the women were ready for this kind of substrate. They had to take a few breaks to dress their legs, seal blisters and corns with plasters. When they passed the energetic labyrinth, before the mountain range, they saw an unusual sight. On the other side of it, on the ground were dozens of burned corpses of various species of animals that apparently innocently wanted to cross the border between countries because it did not exist for them. Moree birds and raidi creatures were the most numerous. The women were aware of the effects of the protective barrier, but watching them live, as well as the unpleasant, suffocating smell in the air, remained in their memory for a long time.

"At least we know the border is not far away." Luka was trying to find some positive in the depressing moment.

The mountain range that they covered two days later turned out to be the most serious challenge, even for Inco residents who had trained in the march. The first two days of the climb only caused pain in the thighs. Then, walking for half a day across the icy ridge killed the shins. The next one and a half days down the slippery slopes additionally strained the knees and ankles. After this grueling stage, the women took a day's recovery break. Anyway, not just any place. On the other side of the mountains, they saw the Ethne Spring and the first signs of new life - vegetation.

Occasional at first, it became more and more lush and colorful with each successive step. The interior of the Glass Dome, which until now each woman had considered a miracle of nature, turned out to be a pile of weeds compared to the vastness of profusely overgrown shrubs with generous flowers. They sat on the soft yellowed moss. Jasmin noticed the insects that had somehow escaped from Floris, but clearly had no intention of going anywhere anymore. All the more so when they are not asked. Women who had never communed with nature before found it difficult to continue their journey. There were signs of blissful happiness on the usually sad, intransigent faces of the slumers. And this kind of reaction in the place where they lived so far could be seen as a sign of weakness. Here, no one was embarrassed. Jasmin thought they looked funny. She liked them for their honesty.

The closer it was to the border, the more women saw other groups, and the machines flying back and forth across the sky, recording everything. Images from cameras placed under their bellies were regularly displayed in Noovack's office. Various emotions could be seen on the faces of the members of the Government who had been debating practically non-stop for many days. Starting from Tatarczyna's excitement, through a slight excitement of Gibbondy, and ending with Davis's apprehension. Noovack had known what she had to do for a long time.

***

A group of slum women merged with another, less numerous group to form a pack. Among them was Jasmin with Victor in a sling. For several days they had wandered along the Ethne, which from its spring turned into a majestic river twenty cubits wide. It was winding calmly, almost silently. The women's march has finally become quite enjoyable, much better than the one over the mountain range. At one point, you could hear an unprecedented sound, as if a river that had been calm so far, met resistance somewhere in the distance. As if something had released a buzzing from the shackles of peace that bound him. The closer they got to him, the louder it got. Eventually the pack reached the culmination of all the noises, so loud that you couldn't hear your own thoughts. As if all the water from all Inco taps was pouring in many streams at once into one small puddle. Here the river lost its depth to value. It began to branch out to the sides, forming a multi-fingered delta at the end of which nothing but fog was visible. The curious women took several dozen more steps to see what was behind her.

And then they saw the Pinati Falls. It was forty cubits high and nearly a hundred wide. Its edge was covered with yellow moss and lush green tufts of water grass. After squeezing between the sharp edges of the rocks, the navy blue water fell vertically into a deep reservoir in which colorful fish of various sizes were swimming. There the water turned turquoise. Its scattered drops released a haze of cool relief, felt even from a distance. Before the water continued its journey to the dam and the artificial reservoir on the Floris side, it had to overcome an obstacle course between mossy boulders and then dash through a few meanders through a canyon with a steep, cliff edge.

Everything around smelled fresh, the air was crystal clear. Jasmin couldn't catch her breath, she was so enchanted by the immensity of wonder. She fell in love with this place. It didn't even bother her that the paradise, she thought of the place, was desecrated by the swarms of women wandering along the shore. They organized one big camping there. They waited for events to unfold. As if they were counting on a miracle, believing they could easily cross the line that literally ran five hundred cubits downstream. There were thousands of women - both slumers and those better-dressed from the first district. Many of them came with whole families, clans or packs. Full age range - from little girls to mature grandmothers. They were all tempted by the prospect of a new life.

"Jasmin? Jasmine!" There was a call that tried to get out above the chattering crowd of nomads.

The owner of the name looked around, but couldn't see anyone who might know her. After a while, in the crowd of people, she saw one waving figure. She began to watch her as the woman pushed her way closer.

"I'm looking for a better life," Tarya said as they greeted each other affectionately. "My husband banished me, he has other women."

Jasmin thought she should ask for details. However, she realized that this would only cloud the cordial atmosphere of the moment. She smiled with palpable empathy.

"And you? What are you looking for in Floris? What's your son's name?" Tarya asked out of nowhere. "I told you there will be a boy."

Many wary looks went to the mother holding the baby. She felt a mass of sharp questions that were penetrating her skin into her body. There were also grimaces on the faces of the pack companions - some looked scolding, others revealed thoughts soaked with meanness. Jasmin had no idea how to react. She hid behind a veil of silence, although she was aware that she was returning to the path of bad luck.

***

Gibbonda's new apartment was divided into residential, business and very private sectors. That's what she called them. The living area consisted of a large bedroom with a wide, fluffy bed, coolant filled with bottled water, a well-equipped recovery room and a spacious wardrobe full of outfits for all occasions. In the service sector there were: a small office, a comfortable room for watching theatremania in various conditions and positions, and a laboratory where the hostess carried out all kinds of tests and experiments on a miniature scale. The third, very private, sector looked smaller than the first two. It means, there was also a bedroom, a coolant, a laboratory or a dressing room, but all rooms were usually half the size. Gibbondy was most likely to be in the third sector. It was to him that three familiar people who looked like two and a half purification had been led to the daily frolics of the evening.

"Stronger," whispered barefoot and half-naked Gibbondy to the bald, shapely slumer striking her with a slippery whip.

The young woman obeyed and smiled at her thoughts.

"Again," Gibbondy said softly through clenched teeth.

The woman licked lasciviously and swallowed again, leaving another mark on the Minister of Health's scarred back. The red of the wounds against the hostess's pale skin looked disapproving, even in the poorly lit recovery room. At this point, a second young person, looking like a GCO officer in full gear, punched Gibbondy with a fist in the stomach. The hostess curled up in pain, but didn't squeal a word. Suddenly the third - in a humaan of garda's outfit, with spiky purple hair and a few round metal inserts on her face - kicked her shin with a boot, giving herself a short shout.

"What are you, underdeveloped?" Gibbondy asked, as if in a whisper, but it sounded like she screamed. "I told you to be quiet."

"Come on, come on, Claire. Will your husband yell at you?" Asked the one who looked like a GCO officer.

Gibbondy narrowed her eyes, pursed her lips and looked piercingly at the girl.

"Do I look like the kind of person who would need a husband, you idiot?" She asked quite softly. "Get out. Enough for today."

All three young women obediently left the playground. Gibbondy rubbed her sore shin and put on a coarse, washed-out bathrobe. She walked towards the door marked with the biohazard symbol. When she lifted them, it turned out that the signage was only intended to confuse potential intruders. Inside, instead of a mini-lab, was another bedroom. In addition to the quadruple bed made of black rods, there were three miniatures of it - baby cots with gray canopies. In each of the cots, one infant slept soundly covered with a quilt.

"My cute," she whispered to the three of them, grinning uneven teeth. "Mommy loves you."

"The other mommy loves you too," said Ana Mariya entering the bedroom. "Did you have a good time?" She turned uncertainly to Gibbondy.

The hostess twitched the left corner of her mouth as if pleased with Ana's jealous tone of voice.

The not ugly yellow-haired girl at the age of four purifications walked over to Gibbondy and stood in front of her. They looked straight into each other's eyes. It looked like an expression duel. Suddenly, they both threw themselves into each other's arms and began kissing fervently as if to bite each other.

"Finally, we don't have to hide," Ana whispered.

Printed in Poland
by Amazon Fulfillment
Poland Sp. z o.o., Wrocław